SQUAT

To Katie

Enjoy!

Eric Klein

SQUAT

ERV KLEIN

ISBN: 978-1-948374-63-7

Hydra Publications

Goshen, Kentucky 40026

www.hydrapublications.com

To Nick Klein, Estill Tolle, and Jimmy Youtsey, who bring out the best in the people who listen, and to my siblings who inspire me.

Chapter One

"I'm *not* leaving until you check it."

She stands in the middle of my service bay like Wonder Woman, her hands on her hips and her spike-heeled feet about twenty inches apart. She is blonde, sassy, and tall, her height accentuated by the stiletto-like heels and her short skirt. Her face is angelic, her voice hard.

"Ma'am—"

"Don't you *ma'am* me. I am *not* your grandmother. One of you guys messed up my car and *you're* going to fix it. Now, get out there and look at it." Her hand flutters in the direction of the door then returns to her hip.

"Ma'a…"

Wonder Woman tilts her head and raises her eyebrows.

"Lady, you need to talk to the service manager. He's right over there."

As I point toward Joe, he scurries away from his desk looking like a rat caught in the beam of a flashlight.

It doesn't matter; she doesn't even glance in the direction I'm pointing. Instead, she raises her left hand from her hip, shifts her weight to her right leg, and points both hand and hip in the direction of a late-model BMW sitting at the curb, saying, "Yeah, and my car's right there."

I search again for Joe, for anybody who can help me, but I'm alone, a matador in the ring with a splint on his leg and a charging bull fifteen feet away.

"Let's go," I sigh.

She smiles and walks out the door, heels ringing like a hammer on concrete with every step. A perfume I've never smelled before but will remember forever drifts on the wind behind her.

When she starts the car, it shakes so hard I'm afraid it might fall apart. I know immediately what's wrong, so I have her shut off the engine and pop the hood release while I go inside to get my BMW manual. After checking the firing sequence, I switch a few spark plug wires and tell her to start it again. The car hums a perfect tune.

"That's the way it's supposed to sound," she purrs just as smoothly. "I'm impressed. How much do I owe you?"

"I can't charge you," I say, lowering the hood. "It was our mistake."

"Wellllllll, not really." Wonder Woman cocks her head to the side and smiles. All the outrage directed toward me only moments ago dissipates as the engine quietly idles.

"What do you mean?"

"You didn't work on it before," she says, turning it off and getting out to stand in front of me.

"I know *I* didn't, but you told me somebody here did."

"Don't get mad, promise?"

I fold my arms across my chest, and she puts her hand lightly on my forearm while I glare at her.

"I didn't mean one of you guys *here* worked on it. Just one of you mechanicky kind of guys." Her nose crinkles when she says "mechanicky." "It was someone who lives in my apartment building. He thought he'd get into my pants by doing me a favor. Fat chance of that."

"So you lied to me."

"Just a liiiittle one." She keeps one hand on my arm and holds the thumb and index finger of the other one next to her face, about a half-inch apart while squinting at me.

I continue glowering at her, and she says, "Okay, I confess. I lied. Spank me."

I guess she thought that would make me laugh. When I don't, she removes her hand from my arm, sighs, and says, "How about this. It's 11:30. Let me buy you lunch."

She's dressed in the latest fashion and has a gold necklace, matching bracelet, and a designer purse which is clearly not a knock-off. Not a hair of her shoulder-length mane is out of place. Her spike heels make her a couple of inches taller than me, and as she stares down from on high, her voice, eyes, and smile all laugh.

My shirt is stained; the front of my pants are discolored from me constantly wiping my oily hands. The only thing I have in my favor is that the stains on my clothes match the grease on my hands.

"I don't think that'll work," I reply. "Anywhere you're dressed for won't let me in looking like this." I sweep my arm downward in front of me. "And you won't feel comfortable anywhere that would let me in."

"Let me decide that. Let's go where you usually eat. Please, you fixed my car, let me buy you lunch. It's 1982; a woman can buy a man lunch without the man getting all crazy."

I sigh and point to the greasy spoon across the street, where my co-workers and I celebrate birthdays, new girlfriends, fresh breakups, and anything else anyone considers worth celebrating. I tell her, "It's not fancy, but the food's good."

"It's perfect. Can you go now?"

"Let me clear it with my boss," I say, shaking my head while wondering what I'm getting into.

"Great," she says, ignoring my body language.

"I have to wash up," I tell her as we walk back into the garage.

She nods. Stopping in my repair bay, she says, "I'll wait here."

After scrubbing my hands with a degreaser, I find Joe back at his desk writing up a report. "Okay if I cut out for lunch?" I ask him. "I don't have anything but that Volvo I've been working on, and he won't be back until four."

"Sure," he replies without raising his head. "Give me thirty-seconds and I'll go with you."

"Nah. Some lady wants to take me to lunch. Someone reversed two spark plug wires and I fixed it for her."

Joe looks past me and stares at Wonder Woman in my repair bay. He lets out a low whistle. "Stepping up in class, aren't you?"

"Don't worry. It's just lunch. By the way, I saw you slinking off when she was yelling at me."

"Knew you could handle it." He continues to ogle her. "But if you need help checking *her* engine, let me know." He waves at her and grins when she wiggles her fingers in return. Apparently she's too far away to hear his comment.

Walking away, I say over my shoulder, "You'll be the first I call."

She smiles at me, again, showing a perfect row of teeth. *All the better to bite me with.* We cross the street, dodging the cars and drawing several honks, which she ignores.

Inside the café, we slide into an open booth and she extends her hand.

"My name's Pam. Pam Gerard."

"I'm Bob. B-O-B, Bob." Damn! I can't believe I said that.

"Nice to meet you B-O-B, Bob." Her bemused smile says she knows she's making me nervous. Her twinkling eyes make it clear she enjoys doing so.

Over lunch, I learn that she is thirty-five, has been married once, and that it will only happen again if she's really, really drunk. She works in pharmaceutical sales and puts out a steady patter of flirtatious comments which keep me constantly off-balance.

After lunch, she invites me to a party at her place the following Saturday. "There will be about forty people there. You'll love it!"

What I hear is, "There will be about thirty-nine strangers and you. You'll have to meet everyone and remember their names and occupations because there will be a quiz later."

"I don't think so. I'm not good at meeting people."

"It'll be easy. They all have cars. They can all use a good mechanic. Think of the exposure you'll get; you can line up a lot of work."

"What if we go to a movie, just the two of us?"

She laughs out loud. "*Come on.* My friends are just people who enjoy getting together and knocking down a few. What's the worst that can happen?"

"I think a movie would be better."

"How about dinner, instead? Movies are for old married couples. We'd sit next to each other for two hours without talking and learn absolutely nothing about each other. I prefer to find out who B-O-B Bob is."

I haven't gone out in such a long time that the guys I work with claim I'm a "legal virgin." One night after work, we were drinking a few beers, and Joe said, "It's like a missing person being declared dead if they aren't found in seven years. Since you haven't got yourself laid in seven years, you could have yourself legally declared a virgin."

I had grinned sheepishly. He was right, but Pam seems interested in me. Maybe I don't have to be a legal virgin the rest of my life.

"Okay, dinner," I say. "When?"

"Tonight. If I give you time to think about it, you'll back out. Seven o'clock at Cromwell's."

She has picked a moderately-priced restaurant on the near north side in a residential area. She tells me later that she picked it deliberately so that if I insisted on paying, it would be in my price range.

———

During the next two and one-half years, I learn that she drinks enough for me to hold out hope for marriage; she is boisterous, friendly, and always ready to party; and she appreciates my dependability; if she needs a date for a family wedding or a company function, I am always available.

There are two other things I learn. The first makes me aspire to stay in Chicago the rest of my life. The second is the reason I leave.

When we are together, she makes me feel that I am the most important person in her world.

When we aren't together, she isn't alone.

Chapter Two

"You'll be back." Joe is smiling at me as if to add, "With your tail tucked between your legs," but he knows I'm hurting, so he holds his tongue.

"I don't think so," I reply. "Pam's been cheating on me the whole time we've been together. Says it's a 'lifestyle choice,' whatever the hell that is."

Joe extends his right hand to me. "Sorry. Let me know when you settle somewhere. I'll give you a good reference."

I thank him; we shake hands, and I walk to my car.

———

At six the next morning, I head south.

After about five hours of traversing Indiana, I cross the river into Kentucky. An hour south of Louisville, I'm hungry, so I take an exit marked *Waynedale*. The County Courthouse is ahead, sitting in the middle of a large roundabout. People on the sidewalk waiting to cross the street wave to me, a stranger.

It's your typical town square, with the whittlers and spitters sitting on benches, the law offices circling the square, and the clock tower with the bell. I've often wondered what it would be like to live in a small town. As pleasant as Waynedale appears, I think I'm going to find out.

I make a mental list of things to do: Find a place to eat, find a furnished room, find a job, forget Pam. The first three should be easy. The last one…

There's a small café about a block off the main square. A flashing sign in the window says it all, *EATS*.

The café is empty except for four people. Two men and two women sit at a table together, talking quietly. When I open the door, they all look up, expectantly, but disappointment covers their faces when they don't recognize me.

I slide into the second booth on the right, where I can sit and watch who comes through the door. Maybe Pam got up at five this morning, trailed me 355 miles south on the interstate, and is about to come into this café. I move to the other side of the booth.

One of the men appears to be about sixty, as does one of the women. The other woman, about my age, stands up and walks over to me with a menu. She is wearing one of those waitress dresses used in small cafés everywhere. The hem of the dress hits her above the knees, but not so high nor so tight as to attract attention. She doesn't wear stockings, and her legs are pale. She is attractive without makeup. Her dirty blonde hair is pulled up on top, and she has a pencil sticking out of it. Force of habit more than curiosity leads me to check her left hand. No ring. Why do I care?

"Hi, Hon. What can I getcha to drink?" She smiles at me. It's a pleasant smile, just not as pretty as Pam's. A few crows' feet gather around her eyes.

"Tea."

"Sweet or unsweet?" I hadn't realized how far south I have driven and wonder if the sandwiches will be served with grits.

"Unsweet. No lemon." Does the expression on her face say, *Yankee*? No. It says, *Damn Yankee*.

When she leaves, I am alone with my thoughts until I hear the older man ask, "You ain't from 'round here, are ya?"

News travels fast in small towns. I turn my attention to the source of the voice. He is a big man, and his gaze is steady. I can see it isn't going to leave me until he gets an answer, even though he already knows I "ain't from 'round here."

Even seated, it's obvious he would tower over me. I gauge him to be about six feet four, maybe five, a good eight inches taller than my five feet eight. His hair is snow white and he has a scraggly beard that might have a bird's nest in it. He doesn't have a single tooth in his mouth, and I remember a joke we used to tell in school about the toothbrush being invented in Kentucky because if it had been invented anywhere else it would be called a teethbrush. His belly is massive and pushes hard against his coveralls, which could use an oil change. Under them, he wears a long-sleeved shirt that appears to be the top half of a set of long underwear. Something is odd about his glasses, but I can't figure out what it is until, as if on cue, he reaches through the left pane to scratch his eyelid and I realize the lens on that side is missing.

"No, I'm not from around here. I'm looking for work, and a place to live."

"Well, there ain't much work in this town, but if you want a room, when you leave outta here, go left two blocks to Lincoln Street, turn left and watch for the 'Rooms' sign on the right. They got a room available. Damn good people, too."

"Thanks. I'll check into that. My name's Bob."

"Hey, Bob. I'm Steve. This here's my wife, Lou."

I nod at Lou; she returns it.

She's as round as she is tall, with dark hair that has to get its color from a bottle. Although much shorter than Steve, she is still tall for a woman, about my height. Her clothes are as old as Steve's but much cleaner. She appears to be a person who takes great pride in her appearance, and she gives me a smile which resembles the waitress's.

Steve jerks his head toward the other man and says, "This here's my brother, Squat. We call him Squat 'cause when he was about five I told him, 'Boy, you don't know squat.' He told me, 'Do so. I Squat!' After that, he wouldn't answer to anything else. Been Squat so long I don't reckon I remember his real name."

Squat looks as if he's heard the explanation of his name a few too many times but seems totally at peace with his surroundings, the company, and me. He waves without looking. He's a little heavy, with a short haircut and muscular arms and appears to be about ten years younger than Steve. It's hard to tell, though, since my view is from his side. I suspect he might be mentally challenged, especially after Steve's explanation of his name.

As the waitress approaches my booth with a large glass of tea, Steve proclaims proudly, "And that's our daughter, Sally. She owns this place and makes a good livin'. Purty thang, ain't she?"

Sally shoots daggers in Steve's direction and says, "Papa, hush!" She, too, seems to have heard that introduction a few too many times, and she *does* take offense. She lays a menu in front of me and cautions, "Don't mind him." Turning her head so her voice will carry to the rest of the room, she raises it and continues, "He's a cantankerous old cuss." Then, looking at me, she says, "I'll give you a minute to decide."

She walks back to the table where her parents and Uncle Squat are sitting, and I can hear her quietly fussing at her father for the way he put her on display. "Like I was a cow in the county fair," she grumbles.

Steve tells her that she needn't worry; I didn't look interested in her, anyway. Her fussing rises an octave. If I don't order soon, we might have a full-blown family night at the fights, so I wave to Sally to come back over.

"What's good?"

"My specialty is fast. If you want good, there's a steak house eight miles over in Grove's Point. You want fast, I can fix you a chicken sandwich with chips, an' it'll fill ya up."

"I'll have a chicken sandwich with chips."

"Good choice." Did Sally wink at me? Didn't matter, Papa was right. I'm not interested in anybody this soon. She turns and walks to a counter where she puts my order on a spindle, spins it around for the cook, then goes back to the table with her family.

Steve isn't ready to let go of me yet. "What in the world brings you to Waynedale without a job?"

"I wanted to get away."

"From what?"

Sally glances at me. Her expression says she knows exactly what I wanted to get away from. "Papa," she says, looking back at Steve, "let the man alone. He don't owe you his life story."

But I feel comfortable talking to this man who is so accessible, so I reply, "I've always wanted to live in a small town. I thought it was time I tried it."

"Where you been livin'?"

"Chicago."

"Yeah, we're a little smaller than Chicago." Despite his gross understatement, Steve's expression is impassive.

Without even looking in my direction, Lou announces, "Chicago's too big for me. I'm a small-town girl. Always have been, always will be. Ain't that right, Stevie?"

Steve neither confirms nor denies her statement. He is on a fact-gathering mission, and he hasn't gathered all his facts yet. "What kind of work you do?"

"Auto mechanic."

Squat immediately turns and stares at me, a smile creasing his cheeks, which are wrinkled in a way that only comes from smiling a lot.

"Best place in town for repairs is Jacob's about three blocks from here. Come to think of it, it's the *only* place. Don't think he's hirin', though." He looks at Squat and asks, "Jacob hiring?"

Squat shakes his head and returns his attention to his sandwich.

Sally and Lou have their heads together, talking low, so Steve and I chat back and forth.

"I don't know how you stand all that snow in Chicago," he says.

"You get used to it."

"Small towns are better. When you need help, everbody's there."

"But there are more people to call on in Chicago."

"You better learn to hunt."

"I'm a city boy."

"Not if you're gonna live here."

The cook appears behind the counter between the diner and the kitchen, places a plate on the counter, and calls, "Order up."

As Sally sets the sandwich in front of me, I thank her then mentally go over my to-do list. I am about to eat and have a lead on a room and a job. The job lead isn't good, but it's a start. I'll have to wait on solving the fourth item.

Squat is content to wait, too. He glances around without ever making eye contact with me then finishes the sandwich he's been working on since I walked in.

Steve, Lou, and Sally resume their quiet conversation.

Sally is right. The sandwich won't win any awards, but it was fast and it fills me up. Just as I finish it, Steve, Lou, and Squat get up to leave and Steve reminds, "Don't forget to see about that room on Lincoln Street."

I wave and say, "I won't."

Sally, not the least bit scarred by Steve's attempts at match-making, kisses each of them on the cheek.

As they go out the door, Squat raises his arm and waves at me without a word or a look.

I wave back, but he has his back turned to me, so I call out, "Bye, Squat."

He again waves without turning.

Sally and I are alone in the diner except for the unseen cook, but before either of us can say anything, another group comes in. They could be the coffee klatch of Waynedale, turned loose for the afternoon. Five women, all appearing to be in their sixties or seventies, laughing, talking, and glancing at me, pull two tables together in the middle of the café and proceed to hold court, with many a sideways glance at me.

As Sally walks around them passing out menus, she is the recipient of a few nudges designed to send her in my direction.

After the third push, she informs them, "Next one of you that sticks her bony hand in my ribs is gonna pull back a bloody stump."

The women cackle.

"Sally, you've got to be out there. You gotta strut your

stuff." This from the one whom I would guess has strutted more stuff than the other four combined.

"I tell you every time you come in here, I don't have any 'stuff' to strut, and I got no interest in struttin' it, anyway." It's good-natured teasing, but Sally appears in no mood. I wonder if she's ever been in the mood.

I can understand where she's coming from, though. I haven't been in town an hour, and Sally's father, and now this gang of five have tried to push her into my arms, figuratively and literally.

I don't revel in all the attention, either, although I had encouraged Steve when I answered his questions. But I am embarrassed for Sally. I get up and walk to the cash register to pay my bill.

"I'm sorry for all the commotion," Sally reveals as she takes my money. Her eyes show nervousness.

"Not your fault. People sure are interested in your private life, though."

"Yeah, welcome to Mayberry. You can't smoke a cigarette without someone talkin' about your breath. You sure you wanna stay here?"

"No, but I'm sure I'll give it a chance. Besides, I don't smoke."

She laughs a self-conscious chuckle, and for the first time, I think that she may not be put off by attention from me, just from the unsolicited advice from Papa and the women on how to get that attention.

The one I've identified as the gang leader is telling the others, "So I told him, 'Honey, if you're gonna get engaged, get her a flawless diamond. They hock for a lot more!' "

Laughter, interspersed with comments like, "Land sakes," "Lawdie," and "Oh, Clare, you are the darnedest" fill the café.

I smile again at Sally, who is holding my change out to me. I tell her to keep it and turn toward the door.

As I pass the table where the ladies sit, I hear, "'Bye, now," "Her name's Sally," "Don't be a stranger," and "Y'all come back," the last one despite me being by myself.

As I close the door, I hear gales of laughter. I walk to the car, smiling.

Chapter Three

Steve's directions are flawless. In two minutes, I'm in front of a large, two-story house with a porch which wraps around two sides and is deep enough to have two swings, the first to the right of the front door, facing the street, and the second at a ninety-degree angle to it. Three people sit in the swings. There is a sign announcing, *Room for rent* in the yard.

As I walk up the sidewalk, I hear a vaguely familiar voice shout, "Hot dang, you found us!" followed by a loud laugh. It's not until I'm on the steps and the sun is out of my eyes that I recognize Steve and Lou in one swing, Squat in the other.

"This is your place, eh?" I ask, amused that Steve gave me directions to his own rooming house without telling me it was his.

"Sure is," says Steve, quite pleased that he put one over on the new guy. "Mama and Daddy left it to me with the understandin' that Squat here gets to stay with me. We had three extra rooms. Turned one into a coupla baths, and rent out the other two. Wanna see yours?"

The assumption that one room is already mine welcomes

me. I like Steve more all the time, and the smile that dominates Lou's face reveals all I need to know about her. I'll be staying here if Squat doesn't mind. His smile is as big as Lou's. I'm home.

————

On Monday, I go to Jacob's Garage to talk to the man himself.

Squat greets me with his now-familiar no-look wave.

Steve is right; Jacob isn't hiring. Squat is Jacob's only employee. He fetches soft drinks for Jacob, sweeps the floor, and waves to everyone who passes. I'll have to expand my search.

When I get back to the house, Lou meets me at the door with a smirk on her face and her eyes dancing. "You sure don't waste no time, Mr. Big City." She holds a pie out to me.

"What're you talking about, eh?"

"Clare Jackson, the queen bee of society here in town. Says she met you Saturday at the diner. She brought this pie over 'just for Bob.'" Lou's voice rises an octave when she says "just for Bob." "You wanna tell me 'bout it?"

"Tell you about what?" I can smell the pie, and as I take it from her, I feel its warmth. "What kind is it?" I follow her into the kitchen, set it down on the counter, and peek under the wrap covering it.

"Apple." She stares at me with her hands on her broad hips. "Clare said she hopes you love it. Said she would've made your favorite if you'd shared what it was, but you didn't. Well, Mr. Big City, what *did* you share with her?"

"It's Bob, B-O-B, Bob. Please, stop calling me 'Mr. Big City.' And who's Clare? I didn't meet anyone at the restaurant except you, Steve, and Squat."

"And Sally. And, apparently, Clare Jackson and Louise

Muldraw and Pauline Wilson and Wanda Polk and Mabel Mason. Oh, you men and your short memories. Love 'em and leave 'em. Us womenfolk don't stand a chance." Lou shakes her head, clucks her tongue, and opens the refrigerator.

Sarcasm? Jealousy? Teasing? I don't know Lou well enough yet to figure it out. "Lou, please, explain what's going on. Are those the five women that came in as I was leaving?"

"You were leaving? Why, the way Clare talked, you became best friends with her and the Waynedale Mafia, as they call themselves. Surprised you ain't got a date with one of 'em, or *all* of 'em, tonight."

Denial is getting me nowhere, so I change tactics. "Who says I don't?"

Lou is getting something out of the refrigerator, but she whirls around and, placing one hand on her hip, declares, "If you're not gonna be here for supper, you best be lettin' me know."

"I'm here for supper. We'll have the pie for dessert."

"Humph. Won't be as good as one of mine." She lifts the foil covering the pie and with a frown on her face, adds, "Guess it'll be okay."

"Hey, Lou, did Clare say how she found out where I lived?"

"Said she figured you'd be here in one of our spare rooms, the way you was all moon-eyed over Sally."

"The way I was moo…"

Lou begins to smile. She winks at me and says, "Gotcha. Anyway, Clare said to tell you, 'Welcome to Waynedale. I hope you like it here.' What she meant was she hopes you settle down with some nice young woman, maybe somebody with a diner. We'll leave names out of it."

"Thank you for your subtlety."

Lou turns her back to me and begins working on supper.

Over her shoulder, she says, "Yeah, and don't forget to write Clare a thank-you note. That's the way we do things here, Mr. Big City."

———

That night, after supper and another round of teasing from Steve and Lou over the apple pie, we gather on the porch, and I observe the pecking order for the swings. Steve and Lou are in the same one from which they greeted me on Saturday. Squat sits in the middle of the other, but as I stand to the side, he scoots over and pats the seat next to him.

I smile at him and sit down. The pecking order is adjusted.

We sit quietly for a few minutes, then Steve asks, "So, Bob, you got family in Chicago?"

"I was an only child of two only children. My mother's dead, and my father and I don't get along. That's about it."

"Well," huffs Lou, "I can't imagine 'that's about it.' There's gotta be more to it than that. What's your daddy do?"

"You mean, what did he do that we don't talk?"

"No, Honey," she says. "You're the young 'un so I figure that's *your* fault. I mean how's he make a livin'?"

Her assumption takes me aback, even though she sounds non-judgmental. "I can't say that I know for sure. He used to be an engraver."

"What'd he engrave?" Steve asks.

"He worked at a print shop. He engraved the printing cylinders that printed magazines."

Lou looks at me dead-on. "Okay, now, what'd cha do?"

"I beg your pardon?" I'm still not used to her thick southern accent.

Steve translates. "How'd ya make your old man mad? D'ya knock up the neighbor girl?"

"*Steve!*" Lou turns to me and says, "Ignore him. He's an idiot."

"No, Steve, I didn't get anyone pregnant. I'd rather not talk about it, eh?"

"No," Steve responds, "It ain't 'eh.' You gonna be livin' here with us; seems we oughta know why you and your daddy ain't talkin'."

"I came here for a new start, not to rehash old problems. Let it go."

"You ain't in trouble with the law, are you?" he asks.

"Stevie," Lou says, placing her hand on his arm, "I wanna hear more 'bout his family, too, but we ain't got a right to be rude." She turns to me. "Bob, when you're ready to talk 'bout your family, you say so. Maybe tomorrow."

Steve stares toward the street, pretending he's not interested.

"Let's just say I'm not in trouble with the law. I had woman trouble and preferred to get away."

Lou nods as if to say, "Go on."

"My father and I were oil and water, and I don't choose to talk about him, nor do I anticipate wanting to talk about him tomorrow."

Lou frowns.

"Humph," is all I hear from Steve.

We talk and don't talk, about the weather, Steve's garden, and all the other little things people talk and don't talk about until, finally, as the sun begins to set, I get around to asking if there are any other garages around.

"Yeah," Steve says. "You got Grove's Point nine miles from here. They're a lot bigger than us, 'bout 15,000 people. Got a Ford dealership there, plus a few garages. You might find somethin' over there if you don't mind workin' in the big city."

"Steve, remember where I came from?"

"Oh, yeah. I forgot. That's why Lou always calls you, 'Mr. Big City.'"

"Not always," says Lou.

"No, just every time you refer to him," says Steve, chuckling.

"How do I get to Grove's Point?"

"Go up to Main Street and take a left. In nine miles, you'll be in Grove's Point."

"Eight," Lou corrects.

"What?" asks Steve. He looks at Lou and frowns.

"Grove's Point is eight miles. I clocked it last time I drove over there."

"Bob, when you go tomorrow, maybe you could take Lou's car and have them check the odometer. It appears to be off about one mile for every nine she drives. Better yet, check it yourself, you bein' a mechanic and everything. Maybe you can give me a break on the cost."

"There ain't nothin' wrong with my odometer, and my hearin' is fine, too," Lou fumes.

"Well, I've lived here all my life and Grove's Point's been nine miles since I was a kid. Don't recollect anybody movin' it a mile closer. No, ma'am, not in my lifetime."

I get up about halfway through Steve's comment, and as I go inside, I hear Lou growl at him, "Steve if you don't..."

I start up the steps toward my room and don't hear Steve's fate if he doesn't. I'm asleep in less than ten minutes.

————

The next day, I drive over to Grove's Point and find the Ford dealership, where I talk to the service manager, a man about my age named Jake.

"Perfect timin'," Jake says. "Lost one of my mechanics last

week when he joined the Army. Won't be around for a few years."

"I've got references."

"Don't need 'em. I already got calls from both Jacob and Steve. Said to give you a try." He glances down at some papers on his desk then asks, "How'd you find your way to Steve's house? He's had that room for five years, I bet, and never had anyone rent it before."

We talk about my arrival, and when I mention Sally, Jake's eyes light up. "Sally's a good ole girl," he says with a smile. "Used to skinny…, ah, swim with her when we was in high school." He looks over my head as if remembering something, and his smile broadens. "Next time you see 'er, tell 'er ole Jake says 'hey.'"

"I'll do that."

The pay isn't what I made in Chicago, but neither is the cost of living, so I take the job, and that night I offer to take Steve, Lou, and Squat out to dinner to celebrate.

"We'll go to Sally's," Lou says, her voice rising. "She'll wanna know, too, and she's workin' tonight. And by the way, our evening meal is supper," Lou corrects me. "Dinner is at noon."

Squat hears "Sally's" and starts hopping from one foot to the other. I had something a little fancier in mind, but the handwriting's on the wall; if we eat out, whatever we call it, it'll be at Eats.

When we get there, I relay Jake's hello.

"Yeah?" she asks, raising her eyebrows. "How's ole Jake the Snake doin'?"

"He's fine," I say. "Jake the Snake, huh?"

Sally peeks at her parents. They aren't listening, so she leans in close and whispers, "Best endowed boy in high school. All the girls used to call it 'the snake.'"

When she pulls back, I stare at her, wide-eyed.

She smiles and winks at me. I can't determine if she's joking or serious, but this opens up a side of her I hadn't expected. Maybe she isn't always so dour.

———

Just as Steve adapted the house to make a place for boarders, he, Lou, and Squat adapt to make room for me. At first, I eat breakfast with just Steve and Lou, but soon Squat starts getting up to eat with us.

Steve says this is new. Squat doesn't like to get up early, and he hates to change his routine. It's a short walk to Jacob's and he could sleep in until 7:30 if he wished, but soon he's showing up for breakfast at 6:45. Sometimes, I catch him watching me. When I do, he looks away really quick.

Lou fixes a sandwich for me to take to work, and I leave about 7:30. It only takes about fifteen minutes to drive the eight miles—Lou was right—between towns, yet I'm entering another world. Grove's Point is tiny after living in Chicago but —Steve was right—compared to Waynedale, it's the big city. I'm home about 5:15 most nights and we sit down to supper at 6:00. Sally frequently joins us.

At supper, Squat always sits on Steve's right. According to Lou, it's been this way since she and Steve have been married. About the middle of the second week, though, he starts sitting on my right.

"What's the matter, you don't wanna sit next to me anymore?" Steve asks the second time it happens.

"Steve, honey," says Lou, "let Squat sit wherever he chooses."

"He can sit wherever. I'm just curious to know why he

23

hankers to change. Twenty-five years he's sat next to me, now all of a sudden, he decides to change. What's up?"

Squat appears to be uncomfortable, like he just farted. Suddenly, he pushes his chair back, almost knocking it over, and bolts from the room.

Steve shakes his head as I process what just happened.

"Now see whatcha done?" asks Lou. "There's no harm in him sittin' next to Bob if he fancies it."

Steve looks at me for support; he doesn't get it. He grumbles, "I didn't say there was any harm. Just wonderin' why the change. You know how he hates change."

I realize I am in the middle of a family feud, my first since moving out of my parents' house. Squat's seating adjustment is, apparently, a seismic shift in the family dynamic, but neither Steve nor Lou raise their voices. If this had been my parents, my father would have been yelling and shaking a fist.

All throughout supper, Steve and Lou appear fine with each other, so when we finish I ask, "Lou, could I get another plate of food?"

"Honey, I'll fix you a plate but when you gonna eat it? You just ate 'nough to feed an Army."

"If it's all right, I'd like to take it up to Squat. I don't want him to miss a meal because of me."

Steve snorts. "Miss a meal? You afraid that boy's gonna skinny up and die? Don't you worry 'bout Squat. He'll be sneakin' down here about ten tonight gettin' a big slice of that cake I'm gettin' ready to cut into."

"If it's all right, I want to take a plate of food up to him."

Lou smiles at me like a mother smiles at a son who's just done good and says, "Wait here. I'll have it in a jiff."

Steve snorts again. "You gonna spoil that boy," he says, but I know he doesn't mean it.

Lou is gone for about two minutes, during which Steve and I sit there in silence.

Just before she returns with a plate heaped with food, Squat peeks around the corner then walks over and sits down next to me.

Steve is getting ready to speak, so I shake my head ever so gently, and he remains quiet.

Lou doesn't break stride. She breezes in and sets the plate of food in front of Squat, saying, "See what I got for you, Squat? You comin' back down saved Bob the trouble of bringin' it up to you. He was gonna, you know."

Squat glances at me then stares down at his lap. "I know."

I glance from Lou to Steve, surprised. This is the first time I've heard Squat talk.

Steve walks out on the porch, but I sit with Squat while he eats and Lou clears the table.

When Squat finishes, he and I join Steve on the porch. Five minutes later, Lou joins us. Nobody has much to say.

After a while, I look at my watch and observe, "I believe *St. Elsewhere* is coming on TV about now. I think I'll go up to my room and watch it."

"Honey, you can watch it in the living room. Won't bother us none, will it, Stevie?"

Steve just grunts. I think he's asleep.

"Maybe not," I say, "but I've been here for almost two weeks now and I haven't seen that TV on yet. I think I'll just watch it upstairs."

"Suit yourself."

My room is in the front corner of the house and it is big. It has windows on two walls. The front one faces the street, the side one the neighbor's house, which is about 100 feet away. A double bed has a small table next to it with a lamp. It butts against the wall with the door into my bath and there is a chair opposite it. On the last wall is a dresser with a small TV sitting on top of it. As I drop into the chair, I notice Squat peeking in.

"You can come in and watch with me if you'd like," I call to him.

He is inside in a flash and sits down on my bed.

When the show is over, he says, "I like Tommy." Tommy is autistic. I start to ask Squat if he's autistic but think better of it.

"I go bed now," he says and walks out of the room. As he reaches the door, he raises his hand in the no-look wave to which I'm becoming accustomed.

Chapter Four

After three months in Waynedale, I'm pleased with how easily I have made the transition. Most of the credit for this goes to my new family. I have supper with Steve, Lou, and Squat every night, and Sally is there frequently. It's like I grew up in this house.

I'm beginning to know people around town, and they greet me by my name. That never happened in Chicago. The Waynedale Mafia have each stopped by separately to ask, "Are they treatin' you right?" The first time Lou hears one of them say this, I see darkness descend over her face.

Pauline Wilson is the last to visit. As soon as she leaves, Lou, lightning flashing in her eyes, asks me, "How do they think we'd be treatin' you?" Her lips pucker as if she just sucked on a lemon.

I shrug and shake my head.

In the evening of the Fourth of July, Steve, Lou, Squat, and I walk to the town square, where we meet Sally. The local politicians are trying to get re-elected, and each has fifteen minutes on the steps of the courthouse to "bend our ear," as Lou calls it.

They don't impress Steve, who is shifting from one foot to the other and commenting under his breath about the "idiots we elect."

"Let's go," he urges Lou. "I thought there was gonna be fireworks."

Lou looks at him, puzzled, and says, "There will be."

"Yeah, but when?"

Lou shakes her head slowly. "It's only 7:00. It won't be dark enough for fireworks for another *two hours*."

Steve takes off the St. Louis baseball cap he always wears and rubs his head. His lips move, but no words come out.

Squat is off to the side nodding at everyone who comes by, them nodding back. To any who will listen, he points in my direction and says, "Me and Bob, we mechanics." Then, when they walk away, he treats them to a no-look wave.

Suddenly, Squat points through the crowd. "Miss Clare! Miss Clare!" he calls while hopping a time or two. The Waynedale Mafia has arrived.

"Hello, Darlin'," Clare says to Squat. She glances at me and says to Squat, "You keep an eye on Bob, will you? After all, it's your day to watch him."

"I watch him," Squat tells her, taking a sideways peek at me.

"Good," Clare croons.

They start to walk away, but Clare turns back one last time. "Strut, Sally, strut!" she says.

Sally ignores her but smiles.

The other four members propel Clare down the street toward a sign that advertises funnel cakes.

Finally, Steve waves in disgust at the current speaker, and says, "I'm goin' home. I'll be damned if I can listen to all this hocus-pocus for another hour. Besides, I need to get up early and get to work in my garden. You comin', Lou?"

"Yeah, I think so. My dogs are tired." She takes her left foot out of her shoe and rubs it against her right calf, puts it back in her shoe, and says, "Come on Squat. Let's go home."

"Firework," Squat insists. "Firework."

Lou raises her eyebrows, but Steve is adamant. "We're goin' home."

Squat frowns and moves toward me.

I say, "He can stay with Sally and me. I'll get him home."

Steve shakes his head. "Squat won't wanna be away from us."

But Squat says, "I come home with Bob. Wanna see firework."

"You want to stay?" Steve asks him.

"Yeah."

Lou and Steve both look at each other, and Lou asks, "Are you sure, Honey? Steve and I won't be here, ya know."

"I knoooow," says Squat, making the word sound twice as long as it is. "Go onnnn."

"Okay," says Lou. "Sally, you take care of Squat."

Squat insists, "I come home with Bob."

"Sure thing, Squat. We'll watch the fireworks, walk Sally to her house, then we'll be home ourselves."

Steve and Lou walk away, but Lou glances back twice. The second time she is smiling.

Squat continues to greet people. He seems quite the celebrity around town.

We listen to the speeches, walk around the square, and Sally and I talk about work, her parents, and Squat.

Squat listens but never comments. He does, however, wave to people coming by, always without looking at them.

The fireworks go off at 9:00. They're directly overhead and soon ashes and the smell of gunpowder drift through the air. I feel the sound of the blasts concussing my chest a split second before I hear them.

Shortly after they start, Sally nudges me with her elbow and points toward Squat, who is covering his ears and gazing to the sky in awe.

I spend the rest of the show moving my gaze back and forth from the sky to Squat, observing his reaction to the explosions taking place hundreds of feet in the air, watching his face light up then darken as the fireworks go from one color to another. The grand finale brings a cheer from him. Clapping, he looks over his shoulder at me, smiling broadly.

Squat is walking about ten feet in front of us on the way to Sally's house when she asks me to tell her about my family. "Are they in Chicago?"

Hesitating, I say, "I don't have a family."

"We all have parents. Are they alive?"

I frown, but Sally looks at me and says, "Come on, Bob. You know things 'bout me I don't normally let outside the family. It's time for you to share if this is gonna be a friendship."

She's right. I heard Sally's life story the first week I was in town, much to her mortification. She didn't wish for me to hear how much trouble she had when she first started having periods, or how she wet the bed until she was a teenager and the medicine she took to fix that. Certain things a person wants to keep within the family, but Steve and Lou are talkers, at least when it comes to their pride and joy, and Sally quickly accepted me as part of the family.

Once I was in, she didn't get embarrassed when they told me about her disastrous luck with men. She even revealed a few secrets her parents didn't know about, such as the summer after her junior year in high school when she was a governor's scholar. She was staying in a dormitory at the University of Kentucky but spent most nights sneaking in and out of the room of a young man from Corbin.

It is only fair I share a little with her, so I say, "My mother died shortly after I graduated high school. I haven't seen my father since her funeral. We had a falling out in the spring of my senior year. He thought I was a great baseball player, would go to college, and he'd be able to sit in the stands basking in parental glory."

"And you didn't want that?"

I shook my head. "I enjoyed working on things. I started taking toys apart and modifying them when I was barely walking. When I was twelve, I worked on a car with a neighbor. From then on, sports came second."

"Didn't your father want you to be a mechanic?"

"No. He didn't understand it. Said I was throwing my life away. He got angry after the last game of my senior year. A recruiter asked to talk to me about playing college ball, and I blew him off just as my mother and father walked up. My father told me I should at least talk to the recruiter, that I could go to college on a free ride, maybe get picked up by the pros in a few years. He mentioned how much money professional baseball players make. By this time, the recruiter had walked away. I told dad college wasn't in my future. I wanted to be an auto mechanic."

"What did he say to that?"

"He said, 'You're throwing away a college education.'"

Sally stops walking, so I stop, too. She stares at me and says, "Did you ever consider he was right?"

"He didn't give a damn about me getting a college education. He needed me to play ball, and I didn't want to. He told me boys dream of having my talent and that I shouldn't throw it away."

"Bob, please don't think I'm tellin' you that you're wrong, but he makes a very persuasive argument, even without bein' here." Sally smiles, but the disapproval comes through.

"Okay, first, I wasn't that talented. Second, I didn't dream of playing ball, he did. It's my life, and I have to live it the way I choose. He told me I was throwing my life away working on cars. He thought mechanics were lowlifes. I don't think I've thrown my life away, do you?"

"It's not for me to judge whether you've thrown your life away. It just seems you're bein' too hard on your father. You could have at least tried his way. You always had the opportunity to walk away later, but you didn't even try."

She is still smiling at me, but I'm no longer smiling back.

"So you're saying I'm wrong, too?" We have reached Sally's house, a small cape cod about four blocks from her parents.

Squat, about twenty feet in front of us, stops first, points at us and says, "I see you," his catch-all phrase for when he is happy.

"I'm not sayin' you're right or wrong. But what's it been now, over fifteen years since you even talked to him? And it's all so minor. Don't you think you could call him?"

I consider discussing the rest; the times he got drunk and blackened my mother's eyes then split my lip when I tried to get between them, the drinking binges that sent fear through mother and me.

My mother always said, "Keep it in the family." Are Sally and I enough of a family to share this? I'm not sure I can explain how one argument grew out of all the anger I felt toward my father.

"He was an SOB then and he's an SOB now." I hope to leave it at that.

"How can you be sure?"

"A leopard can't change its spots."

"Your father's not a leopard. He's a thinkin', reasonin' human. Give him some credit."

I clench and unclench my fists. "Why don't you give me some credit? I think we've talked about this enough. Let's agree to disagree because I'm not going to change my mind on this." I can't bring myself to reveal how afraid I was, not yet.

Sally is on the sidewalk leading up to her front door. She looks at me and says, "I just think you should consider the possibility that you're wrong. I say that as a friend." Before I can reply, she turns and goes inside.

I stand there on the sidewalk gazing at the house, watching lights come on as Sally moves toward the bedroom until I hear Squat say, "I see you!"

I say, "Squat, I better get you home before Lou sends out a search party."

We set off for home, side by side.

"I like firework," he tells me.

"Me, too." I look at Squat. Maybe it's his carefree attitude, but his appearance says he's about my age, even though I know he's in his early fifties.

"We mechanics, Bob. We do same thing."

"Yep," I say, "we're two peas in a pod." I start to put my arm around his shoulder, but he moves away.

"No hugs."

"Okay," I say. "No hugs."

33

———

The next day, Steve is in his garden when I leave for work. He's still there when I get home.

"Did you spend the whole day out there?" I ask.

"Nah," he says. "You've heard that sayin', 'Mad dogs and Englishmen go out in the noonday sun?' I come in about ten every day, rest, have lunch, read a little, sometimes I take a nap. Then about four, I go back out. I love my gardenin'. Most of our vegetables come from it."

"I've got a brown thumb."

"Not everbody enjoys it, but it keeps me young. Besides, what else do I have to do?"

I don't know the answer to that. I have yet to figure out what Steve does, besides gardening and piddling around the house.

———

That night, Sally comes to eat. Neither of us are too sure where we stand with the other, so we don't say much, but after supper she whispers, "Let's take a walk."

"Okay," I say, and then to Lou and Steve, "Think Sally and I will take a walk."

"You should do that," booms Steve. "When winter gets here, it'll be too cold to walk in the evenin'. Course, the advantage you'll have then is there'll be mistletoe a hangin' all over the place."

I start to respond, but Sally tugs on my arm, and says, "Let it go."

We head out on a meandering path around town, neither saying much, until we end up at the park just off the town square, the scene of the fireworks the night before. Thin, early vapors of night are descending around us as Sally scurries ahead of me and sits on a bench, patting the seat next to her as if I were a recalcitrant child.

"Can we talk about last night?" she asks as soon as I sit down.

"Not sure we need to. You think I'm a bastard about my father, I think he's the bastard, and I won't change my mind. What's to talk about?"

"That's why we should talk. I realized after I went in the house last night that it shouldn't matter to me what kind of a relationship you have with your father. If we were datin' that would be one thing, but there's no romantic spark 'tween us, is there?"

"Naw," I say. "I'm beginning to understand what someone meant one time when she told me she liked me too much to love me. I enjoy being with you, but I don't feel too much down below when I think about you, if you know what I mean."

She nods and smiles. Then, glancing away, she says, "It's a shame, really. Papa will be so disappointed. I think he's more interested in us gettin' together than anyone that's ever come around."

"At the risk of being as nosy as Clare Jackson, why haven't you ever married? Is it one of those deals where you're a confused actress?"

She shakes her head slowly. "What *are* you talkin' about?"

"You know, 'I started out to be a thespian, but I ended up a being a lesbian.'"

Sally laughs, shakes her head, and says, "No, I'm definitely interested in men. It's just that in a small town when you've been skinny dippin' with every male within five years of your age, you have to broaden the search beyond the pool you been swimmin' in. I've never been away from here, and there ain't that many strangers that come through. You're the first in a while, in case you hadn't noticed."

"Yeah, I noticed. Think you'll ever meet Mister Right?"

"Not sure, but we're startin' to get a little far afield here. Let's clear up last night first."

"Okay," I sigh, "what about last night?"

"There's a lot of things that can mess up friendships, right?" She scrutinizes me, holding her hands out as if balancing some unseen object. My amusement must be showing because she squints and asks, "What?"

"If someone cut your hands off, you wouldn't be able to talk anymore."

"God, you're hard to talk to." She rolls her eyes then pats my arm. "I'm just sayin' let's be friends. Let's let each other have his opinions and express those opinions and not let it get in the way of our friendship. Does that make sense?"

"Kind of. Are you saying you were wrong the other night?"

"*No!*"

I wince as her voice concusses my ears like the fireworks.

Then, in a conversational tone, she continues, "I'm sayin' it doesn't matter if I was wrong or you were wrong, although for the record I think you *were* wrong, and I think you'd be a lot happier if you at least reached out to your father. But you're not gonna, unless someone way smarter than me figures out a way to get you two talkin', so I won't be mad at you for bein' a pig-headed mule if you won't be mad at me for bein' right. There, does that make sense?"

"It didn't, until you put it so diplomatically."

Sally ignores the sarcasm. "So we're not mad at each other?"

"What, you turn down a proposal of marriage that I never

make and I'm not supposed to be mad?" I am laughing as I say this, and Sally begins to laugh, too.

She leans into me for a moment, but just as I reach to put my arm around her, she straightens up and looks at me.

"Okay, let's get to the issue of you and me as more than friends. We've known each other for what, four months, now? We've had supper about four nights a week—"

"Always in the presence of your parents."

"True, but we've been together a lot and—"

"We haven't been skinny dipping yet."

"No, we haven't, and if I was you, I wouldn't hold my breath, either. Gravity's done some nasty things to me since the last time I did that." She pauses for a minute then asks, "Where was I? Darn, you can get me off the subject."

"We were having supper with your parents."

"Oh, yeah. Okay, we've spent a lot of time together and you've never even tried to kiss me."

"Do you want me to?"

She shakes her head. "Not anymore."

"But you did?"

"Yeah," she nods.

"What changed?"

"I'm not sure. You just kinda became a brother, you know what I mean?"

"I think so. When I first came here, it was just too soon after…well, too soon. By the time I began to think about you as a woman, I was already thinking of you as a sister."

She leans back and stares at me. A look crosses her face that I can't quite figure out. Disappointment? Anger?

"Does that make you mad?" I ask.

She weighs her words for a moment then turns away, and says, "Not mad, sad. In the right circumstance, I think we'd be good together."

"What circumstance would that be?"

She turns to face me, her eyes staring into mine, all the way down into my soul. "Maybe if that torch you're carrryin' wasn't big enough to set fire to the whole town."

I look away. After an awkward pause, I ask, "That obvious, huh?"

"Jeez, Bob, do you think we're all stupid? We're small-town maybe, but we can see when an open sore comes through."

"Whew! For a sister, you can be pretty mean."

She laughs, puts her hand on my knee, and declares, "Sorry."

"Can I ask a favor of you?"

"Sure," she says. "What is it?"

Her hand on my knee is suddenly hot, and for the first time since I left Chicago, I feel a stirring, not quite a hunger, but certainly a stirring.

"Will you give me another chance? Maybe I'm ready to kiss you now."

Sally leans back and withdraws her hand. She stretches, arching her back, her breasts pushing forward. I imagine her doing that on a riverbank wearing nothing but water. I don't care what Sally alleges about gravity, all of a sudden, I want to swim naked with this woman.

"Well?" I say.

Her face contorts and she says, "I'm thinkin'."

After what seems like five minutes but is probably five-seconds, she announces, "I'm sorry, Bob. It's just not there anymore." She smiles gently as she says it.

I'm disappointed but not surprised and I smile back, even though I feel a knot in my stomach. Pam wins again.

She touches my arm. "But we're brother and sister, right? I could use a brother, and you need female companionship in the worst way."

"I've *had* female companionship in the worst way."

We both laugh, but I add, "You're right. I could use a sister. And about that kiss..."

The laughter stops, and she appears apprehensive, but she needn't be. I lean toward her and kiss her cheek.

Chapter Five

On a Saturday morning in early September, Steve comes to my room and asks me if I can help him.

"Car problems?" I guess, as he leans against the door jamb breathing heavily from coming up the stairs.

"Nah. The Waynedale Mafia's comin' for dinner tomorrow. Lou always tries to impress them, 'specially Clare, so I gotta put the trim up around the door to the screened-in porch."

I had noticed the door with no trim the day I moved in and had asked Steve about it.

"You see," Steve had told me, "Lou always wanted a porch, so 'bout a year ago I built this one right offa the kitchen. Cut the door in where a window used to be and built it all by myself. Well, Squat handed me tools, but I did all the work. I never quite got the trim put up round the door, but I'll get to it someday."

That discussion had occurred six months ago; "someday" has arrived.

"Can you help me?"

"Sure. Let's get started." I move toward the door.

He holds his hand up like a traffic cop. "Not so fast, Mr. Big City. I ain't ready to get started yet. I gotta get my tools together and run an errand. We'll get on it about noon."

I take a slow walk around town, get back around twelve, and find Steve on the screened porch.

"Let's go," I say as Steve turns on the TV.

"Ball game's about to start. We'll do it at halftime."

"I thought you wanted to get this done."

"Sure, I do. Don't you think for a minute that I don't wanna get that trim put up, but this is the big game I been hearin' about all week. At halftime, we'll knock that trim out, and be ready to watch the second half."

Steve and I sit down in front of the TV. About ten minutes into the game, Lou sticks her head through the door and says, "I thought you was gonna put the trim up." That's not her happy voice I'm hearing.

"Halftime, Honey, halftime." Steve's eyes never leave the TV.

At halftime, Steve and I both stand up, but instead of heading to the basement for tools and trim, Steve walks to the TV and changes the channel. A second game is just kicking off. "Don't you want to do the trim now?" I ask.

"Nah, we'll do it at halftime of this game." Steve sits back down. There's nothing for me to do but to join him.

Ten minutes go by, and Lou's head comes through the trim-less doorway, again. "When's halftime?"

Steve dismisses her with a wave. "Not yet."

Lou stares for about ten-seconds, looking from Steve to me, and back. Steve's eyes are still glued to the TV. I begin to sense that I am in the presence of a master.

At halftime of the second game, Steve gets up long enough

to change back to the first game, but this time Lou must hear the clicking of the channel selector.

She comes in and asks what's going on, and Steve croons that the trim will be up as soon as the game is over; this is the game of the year, maybe the decade, and surely, she doesn't want him to miss it.

"I want the trim up for the Mafia's visit, that's what I want." Ice hangs from each word.

"And you'll have it," Steve chortles. "You'll have it." Each word is a joyful celebration of a job well-done, anticipated.

Another station change, and I hear Lou starting to prepare supper in the kitchen. The last game ends at 5:15 and Steve, finally energized and focused on the task at hand, stands up and announces, "Time to get that trim up."

Just then, Lou hollers, "Steve, supper's gonna be ready in 'bout ten minutes. You and Bob get washed up and eat while it's hot. You can fix the trim after we eat. Tell Squat to wash up, too."

"Your wish is my command."

I don't believe that for a minute, and the look Lou gives Steve says that she hasn't believed it for about thirty years.

Sally arrives just as we sit down, smiling and hugging everyone. Supper consists of pork chops, mashed potatoes, vegetables from Steve's garden, and small talk about my job; am I liking it, can I maybe listen to Sally's car some time, the engine seems to be misfiring, and the latest gossip from Eats. The Mafia was in again today and Clare asked Sally about me.

"What did you tell her?" I ask.

"I told her I guessed you were okay, and she said she would be over here tomorrow for dinner and would get to check on you herself. I think you're 'bout to get another pie."

Lou harrumphs at that news.

As supper ends, Steve stands, ceremoniously. Rubbing his

ample stomach, he regards me and commands, "Let's go put up that trim."

We walk to the basement where Steve has a workshop and a bumper pool table.

"Wanna shoot a game?" he asks, picking up a pool cue.

"Steve, we really ought to get that trim put up."

Upstairs, I can hear Lou and Sally talking quietly as they clean up after supper, unaware of the insurrection being plotted in the basement.

Steve slowly shakes his head, all the while making a "Tsk, tsk" noise. Then, he says, "I don't have enough trim for that door." There it is, out in the open. When was he going to tell Lou? There is no desperation in his voice, nor do I hear any remorse, just the simple statement; there's no trim, let's shoot pool.

At least *I* don't have to answer to Lou. I hope.

"There's just one thing," says Steve, chalking up a cue. "These balls make a lotta noise when they fall in the hole. When either of us shoots, the other one has to put his hand under the hole and catch the ball if it goes in, so's Lou won't hear it."

We shoot four games of bumper pool, catching each ball as it falls through the hole. I am just lining up what will be the winning shot in the fifth game, when suddenly I hear very loud footsteps coming down the stairs. I survey Steve for guidance, but he's turning in a circle and waving his arms in the air like a drunken sailor trying to dance, all the while, saying, "Act natural. Act natural."

A thought crosses my mind, and it's not pleasant. We're dead meat. I attempt to hold the cue steady as I sense doom arriving.

Lou explodes through the door, moves quickly around the table, and picks up the ball before I can shoot it.

I start to protest but think better of it. Steve will know what to do.

"*Why aren't you puttin' up the trim?*" Each word is a cannon shot coming out of Lou's mouth.

Steve looks befuddled, and I realize that he hasn't planned this far. He rubs his head as if he can push an idea right into it, but all he can come up with is the truth, and that's not going to set us free.

"Honey, I don't have any trim," he whimpers.

I am so disappointed. Where did unflappable Steve go?

The cannon roars again. "*Go buy some.*"

Damn, I think, why didn't Steve think of that, preferably at noon?

Steve raises his eyebrows, and relief crosses his face. "Good idea. What time does the hardware store close?"

I say, "Seven on Saturdays. I saw it on the door when I walked by there this morning."

"What time is it?" Steve is excited now. Not only does he have a plan, but it will work.

I glance at my watch. "6:58."

Steve grins sheepishly at Lou, who slams the ball down on the pool table and stomps upstairs, making somewhat more noise than when she came down.

"Ya know," Steve drawls, totally regaining the cool that had evaporated in Lou's presence, "there's some good come out of her findin' out."

"Yeah? What would that be?"

"We don't have to catch the balls anymore. I believe it's your shot."

We play two more games, letting the balls settle into the holes with a satisfying thump while upstairs Lou is methodically dismantling the kitchen. Pots clang, doors slam, and feet stomp. I begin to wish I knew a secret passage from the basement to my room that could take me there without crossing Lou's path. She is not a small woman.

After about ten minutes, Steve realizes that I am too rattled to give him any serious competition and that he will need to rebuild the kitchen if he doesn't do something soon. He walks over to a loose stack of wood and bends over, farting when he does. He starts sifting through the pile and pulls out a very fine piece of woodwork, about eight feet in length. Almost to himself, he mutters, "That should work."

He reaches into the stack again, as if he knows where to grab, and pulls out a second piece. Another reach and he snags a third piece accompanied by a second fart. "I think we got it," he says.

I give the trim a once-over. Not only are the three pieces not the same width, but none of them has the same shape as either of the other two; they aren't even the same type of wood.

"I don't think Lou will like that," I tell Steve as I follow him up the steps. That doesn't matter to him. Thankfully, Lou has left the kitchen and is not in sight. Sally, probably in anticipation of things to come, is gone also.

Steve quickly cuts a forty-five-degree angle on each piece of trim. Then, using my measurements of the lengths needed, he cuts the three pieces to length. He nails them up, stands back, and admires the door as if it is a museum piece. "There ya go," he drawls, sounding quite pleased.

I point out, one last time, that the trim does not match in style, type of wood, or width.

"Beggars can't be choosers," he says.

The only choosing I see in our future is Lou choosing which of our heads she puts knuckle bumps on first. The begging will be both of us begging her to pick the other one. I don't choose to be in the room when she sees this, so I head quickly upstairs. As I close my door, I hear Steve calling, "Lou, Honey, come look. I put the trim up."

I love the exaggerated way he tells the truth.

———

The next morning, I hear Lou and Steve bustling around in the kitchen, so I go down to see what's happening and walk right into what I imagine a shark feeding frenzy on dry land would look like. Sally has come over, and she and Lou are cooking, baking, and ordering Steve around. No sooner do I walk through the door than Lou instructs me to "peel those taters," waving vaguely in the direction of a large bowl of potatoes on the counter.

I figure that since she didn't come into my room in the middle of the night and beat me senseless with a baseball bat for my part in the door-trim escapade, I should help out. Getting a knife out of a drawer, I start to peel what seems to be a one-week ration of potatoes for Fort Knox.

I've been peeling "taters" for about thirty-seconds when Lou steps next to me and asks, "What *are* you doin'?" She reaches for the knife in my hand and disarms me as smoothly as if she were a Navy seal.

"Lou, *be careful,*" I say. "Don't be grabbing for a knife when I'm using it," but the knife is already out of my hand.

"You can't peel taters with this," she says, holding the knife about three inches from my nose. "Get the tater peeler."

"I didn't know we have a tater peeler. Where might we keep it? In the tater peeler drawer?"

Lou glares at me, opens another drawer, and pulls out an instrument that I vaguely remember from my youth as a potato peeler. She hands it to me and as she walks away. I hear her muttering, "Can't hang trim. Can't peel taters. Good thing he can fix cars."

At 11:45, Lou notifies me to go get dressed.

"I am dressed." I catch a glimpse of Sally over Lou's shoulder shaking her head. Too late.

"You gotta put on some nice clothes. Imagine you have a date." Lou furrows her brow and frowns. "No, that won't work; ain't nobody got that vivid a 'magination. Pretend you're goin' to church. You *have* gone to church sometime in your wretched life, haven't you?"

"Every Christmas and Easter for eighteen years."

I beam proudly, but Lou glares at me as if I am Judas and just betrayed Jesus. "Go put on something you'd wear to church if you was goin'," she barks and sends me off with a wave of her hand. Sally and Steve are standing behind her, trying to keep their laughter out of her sight. I go upstairs to put on "something I'd wear to church."

While I'm changing, I hear the doorbell ring, a rush to the door, and a cacophony of voices. The most recognizable one belongs to Clare Jackson, but the rest of the Mafia's ring through, too. I descend the stairs just as I hear Clare asking, "So where's that Bob?"

I say, "Here I am, Ms. Jackson."

She whirls around and sees me coming down the steps.

"Ms. Jackson? That's my mother, and she's *dead*. I'm Clare. You remember me?"

"I sure do, Ms. uh, Clare."

She is holding out a pie to me. "I made this just for you," she says.

Lou is standing behind her, mouthing, "Just for you," her head rocking back and forth.

"It's apple. I hope you like it."

"It sounds wonderful. Do you mind if I share it with everyone? We'll have it with dinner."

"Well, I did bring a pie for dinner, too." She pauses. "This one's for you." She glances around, saying, "And where's Squat? I haven't seen that boy in forever." She leaves me holding the pie as she searches for Squat.

He comes down the stairs smiling broadly and saying, "I see you. I see you, Miss Clare."

I carry the pie to the kitchen. As I return, Lou calls everyone to the table. There are ten of us at a table for eight, so it is a little crowded. Squat and I sit near the end of the table, with Clare on the other side of me. She regales me throughout the meal with stories of her younger days, when she performed in USO shows.

"I was quite the singer, and I could dance some, too. Performed once on the same show as the Rockettes," she brags, while everyone at the table mouths, "Same show as the Rockettes." At least the story is new to me.

"I didn't know Sylvester Stallone was that old," I say. "How was the Italian Stallion?"

Clare squints at me over her glasses, and I hear a few nervous chuckles around the table. "*Rockettes*," she boasts. "Not Rocky; the Radio City Music Hall *Rawwwwckettes*. No wonder you can't keep a woman. You don't listen."

"It ain't men who can't listen, it's jellyfish," Steve interjects. That tidbit gets everyone's attention. "Here's how it is," he continues. "Ninety-seven percent of all jellyfish can't hear. Don't have a heart or brain, either. Strictly reactin' to their environment." Steve waits a moment for everyone to digest those facts then concludes, "I figure they must all be females." Steve returns to eating, oblivious to the reaction this elicits from the seven women around the table.

Lou starts to respond, but Clare gets there first.

"I don't know what you think men have to be so proud of," she says. "I was readin' just the other day that the first protective cup was used in hockey in 1874 and the first helmet was used in 1974. That means it only took 100 years for you men to realize that your brain upstairs is as important as your brain downstairs."

While the Mafia hoot and Steve scowls, Sally catches my eye and winks; I wink back.

"And when are you gonna get those glasses fixed?" Clare continues. I declare, Steve, you've been missin' the lens out of that one side for nigh on a year, now."

"They want two hunnerd dollars just to put a lens in," Steve complains. "That's not my bad eye. I see just fine as long as I have the lens in the other side."

"You are cheap, you know that, don't you?" Pauline asks.

"He thinks it makes him appear eccentric," says Lou.

"I *am* eccentric," Steve replies.

"You're an old fool," scolds Mabel.

After dinner, Steve asks the Mafia if they'd like to see the trim that, "Bob an' me put up just yesterday."

"Steve, I didn't do anything," I say.

"What're you talkin' about? You were with me all the way."

"No, not really." I require no credit; I prefer no blame.

"Well, anyway," says Steve, escorting the women down the hall toward the porch, "It's another example of the fine work I do with my hands." He gestures grandly toward the door, his fingers spread widely.

The Mafia study the mismatched, unpainted trim.

Finally, Pauline, pulling her glasses down and tipping her head forward so she can see over them, asks, "Steve, is it my glasses, or does that not match at all?"

The others mutter agreement.

"Well, it ain't necessarily supposed to match," says Steve. "Who says each piece of trim has to match?"

"Every carpenter I've ever known!" exclaims Clare. "It's a wonder Lou stays with you."

"Lou's in love with me, Clare. Ain't love grand?"

"Love may be grand," sasses Clare, "but a divorce is about a hundred grand. You best get some matchin' trim up there before Lou kicks your ragged butt outta here."

The Mafia nod their heads, hang their purses over their arms, and to murmurs of "That old fool" turn and leave.

Chapter Six

I have very little opportunity for interaction with customers. I'm told which car to work on, and the service manager talks to the owner when he picks it up.

This morning, I replaced the alternator on an eleven-year-old car, and when I pulled it outside, I noticed the windshield was filthy. After I cleaned it, I gave the ticket to the service manager and told him it was ready.

———

A few hours later, I'm startled when I hear a woman behind me speaking my name as a question.

"Bob?"

I'm sitting at the desk in my repair bay eating my lunch and reading the paper. Turning, I see a woman about my age standing there.

"That's me. What can I do for you?"

She hesitates when she sees the sandwich in my hand. My boss back in Chicago once asked me if I thought a woman knew that men decide within ten-seconds of meeting her whether we want to sleep with her. I told him I didn't think most men thought that way, and he laughed at me.

She's about five feet two, dressed casually in new blue jeans, an old sweatshirt, and a St. Louis Cardinals baseball cap. She has a pleasing figure; she'd probably like to lose ten pounds, but I wouldn't take away an ounce. Even beneath the sweatshirt, I can tell that her breasts are either very firm or she has a bra with magnificent support. Her curly red hair pulled into a ponytail through the hole in the back of her cap reminds me of a movie star I saw once at Grant's Park in Chicago. Her cobalt blue eyes and toothy smile look nervous, perhaps even timid, and I suspect she's embarrassed for interrupting my lunch. Her face is as pretty as I have run across since I've been in town, and her jeans are tight. I'm dying for her to turn around so I can check out her butt. Five-seconds in, the answer is yes.

"I'm sorry. I didn't realize you were eatin'," she says with a Kentucky twang and a husky voice that seems to have smoke rolling off it. "I wanted to thank you for cleanin' the inside of the windshield on my car. Nobody's ever done that before."

I smile at her. "Yours was the one with the big smudge on the inside?"

She nods. "It's so hard to clean the inside."

"I know. I've got a little gadget that pivots and holds a cloth against the windshield. It makes it a lot easier." I set my sandwich down and stand up.

"I need to get one of those," she replies, glancing around. Returning her gaze to me, she says, "My name's Nellie McDonald." She steps toward me then leans, like she doesn't want to invade my space, and holds out her hand.

I wipe mine on a napkin and take hers. It's warm; must have been in her pocket.

"Ah, a wee Scottish lass." I do my best brogue, which is terrible, but Nellie smiles an appreciation for the effort.

"Actually, no. That's the only thing I kept after the divorce. Everything else went to pay off my ex-husband's bills."

I still haven't gotten used to the openness of the locals. People around here seem to think they might as well share everything since everybody knows everyone.

They don't mind questions, either, so I ask, "Is he still running up those bills on you?"

"No. He was a semi-professional drunk when we divorced five years ago. 'Bout a year later, he turned pro. Got drunk one night and passed out in the gutter durin' a rainstorm. Too bad for him 'cause the drain was stopped up and the dern fool drowned. Left me with a ten-year-old daughter who needs a daddy."

She stops talking suddenly, clenches her eyes closed, and flinches. After an uncomfortable pause, during which she opens, then rolls her eyes, she says, "I know. Too much information."

To change the subject, I say, "My name's Bob, but then you knew that."

She smiles and exhales. "How long you been here? I don't remember you, and when you've got an eleven-year-old car, you usually have a close relationship with your mechanic."

"About six months. I moved here from Chicago."

She raises her eyebrows. "You got family in the area?"

"No, just needed a change."

"Woman problems, huh?"

"You been reading my mail?"

Her laugh is as seductive as her voice. "There are only two reasons people move here from places like Chicago. One's to come home and take care of parents. The other is to run away from somethin'." She points at me and adds, "Or somebody."

"You got it." I raise both arms, then let them drop to my sides. "I got dumped, so I took off. End of story."

"Doesn't have to be. It could be the beginnin' of the next chapter. I'm definitely better off without my no-good, dead-beat, lyin', cheatin', two-timin', double dealin' bum ex."

I raise my eyebrows in shock.

"Too harsh?" She frowns and cocks her head as she appears to ponder her own question.

I drop my eyebrows and smile. "Maybe a little."

She shrugs, glances at Jake's desk, and says, "Your boss is lookin' at you. Wanna continue the conversation when you get off work? Do you know where the Grandview Inn is?"

I'm superstitious. I don't believe I should start a relationship in the same manner as with Pam, but I *want* to get to know this woman. I *need* to get to know this woman.

"Is that out on Waynedale Road? If so, I pass it every day on my way to work."

"Yeah, that's it. The best bar in these parts, and you can get a sandwich, too. What time you get off?"

"Five." I should call Lou and tell her I'll be late.

"I'll meet you there a little after five. I gotta make sure Jenny's got supper."

"Your daughter?"

"Yep." She's fifteen now, and I can't just take off without knowin' she's got somethin' to keep her busy or she's liable to get in trouble. She's drawn to...what did my divorce lawyer call them?" She pauses briefly, then announces, "Attractive nuisances. She said it was a term in personal injury cases but it fit my ex, too, and it certainly describes a lot of my daughter's boyfriends."

"Sounds like a handful."

"She is. But what should I expect? She got half her genes from the everlovin' bum I married."

"Sure did."

"Anyway," Nellie says, "I'll meet you there a little after five. We'll have a few laughs."

"Okay."

The whole idea of a night out snuck up on me so quickly that I didn't have time to get nervous, say no, or use any of the defensive strategies I usually rely on to fend off fun. When she walks away, I realize just how much I'm looking forward to it. She has the best butt I've ever seen.

———

The inside of the Grandview Inn is so dark I can't find Nellie when I first walk in. Shapes move about in the dark, and the jukebox is playing a song about trucks loaded up and heading eastbound and down, whatever that means. After a few seconds, my eyes begin to adjust, and I walk toward a waving arm.

As I slide into the booth, Nellie greets me with a big "Hi!" and a smile as wide as Texas.

Just then, the waitress shows up with a beer. Placing it in front of Nellie, she turns to me and asks, "What'll you have, Sugar?"

"The same," I say and tilt my head toward the bottle Nellie is raising to her lips. She has lost the baseball cap, and her hair cascades onto her shoulders. The sweatshirt is also gone, and the blouse she is wearing leaves no doubt that a bra is not the secret to her success. I'm hoping she kept the jeans.

We talk about the weather while we wait for my beer. I complain about the September heat, but Nellie insists I'll get used to it. After my beer arrives, Nellie says, "So this after-noon, all I learned 'bout you is that you're a fugitive from some dragon lady in Chicago. What's your story?"

"Not much to tell. I was with Pam for two and a half years, but she just wasn't ready to settle down, so I decided it was time for me to move on. Last April, I got in the car and headed south. Stopped in Waynedale for lunch and decided to stay for a while."

"For a while? So it ain't definite you'll be stayin' here?" Her husky voice and opulent lips have me thinking like a man.

"Nothing's definite, but I'm enjoying my stay."

"What're you hopin' to find?" When she folds her arms on the table and rests her chin on them, she looks like a pixie. She shows me an enigmatic smile that leaves me guessing what is going on behind those cobalt eyes.

I think for a minute then reply, "I'd like to belong, to have a family. When I have a conversation with someone, I want the other person to understand me."

Nellie wags her head back and forth and raises her eyebrows, so I continue.

"With Pam, I had that. At least, she knew what *I* was thinking, but it wasn't mutual. I had no clue that she was seeing other men. And by the way, she wasn't a dragon lady. More like a twelve-year-old with an ID."

Nellie sits up and purses her lips. "Sorry 'bout that. Most of the men I've met have nothin' good to say about their exes. As for you not havin' a clue about what she was thinkin', none of you guys do. Ever hear 'bout the little old man that had lived a good life, so God visited him and told him He'd grant the man one wish?"

"Variations on a theme. What's yours?"

"God says, 'Tom, you've obeyed my commandments, always did your best to do right. Sure, you've slipped a few times, but I'm willin' to forget you and the owl.'"

"Owl? How can God forget some guy messing around with an owl?"

Nellie's jaw drops and she looks away, then back. "Boy, you sure jump to conclusions. I never said he was messin' with the owl. I just said God was willin' to overlook it." She leans toward me. "Do you wanna hear this story or not?"

"Yeah, I want to hear it." Working hard at keeping a straight face, I say, "I just hope it wasn't a spotted owl. They're protected."

She puts both hands on the table, palms down, and her voice becomes brusque. "*Will you forget the owl?* You're ruinin' my story!" Her eyes sparkle as she laughs.

"Okay, Okay." I laugh, too, and raise my hands. Leaning back, I hold up two fingers in the direction of the waitress and point at our table.

"Anyway, God asks him what he wants. The old man professes, 'I'd like to take my wife to Hawaii for vacation, but she won't fly. Can you build me a bridge to Hawaii so we can drive there?'

"God told Tom, 'Yes, I can do that, but I won't. Boats will have to go around it, sea life will be disrupted. Besides, I don't think anyone else will ever use it. Nobody will drive that far, except you. Can you think of anything else?' Tom thinks, then replies, 'I've been married forty-five years. My wife and I raised three daughters and a son. I never had any trouble understandin' my son, but the women in my life! I don't have a clue! You created women; can you explain them to me?' God sighs and asks, 'Do you want that bridge to be two-lane or four?'" Nellie studies me for a minute. "So you see," she explains, spreading her hands about a foot apart with the palms up, as if she's releasing the idea for my consideration, "we're a mystery, even to God." She sounds pleased to be part of the mystery.

"I get the point, but it baffles me that God could forget the thing with the owl."

"Damn," she grumbles, slapping her hand on the table, "I'm sorry I mentioned that owl! Can we talk about somethin' else?"

Laughing, I ask, "What do you want to talk about?"

The waitress stops by to pick up our empties and drop off two more beers.

"Thanks," Nellie says, glancing up at her. "Can we get a sandwich?" Looking at me she asks, "You wanna get somethin' to eat?"

"Sure."

We give the waitress our order, and when she walks away Nellie says, "So you're enjoyin' your stay. Does that mean you've found someone that reads your mind? Do you really want that? Want someone to know your every thought? Wouldn't that be scary'?"

"No, no, no, and yes."

Nellie leans toward me and squints. "What're you talkin' about?"

"No, I have not found someone who reads my mind. No, I would not want that all the time. No, I do not want someone to know everything I'm thinking. And yes, I would find it intimidating."

She grins when I start talking and is laughing by the time I answer the last question.

"Sorry. I have a habit of firin' off too many questions. But I do think you're bein' a little rash, wantin' someone to read your mind."

I watch one of the pool players walk to the jukebox, where he studies the selections, finally dropping a coin. He returns to the table as his choice fills the bar with a man's voice asking a woman if he says she has a beautiful body will she hold it against him? Glancing at Nellie, I wonder the same thing. But it's not just physical; I love talking to this woman.

"You misunderstand," I say. "I don't want someone reading my mind. I need someone to know me, to understand me, to accept me and my old-fashioned ways."

"Like what?"

Scratching my head, I say, "I think a man should hold the door for a woman, should stand up when she comes into the room, should—"

"Respect her?" Excitement creeps into Nellie's voice.

"Yes, should respect her."

"You're a keeper," She blurts, a large smile on her pretty face. "So this didn't impress, what was her name, Pam?"

"Not at all."

Loud cheering and yelling break out by the pool table, and a skinny guy with a weak mustache high-steps around the table while punching his arms in the air, a cue stick held firmly in his right hand.

"Jasper finally won a game," mutters Nellie, shaking her head. "He's been playin' here forever, and I don't think he's ever won before." Nellie watches Jasper's celebratory lap around the pool table, grinning, then she turns back to me and asks, "Why should a man open a door for a woman?"

"Opening a door for a woman is a courtesy, not a show of strength to the weaker sex. But if a man is loaded down carrying stuff, a woman should open the door for him. Each couple has to negotiate their relationship. When they do, it's nobody else's business."

"And you and Pam couldn't negotiate the relationship?"

I think before answering. "That's the simple way of putting it. We probably weren't looking for the same things from the get-go. It just took me a while to understand that."

Nellie leans back and folds her arms. "Two and a half years? You're a slow learner."

"Ouch." I flinch and take a long drink of beer.

"Sorry, but come on." Her voice rises. "That whole time you didn't know she was runnin' 'round on you?'"

"Yeah, you're right," I shrug and rub my chin. "It's just that most people are a little gentler than you in pointing it out."

She starts to say something, but our sandwiches come and break our train of thought. We talk as we eat, about where I am living and does she know anyone in Waynedale, specifically Steve, Lou, Sally, and Squat, but they are all new to her. Nellie is a beautician. She works in a shop owned by someone else, has no desire to have her own place, loves country music, live theatre, and camping.

Finally, sandwiches finished, Nellie drains her beer and announces, "I've got to get home and check on Jenny, but this has been fun."

"Yes, it has," I agree.

We slide out of the booth and walk toward the door. Just about everyone in the place, including Jasper at the pool table, tells her goodbye, and the men size me up. The looks on their faces say they are not impressed.

I hold the door open for her and let her walk ahead of me, noticing she's still wearing the jeans. After checking out her butt, I resolve to follow her to the ends of the earth as long as she has them on.

As we walk to her car, I wonder if I should kiss her.

She answers that question by holding her hand out to me and saying, "Well, goodnight."

"Goodnight," I say, shaking her hand. Maybe next time.

Chapter Seven

The mid-September heat has lingered into the evening, something I'm not used to. By this time of year in Chicago, the days cool off quickly so when I get home a little after eight, I'm surprised to find Steve, Lou, Sally, and Squat sitting outside in the swings.

"What's her name?" Steve calls out as I come up the walk.

"Who said it was a she?" I holler back.

"You did, when you called to tell me you'd be late," Lou exclaims as I mount the steps.

Squat says, "I see you; I see you," and Sally is watching me like a mother watching a son ride a bike for the first time, proud of his accomplishment but fearful he will fall because he's not very good at it.

"You don't need to know everything," I assert, climbing the steps. "We stopped for a beer; isn't that enough?"

"No," Steve, Lou, and Sally answer in unison, causing all of us to laugh.

"She's just a customer who wanted to thank me for cleaning her windshield."

"Cleanin' her windshield? Is that what you call it these days?"

Ignoring Steve's comment, I drop down in a rocking chair. "Her name's Nellie McDonald. She lives in Grove's Point and has a fifteen-year-old daughter."

Steve shifts from leering to fatherly. "Bob, it's a lazy man that marries a woman with children."

"The subject of marriage didn't come up."

Lou exclaims, "Oh, it came up. You bein' a man, you just didn't realize it."

Sally smiles, and I begin to wonder about this small-town-everyone-knows-everything-about-everybody atmosphere. I remark that I'm tired and heading to bed.

As I stand up, Steve opens his mouth, and his lips flop in on his gums, but it is Sally who speaks. "You sure it's not goin' to bed that got you tired in the first place?"

Laughing loudly, Steve throws his head back, and I see there are no teeth in his mouth.

"Where are your teeth, Steve?" I ask him.

"Upstairs. They broke, so I'm fixin' 'em."

"How are you fixing them?"

"I glued 'em with crazy glue. Should be dry for breakfast. You wanna borry them? Maybe sweet Nellie would like you better with a new set of pearly whites."

"No, I don't want to 'borry' them." The first time Steve asked me if he could 'borry' a tool from me, I had to ask him to repeat it three times before I figured out what he was saying. "Why don't you take them to the dentist to be fixed?"

"Nope," he declares, shaking his head. "If I can't fix 'em, they can't be fixed. Besides, the dentist charges too much."

"Well, I hope you have them in at breakfast. I hate to think of you gumming your bacon and eggs."

I move toward the door, but before I can go inside, Sally says, "Bob, it's only eight-thirty. Let's take a walk."

She's right; it's way too early to go to bed, but I hesitate, making excuses. "It's getting dark; we won't be able to see. Besides, Squat and I usually watch some television before bed, don't we, partner?" I look at Squat, who holds a thumb up.

"We'll stay on the sidewalks and I've got a flashlight in my pocket. Uncle Squat won't mind, will you?"

We both look at him.

He waves his arm dismissively, and says, "Go onnnn."

Sally gets up from the swing and says, "Let's go." She walks to my side, loops her arm through mine, and pulls me toward the steps.

We walk silently to the sidewalk, her arm still looped through mine, and soon the house is out of sight.

After a few minutes of quiet companionship invaded only by the chirping of the crickets, she asks, softly, eyes straight ahead, "So what was her name?"

"I told you, Nellie McDonald."

"Not your date tonight. The woman that ran you out of Chicago. Don't you think it's time you told me about her?" she asks in a matter-of-fact tone.

"Why do you want to know about her?"

"A little bit curiosity." Sally is studying the other side of the street, but I see nothing over there that calls for such scrutiny. "But mostly, you are thirty-five years old and in this whole world, you got no one to talk to. I *dare* you to have a serious conversation with my father; my mother will blab whatever you say to the Mafia, and they'll tell everyone in town; even if you were talkin' to your father, he's not here, and Squat won't understand. That leaves me."

"Why is it so important I talk about her?"

A breeze, the first cool one of the evening, stirs through

our hair, and I hear the exasperation in Sally's voice as she says, "You're startin' a relationship with a woman you just met and you're still mopin' over the woman you left in Chicago. If your new relationship is gonna stand any kind of a chance, you've gotta put the old one to rest."

"Why do you say that?" I'm hoping I can make this conversation a philosophical discussion about getting over a broken heart rather than continuing this specific topic about my failed relationship.

"Well, since you're a man, you'll put your ex-girlfriend on a pedestal and compare Nellie to her. You're gonna remember only the *good* things about the ex while seein' the good *and bad* about Nellie. If you talk about the ex to me, I can tear her down and you'll begin to understand her faults. So let's start with an easy question." She stops suddenly, making me stop, too. Staring at me, she asks in a voice that declares she *will* have an answer, "What was her name?"

Looking away I say, "Pam Girard."

"Okay, now we're gettin' somewhere." She puts her hand on my chin, turns my head until we are face to face, and says, "And don't go all mopey on me." I meet her gaze, and she continues, "I think she was a fool to let you go. Now, fill me in about her so I can start blackin' her teeth and drawin' horns on this image you have before you start singin' her praises to Nellie." She still stares at me, smiling the smile you give a friend when you are absolving him of a mistake, not because he deserves absolution but because he is your friend.

"We dated for two and a half years, and I was ready to get married."

"But she wasn't?" Sally pauses until I nod then continues. "Do you know why?"

"Pam enjoyed playing the field. I didn't realize it until I had fallen in love."

64

"How'd you meet?"

I tell Sally about Pam coming into the garage, and she immediately remarks, "Just like you met Nellie." When I agree, she shakes her head. "You have no imagination."

"Yeah, well, I'm a creature of habit. At least when I met Nellie I didn't introduce myself as 'B-O-B Bob.'"

"What?" She squints at me and shakes her head, so I explain my inclination to spell my name when nervous.

"Oh, man," Sally chuckles. "You *really* should get out more."

I smile weakly and Sally says, "Hey, I'm teasin'."

I take a deep breath and let my gaze drift skyward. The first few stars are glowing, and I wonder if our planet appears as peaceful out there as the stars do from down here. "I know," I say. "I just get a little depressed when I talk about Pam."

We start walking again, and Sally suggests, "Let's work through that; Nellie deserves a chance. So you met Pam at the garage and had lunch. Then what?"

"We had dinner that evening."

"You mean supper?"

"Right. I forgot. Dinner's a big meal at noon."

Sally nods and says, "And you poked her that night?"

"No, I didn't poke her that night, as you so *elegantly* put it. After din...supper, she invited me back to her place, but I said no."

Sally looks at me and her eyebrows rise.

"I wanted it to be my idea."

"You and your male pride." Sally laughs.

"Yeah. But it wasn't long before I was sleeping over on a fairly regular basis. I was in love."

"You were in heat." She nudges me with her elbow, and I chuckle.

"When did you find out she was sleepin' around?" Sally asks.

"Not for a long time."

"Ignorance is bliss, huh?"

"Sure enough."

"And you are very blissful."

"Don't get me laughing," I say, starting to laugh.

We stop, and Sally places her hand on my cheek.

I take it in my hand, move it to my mouth, and kiss her palm. "Her job required frequent travel, and she finally told me she saw other men when she was on the road. She said I could go out with other women, but I told her I wasn't interested."

We have to step apart to let a girl on a bike ride by.

The girl yells, "Sorry," and when we start walking again, I feel Sally take my hand in hers.

"What a sweetheart," she declares, shaking her head. "She was quite a swinger. I wonder what she saw in *you* in the first place."

I turn to look at Sally, surprised she would say something so hurtful. She quickly adds, "Not that you're not a catch, but you seem so…ah…different from her."

It's obvious she didn't mean what she said maliciously, so I answer her question and ignore the implication.

"To this day, I don't know. But one night when she was on the road, I got lonely and called her. She told me she was in bed, and as we were talking, a man's voice asked her who she was talking to. I heard her say, 'Just a friend back home,' and I asked her who she was with, but she couldn't remember his name. She had just fucked him and she wasn't even sure what his name was. I hung up on her, and when she got home, we argued about it for days, mostly just repeating ourselves.

Finally, she told me I could take it or leave it, so I left." I shake my head.

"Have you talked to her since?"

"Just once. I called to tell her I was leaving Chicago, and she asked where I was going. I told her I wanted to buy a little house in a one-horse town. She said, 'Good luck with that,' and hung up. I don't think she was alone that time, either."

Neither of us speaks for a while, then Sally says, "Okay, here's the plan. You are *not*, under any circumstances, to discuss Pam with Nellie."

"Too late."

Sally stops and releases my hand. Putting hers to her cheeks, she stares at me and groans. "Ahhh, shit. Why'd you have to go an' do that?" She stomps her foot. "Shit, shit, shit. What'd you say? Tell me everything."

"Not that much. She called Pam a dragon lady and I said she wasn't that bad."

"Wasn't that bad? *Are you out of your mind?* She was sleepin' with everbody in the country except for me, and I wouldn't be surprised if she was that bimbo comin' on to me up in Louisville a few months back." She stops and shakes her head slowly, then gathers her thoughts. "What else did you say to Nellie?"

"Nothing," I lie. "We didn't talk about her too much."

Sally's expression says that she doesn't believe me, but she lets it go. "From here on out no more talkin' about Pam to Nellie, got it?"

"Why? It might be therapeutic if I talk about her a little."

"From now on, you get your therapy from me, B-O-B Bob, not Nellie. I mean it. I love you like a brother, and I'm tellin' you as a woman you keep shootin' off your mouth about your ex and you will absolutely ruin it with Nellie. And another thing, the first chance you get, you give her a big, wet kiss.

None of this on the cheek stuff. I mean the kind of kiss you *should* have given me the first time *we* were alone."

I am clueless, but she is so adamant about everything that I agree to do what she is saying. When relief floods her face, I ask, "But what do I do if she *asks* about Pam?"

"You respond, 'Gee, honey, that was so long ago, you've driven every thought of her right out of my mind.' And you smile your best 'I'm so stupid' smile. You know, the one you're so good at, and you say it every, *every* time the subject of Pam comes up. Jeez, how are we ever gonna get you laid if you do such dumb things?"

I fold my arms across my chest. "I'm okay with you giving me direction on this, and I'm okay with talking only to you about Pam, but *you* are not responsible for getting me laid, and you need to back off a little on how dumb and naïve and stupid I am." She stares at me blankly, and I add, "Even if it's true."

She nods, slowly, understanding creeping across her face. The first time I met her I wondered if Sally was ever anything but sullen. Tonight, I have seen more sides of her personality than I think Pam even has; anger, affection, incredulity, frustration, and finally love. Sibling love, but love, nonetheless. She hugs me and whispers in my ear, "Nellie is one lucky woman. If she *ever* hurts you, call me. I'll help you hide the body."

———

The next morning Steve has his teeth in his mouth and a hammer in his hand.

"How do they feel?" I ask him.

"What?"

"Your teeth."

"Oh, yeah." He rubs his lips. "Not too bad. There's a little ridge where I glued 'em. I might have used a little too much, but they'll do for now."

"What's the hammer for?"

"I gotta fix the 'frigerator."

"With a *hammer?*"

"I'm gonna fix it," he says, his jaw jutting out, "or *break* it."

"Good luck."

We eat breakfast mostly in silence. Once, Steve peers over the paper and asks whether I know anything about refrigerators. I deny any knowledge, and he disappears behind the paper again.

At work that day, I stop long enough to call Nellie at the beauty parlor. Someone else answers, and I have to wait a minute for her to pick up the phone, but soon I hear, "Hi, Bob. How you doin' this mornin'?" Her smoky voice puts my imagination into overdrive.

"I'm great. You?"

"Ahh, Jenny's already in trouble at school. Been back a week and already she's been to the principal's office. It don't matter what I tell her, she's gonna do what she's gonna do, and I'm gonna have to clean up the mess."

"I hope you get it worked out."

"Oh, I will. She'll be eighteen in approximately two years, ten months, three days, and thirteen hours, give or take," there is a pause as if she is calculating, "seventeen minutes and thirty-seven seconds. Then, if she gives me any shit, I can kick her freckled ass out."

"Not that anybody's counting, though, right?"

Nellie laughs out loud. "That's right. Who's countin'?"

I say, "I called to let you know I had a really good time last night. I'd like to do it again sometime."

"You mean when you said you'd call, you meant it?"

"Yeah, I meant it. I take it you're not used to honesty."

"Not when the subject is 'I'll call you' and the speaker is male."

I put my hand on my chest as if Nellie can see me. "Sorry people of the male persuasion have such low credibility. Do us both a favor and don't lump me with the rest, okay?"

"I'll try but, well...I had a bad experience with the only man I've been serious about since the divorce and it's really hard for me to be trustin'."

"Are you asking me *not* to call?" I feel my world sliding to the edge of a precipice. My heart begins to beat faster.

"I don't know, Bob. That whole 'let's have a beer' thing kind of snuck up on me."

"How could it sneak up on you when it was your idea?" I'm holding the phone in my right hand and spread my left arm wide to my side, the palm of my hand up.

"I know, it don't make sense. I was only lookin' for a night out; I didn't expect us to hit it off so well."

"So you're saying you'd like to take a chance but you're scared?"

"Yeah," Nellie replies. "Damned scared."

"Me, too. Want to be damned scared together?"

There is a crescendo of silence.

I ask, "Are you still there?"

"Yeah," she replies, softly.

"Want to be damned scared together?" I repeat, rubbing my finger on my desk. I expect at any minute for the phone to crumble under the pressure of my grip.

"I think so." Even softer.

Ignoring the equivocation, I ask, "How about Friday?"

"I guess, but you have to be patient with me."

"You said yourself that I'm the slow learner. I think I can be patient." My hand is on my chest, again.

"Yeah, well, sometimes slow learners turn out to be fast

talkers. I don't want to get hurt, and I've got Jenny to think about."

"How about we take it one date at a time?"

"Okay." I think Nellie is crying.

We work out time and directions to her house, but I go back to work wishing I knew the missing parts to Nellie's story.

———

When I get home, the refrigerator is sitting at the curb with the door removed, and there are marks on it where it has been beaten with a hammer. There's a new one in the kitchen. Neither Steve nor the hammer is in sight.

Chapter Eight

"Don't do that," Nellie orders one night as I caress her breast during a kiss.

We've been dating for about a month, and she has made it clear we won't be doing more than a goodnight kiss until she's ready. It's something of a relief for me, after Pam's aggressive style. Nevertheless, as we sit in my car outside her house, I remember what Sally said about not being slow with my affection.

"What's wrong?" I ask.

"I'm just not ready, yet."

"Well, I am, so anytime you decide you are, please say so."

———

Two weeks later, she does just that.

Nellie and I go to the Grandview, have a sandwich, dance to the jukebox, watch Jasper lose three more games of pool despite having come over to Nellie to get a kiss on the cheek "for luck," then drive to her house where she invites me in for coffee.

As we walk into the kitchen, I ask, "Where's Jenny?" I still haven't met her, and on more than one occasion, I've teased Nellie that maybe she doesn't even exist.

"Jenny's not...not gonna be home tonight," she mumbles, turning away. "She's stayin' at a friend's house." Nellie walks to a window and tugs the already closed curtains together. Then, looking over the top of them, which only cover the bottom half out the window, she says, "I stopped at the drugstore today and got you some...uh, toiletries." She turns and gazes at me, smiling. She begins to curl a lock of hair around her finger, something I've noticed she does when nervous.

"Do I need them?"

"You do if...if you're gonna spend the night."

How did my throat go so dry so fast? "Am I going to spend the night?" I ask, hoarsely.

"If you want to." She pauses, then asks, "Do you want to?" her voice quavering ever so slightly.

I pause to contemplate what lies ahead. When I look at her, she is no longer smiling and appears hurt. I realize how long the pause has been.

"*Yes*," I practically shout, walking towards her. "I want *very much* to spend the night."

Nellie's face brightens. She takes me by the hand and leads me to the staircase. Holding hands while climbing stairs feels clumsy, and when we get to the second floor, she gestures toward an open door and says shyly, "All your stuff's on the first shelf of the medicine cabinet, but let me in there first."

She walks into the bathroom, closing the door behind her. This is the first time I've been upstairs in her house, and I stand awkwardly in the hallway. There is a door on each side of me, both of them closed. With nowhere to go, I study what appear to be family pictures hanging on the wall as if there will be a quiz on them later.

The first is clearly Nellie and Jenny and appears to be fairly recent. Nellie has her arm around the shoulder of a teenaged redhead who is her spitting image, but shorter and less curvy. They are both smiling, and Jenny's arm is draped loosely around Nellie's waist. The next is a little redheaded girl, about five, standing next to a bike. At first, I think it's Jenny, but then I notice the older cars in the background and realize this is Nellie, a freckle-faced little girl beaming at the world with what must be her prized possession, based on the size of her smile.

There is one of Nellie holding Jenny as a baby, with an older couple beside them. Could these be Nellie's parents? She told me once they moved to Florida about ten years ago, but that she's not close to them.

There are a few more, but before I can look at them, the door to the bathroom flies open, and Nellie emerges, wearing a flannel robe. She quickly says, "All yours. I'm gonna turn back the bed. Come in when you're ready." After disappearing into the door on the left, she leaves it slightly open and very inviting.

In the bathroom, I find a toothbrush, toothpaste, mouth-wash, a razor with shaving cream, some deodorant, and four different types of condoms. I spruce up a little and carry all four condoms into the bedroom, where Nellie is in bed with the covers up to her chin and her red curls spread wonderfully across the pillow. The robe is draped across a chair, and the dim light from a lamp on the single bedside table accentuates the color of her hair. One whole wall is covered with pictures of Nellie and Jenny white water rafting, hiking, and riding bikes.

Holding up the condoms I say, "I hope you don't think I

can use all four of these because if you do, you're going to be disappointed."

"No, dummy," she coos in the sexiest voice that has ever called me dummy. "I just thought we might want some choice. They're all different; textured, lubricated, plain. I thought about gettin' a glow in the dark, but if anyone in the checkout line saw me, well...it's a small town." She no longer sounds shy.

"Gotcha. I was afraid you expected me to be some sort of super stud. Not that I wouldn't mind needing all of them in one night, but I'm not eighteen anymore."

Pulling her pale white arms from under the cover and extending them and her gaze toward the ceiling, she declares, "And on behalf of all the women in the world, let me just say, thank you, Lord!"

"Okay, smart aleck. Which one of these do you want to use?"

"How about you get in here with me and we'll worry about that in a few?"

Putting the condoms on the bedside table, I self-consciously undress to my underwear. When I slide into bed, I reach out and realize she is naked. I start to say something I think is clever, but before I can, she is kissing me.

She soon pulls off my undershirt and shorts and pushes herself against me as I wrap her in my arms. Putting her mouth to my ear so close I feel her damp breath, she nips my lobe and whispers, "You *are* spendin' the night, aren't you? 'Cause if you're gonna get up and go home in about fifteen minutes I'd rather not even get started."

My hand wanders over the butt I've lusted after since the first time I saw it testing the seams of her blue jeans. "I'm spending the night. And in case you've missed it, *I'm* already started," I say, my erection pushing against her thighs.

Our hands are touching each other everywhere. I want to slow it down; no, I want to speed it up; I don't know what I want, but desire envelopes me. I whisper, "I'm beginning to think that four rubbers might not be enough."

Nellie laughs out loud, and I ask her, "Was it that funny?"

"No." She smiles and gives me a kiss that I want to last all night. When she finally pulls back, she says, "It was that perfect."

———

When I get home the next day, Steve and Lou aren't around. According to Squat, they've gone to Bowling Green to visit some friends. He and I watch football all day and order a pizza for supper.

Squat admits that he missed watching TV with me on Saturday night. I feel bad about that, but can't stop thinking of my night with Nellie, so I warn him that it may happen more in the future.

Most nights, he and I spend an hour or more in my room, him watching TV, me usually reading. Sometimes, we talk about his day at Jacob's, and he asks me about the cars I worked on that day. When he does, I tell him about a mechanical problem and how I fixed it.

He always nods and declares, "That what I do, too. We mechanics, right?"

I assure him we are, indeed, mechanics.

I am flattered by the way he emulates me and enjoy his quiet companionship, but after last night, I want to be with Nellie as much as possible. I tell him that we'll still spend time together and if he has a mechanical problem with a car he can ask me about it and we'll talk it through. This makes him happy.

We hear Steve and Lou come in about nine and I ask Squat if he is going to go downstairs to say hello.

He shakes his head. "I stay here with you."

"Okay." We go back to watching TV.

A little while later, Lou shouts up the stairs, "Everbody in for the night?"

I shout back, "Sure are. Did you have a good visit with your friends?"

"Yes, we did. You?"

"Can't complain." I can hear Lou's all-encompassing harrumph from downstairs.

"Goodnight," I call out, laughing.

"Not as good as last night, I bet," Lou fires back. I don't respond but instead glance at Squat and point toward the door.

"Night, Lou," he calls out.

"Squat, don't you keep Mr. Big City up too late. He needs his rest."

It's not clear if Lou is mad, jealous, or just curious, and right now I don't care. Besides, I'm sure to find out which it is at some point.

———

At breakfast the next morning, Lou demands to know when she's going to meet "this Nellie woman."

"I'm working on that," I tell her, "but first I should meet her daughter. I don't think I should be bringing Nellie around here until our relationship is a little farther along."

I notice Steve's not saying anything and his mouth resembles a pothole in the middle of the highway. To change the subject, I ask him if there is something wrong with his teeth again.

Lou shakes her head, scowling. "He broke 'em again, last night; *sat* on 'em. He glued 'em again just before breakfast, but the glue needs to set up. I'd say that relationship's far enough along. You didn't even come home Saturday night. Not a phone call, nothin'. You think nobody worries 'bout you? Keep on, and we won't."

I smile as I remember Saturday night.

Lou places both her hands on the table and leans forward, staring at me. "Wipe that silly smirk off your face. You look like a teenager tellin' his buddies about his first time."

I smile even broader, and Lou, shaking her head, walks toward the stove.

Over her shoulder she says, "You get this daughter met, then you bring 'em over here for supper. You're always over there, and it's time I check her out." She is spooning hot cereal into a bowl for Steve.

"Lou, I was with you until that 'check her out' comment. She is not someone who needs your approval."

Lou carries the bowl of Cream of Wheat to Steve, sets it down, then puts her hands on her wide hips and glares at me. She's a large woman, anyway, almost as wide as she is tall. When she stands like she is now, she resembles Mount Everest.

"I'll make the call today," I pledge.

"Humph," she grunts, her face still twisted in a scowl.

I turn to Steve and say, "You should take your teeth to the dentist and get them fixed right." He is quietly eating. The only time he is quiet is when he doesn't want to be drawn into a discussion with Lou.

Steve shakes his head, causing his beard to flop back and forth. "Costs too much."

Another of Lou's harrumphs, and I am out the door, on my way to Grove's Point and work.

———

When I call Nellie on my morning break, she says, "Hey, big guy! And I mean that in the best of ways!" That voice. Those words. I start getting hard.

"Hey, Sweetheart. Are you busy?"

"I'm waitin' for a customer's hair to dry. I've got about ten minutes."

"Great. I've been thinking about meeting Jenny. Don't you think it's time?"

"Aww, you're so sweet. Soon as you bang me you get all paternal toward my daughter."

"I hate that word."

"What, *bang?*"

"*Yes.* I wish you wouldn't use it."

"Why?" Nellie sounds curious.

"It sounds so impersonal. Anyway, how about the three of us get a pizza Friday night?"

"I'll ask Jenny. Friday's usually her night out with her friends, so she may not want to spend time with her mother and the guy that's *bangin'* her." I hear her giggle.

"And just how does she know I'm *banging* you, as you insist on calling it?"

"When she cleaned the bathroom, she saw a used condom in the wastebasket. Two, actually. She couldn't wait to tell me. I thought I told you to flush them down the toilet."

"You shouldn't flush them. They don't dissolve and they can stop up your toilet."

"Whatever. If you're gonna leave your used condoms lyin' around where my daughter can find them, I can say you're *bangin'* me. Besides, I like the idea of you *bangin'* me."

It was as if she wanted to bang me over the head with that word. "Can we get back to Friday night?"

"Sure. Jenny wants to meet you, too. Says any guy our age that needs two rubbers in one night deserves checkin' out."

"Goodbye, Nellie. Hope your day goes well."

"Bye lover-boy. I'm gonna get some more condoms on my way home. Any preferences?"

"Your call. Just no glow-in-the-darks."

Chapter Nine

Nellie calls me at work on Wednesday and tells me to come by about seven on Friday.

"Jenny's eager to meet you. She was goin' to a friend's house, but she blew that off right away. I hope she's not buildin' you up too much in her mind."

"Why would she?"

"She's got some issues with me datin'."

I've been writing a repair report while listening to her, but I put my pencil down. "Anything you want to warn me about?"

"Not yet, but there are some things we may need to discuss, dependin' on how things go Friday."

"All right. I'll leave it to you to bring it up." I wish Nellie would quit being so secretive.

———

When I arrive at Nellie's on Friday, it's still light, but barely. Three girls are sitting in a swing on the porch, despite a chill in the October air. They're all wearing jeans and hooded jerseys, and I can't make out any of their features, but can hear them giggling and whispering. I overhear "He's cute!" and "No, he's *really* cute."

There are eight steps up to a large front porch on the front of the house, with the swing perpendicular to the house at the far end. I scratch the back of my neck and start up the steps, but then Nellie comes out the door, so I back off the steps and wait for her on the sidewalk.

Nellie snaps her fingers and points at the girls, saying, "Behave." She smiles, comes down the steps and says, "You've drawn a crowd."

I'd like to take her hand, maybe kiss her on the cheek, but Nellie is watching Jenny and her friends and keeping some distance between us.

"Jenny, come here. Judy and Meg, y'all come down here, too." As the three walk down the steps, a skinny redhead in front and the other two a step behind, Nellie says, "Bob this first one is my Jenny. Judy and Meg are her friends, and they're gettin' ready to leave, right girls?"

"We'll come along if you want." I'm not sure if it is Judy or Meg that makes the offer.

Nellie demurs. "Not tonight. Maybe some other time."

"Hi," says Jenny. She is about three inches shorter than her mother and thinner, but the resemblance is clearly there, starting with beautiful tangles of red hair peeking out from under her hood, and magnificent blue eyes. She puts her arm around her mother's waist and appears to pull Nellie toward herself, away from me.

"Nice to meet you," I say, wondering if she told the other two about finding the condoms. Considering the way they are all giggling, I'd say it's likely. Turning to them, I ask, "Which one's Judy and which one's Meg?"

"I'm Judy. She's Meg," says the shorter of the two. "We're the Three Musketeers."

"Yeah," Meg chimes in. "One for all and all for one!"

Nellie hugs each of them and says, "Okay, girls. We're off to supper. See you later."

Judy and Meg start walking away but Meg suddenly turns around.

"Jenny, quick, come here," she calls, simultaneously summoning Jenny with hurried waves of her arm.

Jenny runs the thirty feet to them and Meg whispers something while giggling. Jenny lopes back to us, a young filly chasing after her mother.

She puts her arm around Nellie's waist again and chirps to me, "Meg thinks you're *hot!*"

Meg and Judy are too far away to hear Jenny's comment, and they keep walking.

"*Jenny!*" Nellie gasps, her eyes narrowing.

I shove my hands in my pockets, look at the ground, and work my toe against a rock embedded in the dirt.

"Oh, Bob. I hope you're up to this," Nellie says, touching my arm sympathetically.

I glance at her and smile. I hope I look confident; I don't feel that way.

I open both doors on the passenger side of my car, and Nellie slides in the front seat, Jenny the back. Nobody says much during the five-minute ride to the pizza place, but when we sit down inside, Jenny begins to pepper me with questions about Chicago.

"I've always wanted to go to Chicago. Did you live there long? Why'd you move? Why here? Do you ever go back? If you go, can we go with you sometime?"

I laugh and Jenny gazes at me blankly, then asks, "What's so funny?"

"You ask questions the same way your mother does," I say.

Nellie shakes her head and looks down at the table, smiling.

"Mom asked you those things, too?"

"No, but your mother asked me multiple questions without giving me a chance to answer any of them."

"Oh," says Jenny, sounding worried. Then her eyes widen and she blurts, "Well, just tell me about Chicago. How's that?"

"That's fine, here's all you need to know. It's a big city with lots of people."

"But what's it like? You know what I mean."

"Yes, I do." I grin at her and she smiles back while Nellie glances from her daughter to me, then back. "Let's see," I muse, "where to start?"

For the next ten minutes, interrupted briefly by the waitress taking our order, I describe the different parts of Chicago, from the lakeshore to the suburbs. I mention things I think would interest a fifteen-year-old girl, but soon Jenny is firing questions at me again, so I answer them. Jenny is a talker, and most of the conversation is between the two of us, with an occasional "That's great, huh, Mom?" directed at Nellie.

Finally, Jenny asks me to promise to take Nellie and her to Chicago sometime.

"Don't be askin' Bob to promise that," Nellie admonishes.

"It's okay," I say. "I never said I *wouldn't* go back, just that I don't need to. But if you both want to go, I can show you around."

That brings a smile to Jenny's face, and I ask her to tell me about her friends. "Judy said you were the three musketeers. Don't girls usually have one best friend?"

"I guess so, but we all met in the first grade, so we just hang. We take care of each other. I don't think I could've gotten through the trial and everything without both of them." Jenny says this very nonchalantly then raises her drink to her mouth. Her lips pucker around the straw as she drinks, and she seems to think I know what she's talking about.

Nellie's eyes grow wide.

"The trial?" I ask.

Nellie immediately retorts, "That's a subject for another time."

I look at Jenny. A cloud passes over her face, but just then the pizza arrives, and we shift our attention to it.

Jenny is easy to talk to. It's as if I've been a friend of the family for years. She reveals that she's glad Nellie has me in her life. "Mother needs some company, and I'm busy with my friends," she says.

"I guess it was either me or a puppy," I say with a grin.

When Jenny laughs, I do, too, but Nellie grimaces. "I'm not used to bein' talked about like I'm not here," she laments. "I don't want you two gangin' up on me."

The evening flies by. At about ten o'clock, I suggest we head home, and Jenny objects, but I remind her that I still have to drive to Waynedale.

"Aren't you gonna spend the night?" Jenny asks. Nellie and I both stare at Jenny and she exclaims, "What? Hey, we're all adults here! Really, I'm okay with it."

Nellie squints at Jenny and says, "First of all, we are *not* all adults. You're *fifteen*. What Bob and I do is *our* business, and I don't care to have my daughter discussin' it with me, Bob, or her friends. Do I make myself clear?" Her chin juts out toward her daughter.

"Sure, fine. Whatever."

Jenny and Nellie both get to the car before I can open the doors for them, and somebody's slams shut, although it's not clear whose.

We ride home in silence, and when we pull into the drive, Jenny hops out and runs inside without saying a word.

Nellie turns to me. "I'm sorry, Bob. She got a little too big for her britches there. I hope she didn't offend you."

"She didn't. I'm sorry it ended on a sour note. I hope you can patch things up."

"Don't worry. This is an everyday occurrence. What surprised me was that it didn't happen sooner. Anyway, at least you two got along."

"You've got your hands full," I say, chuckling.

I put my hand on the back of Nellie's neck and pull her gently toward me, intending to kiss her, but Nellie resists, and says, "She gives me grief all the time. You wanna take her home?"

"I think there are laws against that."

I see the fury in Nellie's face then hear it in her voice. "*I didn't mean to fuck her.* For God's sake, this is my *daughter.*"

"Sorry. It was just a joke."

"It wasn't funny." Nellie sits back and folds her arms across her chest.

I see no good outcome to this conversation, so I say, "I think I should go."

"Yeah, I think you're right."

"I'll call you."

"Heard that before."

"Haven't I called you every time I said I would? I understand you're upset but—"

"Don't be understandin'; I'm not in the mood to be understood. Goodnight, Bob." Nellie starts to push her door open.

"Goodnight, Nell." I try to kiss her, but she turns her head so all I do is glance off her cheek. She gets out, and as I back out of the driveway, I watch her climb the steps as if they were to the gallows.

———

I don't call Nellie until my morning break on Monday. We are both apologetic. Nellie suggests we get together that evening to talk.

"What do you want to talk about? We had a small spat, but it's over; life goes on."

"No," states Nellie. "We need to talk."

"Okay. Grandview?"

"No. Too many people listenin' in. Why don't you come by the house when you get off work?"

"Nellie, what's going on? I think you're making a lot more out of this than there is."

"Maybe I am, and if you don't want to come over here to talk, you don't have to. We can just say it's been real but it's over."

I remark, with equal parts sarcasm, reluctance, and a desire to patch things, "Well, since you make the choices so appealing, I'll be there about five."

"Thanks. And Bob, I really am sorry about the way we parted the other night. There are things you need to know."

Chapter Ten

I have a sense of foreboding when I pull into Nellie's driveway. I tell myself it doesn't matter if she dumps me. She's a fling, nothing more. Buoyed by that lie, I get out and approach the steps. Nellie must be watching for me because as I reach the top step she opens the door. I can see she's been crying. Nevertheless, I say, "How are you doing?"

"Not so good," she mutters, her mouth set grimly. "We need to talk."

"That's why I'm here."

She smiles, wanly, holding the door open to invite me in.

When I'm inside, she walks past me into the living room. There is a fireplace at the far end, which is too clean to have ever been used, with windows on either side of it. A dark blue couch sits against the wall to my right, with a coffee table in front of it. Two chairs flank a large window looking out into the front yard, each with small, mismatched tables next to it. The drapes at the window are open.

Nellie sits on the couch, and I drop into the nearest chair. The coffee table between us has a box of tissues in the middle with many used tissues in several distinct piles. As Nellie sits, she pulls a fresh tissue out of the box and holds it to her mouth. Her eyes are moist and bloodshot.

Neither of us speaks for about ten-seconds. Then, Nellie says, "Jenny's at Judy's house, studyin' for a test. I didn't want her to be here while we talked."

I wait for Nellie to say more, but there is only awkward silence so I say, "Your meeting."

"Yeah, I know. I'm tryin' to figure out where to start."

"How about at the beginning?" I hope my voice sounds supportive. I was defensive when we talked this morning, but seeing how upset she is makes me protective of her.

"Actually, I'm tryin' to decide *how* to start." Her tone is flat, emotionless.

My gaze wanders to the window next to me and what's happening outside. The trees are just beginning to change color, and the sun will be dropping out of sight in a couple of hours. A man wearing a light coat and a hat is walking a dog, and they've stopped for it to sniff at a bush. A couple of young boys are in the yard across the street, tossing a football.

It's interesting how a few words can permanently change lives. Will you marry me? We're going to have a baby. She's dead. When people hear those statements, they know instantly that their lives will never be the same.

Nellie clears her throat and starts talking fast, as if the words need to come out right this instant, or they will stay locked inside forever.

"When Jenny was eleven, the man I was datin' raped her."

My head snaps around and I stare at her.

She has lowered the tissue to her lap. Tears are on her cheeks and her expression pleads with me, but for what I don't know. Her head moves slowly back and forth.

"I thought I was gonna marry him, that he would be her

father. He was good with her." She starts crying, uncontrollably, but manages to talk in bursts through the tears. "He would…take her places…just the two of them. Fathers… fathers do that, right?"

I move around the coffee table to sit on the couch next to her. When I put my arm around her, she leans against me. We sit there for several minutes, her body shaking as she sobs.

When her crying subsides, I say, "Nellie, I'm so sorry. I had no idea."

She sits up, and I remove my arm from around her.

Turning away and dabbing at her nose with the tissue, she says, "I know you didn't. That's why I'm so confused. But the most important job I've got is to protect my daughter, and I've already failed once. I won't let it happen again." She faces me. "*Someone will die* if it happens again."

I have no doubt that she means it. She pauses, as if to let that sink in, then continues.

"So I got mad, not at you, at the bastard that did this to my daughter. But this is the first time I've brought a man around since then, and you were there, grinnin', and…an' jokin' with Jenny the same way *he* used to do. Then, she asked if you were gonna spend the night, and I knew that…that she knew we made love the other night, but it was like she was rubbin' my nose in it, and I realized she's at an age where she's gonna be experimentin' with sex, and her hormones…oh, her hormones are explodin' and her emotions are all confused by what happened, and I can't get her to go to counselin' and, an'…"

Nellie grabs a quick breath, swaps out the tissue for a new one, then continues. "How's she gonna handle her sexuality and sometimes girls become promiscuous when somethin' like this happens, and is she seein' you like Lolita saw Hummert or whatever his name was, an' then you made that crack about sleepin' with her and—"

"Hold on!" I hold my hand up, palm facing her, and the torrent of words stops. She looks at me blankly.

"I never said anything about sleeping with her. You asked if I wanted to take her with me and I said there were laws against that."

Gradually, her face shows acceptance. "Yeah, I know," she agrees. "*Now*, I know. But when you said it, it sure rubbed me the wrong way."

"I can understand *why*. I understand your anger and frustration, and why it was directed at me. I'm sorry I said it, but *please* don't be mad at me."

She begins to cry again, so I put my arm around her and let her lean against me, her tears again becoming sobs. I hold her, kissing her on top of her head, and tell her over and over it will be all right, even though I have no way of knowing whether it ever will.

She sobs for about five minutes this time. When her crying slows, I ask if there is anything I can do to help. She sits up, grabs a handful of clean tissues, and blows her nose.

Her voice is under control as she says, "You've already helped. All day long, I debated how much to tell you. I haven't talked about it to anyone other than to the police. It's been a burden, not havin' anyone to talk to. I always knew if I was gonna date someone I'd have to discuss it with him, but I didn't plan to do it this soon. And I didn't realize how hard it would hit me."

"I wish there was something I could do." Now, *I'm* angry at this unknown bastard who has caused such pain to two people who are becoming important to me faster than I ever expected.

She struggles to find the right words to continue, so I wait quietly and in a minute she does.

"Bob, I'm so confused. I want to say some things that are gonna sound bad, so if anything I say offends you, *please* keep an open mind and understand that I haven't talked to anyone about this before. I really need to talk to you about it, but you can walk away if this is more than you bargained for."

It *is* more than I bargained for, but if I walk away now, I will hurt Nellie as badly as I've ever hurt anyone. Jenny, too, probably.

"I'm staying."

She appears relieved and says, "Thank you. Let me know if anything I say upsets you."

"Fair enough."

She blows her nose, then says, "I haven't dated since… since Jenny was molested. I felt I owed her that. I haven't trusted men and I thought she deserved my undivided attention. Her father had just died. She was never close to him, but she wanted to be. He was a drunk, and he let her down so many times she quit believin' anything he said, but I know she *hoped* things would change. You're the first man I've brought home since she was raped, so you carry a heavy burden. It might not be fair, but it's fact. And then, when we were talkin' the other night, I hadn't seen her act that way in a long time."

"She seemed all right to me."

Nellie pulls back and looks out the window. "I *know*. She was *open*, she *talked* to you. She hasn't talked to any adult like that in a long time, 'specially me."

"Does that bother you?"

She turns and glares at me. "*Damn right it bothers me.* I'm her *mother.* I've been here for her; *you* haven't. Five minutes with you and she's askin' you all about Chicago, and wantin' you to take her there an'—"

"I'm not upset, but let me point out, she didn't ask me to take just her. *You* were included."

Nellie shook her head, still staring at me. "I may have been included in the question, but she wanted you to take *her*." I raise my eyebrows, but Nellie waves her hand, dismissively, and continues.

"Anyway, she opened up to you. She hasn't opened up to me since she was…since it happened. And the… what he did…it was brutal."

She pauses again, and I can see she is conflicted, so I stroke the side of her face and tell her, "We can discuss as much or as little as you want."

She nods, and when she continues, her voice is hard. "He made it a game, and when she realized what was happenin', it was too late." Her fist beats against her thigh several times.

My head is spinning at these revelations, and I see a few stray tears start rolling down Nellie's cheeks again. I put my hand on her shoulder and she leans against me again and cries, although not with the sobs that had shaken her body earlier.

"Take your time," I tell her, putting my arms around her.

A muffled "thank you" comes from my chest, where she is resting her head. Holding her, I let her cry until she begins to talk again.

She reveals that he worked the night shift so he would pick up Jenny after school. When they got home, he always had some pretext to be in her room when she changed clothes. He would tell her she was pretty enough to be a movie star and showed her nude pictures of actresses she admired. Then, he told her that if she wanted to be an actress, she needed to pose for him.

I feel my throat constricting as Nellie relates how he had told her the pictures would help make her a star, but to be really good, he would have to teach her things they did in the movies. So he took her to movies with love scenes then would take her home to "practice." He convinced her it should be their secret, that she shouldn't let anyone know that he was preparing her to be a movie star.

Through it all, Nellie alternates crying, being angry at herself, the rapist, men in general, and filling me in on all the graphic details. I keep reminding her she doesn't have to tell me anything she isn't comfortable with, hoping she will spare me the worst of what he did, but the barn door is open and the horse is running free.

"She *trusted* him," Nellie practically screams at me. She rears her head back and begins to beat on my chest with the hand not holding the tissue. "Jesus Christ, eleven years old and she's bein' *fucked* by some *shitass* I thought was gonna be her father."

I pull her to me so she can't hit me anymore, and envelop her in what I hope is a comforting hug. She grows quiet; I feel queasy.

She has been talking for over an hour, so I let her rest for a few minutes before asking, "How did you find out?"

"Jenny wasn't feeling good, cramps, itching, that kind of stuff." I swallow hard and wish I hadn't asked, but Nellie doesn't notice my discomfort. "I took her to the doctor who told me she had a sexually transmitted infection and that it appeared she had become sexually active. It took the doctor and me both talkin' to her to get her to reveal what had happened."

"What did you do?"

"I called the police. They arrested the son of a bitch and found all the pictures he took."

"What happened to him?"

"He went to prison. Six months later, he was murdered by

several prisoners who didn't appreciate child molesters." Nellie draws in a deep breath then gazes directly at me as if I was the man who had violated her daughter. "I hope it was a sloooow, painful death."

"I don't blame you," I say, feeling anger rising within. "At least Jenny never has to face him again."

She puts her head back on my shoulder and is quiet for a minute. I'm wondering if there is more when she asks, "Why didn't I spot it?"

"Do you really think you could have prevented it?"

Nellie shrugs.

"Does Jenny ever talk about it?"

"Not to me. She may to her friends, but I don't know."

"You said Jenny won't talk to a counselor. Any idea why?"

Nellie has lowered her head against my chest, and I feel it shake. Her voice is muffled as she murmurs, "I was told that's not unusual 'cause the abuser usually manages to convince his victim that it's her fault. Jenny pretends it didn't happen. Sometimes I get angry thinkin' about it. When I do, she blames herself. It don't matter how many times I remind her it's not her fault, she thinks I'm mad at her for lettin' it happen." I feel tears on my shirt where they are rolling down Nellie's cheeks again. "I worry about her. I'm afraid she'll have a distorted image of sex, men, herself. I don't know what to do."

"Can I help in *any* way?"

Her head moves against my chest. "Maybe. I know we haven't been together long, but we've hit it off, haven't we?"

I hug her tight. "Yes."

"And Jenny likes you, that's obvious. So there's something you need to do. The counselor told me if there was ever a man in my life he should do this."

"What is it?"

95

"Tell Jenny that you will never have sex with her."

"*What?*" I pull back this time so I can look at her. "Of course I'm not going to have sex with your daughter!"

"I'm not sayin' you would, Bob. I'm not accusin' you of wantin' to, or anything. But when kids have been abused, they think anyone in a position like that, kind of a father-figure…" Nellie is looking at me, and I raise my eyebrows.

The wrong thing to do.

"Never mind." Her voice goes flat and she sounds alone, adrift on an ice floe with no land in sight. "You're not ready for this." She leans forward, her face almost down to her knees. She covers it with her hands, and starts crying again.

"Wait a minute, Nellie." I put my hand on her back. "Give me a chance, will you? You've had four years to think about this, I've had about an hour and a half, and now I find out I'm supposed to tell your daughter I won't have sex with her. That's a lot to get a handle on in one evening."

Nellie removes her hands from her face and sits up, slowly nodding her head. "You're right. I'm sorry. I appreciate you lettin' me unload on you."

We sit and hold each other, neither saying a word.

After about five minutes, she quietly asks if I'm hungry.

"Not really. You?"

"No, but I got you over here at suppertime, then we talked for almost two hours. I'll fix somethin' if you're hungry."

Nellie's right, it's almost seven. Time has become unimportant, but right now, I have no appetite.

"No," I say. "Are we still an item, as Lou calls it? If we are, I need to talk to Jenny. If we're not, I should go."

There is a brief pause before Nellie replies, "We're as much of an item as you want us to be. My mind tells me to slow it down, but my heart says don't miss this chance, even though there's gonna be some rough spots with me and

Jenny, both. It may not be fair, but you have to earn our trust."

"I understand."

"Okay," she declares, standing up. "I'll call Judy's mom and have her send Jenny home."

While Nellie is on the phone, I go to the window. It's dark now and the lights are on in the house where the boys were playing catch earlier. They're probably finishing their supper about now. I think about what I'll say when Jenny gets here. When I was fifteen, I wanted to have sex with a fifteen-year-old, *any* fifteen-year-old. Now, twenty years later, the idea of sex with Jenny is strange, but the need to tell her I won't is even stranger. *She's a child,* my brain screams. Under my breath, I curse the dead bastard who put me in this situation.

Nellie walks up behind me and puts her arms around my waist from behind. "She'll be right home. She's only five minutes away."

We stand there, her with her arms around me, and me gazing out into the dark with my hands resting on top of hers, until we see a shape coming up the walk.

Nellie lets go of me just before Jenny comes in the door, and we focus our attention on her.

She sets her books down, then sees me and says, "Hey, Bob. I saw your car in the driveway. What's up?"

After an awkward pause during which Jenny stares at me, Nellie reveals, "Honey, I told Bob about...the rape."

Jenny's eyes widen and she looks at me as Nellie continues. "He's gonna be comin' around, so he should know about it, and he needs to make somethin' clear to you."

Nellie turns to me, and I gaze at Jenny. At first, she appears angry but then she spots how awkward I'm acting and her expression changes to confidence.

"Jenny," I start, "first, I am so sorry about...what

happened. I will never do any of those things to you." I glance at Nellie, hoping that's enough, but she's still looking at Jenny, so I continue. "I will not have sex with you. I will not take nude pictures of you."

Jenny smirks, seeming to enjoy watching me squirm.

"I will respect you and your mother, and I will not come between you." Nellie nods approvingly, and I ask Jenny, "Do you have any questions?"

"Yeah." She puts her hands on her hips. "What makes you think I'd have sex with you? Just 'cause my friends think you're hot doesn't mean *I* want you jumpin' my bones."

"*Jenny*! That's enough. Bob's tryin' to explain he won't take advantage of you."

She glares at Nellie for a moment then demands, "What makes you think I'd let him?"

"Nothing. Nothing at all, Honey. It's just that I...we want you to know that you're safe with him."

"I'm not the kid I was four years ago. If some old guy tries that with me now, I'll cut his balls off."

I'm standing to the side, watching the eternal battle of a young woman asserting herself just a little faster than her mother likes. If it wasn't *my* balls resting under the sword of Damocles, it would be fascinating.

Nellie seems confused, and I wonder if this reaction, stronger than she probably wanted, is nevertheless good news to her. Her daughter may not be a woman, but she's not a little girl anymore, either, and men better beware.

"Okay," Nellie assures her. "You can take care of yourself. I'm glad to hear it. Is there anything else you want to ask Bob?"

"Yeah," Jenny says with a mischievous grin. "When are you taking me to Chicago?"

"I'm never taking *you* to Chicago. I will take both of you whenever your mother is ready to go."

Nellie comes over and hugs me, then does the same with Jenny, who wiggles like she doesn't want to be hugged but is smiling.

"Hey, are we ever gonna have any supper tonight?" Jenny asks.

Nellie looks relieved. "Will you stay, Bob? I can order a pizza."

"Sure." I feel the knot in my stomach relax.

"Can we play *Monopoly* while we eat it?" Jenny is already on her way to get the game.

"That takes too long," says Nellie. We'll never finish it."

"Then, let's play until 9:30," Jenny suggests, "And whoever has the most money wins."

And that's what we do, except we never count the money.

———

The next morning at breakfast Lou asks me if Nellie and I had a nice time the night before. I had called to let her know not to hold supper because I was seeing Nellie.

"It was nice. We talked."

"Whadja talk about?"

"This and that, here and there, now and then."

Steve snorts.

Squat says, "Yeah," then he snorts, too.

"Oh, now, that tells me a lot," Lou scolds, glaring at me from in front of the stove. She pours a cup of coffee and walks toward the table.

"Lou, there are going to be things Nellie and I discuss that you don't need to hear."

Steve and Squat jump up like a covey of quail startled by

hunters. "Wastin' time," Steve says, bustling toward the door. "Gotta get out in the garden."

Squat grabs his lunch from the counter and says, "I go work."

I feel like I'm watching a *Three Stooges* routine as they get into each other's way trying to be the first one out the door. As it closes, I hear Steve say, "Ho*oowee*," and Squat reply, "Yeah, hooowee."

Lou continues to glare at me. I am alone in the cave with mama bear.

She sets her coffee on the table, puts her hands on her expansive hips, and declares, "You have this Nellie woman here at five o'clock Sunday for supper, or I'm followin' you on your next date."

"That would be stalking."

"No, it wouldn't! Stalkin' is if you're followin' someone you're obsessed with."

"I rest my case."

She leans forward and places both hands on the table, her stare never leaving my face. "You call it what you want, but if she's here Sunday evenin' I won't have to do it." She smiles. It is the smile of an assassin slicing the throat of a long-time enemy.

"I'll set it up. Is her daughter invited, too?"

Lou sits down and pours some milk in her coffee. "Of course," she snaps, stirring her coffee like she's whipping a rented mule. "You *have* met the daughter, haven't you?"

"Yes. Cute kid. Really sweet."

I smile at Lou but only get a "humph."

Chapter Eleven

Sunday, I sleep in then go for a stroll around town. It's a lazy October afternoon in a sleepy country town; just the opposite of the full-blown brouhaha I find in the kitchen when I get home about four.

"Why do we have to have company for supper today?" Steve asks as he carries plates from the kitchen to the dining room. "The World Series starts today."

I follow Steve to the dining room, while Lou continues bustling around the kitchen, ignoring us both. Steve leaves the plates stacked on the table and returns to the kitchen, so I work on setting them around. Through the door, I see him walking about one foot behind Lou until she suddenly turns around, and he runs into her. They remind me of two sumo wrestlers attempting to shove each other out of the ring.

"Darn, Steve, get out of the way." Lou waves her hands as if she was chasing flies. "I've got supper to fix. Nellie and Jenny will be here soon."

"I wanna watch the World Series. The Cardinals are

playin', and they got all those kids that played up in Louisville."

"I'm sure they'll play that game just fine without you." Lou opens the oven and checks a roast. "This is the first time Bob's brought someone home for supper and it should be special."

Squat ambles into the kitchen. He's as scruffy as a dog's old toy. His sweatshirt is torn and stained. His jeans have a hole in the knee, and his hair is a mess.

"Squat, those clothes won't do," Lou says. "You go up to your room and put on the clothes you wear when we go to the movies."

Squat looks blankly at Steve, who waves toward his room, so Squat retreats.

"And comb your hair," Lou calls after him as she bastes the roast.

"What do you mean, this is the first time Bob has had people come to supper? This wasn't his idea; you insisted they come," Steve whines.

As I fill the water glasses from a pitcher Steve brought into the dining room, he adds, "Besides, Bob wants to watch the game, too."

Not if it means incurring Lou's wrath, thank you very much. Besides, Lou's right. I want Jenny and Nellie to meet my family. Sally is coming, Squat will be here. I'm looking forward to a family supper. I can watch the highlights later.

Lou murmurs something to Steve that I can't quite make out, but it ends the discussion.

Steve rolls into the dining room looking like a storm cloud rolling across the prairie. I try not to appear too happy, but he glowers at me.

"What are you so happy about? You're gonna miss the game, too."

"Oh, go comb your beard. I don't want my girl to see that tangled mess sitting across the table from her."

"*Et tu, Brute?*" Steve pronounces it as if it were spelled "bruut," but the teasing has worked. He smiles, softly, so I take another shot.

"And don't forget to wear your teeth. That mug of yours is a mess without them."

Steve points at me, and drawls, "If she can put up with that mug of your'n, she can put up with me without my teeth. Maybe I oughta leave 'em out. She might wanna do some kissin' later, and if I don't have my teeth in, she might choose me instead of you."

I laugh and Steve demands, "What's funny 'bout that? I've had my share of women kissin' on me."

I laugh again, and Steve says, "It ain't funny." I keep laughing, and he proclaims, "Okay, it's funny, but it ain't *that* funny."

He picks up the silverware and helps me set the table, his easy-going manner having returned. "Tell me about her, this Nellie. What she's got that my Sally ain't?"

I'm folding napkins and when I don't respond immediately Steve says, "I'm just wonderin', 'cause I had you pegged as Sally's type. What happened?"

"Not sure. Maybe it's all the family meals we've had together. She's more like a sister."

"Sister, huh? Why not cousin? In Kentucky, that's okay. There's even a law 'bout it. If a couple gets divorced, they're still cousins."

I laugh, and he continues to grouse amiably. "So I'm not gonna get any grandbabies, is that what you're sayin'? It's not for me, but Lou wants some little ones around here so bad." He's quiet for a moment, appearing to be deep in thought. "Maybe I oughta get her a puppy. What d'ya think?"

I don't know which question I should respond to, but the puppy seems safest. I place the last glass of water next to Steve's plate at the head of the table and ask, "What kind of dog would you get her?"

"Maybe a bloodhound doggie." He draws out the words 'blood' and 'doggie.' "I'd name it Great Reluctance. Then, ever' time I had to go somewheres, I could tell her, 'I'm leavin' you with Great Reluctance.'"

"How long have you been saving that one up?" I ask. I know he isn't getting Lou a dog. She already has two cats, one of which is wrapping itself around my ankles as we speak.

Just then, Lou comes into the room and surveys the table with a critical eye. She directs Steve to remove Felix the cat and close the door so he can't get back in. Then, she moves all the forks to the opposite side of the plates from where I put them and scoots two chairs imperceptibly apart. Now satisfied with the table, she looks me up and down and makes a face like she bit into a sour persimmon.

"Is that what you're wearin'?" Mother does not approve.

I gaze down at my T-shirt and blue jeans. The shirt is about ten years old. It may have a hole or two, but it's clean. When I look up, Lou is still wearing the sour persimmon expression.

"Change," she says and wheels into the kitchen.

Even though she is out of hearing range I say, "Yes, ma'am" and head for the stairs, hoping I can get it right this time.

———

When I come back down, I start toward the living room to wait for Nellie and Jenny when I hear Lou call, "Just a minute, Mr. Big City. I need to see what you put on." She sizes up my khaki slacks and gray polo shirt, mutters a low "Hmmmmm," and returns to the kitchen.

Nellie pulls into the driveway exactly at five, with Jenny waving out the window as if she's trying to flag a cab. She bounds out of the car as soon as it stops and comes loping toward me yelling, "Hi, Bob!" as I come down the steps.

"Hello, you two." I smile at Jenny, who seems to be bouncing on springs. When Nellie comes up, I kiss her on the cheek.

"I think Jenny's had a little too much caffeine today," Nellie announces as we walk toward the steps. Steve and Lou are standing on the porch, and Squat sits in the swing with his legs folded under him.

As we climb toward the porch, I feel Nellie take hold of my left hand. Jenny already has my right.

"Welcome to our home," Lou chirps, hands poised shoulder-high in preparation for hugging. "We haven't heard near nuff 'bout you, Sugar, but any friend of Bob's is sure a friend of ours."

She reaches out and hugs Nellie, who says "Nice to meet you, ma'am."

Lou smiles at Steve and croons, "I just *knew* she'd be polite." To Nellie, she says, "Lou. My name's Lou." Then, turning to Jenny, she coos, "And this must be Jenny. Why, she's an angel, just like Bob said." Lou envelopes Jenny in a mamma bear hug to which, to my surprise, Jenny is receptive.

I hear what sounds like fifteen conversations at once, until Lou looks toward the street and announces, "There's my Sally." As Sally comes up the steps, Lou says, "Nellie and Jenny, this is my daughter, Sally. She owns the café downtown."

"She's my daughter, too," Steve says, proudly.

"That's never been proven in a court of law," Lou declares over her shoulder, and Steve grumbles under his breath.

The women are hugging like it's a family reunion when I hear Squat saying, "I Squat, I Squat." I take Nellie and Jenny over to the swing, and introduce him.

Squat says, "I live here, too. Me and Bob, we live here."

"Bob has told me about you, Squat," Nellie assures. "You're a mechanic, right?"

Squat beams. "Yeah, me and Bob, we mechanics. We fix cars, right, Bob?"

"That's right, partner."

Lou herds everyone into the dining room, along with directions to the bathroom so we can "go wash up."

As Sally is helping Lou put the food on the table, I hear Steve relating to Nellie how he fixed his false teeth with crazy glue.

"In fact," he says, reaching for his mouth, "let me show you what I done."

A sick expression crosses Nellie's face and I say, "Steve, that's not necessary," in a tone reserved for correcting a dog that is growling at a friend.

"I just thought she might be interested," Steve says, withdrawing his hand from his mouth.

"Come on, everbody, set down afore I feed it to th' hogs," Lou cackles in an exaggerated southern accent, as if it needs to be exaggerated. "Nellie, you sit right here next to Bob."

She has directed Nellie to the chair Squat normally occupies, and he immediately steps forward. "That my seat!" he proclaims, "My seat!"

Nellie glances at me, puzzled, and I ask her if she would sit on the other side.

"Sure," she says, patting my arm and moving to the chair on my left.

Lou frowns and shakes her head as Squat sits down in "his" seat. "Squat, honey, I thought tonight you could sit over here with Sally."

He shakes his head, and declares, "My seat." Lou and I make eye contact, and I nod, so Lou smiles at Jenny and soothes, "Hon, you sit over here next to Steve."

When everyone is seated, Lou asks Steve to do a blessing, and Steve looks astonished. "Somethin' we should know about the food? We never do a blessin'."

Lou locks in on him with a glare that could crumble the Pyramids and snarls, "Tonight, we do." I think I see ice forming on her breath.

Steve mutters for a moment and looks at me for help. I fold my hands in my lap and look down, so he commences a rambling request for blessings on everyone at the table plus the cats, each person and cat named individually, good health for several people known only to Steve, a plea for an early spring for his garden, a request for grandchildren so he and Lou can enjoy their golden years, and a suggestion of help for the St. Louis Cardinals in the World Series. "Oh, yeah," he adds, "and bless this food. It shouldn't need it."

"Well, wasn't that nice?" Lou asks, in a tone that indicates it wasn't nice at all.

"Are you a Cardinals fan?" Jenny asks.

"Been one all my life."

Jenny holds her hand up and Steve gives her a high five.

Lou rolls her eyes, and growls, "Steve."

"I will not ignore a young lady's request for a high five," he says, tucking his napkin into his shirt collar.

"Can we watch the game after supper?" Jenny asks Steve.

Lou shakes her head, but Steve doesn't see it. Instead, eyes focused on Jenny, he says, "You bet your sweet a— you bet we can, Honey!"

Jenny beams and looks over at her mom, who shakes her head and says, "I knew you'd find a way to watch that game."

"You know," Steve drawls as we pass the food around the table, "Lou and I consider Bob a son, and Sally has never been married." I glance at Sally, who is staring him down over his mention of her marital status, but he avoids her glare. "And Lou was sayin' just this mornin' how nice it would be to have some grandchi—"

"Don't go there, Steve," I say.

"What? I'm just sayin'—"

"Papa, don't go there," Sally demands.

"Steve," Lou says in her let's-distract-Steve-because-that-will-accomplish-more-than-trying-to-reason-with-him   voice, "why don't you tell Nellie and Jenny about your latest project?"

"What latest project?"

"I don't know, Honey. Whatever it is you been workin' on."

"What're ya talkin' about? What project?"

"Well, if you don't know about it, how am I supposed to know about it?" Lou smiles benignly, and continues, "Did everyone get green beans? They're outta our garden. Steve, did you get green beans?"

"Yeah, I, uh, I got green beans. What project—"

"Well, good. 'cause I could be mistaken, but I believe these are the best green beans I've ever put up. Don't you think so, Sally?"

"Oh, absolutely, Mama. What do you think Bob?" Sally gazes at me, grinning from ear to ear.

I'll play along. "Yes, definitely."

Lou, still smiling her deadly smile, stares at Steve with a look that demands the correct answer. "What about you, Honey? You think these are my best?"

Steve takes a bite of green beans, thinks for a minute then says, "The ones from nine years ago were better."

"Oh, they were *good*," agrees Lou. "But these are better. Actually, I prefer to put up 'maters. How 'bout you, Nellie? You can anything?"

"Sometimes, if I can get some fresh stuff, but Jenny prefers store-bought."

Lou turns to Jenny, "Gracious, child, you just can't beat fresh."

Jenny looks around at everyone and says, "I prefer my food to be zapped good to get rid of all the crawly things."

Lou studies Jenny as if she were an alien needing to learn about earth rituals. "I have a *wonderful* idea. Some Saturday when Sally don't have to work, the four of us, *just us girls*, will get together and put up some 'maters. I got one last batch. We can get to know each other, and talk about, oh, I don't know, just so many things. Nellie, you and I can talk about bein' mamas and Jenny, you and Sally can talk about bein' daughters, and there won't be any men so we can talk about..." she stares directly at me, smiling. "Them, too."

Sally, Jenny, and Nellie, first one, then the next, all agree what a *wonderful* idea that is. I thought all the crap about projects and best beans ever and canning had been about getting Steve to shut up, but it was about separating Nellie from me. I glance at Steve, and he is smirking.

There is more conversation, but I can't hear it over the roar of Steve's eyes saying, "You've been had by the master, Mr. Big City. From the moment you agreed to bring sweet Nellie here, you've been had."

Chapter Twelve

"John and Shirley! John and Shirley!" Squat is pointing across the parking lot at a man and woman about Steve's age. Squat, Steve, and I are in Bowling Green for a football game, while the women hold their canning extravaganza.

We were banished from the house and told not to come back until supper time. "And bring something to eat back with you," Lou added, as we started out the door. "Enough for all of us."

"Why?" Steve demanded. "There will be four women here. Well, three plus Little Bit. Are you implyin' y'all can't throw together supper?"

"Every one of us will be worn out from cannin', 'specially Little Bit. You, on the other hand, will be sitting on your butt watchin' a bunch of overgrown adolescents fight over a funny-shaped ball. The most strenuous thing any of you will do all day is lift a beer to your mouth. The *least* you can do is bring home somethin' for the workers to eat, or would you rather we not have any canned 'maters this winter?"

As testament to how much Steve loves his canned tomatoes, he walked out the door, grumbling, but resigned to bringing supper home.

John and Shirley are wearing big smiles following the Hilltoppers' win. They hug Steve, but Squat fends them off with his "no hugs, no hugs" mantra, all the while backing up and waving his hands in the air. When Steve introduces me to them as "Sally's new beau" I stare at him like he's lost his mind.

"John and Shirley are Sally's godparents," Steve reveals, avoiding eye contact with me. "We grew up together."

"That's right," says Shirley, hugging John's arm and gazing sideways at him with a smile. "John and I were high school sweethearts in Waynedale. Grew up with Stevie, here." She extends a hand toward Steve, who beams at her. "John and I got married while we were at Western Kentucky; been livin' in Bowlin' Green ever since." She looks me up and down until I know how a pork chop in the butcher shop window feels. Finally, she says, "So you're Sally's beau, huh?"

Before I can correct her, John asks Steve, "I take it Sally finally got over what's-his-name?"

Steve nods, somberly. "Never did know what she saw in him."

"I know 'zactly what she saw in him," chirps Shirley. "He was a gooooood-lookin' man. I'll never forget ole what's-his-name. Had one of my three all-time favorite butts."

"*Really?*" questions John, sounding indignant, but smiling. "And who are the other two?"

"Why *you* are, Darlin'. *Both* of them," she reveals with a smile and a kiss on his cheek, to which John rolls his eyes.

Squat has been attempting to say something since he first spied the couple, and finally, he blurts, "Bob a mechanic, just like me."

"Well, ain't that nice," says Shirley, turning to me. "It's

good to meet you, Bob, and don't worry, you're *almost* as good-lookin' as ole what's-his-name."

"What *is* his name?" I ask, for future reference, historical significance, and purposes of blackmail.

"Charlie," says Steve. "But you 'da man, now!"

"I am *not* Sally's beau," I state but realize immediately I've been just a touch too emphatic in my denial. Shirley seems disappointed, so I quickly add, "She's not interested in me."

Shirley smiles at me, sympathetically. "I think it's gonna be a long time before she's over ole what's-his-name. Hey, guys, we're headin' to a friend's house for supper. Why don't you come along? They always have enough for extras."

Steve shakes his head. "Can't. We gotta bring supper home. Lou and Sally been cannin' all day with a coupla friends of Bob's. If we don't get there with supper, nobody eats."

"Cannin'! Yuk." Shirley crinkles her face. "Why's Lou do that when she can buy anything she needs at the store?"

"She's gotta do somethin' with everything I grow in the garden. Otherwise, why grow it?"

"My point exactly," advises Shirley. "Why *do* you grow it?"

"Lou won't have anything to can if I don't."

Shirley cocks her head to one side, then very slowly shakes it. "Whatever," she drawls. "Hey, you guys got plans for Thanksgiving?"

"Yeah. I don't know what they are, but the house will be full. Lou's prob'ly gonna insist on Bob's friends comin' over. How 'bout you join us?"

"Can't," says Shirley. "This is the year for all my family to come to our house."

We all stand there, awkwardly, for a few seconds, and then Shirley says to Steve, "We gotta get goin'. Come here, you old fool, and give me a hug."

She hugs Steve again as Squat moves out of range.

Shaking my hand, Shirley advises me, "You be patient, Bob. She'll get over ole what's-his-name someday."

As they walk away, Steve asks, "Squat, you in the mood for pizza?"

"Pizzzzza!" yells Squat as we turn and head toward the car.

I tell Steve, "That will make Jenny happy, too."

"Then, pizza it is. We'll run through Grove's Point on the way home and get a couple."

On the ride back, Squat talks about the ball game for a while then falls asleep in the back seat. That's when Steve glances at me curiously.

"So you and Nellie, it's gettin' serious, huh?"

"Yeah, it is. I told you that when they came over for supper two weeks ago. She's a good person and I enjoy being with her and Jenny."

"Sally's a good person, too."

"I know. She's a good friend."

"*Huh*. Friendship don't get me no grandchildren."

"You need to talk to Sally about that. I can't help you."

He lets go of the wheel, throwing his hands in the air. "You could if you wanted to."

I shake my head. "Takes two to tango. It ever occur to you that maybe Sally doesn't *want* to have my children?"

"Yeah, I know that. It goes without sayin' she can do better, but damn, at her age, she can't be *too* picky."

"Since it goes without saying, why'd you have to go and say it?" Steve is yanking my chain, but if I don't respond, he'll lose interest, and I want to keep him talking. There's something I want to find out about.

"Oh, come on Bob." Steve shakes his head and adds, "Don't take it personal."

I grin. There's so much I can do with that response. "You tell me I'm not good enough for your daughter then say don't take it personal? How am I *not* supposed to take it personal?"

"Anyway," says Steve, waving his right hand at me dismissively, "she's pretty, got her own house, her own business." Almost as an afterthought, he adds, "Still got all her teeth; that's important. Gets a little cranky but, hell, you get that with any woman once a month."

It's time to use Lou's trick, so I change the subject to the one I want to talk about. "Fill me in on Charlie."

Steve shakes his head as if he's trying to lose a bad memory. "He's from up in Louisville. City slicker, like you, 'cept smoother and taller. Handsomer, too." He gives me a grin that I ignore. "Sally went up there for the weekend with a friend, met him somewhere, and the next thing I know he's sittin' across from me at Sunday dinner. Not supper, mind you; *dinner*. Sally was head over heels. Warn't three months before they was engaged."

"What happened?"

Steve shrugged. "He got married, Sally didn't. Come to find out he had a fianceé up in Indianapolis. Sally took it hard, so did Lou. Didn't bother me none; I thought he was a dipshit." Steve pauses then adds, "Did have to run up to Louisville, though."

"Why?"

"Had to tell Charlie somethin'."

"What?"

Steve shakes his head imperceptibly and stares straight ahead.

"You going to tell me?"

He glances over at me then back to the road, and says, "All right, but you don't breathe a word of this to Sally, 'cause she don't know 'bout this. Lou don't, neither."

"It stays in this car."

He checks on Squat in the rear-view mirror. I look over my shoulder and see that he's still asleep, and Steve continues. "Sally was hurt. She'd had boyfriends, lots of 'em, but this was different."

He pauses again, and I ask, "How long ago was this?"

"Coupla years. Like I say, it wasn't her first rodeo, but it *was* the first time she was engaged. Let me tell you somethin', Bob. If you ever have a child, you'll know 'zactly what I'm talkin' about. It don't matter how old they get; ever' time you gaze in their eyes you see the first time they cried and you couldn't make it better. I just couldn't let him think he'd gotten away with what he'd done to my Sally."

"Okay."

"So I drove up to Louisville and found his house. When I knocked on the door, that woman he married 'stead of Sally opened it. I told her to get his sorry ass front and center. When he come to the door, I told him if I ever found him sniffin' round my daughter again, I'd hunt him down, cut off his head and shit down his throat."

Steve is frequently cantankerous, but this is the first time I have ever seen malevolence. I make a mental note to *never* hurt Sally.

"What'd he say?"

"He said, 'Yes, sir.' If he hadn't said 'sir' I'd a done it right then."

I study Steve, intently, his eyes staring fiercely at the road.

I wish he was my dad.

———

Every window on the kitchen side of the house is fogged over when we get there, and as we walk inside, the women look limp as dishrags hanging on a line.

"Open a window," yells Steve, as the heat and humidity hit him. "Hell, open a bunch of windows."

I set the pizzas on the kitchen table, which Jenny has just wiped clean, and start opening windows. Sally and Nellie are carrying large pots to the basement. On the counters sit rows and rows of tomatoes in glass jars.

"I've made up my mind," Jenny moans as she drags over to me. "I'm stickin' to store-bought. I don't *ever* want to can again."

Putting my arm around her shoulder, I kiss the top of her head and say, "Poor baby."

"Who won?" asks Lou, approaching Steve with a kiss.

"Hilltopper! Hilltopper won!" shouts Squat. "Me and Bob see it."

"Yep," says Steve, ignoring Squat's omission of him. "They always win when I'm there. Course, I wasn't sure 'bout today since I had Mr. Big City with me. Didn't know what kind of mojo he'd be bringin'."

Nellie returns from the basement and comes over to where Jenny and I are standing.

I slip my arm around her waist and stand there between the two. Both their eyes are dancing, so I ask what they've been talking about all day.

Before either can answer, Lou starts waving her hands in the air and declares, "Nope. Can't discuss that. When we're cannin', all talk is girl-talk, and all girl-talk is confidential. But I *will* tell you this much, B-O-B Bob, I learned a lot about *you*."

"Yeah," says Jenny. "*A lot!*"

"I didn't think anyone here knew a lot about me," I laugh.

"We don't," says Sally, walking by. "We just made it up,

right, Nellie?" she pokes Nellie with her elbow as she carries drinks to the table.

"Right." Nellie puts her arm around my waist and pinches my side.

"Okay, be that way," I scold. "I learned a few things today, too."

"Oh, yeah? What?" Sally asks. She stops putting drinks out and focuses on me. Her mouth, smiling just a moment before, is now set in a grimace. Can she know what I'm alluding to?

"Nope," I reply. "When we're at a ball game, all talk is guy-talk, and all guy-talk is confidential. Right Steve?"

Steve laughs, rubs his ample sides, and agrees, "That's right, Little Bit. Bob's absatively right."

He continues laughing as we sit down. Nellie is on my left and I feel her place her hand on my knee under the table.

Squat takes his usual chair on my right and says, "Pizzzza!" to no one in particular.

I wink at Sally across from me, and she winks back then turns her attention to her father.

Steve is regaling everyone with stories of our adventures in Bowling Green, and if only half of what he is saying had a grain of truth to it, Marco Polo's exploits would pale in comparison. Lou is passing out pizza. Jenny, sitting next to Steve, shows him a blister she got on her finger and he, interrupting his narrative, says, with a great flourish, "Ah, my poor Little Bit," and kisses it gently. Nellie is grinning innocently as her hand drifts north on my leg, the way Pam's used to do at dinner parties.

I wonder what Pam's doing right now.

Chapter Thirteen

Nellie has just awakened. She rolls on her side to face me, props her head on her hand, and asks, "What're you thinkin'?"

I shake my head as my eyes roam the room but focus on nothing.

"You seem so far away."

I've been sitting up in her bed leaning against the headboard for about an hour while she slept. Jenny stayed with Sally last night after the canning extravaganza, so I came home with Nellie, but Pam stayed in my head. I feel guilty that my ex inspired me last night while Nellie was moaning in my ear.

This morning, Pam is still in my thoughts. I try to chase her out but only succeed in pursuing her memory around the bed a couple more times.

I put my arm around Nellie, and she snuggles against me, smiling shyly. I can't reveal what I'm *really* thinking about, so I say, "I was thinking how great these last few months have been. I have everything I could possibly want."

That's true, so why, in my mind, am I motor boating Pam's breasts?

Nellie puts her head on my chest and I feel her hand moving south on my body. "You know what I want?" she murmurs.

"I hope it involves what you've got in your hand."

Nellie grins at me then disappears beneath the covers. For the time being, Pam's memory fades.

———

I have every reason to be content; Thanksgiving and Christmas are the best I've ever had, and Nellie and I have a comfortable routine. Lou insists that Nellie and Jenny come to supper every Wednesday, and Nellie, Jenny and I have a Sunday night ritual; supper at their house, then after we wash the dishes, a game of Monopoly around the kitchen table. Nellie and I also get together at least one other night, just the two of us.

Nevertheless, I'm living my life as if I'm peering through a fog. I can see what's going on around me, but nothing is in focus. When we play Monopoly, Nellie's hand on my thigh during the game at first reminds me of pleasures to come, but as the weeks go by and the fog of discontent settles in, it reminds me too frequently of times past in Chicago.

Nellie doesn't catch my confusion, but Sally does. Sometimes when we're together, she leans over and whispers, "Time to come home." I don't understand how she knows; she claims she sees it in my eyes.

Early in the new year, events with Jenny take my mind off of Pam.

After our talk about me not having sex with her, Jenny goes through a succession of boyfriends, some of whom last no longer than a thunderstorm, but with the same cataclysmic upheaval. Nellie is concerned about her, and I am clueless, so on a Sunday in late January, while I'm waiting for my Chicago Bears to play in the Super Bowl, we sit down across from each other at her kitchen table and she educates me.

"Jenny has a lot of issues," she starts. "First, her teenage hormones are runnin' wild. She's got urges just like you and me, only stronger. She ain't used to them and don't have a clue how to deal with them. Second, she was rejected by her daddy."

"Her daddy died; how is that rejection?"

"Her daddy was a drunk. He could have stayed sober for her sake, but he chose booze. That's rejection."

"That's a stretch."

"I know, but that's what the counselors told me. And there's more."

"There usually is with women."

Nellie's face flushes and she glares at me. "I'm tryin' to have a serious discussion here. If you don't wanna be part of it, I got better things to do than to have you make jokes about my daughter's problems."

"I'm sorry. Inappropriate."

She thrusts her jaw out and squints at me. Apology insufficient. She purses her lips, making her mouth wonderfully kissable, but I know better than to do so. I attempt the apology again.

"*Totally* inappropriate, and I'm *very* sorry," I say, placing my hand on top of hers.

After a pause, she continues. "Bein' raped makes her question her self-worth. Why did he do this to her? Did she deserve to be abused? She might try to prove that she is worth something by seekin' attention from men. That's why you had to tell her you wouldn't have sex with her, to let her know she don't have to do that with you to have your approval. That makes sense, don't it?'"

"Yes," I acknowledge. I remove my hand from hers and lean back in the chair. "It didn't when you first told me, but it does now."

"But it don't have to be you. She could still experiment sexually with other men."

My eyebrows rise in surprise. "What are you going to do?"

"I'm gonna get hold of one of the counselors I talked to right after it happened, but I need to ask a huge favor."

"What?"

"I'd like you to go with me." Nellie sees the surprise on my face, and before I can say anything she continues, "I wouldn't ask this if I didn't think it was important. Jenny respects you. She hasn't had a strong man in her life, and if we're gonna make a go of it, you gotta be involved."

When I awoke this morning, I thought the biggest thing happening today was a football game. Life sometimes gives us a twist we're not expecting. I've always known that if Nellie and I stay together, sooner or later, we will have to define my relationship with Jenny. A football game, even a Super Bowl, doesn't seem so important now. And yet, I hesitate.

"Bob," she asks, putting her hand on mine and gripping it, "will you go?"

I pull my hand from hers, spread my arms out to the side, and say, "What do I have to bring to the table?" I'm nervous and a little scared. "Jenny is pretty headstrong."

"No shit, Sherlock." Nellie crosses her arms across her chest. "We need to be united. Are you with me?"

"Of course," I reply, hoping to sound emphatic, decisive, even as I feel insecure, inadequate.

We encourage Jenny to go with us by telling her that we're starting to meld into a family, so it would be good to talk to an expert about family dynamics in a non-traditional household. She doesn't buy it, so Nellie and I go alone every Tuesday evening.

———

Shortly before spring break, Nellie and I return to her house following a session, but Jenny is not in sight. She is usually very conspicuous when we return, as if to be sure we know she didn't go with us. This time, however, as we stand in the kitchen discussing that evening's session, Nellie realizes the house is quiet except for muffled noises from upstairs, as if someone left a radio on.

"Where's Jenny?" She looks at me, then quickly walks to the living room, calling, "Jenny, where are you, Honey?" As she goes upstairs, I hear the sound of scurrying feet. Moving to the bottom of the steps, I hear Nellie call Jenny again, and then the door to Jenny's room flies open; a naked boy bolts into the bathroom carrying his clothes.

"*Oh, Jenny!*" Nellie shouts when the boy almost knocks her down. She goes into Jenny's room and closes the door. I hear them arguing, but the door is closed, and they're both talking at the same time, so I can't make out what either is saying. I go into the living room and sit down.

As I stare out the window, trying to figure out what I should do, I hear loud steps on the stairs, and the boy comes bounding down, buttoning his shirt and carrying a jacket. He darts out the front door and heads down the street on the run. He is the latest thunderstorm, a boy Jenny calls "Snake" in a way too affectionate tone of voice.

Nellie emerges from Jenny's bedroom, saying over her shoulder, "Put some clothes on" then shouts toward the bathroom, "Snake, get out here." There is murder in her voice.

"He left," I call up to her.

Nellie quickly comes down the stairs into the living room, clenching and unclenching her fists. Her eyes are darting from left to right, and she's licking her lips. "I got a full-blown rebellion goin' on up there," she says. "I'm hopin' maybe some third-party intervention will help. Let's go." She turns and heads for the stairs.

When I hesitate, she glances over her shoulder and snaps, "*Come on.*"

"Oh, you mean me?"

"Jeez, Bob, who the hell do you think I mean? *Let's go.*"

Nellie is halfway up by the time I reach the stairs, and as I climb them, I wonder how many steps there are on the gallows.

In her room, Jenny, barefoot, and wearing shorts and a T-shirt, is pacing like a tiger in a cage. She looks as if she just threw her clothes back on; her hair is a mess, and her underwear is lying conspicuously on the unmade, rumpled bed. There's a large hickey on her neck.

"Guess who's in love?" Nellie asks in a sarcastic voice, drawing my eyes away from Jenny.

"*Mom!* Why can't you accept the fact that I'm almost a woman?"

"'Cause fifteen is not 'almost a woman', is it, Bob?" She stretches an arm in supplication toward me.

That's a lose-lose question if ever I've heard one. I look at Jenny and remember being fifteen and in love. Then, it hits me; I wasn't in love, I was in heat. I shake my head slowly and ask, "Do you *really* think you're in love with Snake?" Even as I say it, I can hear the condescension in my tone.

Jenny stops pacing and crosses her arms in front of her, stretching her shirt tightly. "I don't *think* I'm in love. I *am* in love."

"Okay, but there's a big difference between love and sex, right?" I rebut. "I think what your mother is getting at is that while your body is maturing…" I inadvertently let my gaze drop to her chest, where her nipples are showing clearly through the thin fabric of her T-shirt and there's no mistaking that her breasts are now almost the same size as her mother's. Quickly returning my eyes to her face, I see triumph in Jenny's eyes and hope Nellie didn't catch me glancing at her daughter's breasts. Taking a deep breath, I continue, "…emotionally, you may not be ready for sex."

"So what you're sayin' is it's okay for you and my mother to fuck but not for me."

Nellie points at Jenny and says, "I won't put up with that kind of language, young lady."

I glance at Nellie then turn my attention back to Jenny. "No, I'm not saying that at all. What I'm saying is…" My voice drifts off as I think, *What am I saying?*

I'm holding my arms out with my palms up, hoping to catch an idea, anything that will calm Jenny, mollify Nellie, and make sense. I slowly shake my head and turn toward Nellie.

She mouths, "Come on, Bob," but I can't think of anything to say. She throws her hands in the air and lets them slap against her legs, shakes her head, and turns her back to us. She raises her hands to her face, and her shoulders heave as she tries to regain her composure.

The words of the counselor come back to me, so I regurgitate them to Jenny. "Actually, yes, as unfair as it may seem to you, that's *exactly* what I'm saying."

Nellie studies me from behind Jenny. "Because of our age, we're better able to gauge the emotional maturity of our partner and know the consequences of our actions."

Nellie turns back toward us, nodding her head toward Jenny and extending her arm toward me.

Jenny frowns, her eyes narrowing. "That's just some *crap* the counselor told you to say. You don't know *anything* about how I feel, and you're *not* my father."

Game, set, and match to Jenny.

I look at Nellie for help, but she's as lost as me, so I think about what the counselor suggested I say when Jenny challenged my role in her life.

"No, I'm not your father," I say, "but I'd be proud to be."

"Yeah, *right*." Jenny shakes her head.

"Yes, *really*. I *care* about you. Give me a chance, girl. Sometimes, fatherhood is an accident. Some men father children and don't even know it. I *choose* to be with you and your mother."

That seems to surprise Jenny, and she pauses for a moment then confirms I've scored a point when she growls, "Shut the fuck up," and glares at me, belligerently.

"*Language, Jenny!*" Nellie says.

Glancing at Nellie, as much to escape Jenny's withering stare as to find help, I say, "Nellie?" hoping she has something that will work since this is *not* going the way the counselor said it would.

Nellie says, "I know it's hard for you to understand now—"

"But someday I'll thank you for this? Is that what you're gonna say, Mother? 'Cause if it is, save your breath. I'll *never* forgive you for runnin' Snake off."

"*Wait a minute*," I growl, and Jenny's head snaps around to look at me. She appears taken aback by my anger. I point at Nellie, and say, "Your mother didn't *run* Snake off. He was in full flight and halfway down the street when she came looking for him."

Jenny glares at me; her eyes are lasers trying to cut me in

half. I begin to comprehend how mad she is at men, her mother, the world. We stand there, silently. Every one of the counselor's suggestions has failed.

It is so quiet I can hear the clock on her desk ticking, and I count off ten-seconds then remember a stunt one of my coworkers in Chicago used to pull.

Quietly, I say, "I want to tell you something that might help you understand what we're saying. Can I speak the fuck up?"

Nellie's voice catches me off guard. "I don't need that language from you, eith—"

I glance at Nellie and shake my head, imperceptibly, surprised when it stops her in mid-sentence.

Jenny still glares at me then quickly smiles. It's not clear to me if she appreciates the disagreement occurring between her mother and me, or my attempt at humor. When she sits on the bed, however, the smile disappears; she glowers at me again but is quiet.

I say, "I was at a friend's house one time. He was not a teenager, he and I were in our late twenties, and he considered himself quite the ladies' man. Jason told me he could help me 'get a woman,' as he put it. He showed me a drawer full of cheap earrings and told me he used them to convince girls to have sex with him."

Jenny looks puzzled. "I didn't understand it, either," I continue, "so I asked him, 'How do you use earrings to get sex?' He said that if he couldn't get a girl to go to bed with him, he'd take her out to dinner at a nice restaurant and tell her, 'I wish you had known my mother.' You see, Jenny, his mother was dead."

Jenny is still glaring at me, but she glances at her mother, apparently to see if her mother knows where I'm going with this, but she shakes her head at Jenny. "He'd coo to his prey, and I call them 'prey' because that's all they were to him,

'Mom would have liked you.' Then, he'd declare, 'Mom told me on her death bed that someday I'd meet a special girl, and she wanted that girl to have the earrings my father had given her on their first anniversary.' Then, he'd give her one of those cheap pair that he bought a dozen at a time, and he'd tell her, 'These are the earrings. Mom would have wanted you to have them.'"

Jenny's eyes widen and I hear Nellie gasp.

Jenny shakes her head. "He wouldn't."

"Yes, he did."

"And it worked?" Jenny asks.

"*Every* time, according to him. And the women never heard from him again. See, it was just a game to him, but for them, it could lead to pregnancy or, or…" The phrase "a dose of the clap" keeps running through my head, but I'm not about to say *that*.

Nellie saves me. "A sexually transmitted disease."

"Yeah," I say. "And a broken heart."

"That is so sleazy." Jenny studies her hands resting in her lap, for the first time since I entered the room not challenging one of us with her belligerent glare.

"That's my point. When a guy doesn't care about your emotional vulnerability, he will manipulate you. Jason didn't care about the women. All he cared about was getting them into bed. I'm not saying it happened with Snake, but it could."

Jenny mumbles, "Snake wouldn't do that; we're in love."

"If Snake loves you, why did he leave you to deal with us alone?" I ask.

Jenny jerks her head up, and her eyes flash at me again, but it's not clear who she's mad at now, me or Snake. Probably both. She begins to cry. Pointing to the door, she orders, "Both of you, *leave*." Neither of us moves, so she shouts, "*Why won't you leave?*" and pounds her fists against her thighs.

127

"Because we love you," Nellie says. "We love you whether you want us to or not. Honey, I understand how it can be. First time I met your father, I couldn't say no, and nine months later, I had you. I'm not wishin' you away, but I lost a lot of opportunities when I got pregnant at sixteen. I don't want that to happen to you."

Nellie pauses for a moment before continuing, "I'd like you to wait, but even more, I want you to be safe. Did you even think of pregnancy? Or STDs?"

"No," she says, her voice muffled by her crying.

"This AIDS thing is really scary. If I get you some condoms, will you try to wait? But if you can't, will you promise me you'll use them?"

She screws up her face. "That's creepy. My mother buyin' me condoms."

Nellie sits down next to her on the bed. "No creepier than for me to be buyin' condoms for my daughter," she says, daring to put her arm around Jenny's shoulder. "But I'm willin' to get over it if you will. What d'ya say?"

"How 'bout you just put some in the closet in the bathroom." She waves her arm in the general direction of the door. "Then, Bob can use 'em, too. It won't be like they're just for me. That'll work, won't it, Bob?" She looks at me for support.

"That'll work," I say, shoving my hands in my pockets. The less we talk about the household condom supply, the happier I'll be.

"But what do I tell Snake?"

Nellie brushes a stray hair out of Jenny's face. "What do you *wanna* tell him?"

"I wanna say I prefer to wait, but what if he breaks up with me 'cause of that?"

"Don't you see?" I ask. "If he won't wait for you to be

ready, he's only in it for himself. Don't fall for the earrings, sweetheart. They're not real."

"Yeah," suggests Nellie, gently hugging Jenny, "any guy that can't wait for you is not worth havin'."

Jenny wipes away the tears and smiles at the hug. I can't tell if she accepts the support we're offering, but it's all we've got at the moment.

"Anything else?" I ask.

"Yeah," Jenny says, her gaze on me. "When you takin' us to Chicago?"

I'm delighted to change the subject. "How about spring break, if your mother and I can get off?"

"Can we, Mama?" she asks, sounding as relieved as me.

"We can," assures Mama.

The next day, we begin to plan our trip. In a city of over six million people, what is the chance of bumping into one specific person?

Chapter Fourteen

Nellie and I laugh as Jenny bounces up and down in the back seat of my Chevy.

"Chicago will be the largest city I've ever been to," she gushes. "Are you gonna show us where you lived and where you worked? What all are we gonna do?"

"I want to show you some of the museums," I tell Jenny, glancing at her in the rear-view mirror. "The Museum of Science and Industry is my favorite, with the only captured German U-boat from World War II."

Jenny frowns.

"Or if you don't like that, there's the Field Museum of Natural History."

"What have they got there?"

"Among a lot of stuffed animals, they have some elephants and two man-eating lions."

"How do they know the lions were man-eaters?" Nellie wonders.

"They preyed on a crew that was laying a train track. I saw a movie about them as a child, called *Killers of Kilimanjaro*."

"Cool," Jenny says.

"And there's the Art Institute of Chicago. They have a wide variety of art with special exhibits that change frequently. Their modern art section is one of the best."

Nellie puts her hand on my knee. "Let's not forget that Jenny's fifteen. She might not want to spend the whole time in museums."

I'm not sure if Nellie is saying that for Jenny's sake or her own, but I switch gears, anyway. "We've got to walk up and down the Magnificent Mile and spend some time at Grant Park. Something is going on there all the time."

"Like what?" asks Jenny.

"Music concerts or fireworks or special festivals where you can get all sorts of food that's not good for you. Oh, and the zoo's up on the near north side. You've got to see it."

"That's what I'm talkin' about," Jenny declares. "This is gonna be great. What's the Magnificent Mile?"

"A lot of famous department stores. Even if you're not into shopping, we should walk around and see the buildings."

"I'm countin' on you, Bob. You take us and I'll go." Jenny's face is shining as she says this.

The city comes into view, a view I took for granted when I lived here. After being away for a year, though, I share Nellie and Jenny's wonder at the sight of gleaming skyscrapers and seemingly endless streets. I'm glad I don't live here anymore, but I am in awe of the majesty of it.

We drive north on the Dan Ryan Expressway, and I long for the quiet roads of rural Kentucky. I was once a pretty good urban driver, but after one year away, I am intimidated by the kamikaze driving, as cars ride my bumper and cut over in front of us.

We check into a hotel on the north side, near the Zoo, and begin to make the rounds. Jenny and Nellie are dazzled by the skyscrapers. They both insist we go to the top of the Sears Tower and the John Hancock Tower, and are amazed that I lived in Chicago for thirty-four years and have never been to the top of either.

"I'm scared of heights," I confess. "I don't even like being this tall."

We start with the museums and spend the better part of the day at the Museum of Natural History. I had forgotten the wonderful taxidermy exhibit and the stuffed animals, and Jenny is enthralled.

Besides the touristy things, Nellie tells me she wants to take what she calls 'the Bob tour,' which consists of where I worked, lived, studied, and played, so on Tuesday we drive by the garage where I worked, the schools I attended, and finally, the house where I grew up.

"Do you think your father still lives there?" Nellie asks.

"No idea." I see her start to say something, so I add, "We're not stopping; I don't even know if he's still alive."

Nellie folds her arms in front of her. "It just seems that if you're on the same street where he lives you might stop in to see him and, oh, I don't know, *introduce your friends.*"

"Yeah, Bob," Jenny chimes in. Someday in about five years when you and Mom are in nursin' homes, you'll be wantin' me to stop by and see you."

Nellie throws a withering glare toward Jenny, who looks back at her wide-eyed and says, "Whaaat?"

I ignore her comment and go back to the original subject. "I hope this whole 'Bob tour' isn't some setup to get me together with my father because if it is I will be really pissed."

Nellie gazes out the window, and says, "Okay, be that way. But mark my words, there's gonna be a day when you regret bein' so bullheaded."

We drive in silence until a few minutes later, when Jenny observes, "You should be a little nicer to me. After all, I'll be decidin' which nursin' home at least one of you will go to."

"Jenny, just hush," I snap. As we drive toward Grant Park, we are all sulking.

————

The Chicago schools appear not to be on spring break yet since Grant Park is not crowded and nothing is happening. I shiver as the early spring chill cuts through my windbreaker.

Nellie points to a kiosk that has a list of upcoming events, so we read its posts. There will be five bands playing Saturday morning starting at 9:00 a.m. We are planning to leave Saturday morning, but this is the type event I want them to see.

"I have a suggestion."

Both of them look at me, Jenny eagerly, Nellie more complacently.

"Instead of leaving Saturday morning let's pack the car, come down here for the music and leave mid-afternoon. If we leave by three, we can be back in Waynedale by about ten or eleven, even with the time change. We can sleep in Sunday and be rested for school on Monday." I say this last sentence while focusing on Jenny.

Her face contorts, and she says, "Don't mention school. I've got four more days here and I'd like to enjoy myself."

Nellie is examining the list. "I don't mind stayin', but I'm not familiar with any of these groups. Do you know who they are?"

I recognize a few bands that have been around Chicago a while. "Yeah, I've heard of most of them. The reason you haven't is that there's no fiddle or twang in their voices. I think you'd enjoy them. It's pop, but not hard rock. Kind of a northern version of southern rock."

"That sounds good," says Nellie. "You wanna hear a northern version of southern rock, don't you, Jenny?" She sounds sarcastic as she repeats my description, but she smiles, so maybe she's finished sulking.

"Yeah. Can we stay a little later, Mom? I wanna hear them."

After weighing the suggestion, Nellie responds, "If we can all agree to drop the bickerin', I guess we can. If not, we may as well head home now."

I hold my hand out to my side and make a motion like I'm dropping something.

Jenny laughs at me and makes the same motion.

"Okay, then," Nellie agrees, "We stay. Let's walk over to that fountain over there. I wanna take your pictures." Nellie is pointing in the direction of the Buckingham Fountain, so we all head that way.

We spend the next three days touring Grant Park, the zoo, the art museum, and the city in general.

On Friday, we go to the top of the John Hancock Building, where I stand well back from the glass as Jenny presses her face against it to get a better view. She is racing around calling out the places we've been that she can see. I attempt to look out the windows without focusing downward and am relieved when finally her interest wanes and we return to Earth.

At the hotel, they are climbing the steps in front of me and Nellie is dragging. She has one hand on her knee, pushing as if to help herself up, and the other hand is on the rail. I hook my hand in her belt and lift, eliciting a groan.

"What are you groaning about?" I ask her. "I've got the heavy end."

She stops suddenly, and my face bumps into the heavy end. I try to bite her, but she knows that move and pulls away.

Jenny chortles, "Yeah, Mom, your butt's the heavy end."

"My butt's not fat. It's pleasingly plump," she says indignantly.

I pat it, affectionately.

"Not in front of my daughter, I'm wholesome."

"Yeah," I think, "and right now I'd sure like to hold some." Nellie and I haven't been alone since we left Waynedale.

———

Saturday morning, I walk next door to Nellie and Jenny's room and knock. "Is everybody ready?"

The door opens a crack, and Jenny sticks her face out. "Give us five more, Mom's still half-naked." Her eyes widen. "Hey, you wanna see her?" she asks, leering at me.

I do, but I'm not going to tell Jenny that. "I'll be down at the car waiting. When you're ready, wave to me and I'll come help carry the bags."

"You got it, Big Guy."

I do a double-take. Why do I have to be Big Guy or Mr. Big City? What's wrong with Bob?

A few minutes later, the car is loaded and we're on our way. We drive as close to Grant Park as we can get and walk the rest of the way, arriving just in time to hear the first band cranking it up. They are a little heavier metal than Nellie and I care for, but Jenny is enraptured. After a short break, the second band is what I had promised Nellie, not outright country but certainly not heavy metal, either.

"Anybody want a hot dog?" I ask. We didn't eat breakfast and I'm hungry.

They are, too, so I set off for the concessions. The line is short, so I am quickly on my way back, balancing three hot dogs and drinks.

Glancing down to make sure the drinks are not tipping, I hear a familiar voice say, "Bob, is that you?" When my head jerks up, I am staring at a very familiar, very beautiful face.

Pam glances down at the food I'm carrying. "You must be hungry." She is smiling at me and looking damned good. She tries to hug me, but with the drinks and dogs that's not possible, so she kisses her hand and touches it to my cheek.

"What are you doing here?" I ask.

"I'm here with the gang. What about you? Have you moved back to town?"

"No, actually, I'm here with some friends from Kentucky. They wanted to see Chicago, so I told them we'd come up for a few days."

"So how long are you staying? Can I meet your friends?" Pam sweeps the crowd with her gaze as if she'll be able to pick them out just knowing they're with me.

"Actually, we're leaving as soon as the concert is over."

"Stay over tonight and we'll have a party. How many guys are with you? I'll get some women to keep them busy and you and I can have some fun."

Damn my imagination. It takes all my strength to reply, "No, we can't. Work and everything; we've all got to get back." I'm about to drop the drinks, so Pam helps me steady them. When our hands touch, it feels like electricity running up my arm.

"What, someone has to work tomorrow? What's there to do on Sunday in your one-horse town?"

"Listen, I've got to go, but it was sure good to see you." I'm rearranging the drinks and glad I'm about to get away from her, when I notice Jenny coming toward us.

Jenny never hesitates as she walks up. "Hey, Bob, we thought you might need help, so I came lookin' for you." She is talking to me, but she and Pam are sizing up each other.

"Well, B-O-B Bob, who do we have here?" asks Pam. "You're picking them a little green these days, aren't you?" She smiles condescendingly at Jenny, who frowns.

"This is Nel, I mean, Jenny. Jenny this is, this is—"

"Pam," Pam finishes for me.

As Pam stares at Jenny, I add, "Jenny's mother and I are friends. I told them I'd bring them to Chicago, so here we are."

Pam's eyebrows rise and her mouth forms an O. "Well, Jenny, it's nice to meet you. Why don't I walk back with you and meet your mother?" Pam is smiling like a parent who catches her child with his hand in the cookie jar.

"We're right over there," says Jenny, pointing in the direction where we have a blanket spread. "Come on, I'll show you. I *know* Mom will wanna meet you."

Oh, boy. I feel a knot in my stomach as I walk a few steps behind Pam, where I can't help but notice her ass swaying back and forth, and I wonder who's been leaving fingerprints on it lately.

Balancing the hot dogs and drinks slows me down, and when I get to the blanket, Jenny is already introducing Pam to her mother. All three are smiling, but Nellie's seems forced, Pam's smug. Jenny is having the time of her life.

"How did you two meet?" Pam asks Nellie.

"Bob worked on my car and did such a good job I wanted to thank him."

"Ah, yes," Pam coos and gives me a knowing smile.

Turning back to Nellie, she says, "I was just offering to get some of the gang together tonight so that Bob could see them, but he tells me you're leaving this afternoon. Is there any way you could stay until tomorrow?"

"We've already checked out of our room," says Nellie.

"Stay at my place. Bob knows it's big enough for everyone." Turning to me, Pam declares, "In fact, I think you still have some pajamas there. Practically brand new. You never wore them much, if I recall. Least, not the bottoms."

Nellie glares at me then turns back to Pam. "I'm afraid we can't. Jenny has to be back in school Monday, and I've got to be back at work."

"What do you do?"

"I'm a beautician."

"Really? Maybe if you stayed over, you could give me a few pointers. I love your hair. It's so retro. The 1950s all over again."

Nellie runs her hand over her hair as if to reassure herself that it hasn't fallen out. "You don't need any pointers from me," she says. "Your hair is beautiful."

"Thank you, but when you're meeting with doctors every day, you've got to be at your best. Did Bob tell you I'm in pharmaceutical sales?"

"No, Bob doesn't talk about you."

"Oh? Then, *we* need to talk. Please, stay."

Nellie thinks about that for a minute. "Maybe you can stay and listen to the music with us, and we can talk now."

"No," says Pam. "I'm with a group over by the fountain. They're expecting me back. If you change your mind about staying, Bob's got my number."

Looking at me, she adds, "It hasn't changed, Tiger." I again feel the heat of Nellie's glare.

Pam comes over and hugs me a little too long. Her lips graze my cheek with a kiss, and then she whispers in a voice only I can hear, "You can do better. Call me."

I don't watch her walk away, but out of the corner of my eye, I can see Jenny smirking and Nellie glowering. I take a deep breath, exhaling loudly. It's going to be a long drive back to Waynedale.

Chapter Fifteen

Nellie broods over Pam's overt friendliness toward me most of the afternoon. At 2:00, an hour earlier than we discussed leaving, she announces it's time for us to leave, setting off incessant complaints from Jenny. The last band is still warming up, and Jenny and I both want to hear them, although for different reasons.

Jenny is enjoying the music and people-watching. I want to delay the drive home as long as possible to give Nellie time to cool off and see that the chance encounter meant nothing to me. Of course, it would help if that were true. The more I tell her it is all over, the more she talks about the long hug Pam gave me.

"What'd she whisper in your ear?" she asks, as we gather our things. "You think I didn't notice that?"

I shrug.

"You may think it's over, but she sure don't," Nellie says as we walk to the car. We are breaking a tacit agreement that we won't talk about our relationship in front of Jenny, who is soaking it all in.

"Okay," Jenny says from her position five feet behind us, "We knew Bob had a girlfriend in Chicago. Now we know she's hot. What's the big deal?"

Nellie spins around and raises an index finger just under Jenny's nose, bringing her daughter to an abrupt stop. "The 'big deal,' young lady, is that it's none of your business. This is a private conversation." She turns and again walks toward the car.

"Not if you're gonna talk about it on a street in downtown Chicago."

She has a point, but Nellie ignores her. As soon as we are in the car, Nellie insists, "Why don't you just admit that you still have feelings? It'll make it easier on both of us."

I mull over that option. How do I explain that even though I have feelings, and may always have feelings, they don't matter unless they are reciprocated?

I love Nellie, but right now, Pam is in my head, her scent in my nose, her voice in my ears. I can't help it. Damn, why did we have to come to Chicago?

I glance in the rearview mirror and see Jenny sitting there. Nellie and I have come so far with her, teaching her that not all men are scum. If she knows how I feel about Pam, how will that affect her attitude toward me? Toward men?

I can't explain my feelings, so I deny them.

"Nellie, I love you. You're the one I want to be with."

"Yeah, right." Nellie crosses her arms and stares out the passenger window.

The miles start to slide away, and an hour later when I peek in the rear view at Jenny, she is asleep. We are south of Indianapolis when her voice startles me; I don't know how long she's been awake.

"So Bob, I had a great time in Chicago. You think we can go back sometime?"

Nellie answers for me. "We will *not* be returnin'. I've seen enough to last a lifetime." Nellie has been facing out the side window since we left Chicago. Now, she turns to look out the front. When I glance at her, I see a tear on her cheek.

"I haven't," Jenny replies. "I think I could live there." I look at Jenny's reflection in the mirror, contemplating whether she is just stirring the pot, but her face gives up nothing.

"You can live there when you're an adult, just don't ever expect me to visit."

With that settled, silence envelops the car. When traffic permits, I glance at the landscape and remember that the last time I came this way, I thought it was the worst trip of my life. Now, that journey has competition.

———

It's dark when we get to Grove's Point, and Nellie and Jenny are both asleep but awaken when I shut off the engine. I help them carry their bags into the house, not sure what's going to happen.

Inside, Jenny ignores her mother but hugs me, saying "Thanks, Bob. I had a *great* time."

When she goes upstairs, Nellie turns to me and states, "Maybe we should to take a little time off." I start to protest, but she speaks again before I can. "We both got things to sort out."

"She's not interested in me."

Nellie's eyes darken. She turns and walks into the kitchen, me following her. When we get in the kitchen, she turns and demands, "What about you, Bob?" Her finger is on my chest. "Are *you* interested in *her*?"

"It doesn't matter; she's not interested in me."

"You just don't get it, do you?" With every word, her finger punches my chest. "I don't give a shit if *Pam* is interested in *you*. Are *you* interested in *her*, you *dumb fuck*?"

I don't think any woman has ever been this angry at me. Her gaze shifts to over my shoulder, and she yells, "*Jenny, get the hell out of here!*"

Glancing over my shoulder, I spot Jenny just as she wheels around.

She runs back up the stairs and slams the door to her room. I hadn't heard her come down.

I study Nellie's expression but don't recognize the woman in front of me. As we watch each other, she growls, "*What?* She came down here knowin' we were arguin'. She needs to stay out of this."

"You're angry at me and you're taking it out on her. That's not fair, but then, neither is being angry at me."

"I'm angry at you 'cause I thought I knew where we were headed, and now I don't. We're gettin' to the point where I shouldn't have to worry about what's in your head, but I saw the way you looked at her. You're not over her."

"That's ridiculous," I say, knowing full well it's not.

"You probably had a hard-on when she hugged you, you son of a bitch." She waits for me to deny it.

I turn away, afraid of what my eyes might give away.

She puts her hand to her mouth and gasps. "Oh, my God, *it's true*. Goodbye, Bob. Come back when it's *me* on your mind." She pushes me toward the door, crying, but I don't move. I reach out to hug her, but she pushes me away.

"Nellie, wait. Let's talk."

She begins to pace around the kitchen table. "*About what?* I won't be a sideshow."

"You're not a sideshow," I shout, banging my hand on the table, making her jump. Without thinking, I add, "All right, I've still got feelings for Pam, but they don't matter. She and I are through." I spread my arms wide. "*This* is where I want to be."

"I wish I could believe that." She covers her face with her hand and is sobbing. "Get out of my house."

I don't move.

"*Now.*"

"So just like that, it's over? This doesn't make sense. You knew I had a past. Hell, so do you, and a daughter to show for it."

"Yeah, but *my* past is dead. Can't be more over than that. *Yours* is not only alive, but she's *stalkin'* us."

"That's *crazy.*" I hold my arms out to my sides. "She's over three hundred miles away, and all she's capable of is a fling. I want a relationship."

Nellie shakes her head. "It don't matter if she's on the other side of the world if she's still in your head. You get her out of there and we'll talk. Till then, I don't wanna see you."

She follows me through the living room.

On the porch, I stop to say something, but she slams the door.

It is only later that I remember Jenny. I should have said goodbye.

———

When I get home, Sally is waiting for me on the porch. I'm not even halfway up to the house when she shouts, "I can't believe you told her you still have feelings for Pam."

"I can't believe she called me a dumb fuck."

"You are a dumb fuck, you *dumb fuck*. You *never* tell a woman you claim to be in love with that you still have feelings for an old girlfriend. Don't you know anything?" Sally sounds as offended as Nellie.

As I reach the top of the steps I grouse, "I know that I've already had one woman kick my ass up between my ears tonight. I don't need it again."

Sally stands between me and the door. We're close enough that I can smell her chewing gum, and she softly says, "Right. You're right. Let's talk."

"Not tonight. I've got to think things through. I'll call you tomorrow, okay?"

I start to walk past Sally, but she grabs my arm. "Come here, dummy." She puts her arm around my neck, pulls me toward her, and kisses my cheek.

"If I know Nellie, it ain't over yet. But you got a mess to clean up, mister."

She lets me go, smiles awkwardly, then turns and walks down the steps.

I go into the silent house and realize that everyone is in bed. Looking out the window, I watch Sally in the light from the street lamp until she disappears around the corner, and then I go back out onto the porch. It's chilly, so I walk to the car to get my coat. Returning to the porch, I sit down in the swing, using the coat as a blanket. In a while, I am cold again, so I go inside to bed.

————

The next night, it's Lou's turn. As she cleans up after supper, she demands for me to explain how I could have done this to Nellie and what's to become of Jenny.

"That girl needs a father. If *you're* not gonna be there, who is?"

"Lou, you're talking to the wrong person. I'm not the one who asked for some time off."

Steve is sitting at the kitchen table, finishing his sweet tea. "I can't believe you just let her dictate how it's gonna be," he says, his false teeth clicking as he pushes on them with his tongue. "There's more'n one 'tater in the patch. Let her know a man's gotta do certain things, and a woman's gotta accept 'em. Remember what Tammy Wynette said? 'Stand by your man.'"

Lou stares at Steve with her mouth agape and waves her hand dismissively. Turning to me, she says, "Don't listen to that man." Her eyes narrow, and she puts her hands on her hips. "You gotta 'pologize to her. Buy her some flowers, grovel, whatever it takes, but you gotta get her back. She's too good for you, but that child, Little Bit, needs you. Now, git to it."

Lou grabs my shoulders, turns me, and points me toward the door. With one hand pushing between my shoulder blades, she swats me on the butt with the other and shoves me toward the front porch. It's too cool to sit out there tonight, so I head to my room.

Squat is waiting at the top of the steps, holding the white bear which Steve and Lou gave him the previous Christmas. It's his security bear that he always carries when he's nervous. He follows me into my room but doesn't turn on the television. Sitting on my bed with his legs folded and his bear in his lap, he gazes at me and asks, "Is Nellie gone?"

"I think so, yeah."

"Why?"

"I'm not sure."

"Come back."

"I wish it was that easy, partner. I really do."

"She come back. She nice."

Squat looks like I just kicked his dog. "Hey, Squat, maybe tonight you should watch TV with Steve and Lou down in the living room. What do you think?"

He shakes his head. "I stay."

"Then, let's get off the subject of Nellie, okay?"

"Why?"

"Because I…" My voice trails off as he stares at me expectantly. "Squat, how about we walk up to the ice cream store and get a cone. Might make us both feel better, eh?"

"Yeah," he says, visibly brightening. "I like *peppermint.*"

We invite Lou and Steve, but they're not interested, so Squat and I walk the three blocks to the ice cream store and get a double. I watch Squat happily devour his cone while repeating, "I love peppermint" between bites.

After he affirms his love for peppermint the fifth time, I ask him, "You like peppermint?"

Smiling happily, he shakes his head. "I *love* peppermint."

Laughing, I take another bite of my vanilla.

———

After forty-five minutes with Squat, I'm in a better mood.

When we get home, he follows me to my room, turns on the TV, and drops onto my easy chair. The show is about an idiot husband who infuriates his long-suffering wife. It hits a little too close to home, and when they patch things up just before the closing commercial, I wonder why I can't have sitcom writers plot my life. Every argument settled in twenty-three minutes. The next show is more of the same, albeit with a new idiot husband and a different long-suffering wife, so I pick up a book, sit on my desk chair, and start to read.

When the second show ends, I hear the news begin. Squat never watches the news. I glance at him. He has dozed off, so I gently shake his arm.

He appears to be puzzled then realizes he's been asleep. "I go bed," he tells me.

We exchange good nights and he walks to the door, where he pauses.

I wait for him to gather his thoughts, wondering what he wants to say.

Finally, he advises, "You wait. It be okay." He is gone before I can reply.

I read until 2:30 in the morning, but when I put the book down I have no idea what it's about.

Chapter Sixteen

It was the phone call I half-expected, maybe wanted, constantly dreaded.

"Hi, stranger. Remember me?"

The voice sends a shiver down my spine. "Hello, Pam." Do I sound too enthusiastic? Not enthusiastic enough? It would be easier if I knew how enthusiastic I actually am.

"So I enjoyed seeing you last month and meeting what's-her-name and her daughter, whatchamacallit. Sorry we didn't have more time to visit."

I start pacing, imagining the corners of Pam's lips curling up as they always did when she teased me. "Oh, I think you had plenty of time," I tell her. The phone cord only stretches three feet in any one direction, so I take two steps and turn, take two steps and turn, eyes on the floor.

"Not sure why you say that. Hey, have you and old what's-her-name bought a house yet in that one-horse town? What's it called? Waynewale, eh?"

"Cute. Waynedale." I pause, wondering how much to tell. "I'm not sure this is the right town."

"What? There's trouble in paradise? Does that mean things aren't working out with what's-her-name?"

"Her name, as you well know, is Nellie." My knuckles are white from squeezing the phone. "We've decided to take a little break for now. And my leaving Chicago was never about meeting someone; it was about finding out who I am."

"Wow, that's beautiful. What self-help book did you read that in?"

"What do you want, Pam?"

"To see you. Can I come for a visit, stay a few days?"

"I don't think that's a very good idea." *If it isn't a good idea, why am I getting an erection?* Step, step, turn; step, step, turn.

"Oh, come on. Let bygones be bygones. I bet it's been a long time since you had anyone roll you as good as I can."

My mind fills with memories of Pam; the way her skin felt when I caressed it, how her kisses tasted, the scent she dabbed behind her ears, the feel of her breasts crushed against my chest.

I know that if Pam visits it will infuriate Nellie, but I rationalize. Nellie and I are still on the sabbatical *she* wanted, and she did tell me to settle on where my future lies. What better way than to have Pam visit?

I stop pacing. "When did you have in mind?"

"The end of the month." Her voice is as excited as a puppy with a squeaky toy. "I can leave work early the twenty-sixth, drive down, and be there in the evening. At least I think I can. Where is Waynewale, anyway?"

"You should fly. Get a flight into Louisville and I'll pick you up."

"How will I get around while I'm there? Don't pick me up; I'll rent a car."

"You don't need a car to get around here. You can walk. Or borrow my bike. That'll get you around."

"You've got to be kidding me. I haven't ridden a bike since I was nine years old."

"Okay, walking it is, but I bet you'd look pretty good sitting on a bike."

"Of course, I would," she laughs. "I look good on anything. You sure it's a bike you want me sitting on?"

How can she read my mind? Before I can respond, she adds, "I'll let you know when I've got a flight. It'll be great seeing you, B-O-B Bob."

I hang up and catch my grinning reflection in a mirror. *Wipe that grin off your face and figure out how you're going to tell Nellie about this,* I think.

———

The next day, Pam calls again, this time at work, with her flight number and time of arrival in Louisville.

I ask, "How'd you get my work number?"

"A woman never reveals her sources," she teases. "I know how to get what I want."

Even though Nellie and I haven't seen each other since we got back from Chicago three weeks earlier, we've talked a few times. The conversations have been tense, but at least we're communicating. I put off calling her until the next day. Then, when I do, I tell her we need to talk.

"What do we have to talk about?"

"You told me to work things out. I need to let you know what's going on."

"Have you gotten her out of your head?"

"I'd rather have this conversation in person. I think we owe that to each other. Okay?"

She sighs. "I'll be home at five-thirty if you wanna stop

by." She seems to know she's not going to like what I have to tell her.

———

When I pull into the drive, Jenny jumps down the steps yelling, "Bob!" She comes up to me as I get out of the car, and I swear she has grown a couple of inches in the few weeks since I saw her last. She hugs me, enthusiastically, a little tighter than normal and keeps kissing me on the cheek, until I make her stop.

Nellie is less enthusiastic, although she smiles at me. I wish we could just go inside, fix a pizza, and play a game of *Monopoly.*

Nellie advises Jenny, "Honey, I think you need to finish your homework. We'll have supper in about an hour."

"Are you stayin' for supper, Bob?" She flashes a toothy grin at me.

"No," Nellie snaps before I can answer. "Go finish your homework."

Jenny makes a face at her mother, surprises me with another kiss on the cheek, then goes into the house.

"So what do you wanna talk about?" Nellie asks as we sit down on the porch.

I start my carefully rehearsed speech. "The last time I saw you, you told me I had a lot of things to sort through."

Nellie nods in affirmation.

"Well, you're right; I have to resolve how I feel about Pam, only I can't do that with her in Chicago and me here."

"So you're goin' to Chicago." Ice hangs on each word, and her eyes bore into me.

"No, Pam's coming here."

I might as well have punched Nellie in the stomach. Her eyes widen and I hear her gasp. She rocks forward with her arms folded across her stomach and I think for a moment that she's going to be sick. She jumps up, runs into the house, and slams the door. I sit there for about five minutes, hoping she will come back out.

When I finally accept that she's not coming back, I walk to my car. As I drive away, I see Jenny watching me from an upstairs window.

———

Sally and Lou are sitting on the porch when I get home. One look tells me they've talked to Nellie. Lou fans herself with the evening paper, and Sally has her arms folded across her chest. Both have the same fierce frown.

Neither speaks as I walk up the steps and sit down in the swing opposite them. After staring at me during my journey up the walk and the steps, neither will look at me now. Indignation waits ten-seconds then explodes.

"I can't *believe* you're bringin' her here," Sally yells, her eyes bulging and finally meeting mine. "Are you outta your mind?"

"Probably," I admit. "Hey, she took me by surprise. She called and invited herself. What was I supposed to do?"

"*Say no*," Lou thunders, hitting her thigh with the paper. "Bob, we love you like a son, but I don't understand this, not at all." Her lips quiver and her eyes are moist. "I'm not comfortable with her stayin' here." Lou thrusts her jaw forward, daring me to challenge her.

"Then she won't. Maybe I won't, either."

"Maybe you shouldn't," says Sally, but Lou appears horrified at that idea.

"No, no," she says, shaking her head and waving a hand up and down. "I'm not implyin' *you* need to leave. I'm just not comfortable with her stayin' here with you. Think what Squat would be exposed to."

"That's your concern? What a fifty-something-year-old man might see? What about me? Hasn't it ever occurred to you that I might want female companionship now and then? Haven't any of your other boarders had overnight guests?"

Lou stares at me blankly for a moment then mumbles, "We never had a boarder before you." She regains her train of thought, and continues, "But I won't stand by and see Nellie hurt. She's part of our family now, too."

Sally nods in agreement.

"So how do you decide which member of your family to protect? A minute ago, you said I was like a son, but you're sure not helping me out. I can't even have someone who's been important in my life stay here? I've got to put her up in a motel and the closest one's over in Grove's Point, eight miles away? That's going to be a little inconvenient for me."

Lou's fists look like soldiers at attention in her lap, clenched so tight that I think her knuckles are going to pop out of her skin. "She ain't stayin' here. You do what you have to do, but I'll not abide her stayin' here."

Our eyes lock on each other, and I see the determination in Lou's face, but she swallows twice.

Finally, I stand and go inside.

When I get upstairs to my room, I find Squat watching TV. His gaze follows me as I pull my suitcase out of the closet. Opening it on the bed, I throw socks and underwear at it, some of them ending on the floor.

"You go vacation?"

"No, Squat. I'm moving." I pull three shirts off their

hangers and wad them into a ball, getting ready to throw them, too.

He gets up and begins to pace, swinging a fist into the other palm. "*No*," he demands. "Don't go. Stay here."

"Yeah, well, Lou and Sally don't *want* me here. What am I supposed to do?"

"Wait. Wait a little."

I stop balling the shirts and look at him. His eyes are set wide and a tear is on his cheek.

He says, "When you mad, wait until you not mad anymore. Mad does stupid things."

I gaze at Squat. He stands there, clenching and unclenching his fists, his nostrils puffing out and in with each breath, and I realize I am about to walk out on people I love and, just as importantly, people who love me.

Squat and I continue to look at each other.

"Where'd you learn that?" I ask as I slowly return my shirts to their hangers, smoothing them as I do.

"Clare teach me," he says.

After hanging the shirts, I pick up the socks and underwear on the floor.

Squat picks up the few clothes that landed in the suitcase and hands them to me.

I take them from him and as I return them to the dresser I ask, "How'd you get to be so smart, partner?"

He shrugs. "I listen." A profound statement from a simple man. I walk toward him, but he sees a hug coming and backs off. Waving his hands, he reminds me, "No hugs."

"Okay, no hugs." I point at him and say, "But you da man."

He smiles and thumps his chest. "Yeah. I da man. You stay?"

"For now. But I've got to be honest, Squat, I'm not sure how it's all going to play out."

"What you mean?"

"I don't know how long I'll be staying. We'll have to see."

"You stay until you not mad?"

"Yeah. I stay until I'm not mad."

Chapter Seventeen

Pam's flight into Louisville arrives around six-thirty in the evening.

As we drive south on the interstate, I reveal that I've made her a reservation at a motel in Grove's Point. She wants to stay with me, but I tell her Lou and Steve get up early and they're afraid they will disturb us.

"Bull. What's the real reason, eh?"

I glance at her, and she arches her eyebrows and cocks her head.

"Remember the joke about the guy whose brother got him a sweater for his birthday, and it was okay, except he'd rather have had a screamer or a moaner?"

Pam folds her arms in front of her. "I am *not* a sweater," she huffs.

"No, you're a screamer. And a moaner. *We'll* disturb them."

She's quiet for a moment then insists, "Cut the crap. Why don't you want me staying with you, eh?"

"I just told you."

"Hey, I have occasionally screamed, but why do you think I'll be doing it this weekend?"

She's right, and now that she's here, I'm not sure I want to give her a reason to scream. Even though I'm happy to see Pam, the more we talk, the more I want to work things out with Nellie. I need to be honest with both of them; I can start right here.

Taking a deep breath, I ask, "You remember Nellie?" Traffic on the highway is light and I steal another glance at her.

Pam turns away from me to gaze out the window and retorts, "*No*, and when I finish with you, you won't, either." She pauses, then adds, "I thought you two were taking a break."

"We are."

"Fine. Come back to Chicago."

"Why?" I stare at Pam much longer than I should and only look back at the road when my tires hit the rumble strips on the side of the lane. An image of me with Nellie and Jenny drifts through my mind. The three of us are sitting at Nellie's kitchen table, laughing and teasing. Loving.

Pam's voice interrupts my reverie. "I miss you. Is that what you need to hear? Okay, I've said it. I miss you. I'm tired of you being in my head. I want you in my bed."

This time, my mind wanders to Pam's bedroom, and I visualize Pam lying on the bed, naked. I imagine lying down next to her, but before I can touch her, my imagination opens the bathroom door and a strange man walks out. He's naked, too.

I shake my head and focus on Pam's last words. "Does that mean you're ready for an exclusive relationship?" I ask.

She ignores my question. "I miss having you around when I'm in Chicago." She reaches over and massages my neck.

"God, Pam, you are the most selfish bi——" Out of the corner of my eye, I see her staring at me.

She pulls her hand back and folds her arms across her chest.

"Most selfish person I know. You knew why I left Chicago, yet you come down here to talk me into coming back to the *same* situation? What is it with you?"

"*All right*. I'm willing to consider a monogamous relationship if you come back to Chicago."

"Chicago's not my home anymore."

"Okay, we've gotten off on the wrong foot. Let's back up. You're telling me I can't stay with you because Nellie will be upset."

"And Sally, and Lou, and Squat. And probably the Mafia."

"The Mafia?"

I smile and check the rearview mirror. "I'll explain that one later."

"Okay, so I have competition. I can handle that. Let's get to the motel and find out if the bed's comfortable." She reaches over and tickles me in the ribs. "Then, you can show me around town."

When we get to the motel, I carry Pam's bags inside.

As soon as I set them down, she kisses me and grinds her hips against mine. I feel her hand grab me. In the past, that would always get me hard.

Not this time.

Images of Nellie, Jenny, and me run through my mind. We're playing *Monopoly*, watching a movie, having supper. I remember driving to Chicago, with Nellie asleep in the front and Jenny asleep in the back, both of them so trusting of me. I even flash on some of the bad times when we argued, and the scene with Snake. The three of us have *always* worked things out, no matter how bad.

There it is, right in front of me, what I want. I need to tell Pam, but that will be the easy part. How do I convince Nellie?

————

"This is something new," Pam says. "Do you have liftoff failure with Nellie, or did you save this for me, eh?" She is frowning.

"Pam, let's talk." I pause and weigh my words carefully. Standing face-to-face, I gaze into her eyes and swallow hard.

She looks like I just slapped her. Her mouth forms an *O*, her eyes go wide, and she steps back. "Oh, my God," she squeals. "This can't be happening. You're getting ready to claim that you're in love with her. I can't believe this. I can't *fucking* believe this. Why'd you waste my time bringing me down here to Possum Trot, anyway?"

Wow. Telling Pam is even easier than I thought.

"Waynedale," I say, quietly. "I live in Waynedale, although technically we're in Grove's Point right now. Possum Trot is in the western part of the state."

"*Whatever.* Why'd you have me come down here?" Pam sounds more hurt than mad. There's a chair behind her. She sits down and stares at me, her hands resting on the arms of the chair.

I shrug. "It wasn't my idea. You invited yourself."

"Why didn't you insist that I not come?"

"After we saw you in Chicago, Nellie sensed that I still had a thing for you, so she told me she didn't want to see me again until I sorted out who I want to be with. Then, you called and I have to admit I *was* still thinking about you, so it seemed to make sense that you should come. But when I told Nellie you were coming, the shit hit the fan." I sit down on the edge of the bed, facing Pam. "I don't understand it. She told me to figure out how I felt, then when I make plans to do that, she gets pissed. What did she want me to do?"

"Well, not this, obviously," Pam observes.

"No, I'm sure she didn't want me here with you, but we've got a history, too, and nothing any of us can do will change that. Plus, she told me to sort things out."

Pam snorted. "Dear, sweet, B-O-B Bob, naïve as ever. When a woman says to 'sort things out,' she means for you to immediately profess your undying love for her. You're supposed to tell her the other woman is yesterday, not invite the ex to town." She shakes her head but starts to laugh.

"Guess I kind of messed this up, didn't I?"

We remain focused on each other for a moment, and then Pam asks, "Are you *really* in love with her?"

Without hesitation, I declare, "Yes." Finally, I believe it.

"Why? I don't see it. She's a beautician, for crissakes,"

"Why should that matter? She's a beautician, yes, and a lot of other things."

Pam leans forward and says, "Make your case."

I rub my hands together and smile as I think about Nellie. "She's a good soul, cares about everyone. She calls Lou at least twice a week but doesn't even mention *me*. She asks Lou about Squat and Steve, 'Are you okay? Can I help with anything?' And when she and Jenny come to supper, she always brings a dish and stays to help clean up. Steve loves to tease everybody, and she always laughs, but she laughs hardest when Steve's teasing *her*. And talk about quick. Soon as he's finished, she hits him with a zinger.

"She's got her hands full with Jenny, but if you could see the way she looks at that girl. Even when she's ready to throttle her, Jenny is her world. Our friends assure me that she never talks about herself. She asks how *they're* doing. When we're apart, I miss her smile, her laugh, her warmth, even the way her lips pucker when she's aggravated at me."

Pam nods her head slowly. "So I've wasted a weekend, eh? It's really too late for us?"

"Yeah. It's really too late." I feel no regret as I say it.

"Well," says Pam, always ready for some uncommitted coupling, "now that your mind is at peace, you want to see if you can get that pecker up so we have one for the road?" She gets up and walks to me. Standing in front of me, she runs her fingers through my hair then kneels on the bed, one knee on each side of me, and rests her butt in my lap while facing me.

Against my will, I'm getting hard. She used to do this when we were on her couch in Chicago, and I remember where it always ended up. Turning my head away so she can't kiss me, I murmur, "No," and force both of us to stand. "I'll show you around, introduce you to everyone, but we can't have 'one for the road.' It wouldn't be fair to Nellie."

"Man, you're eaten up with her, aren't you?" She sounds impressed.

"Yes, I am. Plus, there's a song they play around here sometimes that sums you up perfectly. It's called 'You done stomped on my heart, and you mashed that sucker flat.'"

Pam does nothing to mask her distaste, so I put my hands on her shoulders. "But whether Nellie likes it or not, it was right for you to come here. Now I know. I'm truly, deeply, madly, in love with Miss Nellie McDonald." The more I think about it, the happier I am.

Pam seems disappointed but not mad. "So what are your plans to get Nellie back, eh?"

I shake my head. "I got nothin'. I hope Sally can help. She knows Nellie and might have an idea." I'm looking at Pam, but thinking of Nellie.

Pam kisses me, gently, but not romantically, and I smile at

her. "Okay," she says, "since I'm here, I want to meet these people. Never met a Squat before." She pauses then says, "Be right back." She walks into the bathroom and closes the door.

I stand there enjoying the clarity of my thoughts. I am a happy man. However, happiness has a short shelf life.

I pick up the phone, call Nellie, and tell her Pam wants to meet with her.

"You tell her we met in Chicago and that was one meetin' too many." I picture her jaw set firmly and her lips pursed.

"Nellie, give her a chance to explain. It's over between us. It's you I want." If I expect Nellie to express happiness at this revelation, I am disappointed.

"Where you callin' from?" she asks, suspiciously.

"I'm here with Pam in her motel room." As I report this, Pam, having come out of the bathroom, grimaces and shakes her head vigorously. Too late.

"Go fuck yourself!" Nellie shouts, and the line goes dead.

Gently placing the phone in the cradle, I say, sheepishly, "I think that went well."

"B-O-B Bob, what is wrong with you? You don't confess to the woman you love that you're in your ex's motel room."

"You sound like Sally."

"Then, it's time I met her. Maybe between the three of us, we can figure out something. Call and ask her if we can come by, and for God's sake, don't tell *her* you're in my motel room."

"Why are you doin' this, Pam?" I study my hands folded in my lap but peek at her out of the corner of my eye. I've never known her to think of someone else's wants and needs over hers.

She purses her lips and looks at me. I can see her brain churning that question around.

After a bit, she reveals, "I realize not everyone's the same as me. I've always taken sex pretty casually."

I smile.

"What?"

Shaking my head, I look away.

"Anyway," Pam continues, "lately, I've been finding out not everyone feels that way. I've had two boyfriends drop me because they're getting married. I've had one married guy drop me when his wife gave him an ultimatum."

She sits in the chair, again, and I sit on the bed.

"What's that got to do with me?" I ask.

"I'm may not be in *love* with you, but I am in *like* with you."

"You silver-tongued devil." That's pretty much what she told me a year ago when I left Chicago, and it hurt me then. Now, it sounds good, and I smile at her.

"Come on, you just told me you love Nellie, not me. Isn't it okay if I *care* about you without loving you?"

"It is," I concede.

"If you and I aren't going to get together, why should I keep you from being happy? I'm a carefree woman, not a vindictive bitch. I've messed things up. Let me help fix them. Let's get you back with Nellie."

When I call Sally, she is ready to close the café but says we can come by.

"I don't know why she wants to meet me, though. I sure don't need to meet her."

As we drive over to Waynedale, I fill Pam in about Sally, her parents, and Squat. She thinks it's 'sweet' that they've 'adopted' me and that Sally and I have a platonic friendship.

We arrive at the café as Sally is cleaning up. I wave to her as Pam and I sit down in a booth. After locking the door and turning the Open/Closed sign to *Closed*, Sally sits down next to me and across from Pam, eyeing her like an old cat watches a big dog.

Pam stretches her hand across the table and says, "Hi, I'm Pam Girard, B-O-B Bob's *ex*-girlfriend."

Sally's eyebrows rise when she hears the emphasis Pam places on 'ex' but still won't shake her hand, so Pam withdraws it.

"Pam," I sputter, "this is the lady I've been talkin' about. She has the best chicken salad in Kentucky and her desser—"

"Shut the fuck up, Bob. I got a call from Nellie right after you called, cryin' her heart out. Says you called her from Pam's motel room. What kind of a moron are you?"

"Yeah," I acknowledge, shaking my head. "That wasn't smart."

"Ya *think*?" asks Sally.

"Give Pam and me a minute to talk to you," I plead. "I've come to some decisions, and Pam understands them, but I need your help."

Pam nods in agreement and smiles at her. Sally's hands are clasped in front of her, resting on the table, and she has a familiar frown on her face. My hope begins to fade.

"Sally, obviously you don't have a good opinion of me," says Pam, "but it's apparent you care for Nellie and Bob. I care for B-O-B Bob, too. He's explained things to me about him and Nellie and, well, I know he's in love with her, so I'd like to help him. I didn't come here to start trouble. What can I do to straighten things out?"

"First thing you can do is stop callin' him B-O-B Bob. I'm sure he's told you by now he doesn't like it."

Pam smiles at me. "Bob," she says.

"Why *did* you come here?" Sally asks. "You met Nellie in Chicago; you had to know it would cause problems for her and Bob, so why'd you do it?"

Pam hesitates for a moment. "Is that important? Can't we just accept where we are now, that B-O—"

Sally cocks her head, questioningly.

"That Bob is in love with Nellie, that I'm yesterday, and that we need to get Nellie to talk to him. Can't we do that?"

Sally glances at me. She has absorbed what Pam said but doesn't respond. Nevertheless, her crinkled eyes and pursed lips relax, and she says to me, "Bob, you knew Nellie was crazy about you and Jenny'd told all her friends she hoped you became her stepfather. Then, you gotta get all moon-eyed over, well, over Pam, here." Sally jerks her head in Pam's direction as she utters her name, giving it the sound of a pejorative.

Pam murmurs, to no one in particular, "I'm so sorry. I just didn't know Bob was happy here."

"Now you do," I tell her, and she nods.

————

We talk for about a half-hour. As the conversation meanders, Pam gradually begins to charm Sally. Finally, Sally laughs out loud when Pam comments that when she first met me, I couldn't get laid in a women's prison with a handful of pardons.

"Dish on 'Mr. Big City,' here," Sally says, tilting her head in my direction as if Pam wouldn't know who she was talking about. "What was he like in Chicago?"

Pam, noticing the distaste on my face, comments, "For one thing, he doesn't like being called 'Mr. Big City' any more than B-O-B Bob."

"Well, then," says Sally, "he really is a big baby, isn't he?"

She and Pam both laugh. I don't care what they call me, as long as they bond.

After a little more teasing regarding my myriad nicknames,

Sally suggests, "Okay, here's what I think we should do. I'll talk to Nellie, let her know I met the dragon lady and—"

Pam's eyes go wide and she turns to me, saying, "Are you going to let her call me that?" but she laughs.

"I'm sorry," Sally replies, "but Nellie and I have taken to callin' you that." She pauses then points a finger at Pam. "I'll tell you somethin', though. Nellie told me the first time she called you that, Bob told her you *weren't* a dragon lady and he didn't want her thinkin' bad 'bout you."

Pam smiles at me, taking my hand and squeezing it.

"But I wouldn't go takin' his hand in front of her, if I was you," Sally warns.

Pam jerks her hand back as if mine was a hot horseshoe.

"Anyway," continues Sally, "I need to tell Nellie I've met you and I believe you two are over. I'll call her tonight when I get home."

"You might not want to call her this late," I suggest.

"Oh, don't you worry about wakin' up Miss Nellie," Sally says. "She ain't gonna be doin' much sleepin' tonight. It's best I call her before everybody goes to bed. That way, she won't accidentally slip into someone's room and carelessly slit a throat."

Pam swallows hard.

Sally smiles as if she didn't just hint at the possibility of murder and mayhem and adds, "You never did talk 'bout you and Bob in Chicago."

Pam regards me. "Let's just say it was long ago and whatever we had is over now."

I nod in agreement.

"Good," Sally responds, slapping her hand on the table. "That's perfect. Be sure Nellie hears you say that. Now, you two scoot, and Bob, if you're gonna be more'n a half-hour gettin' home, tell me now 'cause I won't even bother callin'

Nellie. I'll just call Mama and tell her you are a dirty, lyin', cheatin' scumbag."

"I'll be home in a half-hour."

We stand up, and I hug Sally.

She kisses me on the cheek and states, "This ain't gonna be easy, but that woman really loves you. Lord knows why; I don't see it."

"It's a mystery to me," agrees Pam, putting her hand on Sally's arm.

They look at each other and laugh.

"I'm not sure what I've gotten myself into, gettin' you two together," I mutter.

"Yeah, but you did," says Pam, walking toward the door, "so now you'll have to live with it. Come on, Sally. We'll drop you at your house."

I walk to my car between two of my five favorite women.

Chapter Eighteen

I take Pam back to her motel and then drive home. It's about eleven when I arrive. Lou and Steve have gone to bed, but Squat is standing at the top of the stairs in his pajamas. He has a blank expression on his face.

"Are you stayin'?"

"I'm stayin'."

His shoulders relax, and a smile as big as Texas lights up his face.

I tell him, "I'm sorry for worryin' you. There's been a lot goin' on."

"You stay here forever."

"I don't know about that, partner. You might get sick of me."

We walk into my room, and I sit down in my chair while Squat sprawls on the bed.

"If Nellie and I get back together, we might get married. If we do, we'd probably live in her house."

"You eat supper here?"

"Not every night." Squat's face darkens so I quickly add, "But sometimes, and you could have supper with us some, too. That would be fun, wouldn't it?"

"You live here. We family."

"Let's take one thing at a time."

Squat still appears troubled, and I grapple at ways to explain the situation so he will understand and accept. "Hey, didn't Sally live here when she was growin' up?"

"Yes."

"Well, she's family, too, isn't she?"

"Yeah."

"Okay, and she still comes over and has supper and you see her a lot, right?"

"Yeah." Squat smiles. "She buy me ice cream."

"That's right," I say, "It would be like that. But for right now, I'm not goin' anywhere, and, I'm workin' on gettin' Nellie back."

"Nellie nice."

"I know. No promises, but I hope it'll work out."

Squat smiles widely. "You marry Nellie!"

"Okay, partner, let's not get ahead of ourselves. First, we've got to get Nellie and me back together."

"We will," Squat insists, smiling broadly. "We will!"

———

After Squat leaves, I start getting ready for bed, when I hear the phone ring. No one calls Lou and Steve this late, so I grab it quickly. It's Sally.

"I talked to her, Bob, and she's awful upset. Says you went behind her back bringin' Pam here and she's hurtin'. The good thing for you is that she's still in love with you, but she's gonna make you earn it."

"Did you tell her you talked to Pam and you know it's over between us?"

"Yeah, I told her that, but she's still upset that you brought her to town."

"I didn't bring her here, she invited *herself*."

"Yeah, but you didn't say no. Hey, by the way, why'd you give Pam my phone number here at the house?"

"I didn't. What makes you think I did?" I begin to pace.

"She called me right after I got off the phone with Nellie. How'd she get my number?"

"You're in the phone book, aren't you?"

"Oh. Yeah."

Nodding, I hold my hand out as if Sally could see me. "There you go, then. What'd she want?"

"She asked how it went with Nellie. I gotta admit I had her figured wrong. She may have come down here to lasso you home, but once she figured out you were sweet on Nellie, she set her mind to gettin' the two of you back together."

Man, it would have been so much easier if she'd never come. "I don't know if there's much she can do about that." It would also have been so much easier if I'd never had that first lunch with her. But then, if I'd never met her, I probably wouldn't have had the stimulus to leave Chicago and wouldn't have met Nellie.

"She's gonna give it her best shot." Sally sounds amused.

"What's she up to?"

"Let's just wait and see what happens."

"What's goin' on, Sally?"

"I'm not at liberty to discuss it. 'Night B-O-B Bob." Sally sounds mischievous, flirtatious, and devious all at the same time. She's Pam, all over again.

Before I can reply, the phone clicks dead.

I try to sleep but there are too many images running

through my mind; of Nellie and Jenny, board games, and stolen innocence; of Squat and his faith in me; of Steve and Lou and how close we've become; and finally, of Pam. Even though we didn't do anything, I can hear all the Waynedale women saying, "That's a male rationalization. You brought her here. That's enough."

I'm beginning to understand.

———

Sunday morning dawns warm so I take the newspaper out on the porch. I'm reading words without meanings when the phone rings, and Lou answers it. She says, "Yeah, he's here. Just a minute." The door opens, and Lou sticks her head out. She looks at me as if I just vomited on her porch, and orders, "Git in here and take this call."

It's Nellie. There's no chit chat, just, "Bob, I need to talk to you." I have been summoned by the icy voice of Judgment.

"When?"

"Now." The summons is immediate.

"Is there anything I should know?"

"No. You should come over here now. Can you be here in twenty minutes?"

"I'll have to leave right now to be there that soon."

Lou is walking by, and she stops and glares at me.

"Do it." Nellie is insistent. "I will see you in twenty minutes."

"Wait a minute, Nellie. I want—" The phone clicks.

What I want is irrelevant. My fate will be delivered in twenty minutes and I had best be there to receive it. Lou is still glaring at me.

"She wants to see me," I say, smiling as if her voice had been friendly.

Lou rolls her eyes, shakes her head, and moves on.

As I drive toward Grove's Point, I think about how a person who lives to age seventy will have over twenty-five thousand days of existence with maybe six or eight really critical moments along the way. That thought only adds to my anxiety since it means that if Nellie casts me out, I will have about twelve thousand days to get through without her.

At Nellie's, Sally's car is in the drive; I park behind it.

Jenny meets me at the door, smiling, and very excited.

"Come on in, Bob. We've been havin' the best time visitin'." She spins around and runs toward the kitchen, from which I hear voices, all female, laughing and raucous. They sound like a younger version of the Mafia.

I follow Jenny into the kitchen and there, sitting at the table, are Nellie and Sally. And Pam.

Jenny quickly joins them in the only other chair, grinning from ear to ear. She has been admitted to the inner sanctum of the female kingdom, to help sit in judgment of the poor, dumb male who has arrived.

No one suggests I get a chair, so I stand awkwardly in front of them.

Sally reaches out and gives my hand a quick tug. "Hey, Sweetie," she says.

"What's happenin'?" I ask, hopeful at the light-hearted nature of the greeting.

"Well," explains Sally, "I told you Pam called last night. When I told her that Nellie was still upset with you, 'specially since you called from her motel room, she said she wanted to talk to Nellie, but didn't have any way of gettin' here; would I carry her over this mornin'? I thought about it, and after meetin' her, I could see she had Nellie's best interest at heart, so I said okay. So we came over this mornin', and the four of us fixed breakfast. Did you know Pam had never had grits?"

Sally reaches over and put her hand on Pam's arm, and they smile at each other. "Can't say that, anymore, can you, girl?" Sally asks.

"There's a lot of things I can't say anymore," agrees Pam.

"What else?" asks Jenny, squirming in her chair.

"Let's see." Pam rears back to ponder her answer. "I've never, and I mean never, tried to talk another woman into taking back a man I'm interested in."

The others all nod their heads.

I remain standing, a prisoner before the court. I am encouraged by the familiarity the women show for each other, but none has invited me to sit with them, so I walk to the sink and lean against it, waiting for the other shoe to fall. It is quiet for fifteen to twenty seconds. They're content to let me twist in the wind.

Around this table are four of the five most important women in my life. My past, present, and, I hope, future, are here, and I begin to feel comfortable. If Nellie wanted a public execution, Jenny wouldn't be here.

After an interminable wait, Nellie begins, "So, B-O-B Bob, Pam tells me you were at her motel room last night." The words, each one clipped and precise, slide out of her mouth as if they were letters slipped through a mail slot.

"You knew that already." This is not a good start and not in keeping with the love fest I walked into a minute ago. Despite my desire to fix things, it aggravates me.

"Yeah, but I didn't know the exact *circumstances* of you bein' there."

Uh-oh.

"For example, I didn't know she was just checkin' in and you carried her bag in for her. That's bein' a gentleman and I'd expect that of you. And when she told me she came on to you, at first I was mad, but she explained how she didn't really know you and I were so…" Nellie turns to Pam. "How'd you put it, Honey?"

Pam is staring me straight in the eye and for a moment it seems we are the only two people in the room. Then, she faces Nellie and murmurs, "Destined to be together."

"Yeah, that's it!" Nellie claps her hands, rocks back in her chair, and laughs happily. "Destined to be together. That's good." I gaze at Nellie and smile, grateful for her happiness.

"And then," Nellie continues, "she told me that you turned her down flat, said you couldn't do that to me. Said that's when she knew we were destined to be together 'cause you'd *never* been able to turn her down before."

"Yeah. That…that's what happened," I stutter.

"Bob, I don't care what happened between you and Pam a year ago if it's over now."

Pam and I lock stares again.

"It's over," I say.

Pam's eyes are glistening. She breaks her gaze away from me, faces Nellie and, slapping the table for emphasis, affirms, "Yep, it's over."

I look at Sally, then Jenny, and finally Nellie. Each of them is smiling at me, and I smile back.

"I was afraid you were gonna see Pam and remember all the 'good ole days' and fall into bed with her. When you called me from her motel room, I thought that's what you were callin' to tell me, so I got mad. But when she told me you wouldn't let nothin' happen, I knew you loved me."

Nellie suddenly jumps up and hugs me. I make sure not to look at Pam as Nellie kisses me. It's a quick kiss, the kind a married couple exchange when they see each other at the end of the day. When Nellie releases me, she grabs a chair from her desk. "Here," she offers, pulling the chair between her and Jenny, who scoots over. "Sit down."

Court stands adjourned.

"So, Pam," says Sally, "I never did get you to tell me much about Mr. Big City. Dish."

"I don't think there's much to talk about," says Pam. "More than any man I've ever known, and I've known a few—"

"A mild understatement," I point out.

Nellie slaps my hand and says, "*Bob,*" but Sally glances at me and smiles.

"Okay," says Pam, laughing, "I've known a lot. Anyway, more than with any other man, with Bob, what you see is what you get. He's been here for over a year, now. You know how he is." She surveys the other women then continues. "Now that I've been here, I understand that this is where he belongs. I don't think I can tell you a thing about him that you don't already know."

She focuses on me, and I mouth, "Thank you." She has endeared herself to me forever.

Nellie jumps to her feet and steps behind Pam. She hugs Pam around her shoulders while Pam pats her arm, and yet I do not feel the Earth shift off of its axis.

Jenny shouts, "*Mom,*" dragging it out into two syllables to express her adolescent distaste for public displays of affection between anyone she considers old, like, for example, over twenty-one.

Pam says, "I talked to the airline this morning and I can get on a flight back home today if I can get a ride to the airport."

"Nonsense," says Sally. We got somethin' to celebrate."

"What would that be?" I ask.

"Well, I'm not rightly sure," says Sally, "but I feel like celebratin'."

Jenny and Nellie both agree that we have cause for a celebration, although no one is sure exactly what it is to be called.

"The 'Bob comes to his senses' party," suggests Sally.

Pam winces.

"'The B-O-B Bob-Mr. Big City Extravaganza,'" suggests Nellie.

The others quickly agree that, even though a little long, it works.

"I'm not sure I want to stay for a celebration of Bob choosing someone else over me," Pam declares, a sick smile on her face.

"Please don't take it personally," says Sally. "It's not meant that way. My parents want to meet you. And the Mafia does, too."

Pam jerks her head around to look at me. "You said something about the Mafia yesterday, and you said you would explain it, but you never did. Who, for goodness sake, is the Mafia?"

"Only the high society in town," affirms Sally. "They took a shine to Bob right away. I declare, the sale of apples has doubled since he showed up, just so's they can keep him in pies. We'll have supper at Mom and Dad's tonight, and the Mafia will come over to meet you, too. It's gonna be so much fun. We'll all tell our favorite B-O-B Bob story."

The plan for supper begins to sound like a runaway train, which I seek to derail. "I don't think Lou will appreciate you puttin' all this on her so sudden," I say. "And this is awfully short notice to invite the Mafia."

"Are you kiddin' me?" asks Sally. "Mama's been plannin' this supper since you first told her Pam was comin'; the Mafia's been invited for a week."

I remember the first time Nellie and Jenny came to supper and how Lou worked things around so she could invite both of them to a canning party with Sally. I remember Steve laughing at me and his eyes scolding, "You've been had, Mr. Big City."

Once again, I've been had.

Chapter Nineteen

On our way back to Pam's motel, I thank her for what she said to Nellie.

"Why should I not?" she asked. "To withhold it wouldn't help me and would probably doom you to bachelorhood the rest of your life."

She pauses for a minute, as if contemplating prospects for the rest of *her* life, then continues. "I realized yesterday that I made a mistake running you off, but I don't have to be vindictive. You loved me; now you love Nellie." She reaches over and touches my arm. "And by the way, she and Jenny are adorable." She pauses, again, her eyes pinched and her brow furrowed. I've seen this face before; she is debating whether to share a piece of information with me. Finally, she does.

"I've invited them to Chicago, with or without you."

I smile and nod. "I'm okay with that," I say as we pull into the motel parking lot. There is a spot right in front of her room. I put the car in park, but let the motor run. We focus on each other and she smiles.

"What?" I ask.

She reaches over and puts her hand on the back of my head. "You're not B-O-B Bob anymore. I'll miss that doofus, but I'm happy for you. You've got someone who loves you. Two, really. Jenny's so happy to have you there for her and her mother. I wish it could have been me."

"It could have been."

She shakes her head and turns away. "Naah, not really. We're too different." She looks back at me and whispers, "But I could use a friend in Kentucky."

"Deal." I want to kiss her, not affectionately, more like Sally kisses me, but I realize it could be misunderstood, so I let the moment pass.

She gets out and closes the door. Turning, she leans forward and peers in the open window. "Why don't you come in and wait for me? I want to take a shower and change my clothes. Nellie should see what you passed up."

"Don't overdo it, okay?"

She winks at me.

"I'm serious, Pam. I don't want to screw this up, again. Don't come out dressed like some movie star. Steve and Lou are plain folks. It's important to me that they accept you."

She pushes her lower lip out in a fake pout.

"How about I pick you up about five?" I ask.

"Darn," she teases, going from pout to smile. "I was hoping you'd come in and wash my back when I take my shower."

I open my mouth to speak, but nothing comes out.

Pam straightens up and laughs. "Just wanted to see if *any* of the doofus was left," she sings out, gleefully. "I'll be ready at five, but why so early?"

"You're on CPT."

She cocks her head and looks puzzled.

"Country People Time. Supper is served at 5:30."

She shakes her head. "I could never get used to eating dinner that early."

"Dinner's at noon. You're comin' to supper."

She rolls her eyes but smiles. "Supper. Okay, see you at five." She points a finger at me and adds, "Pick up Nellie and Jenny first." As she walks toward her room, I watch her butt.

Nellie's is better.

———

After I pick up Nellie and Jenny, the three of us swing by Pam's motel where they greet her as if they've known her all their lives. On the ride to Waynedale, Jenny pumps Pam for information about Chicago, telling her that she'd enjoy living there someday.

When we pull up at Steve and Lou's, Jenny and Pam hop out and walk toward the porch. I open the door for Nellie, and she and I follow them a few feet behind. I reach over and take Nellie's hand, and she graces me with a smile. Everyone but Squat must have been watching for us because they come out on the porch in full-welcome mode.

"Mama and Papa," says Sally, "This is our new friend, Pam. Don't believe a single thing that Bob has told you about her."

Steve smiles broadly and Lou is as animated as I've ever seen. She extends her arms and hurries toward Pam. Ostentatiously rubbing her hand on the back of Pam's head, she declares, "Well, well, well. You don't have devil horns at all." Turning to me she scolds, "Bob, why'd you tell me that awful lie. She's sweet 'nuff to be from Kentucky."

I think better of saying what comes to mind about Pam, horns, and the devil.

Lou focuses her attention back to Pam. She then releases

Pam from the Mama Bear hug but continues to hold her with a hand on each arm. "Now, Pam, I hope you see that we've taken extra good care of ole, worthless Bob since he's been here."

"And you've done pretty good," Pam says, "considering what you had to work with."

Steve guffaws, and I start to reply, but just then the Mafia arrives en masse, as always. After introductions, Clare leans toward Pam as if to divulge something confidential, but in a whisper loud enough for all to hear, says, "At first we thought there was somethin' wrong with Bob. Then, we realized he's just a dayum Yankee. Here, Honey. I brought you this pie."

"Where's mine?" I ask.

"You'll get one when you start behavin' again," Clare fusses, wagging a finger at me.

"That's right," agree the chorus, mostly in unison.

As we go inside for supper, I realize somebody's missing.

"Where's Squat?" I ask Lou.

"Ain't come down yet. He's still afraid you're goin' back to Chicago with Pam."

"I told him I wasn't."

"Give him time, he'll be all right. Why doncha go up and get him? Better yet, take Pam with ya and introduce them up there where there won't be so much commotion." She takes the pie from Pam.

I hesitate. Lou's going to let Pam go upstairs with me?

Lou sets the pie down on the hall table, plants a hand in each of our backs, says, "Go, on with ya," and pushes us toward the stairs.

We walk up the steps and I knock on Squat's door. "Squat, you in there?"

"Yeah," he answers, his voice flat and devoid of emotion.

"I got someone who wants to meet you."

I hear Squat walking across the room. When he opens the door, he blurts out, "Are you goin' back to Chaago?"

"No. I'm stayin'. And this is my friend, Pam. She wants to be your friend, too."

"Hello, Squat," says Pam. "It's so nice to meet you."

"Me an' Bob mechanics," Squat informs Pam.

"Is that right? Bob used to take care of my car when he lived in Chicago. I have to find someone else since Bob's staying here."

Squat brightens. "Is supper ready?" He looks at Pam and says, "Bob sit by Squat at supper."

Squat heads down the steps, Pam and me behind him.

———

The supper is great. Steve has his teeth in; he had lost them a few weeks earlier.

"I found 'em a few days ago," he says, smiling at Pam.

"How can you lose your teeth?" asks Clare.

"Hey, if you was as busy as me, you'd lose your mind. Come to think of it, maybe you are as busy as me." Steve smiles, as proud of his clever reply as a dog with two tails.

"Just what do you do that keeps you so busy?" challenges Clare.

"I spend a lot a' time turnin' beer and whiskey into pee." Steve glances at Lou, who is glaring at him, but Pam laughs, so Steve is happy.

"How do you live with this worthless man?" Clare asks Lou.

"He may be worthless now, but I got a plan for when he dies."

"What's that, Mama?" Sally asks.

"Yeah?" Steve inquires. "Not sure I like you havin' a plan for when I'm dead."

Lou takes a long sip of sweet tea. When she has everyone's attention, she announces, "I'm gonna have him cremated and put his ashes in a egg timer. That way, I'll get six minutes of work outta him ever' mornin'."

When the hoots and hollers die down, I ask Steve, "Where'd you find your teeth?"

"Under the seat a' my truck." His statement is greeted with universal disbelief.

"No, that's right," Sally confirms. "I was with him. He was searchin' for a monkey wrench to fix a leak down at the café and he says, 'Lookie here!' He reached under the seat and pulls out the upper plate. After he wipes 'em on his overalls, he pops 'em in his mouth, then says, 'The bottoms must be in here, too.' So he roots around some more, finds the bottoms, wipes 'em off, and pops them in, too." She shakes her head and adds, "I hope I'm adopted."

Everyone except Steve nods, sympathetically.

"I was up in Louisville last week at the flea market," Clare reveals. "Met a woman who says she collects household primitives. Told her, 'You'd enjoy meetin' my friend, Steve.' 'Does he collect household primitives?' she asked me. 'No,' I said, 'he *is* a household primitive.'"

This time, Steve's the only one who *doesn't* laugh.

———

After supper, we all sit on the back porch. Clare stops on the way through the door jamb and studies it. "Steve, you never fixed this trim," she says.

"If it ain't broke don't fix it."

"But it *is* broke," declares Lou. "None of the trim matches."

"Who says it has to match? Some of the finest furniture ever built had different wood in it."

As Lou rolls her eyes, Clare murmurs, "Men. Can't live with 'em, can't kill 'em."

"What'dya know about it, Clare?" Steve asks. "You never been married."

"That's why I understand it. Lou thinks she's gotta put up with you. Well, I'll tell you," Clare rants, turning to Lou, "I know a good divorce lawyer who'll take your case free, just 'cause he knows Steve."

"Yeah," says Lou, "but I wouldn't get my egg timer." To hear her voice, you'd think having Steve cremated will be the high point of their marriage.

Pam and Nellie are off to the side, talking. Pam reaches over and takes Nellie's hand in hers.

After a few minutes of quiet conversation, Nellie gets up and tells Lou, "We've had a wonderful time and appreciate you invitin' us, but tomorrow's a school day, so I have to get Jenny home."

Pam stands. "I'm riding with them. Plus I have an early flight, so I guess I'll be going, too. I appreciate the kindness you showed me, considering I just dropped in, kind of."

"Honey," assures Lou, putting a motherly hand on Pam's arm, "don't you worry 'bout a thing. I blame Bob."

I start to respond, but Lou, without even glancing my way, points at me and commands, "Hush."

Lowering her hand, she continues talking to Pam. "But now you know where we are so you don't have to wait for that slow-movin' man to bring you back down here. You come anytime you want to."

"Yeah," Steve exclaims. "If you come back when we can

make plans, we'll have a good time. I'll show you the swimmin' hole where we go skinny dippin'."

Lou shakes her head, and says, "Don't pay a bit of attention to him. He ain't gonna be skinny dippin' with anybody looks as good as you, Honey."

Steve's eyes light up like they do when he thinks he's got a brilliant reply, but Sally puts her hand on his arm and advises, "Now's when a smart man keeps his mouth shut."

Steve's lips move for a second then stop as a look of consternation crosses his face. To his credit, he keeps his mouth shut.

We sound like a family reunion breaking up. Each of the Mafia has to tell Pam their favorite "Mr. Big City" story, ending with Clare telling her that I eat more pies than any man she knows, to which the Mafia all nod. As if I've asked them for even one of them.

Before we leave, Steve grabs my arm and pulls me to the side. "Quite the embrigglement you got yourself into, Mr. Big City." He grins then puts his hand on my shoulder and says, "Glad you got it worked out. Nellie's a fine woman. You mess it up again, you answer to me."

Remembering what he told me about his trip to Louisville when Sally got her heart broken, I look him in the eye and say, "Yes, sir."

Finally, I get the Grove's Point delegation in the car, and we head out.

During the ride, Jenny and Pam are in the back seat planning a visit to Chicago.

"Jenny," Nellie reminds her, "I'm not gonna let you fly to Chicago on your own."

I hear Jenny whisper to Pam, "Don't worry, I'll get it worked out. You sure I can stay with you?"

Nellie hears it, too, and is going to speak up when Pam tells Jenny, "Only if I hear from your mother that it's okay."

With that, Nellie sits back, her arms crossed firmly on her chest, but she is smiling.

We drop Pam at her motel and make arrangements for me to drive her to the airport in Louisville the next morning. She hugs Nellie and Jenny but just smiles at me.

"What? I ask. "I don't get a hug, too?"

Pam glances at Nellie, who sighs theatrically, rolls her eyes, and says, "Well, okay. For old times' sake, right?"

"That's right," Pam agrees. "For yesterdays."

She sounds sad and hugs me briefly. As she walks away, I deliberately zero in on Nellie so she can see I'm not watching Pam, but as we pull away, in the rearview mirror I see Pam in the window, watching us leave.

When we get to Nellie's, we walk into the kitchen, where she tells Jenny, "Go get your books together for school."

Jenny hugs me, plants a quick kiss on my cheek, and says, "Glad you're back. Don't screw it up this time."

Before I can reply, she dashes upstairs. I look at Nellie, who is leaning against the door jamb with her arms folded. She walks over to me and puts her hands behind my head. Pulling my face toward hers, she whispers, "Yeah, dummy, don't screw it up this time," and gives me a big, wet kiss that lasts about five minutes.

"What brought that on?" I ask when we come up for air.

"I've wanted to do it for a couple of weeks now, but you didn't come by, you dumb fuck." This time, when she calls me that, it sounds affectionate.

"If I remember right, you said we should take some time off."

"But I didn't say you should bring your ex to town."

We stare at each other, and just as I think things are

spiraling out of control again, Nellie acknowledges, "I'm glad you did, though. You know what she told me at the B-O-B Bob-Mr. Big City extravaganza?"

"I'm afraid to ask."

Nellie chuckles then says, "She told me when you left Chicago she was glad, but after you were gone, she started missin' you and wantin' you back. Then, when she saw you here with all of us, she realized you'd never be happy in Chicago again. She asked me to please take care of you 'cause you're the nicest, dumbest, smart man she's ever known."

"What a ringin' endorsement."

"It's about the nicest thing I've ever heard a woman say about an ex. In fact, it set me to worryin' for a minute that she still had designs on you. But then, she took my hand and told me you and I belong together."

"Do you want to ride to the airport with us tomorrow?"

"No, but thanks for askin'. The whole Mafia signed up to come in tomorrow for a rinse and set. I can't pass that up. Can you imagine what it'll be like with all five of them in the shop?" she asks, laughing.

She hugs me again, puts her mouth to my ear, and whispers, "But if you manage to keep your hands off Pam's ass when you say goodbye, come over tomorrow night and you can have them all over mine. Jenny's goin' to a friend's to study for a test."

Nellie kisses me again, even longer and sloppier than the first one, and I feel a pain in my gonads I haven't felt since high school.

Chapter Twenty

I am sitting in my chair, dozing, my book unable to keep me awake. I vaguely remember hearing Squat leave a half-hour earlier, although the TV is still on when Steve's voice rouses me. "What say you and I drive down to Bowlin' Green and go to a ball game?"

He's standing in the door to my room wearing pajamas with feet on them, the kind toddlers wear. They are adorned everywhere with rabbits. He smiles as I gawk.

"You like 'em?" he asks, holding his arms out so I can get a better view. "Lou made 'em for me, and doggone they're comfortable. If you ask her, she'll make you a pair."

"I think I'll pass. What time is it?"

"11:30. So are we on for the game?"

"When is it? I'll need to check with Nellie to make sure we don't have plans."

"Come on, Bob," Steve insists. "Be a man. Just tell her you're goin'. Show Nellie who's boss."

"She already knows who's boss. So do I; that's why I have to ask her. When do you wanna go?"

"The 'Toppers are playin' South Florida next Thursday. Lou says I can go then." I study his face for a sign that he understands the irony in his statement, but he's inscrutable.

"I'll talk to Nellie tomorrow and run that by her."

"Okay, so Thursday, then." He turns to walk away, and I almost fall out of my chair. The pajamas have a drop seat, but it's only buttoned on one side. If I was a child, I'd be scarred for life; I may be, anyway.

———

It is late January, 1988, about a year and a half after Pam's visit, and Nellie and I are engaged. The wedding will be in early December. Lou, as "mother" of the bride, a self-appointed title that no one was going to deny her, is our event planner.

The following Thursday, Steve and I bounce down to Bowling Green in what Steve calls his pick-um-up truck, a raggedy old thing that he drives mostly to keep it running. It's probably twenty years old, and sometime during those twenty years, a good hailstorm left pockmarks on it that make it appear to be recovering from a bad case of acne. There's a spot in the side that looks suspiciously like a bullet hole, although I've never asked. The tailgate is wired shut with baling wire and one front fender has been replaced, probably by Steve. It doesn't fit well and has been painted a slightly different shade of red from the rest of the truck. The paint has brush marks in it. Since the driver's side interior handle is missing, every time Steve opens the door he has to roll down the window and pull on the exterior handle.

Western wins, and Steve is happy, but he appears distracted. As soon as we start home, he says he needs a favor.

"Fire away." Steve snuck some beers into the game, and I'm feeling pretty good after drinking a few.

"I want you to spend a little time with Squat away from the house."

I had slouched down in the seat, but now I sit up and look at him. "Why?" I ask.

"I think it'd be good for him. Ya know he doesn't socialize real good, but he's taken a shine to you. Other than goin' to work at Jacob's, he don't leave the house 'less he's with Lou and me or Sally takes him for an ice cream. I think it'd be good for him. Are you up to that?"

"I don't mind doin' it, but I'm not sure Squat will want to. He didn't even come with us tonight."

"I didn't ask him. Wanted us to be able to talk about this."

"If I'm not over at Nellie's, he and I are in my room watchin' TV, or out on the porch watchin' life go by, so we spend a lot of time together already."

"You think you could take him with you to Nellie's?" Steve glances at me and licks his lips, something he only does when he's nervous.

"I'm not sure. I don't want Squat to feel out of place."

"Now see, that's the kind of notion you need to get over. Squat's *never* out of place; he's just there. You know what would be great? If you could take him to Chicago sometime. Show him around. Since you moved here, he's always talkin' 'bout Chaago, as he calls it."

"Steve, what's goin' on? Are you tryin' to get us out of the house?"

When he doesn't answer right away, I say, "Oh, Lordy, are you plannin' on chasin' Lou around the house naked?"

"Jeez, Bob, restrain yourself. It ain't nothin' like that." He chuckles, and adds, "But that could be fun." Then, he shakes his head, as if to clear it of the image of naked Lou running down the hall, and adds, "Back to Squat."

"I don't mind doin' what you're askin', but you really haven't given me a good reason why you want me to. What's behind this?"

"I want you to get to know Squat."

"I know Squat," I say, smiling at the double meaning.

Steve sighs, then says, "You think you do, but you don't. Talk to him. Find out what he likes. With Squat, you gotta draw him out. He's the same as us, but slow. Some things appeal to him; some don't. You're the first person outside the family he's let into his life."

"I think you're wrong, Steve. I see him around town. Everybody talks to him. He knows everyone."

"Sure, he knows *them*. He gives everbody that no-look wave he's famous for. They don't know *him*, though. Listen to how they talk to him. It's 'Oh, Squat, you got my car runnin' so good,' but what they think is, 'You just push the broom.' You don't talk to him like that. You talk to him about sweepin' as if it's the most important thing that happens at Jacob's. You make him feel important."

"He is important."

"Yeah, *I* think that, and *you* think that but who else? Hell, he tells people he's a mechanic, same as you. You never hear him say he's a gardener, like me, do you?"

We ride in silence for a while, then just as we enter our home county, I see flashing blue lights all around us. Steve glares in the rearview mirror.

"Now what the devil does *he* want?" Steve asks no one in particular as he begins to pull into the emergency lane.

I peer behind us and see a sheriff's car, its roof lights flashing.

Steve brings the truck to a stop, asks me to find the registration in the glove box, then sits there fuming as a deputy sheriff walks up and asks to see his license and registration.

"Where you men goin' this time of night?" he asks, and I hope for once Steve plays it straight.

"We're on our way to a lecture, officer."

Oh, Steve.

"A lecture, huh? What about?" the deputy asks as he reviews the registration.

"The evils of alcohol and late-night carousin'," Steve declares.

We're dead.

The deputy glances up from Steve's documents and asks, "Who's givin' that lecture at this time of night, Steve?"

"Lou, as soon as we get home."

I prepare to be arrested, but the deputy laughs. He puts his hand on Steve's arm and gently shakes it, saying, "Your right tail light's out. Think you can have it fixed by Monday?"

"I got one of the best mechanics in the county sittin' right here next to me," Steve reveals. "Bob, this is Pete Jackson, Clare's great-nephew. Pete, this is Bob. He rents a room from Lou and me, and eats a lot of your aunt's pies without ever offerin' to share." To hear Steve whine, you'd think I stole all those pies from him.

"Heard all 'bout you from Aunt Clare," Pete says, looking at me. "Hope you enjoy eatin' those pies as much as she enjoys bakin' 'em. Will you make sure this old fool gets home safe?"

"Oh, it's my day to watch him?" I ask.

"I know, it's not fair," agrees Pete, "but somebody's gotta do it. Can't believe Lou let him out of her sight." Turning his attention back to Steve, Pete asks, "Hey, how 'bout those Hilltoppers?"

"Quite a night," says Steve. "That's where we been."

"Figured that. Y'all take care, and get that tail light fixed."

He surveys the truck, puts his finger in what could be the bullet hole, and seems about to say something else but just shakes his head. He touches his right hand to the brim of his cap and nods at me, saying, "Nice to meet you, Bob," then walks back to his car.

"First time knowin' Clare was ever a help to me," Steve grouses, but I don't believe him.

When we get off the expressway a few minutes later, Steve asks again, "So you'll take Squat to Chicago?"

"I have to be careful with trips to Chicago. Nellie might think I'm up to somethin'."

"Yeah, well, I figure if you have Squat along you'll be less inclined to look up ole sweet cheeks. Damn, but she's fine."

Ignoring his comment, I ask, "What if I take Nellie along? And Jenny?"

"Isn't there a law against transportin' young girls across state lines?"

Steve winks at me then focuses again on the road. For a moment, I'm angry at him for saying such a thoughtless thing. Then, I realize that he isn't aware Jenny was raped.

"Steve, there's something you should know. I don't want it blabbed to everyone 'cause, frankly, it's nobody's business."

Steve says, "Okay. Let's hear it."

"That no-good son of a bitch!" he thunders when I tell him what happened to Jenny. "How could anyone do that to our Little Bit? Bob, I meant *nothin'*. You know I meant *nothin'*."

"I know," I acknowledge. "Jenny's fairly open about it. All I ask is if she *ever* brings it up, I don't care in what context, don't make a joke about it, okay?"

"You got that. And if you ever think I can help her, you let me know. I'll do anything I can for that kid. That bastard. That rat bastard."

We pull into the driveway, and Steve is unusually somber.

The only other time I've seen him in this mood was when he told me about Sally's cheating fiancé and his trip to Louisville to confront him. He can joke all he wants, but I know if the chips are ever down, Steve is someone I want in my corner.

———

Saturday evening, while Jenny attends her high school's ball game, Nellie and I bundle up and take a walk in the cold night air while I tell her what Steve has asked me to do.

"He's right," she says. "You're Squat's best friend."

"I've been nice to him, that's all."

"Maybe bein' nice to him is all he needs. It gives him a chance to be one of the guys."

"And you're okay if we go to Chicago?"

"Yes." She pauses, then drawls, "but if I find out you and Pam share anythin' more than a handshake, I'll cut your dick off." There's less emotion in her voice than when she asks me what I want for supper. As I gaze at her, she bats her eyes and smiles.

"I'm so glad you've got it in perspective," I say.

———

Before I talk to Squat about Chicago, I spend time with him in Waynedale. I clear it with my boss to take him to work. He hands me tools most of the day, but late in the afternoon, I have him tighten a nut. His tongue sticks out of the corner of his mouth, and the intensity on his face says he's defusing a bomb. Later, as I lean over a fender to reach the alternator, I feel his hand on my shoulder, and he whispers, "Don't fall in."

Next, I take a day off and go to work with him. He shows me the proper way to sweep, stopping me twice to correct my technique. Jacob stands to the side and laughs when Squat tells me, "No, you do it wrong. Hold the broom like you dance with it."

Squat is guileless. In him, I find the innocence of a child, the masculinity of a man, and the hopes of a human. I come to understand that innocence is not weakness, and I seek not to harm people with anger, especially when I'm tired. He shows me that masculinity is not physical strength, but rather maturity, and I become more patient with demanding customers. I learn that hope is not only for the intelligent, but for everyone who loves someone, and I am more hopeful of my future with Nellie, Jenny, and Squat.

"What are you thinkin'?" I ask him frequently.

At first, he is reluctant to share, but Lou reminds me to be patient.

"Nobody's ever asked him that before," she informs me quietly. "It'll take him a little while to get used to it."

Lou is right; in time, he begins to talk;

"I think we mechanics," he says.

"I think you don't sweep good." He smiles.

"I think I want ice cream." He tugs my arm.

"I think we friends."

I ask him about his no-look wave, but he just smiles, as if to say, why do I have to look at someone to greet them? Then, the little shit turns and walks out of my room, giving me a no-looker when he reaches the door. In a half-second, his smiling face comes around the corner and without speaking a word, his eyes yell *"Gotcha!"*

He never overanalyzes. If I tell him I can't do something with him, he doesn't fret about it. He just asks, "Okay, when?"

———

After a few weeks, I ask Steve and Lou if I can take Squat to Chicago, show him where I lived, where I worked. "I think it'll help him know me better," I tell them.

"Honey," Lou says in her easy-going drawl, "he knows you better than you think. He's worshipped you since that first day at the diner. But don't be disappointed if he don't wanna go 'cause he ain't done nothin' like that before."

This time, Lou is wrong. He hops in the air and sings, "I go Chaago! I go Chaago!"

We set the trip for June, right after Jenny's high school graduation, and when Sally hears about it, she labels it, 'Bob and Squat's excellent adventure,' after a movie she read about that was being filmed out in Arizona.

I'm feeling pretty good about it until Squat declares, "We go Chaago! I meet Bob's father!"

Chapter Twenty-One

In early June Bob and Squat's excellent adventure takes off for 'Chaago.' Squat has two suitcases to hold all his clothes.

"Why's he need so many clothes?" I ask Lou as she finishes packing for him.

"Ain't you noticed how often he changes?" she replies.

"Now that you mention it, yes." Squat changes at least three times a day. If he's home, changes come more frequently.

"Why's he do that?" I ask.

Lou shakes her head and puts her hand on my shoulder. "If you figure that out, be sure and let me know," she replies with a motherly smile.

———

The first day, we visit the zoo and walk around Grant Park, but Squat is eager to learn more about my life in the city, so the next day I call Joe, my old boss. He tells me to come around at noon and we'll have lunch. Squat is thrilled that he's going to meet more mechanics.

Most of the old gang is there, and he announces to each of them, "I be mechanic, just like Bob."

The guys tell him they hope he's not too much like me.

After he meets everyone, we walk across the street to the diner where Pam and I had our first lunch. All but one table is taken so five of us squeeze around a table for four, where the conversation quickly turns to my bad luck with women.

But Squat shakes his head. "Bob gettin' married," he announces.

"No way," mocks Joey.

"Yes, way," Squat replies. Everyone laughs, and Squat looks pleased.

"When's the big day, Bob?" asks Joe.

"December."

"I swear," Marty says, "I didn't think you'd ever get married, the way that Pam woman ran you around."

"There were a few twists," I concede. I relate to them how we ran into Pam in Chicago, her visit to Waynedale, and finally, Sally and Pam helping to convince Nellie to get back with me.

"Pam's not so bad after all," I add. "Jenny's even comin' up here to visit with her sometime."

"Damn, Bob, you got a regular harem." Joe leans close and asks, "You nailing all of them?"

Shaking my head, I reply, "I'm not gonna dignify that with a response."

"Okay, so you're not nailing all of them. But you're nailing Nellie, aren't you?"

"You never change, do you, Joe?"

Joe leans back, and says, "Don't get your shorts in a bunch, country boy. I like that southern accent you've picked up."

I smile then gaze at Squat, sitting at a table with three total strangers, laughing and talking. I wish Steve and Lou could see him.

After lunch, Squat tells the waitress, "We mechanics." He waves his arms around to indicate all of us.

She smiles at him, and says, "I bet you're the best, Sweetie."

"Yeah. I best." He grins.

We say our goodbyes to the gang. Then, as we walk to the car, Squat asks, "Where you live, Bob?"

"Just a few miles from here. I'll show you."

When we're in the car, I head to the apartment where I lived after moving out of my parents' house. Along the way, Squat grills me.

"Who there now?"

"I'm sure someone lives there. It's just an apartment."

"Maybe you Papa there."

"No, Squat, my father never lived there. Just me."

"Where you live with you Mama and Papa?"

"Way across town." I have no idea how to describe to Squat my relationship with my father, especially since I've never wanted to explain it to anyone.

"We go there," he says, sitting back and folding his arms across his chest.

"I don't think so, Squat, but here's where I lived when I worked at the garage."

We stop in front of a U-shaped building that is similar to every other one on the block.

"I lived in the back, through that center door," I tell him, pointing to the middle of the building.

"Uh-huh, now other place."

"This is the only place I lived."

"Where you lived with Mama and Papa."

"Why don't we forget that?"

"No," he says, smiling broadly.

I shake my head but resign myself to the fact that I'm going to have to drive him by my childhood home. I hope I can drive by without slowing down.

As we get closer, I point out personal landmarks. "This is the movie theatre I went to as a kid. Here's where I ate when I'd go out. This is the high school I went to." Finally, "There's the house where I grew up."

I see him in front of the house, and I speed up.

"No, go slow," Squat demands. "I wanna see who sweepin'."

I study him closely, too. It's hard to believe that this stoop-shouldered man having trouble moving a broom is the same one who used to send terror into my heart. He seems so feeble now.

"We stop," Squat demands.

I drove for seventeen years in Chicago and never found a parking space. Now I don't want one, and I spot two; so does Squat.

He points to the first. "There," he insists. "*Right there.*"

I reluctantly pull in, about a hundred feet from where my father continues to sweep.

Squat has his seat belt off and is opening the door before the car stops rolling.

"Where are you goin'?" I ask him. "We're not gettin' out. We can see the house from here."

"No. I talk to man. Maybe he know you."

He does, but I don't want to know him.

"Squat, get back in the car," I say as he jumps out.

He's moving more quickly than normal. He lowers his head, swings his arms in front of himself, and is off on his mission.

I get out and run to catch up. Grabbing his arm, I pull him toward the car, but he jerks away.

"Come on," he says, waving his arm to hurry me.

"We don't get along. Can't you understand that?"

"No. He your Papa. Everybody like his Papa."

"I don't."

But Squat is not deterred. He strides toward my father. I'm a few steps behind, caught in Squat's undertow.

As we get within twenty feet, Squat reverts to his shy self. He lags back, so I suggest we return to the car, but he says no.

My father is facing away from us. We can walk right by, and if he doesn't raise his head, he'll never see me. But just as I am rushing past him, Squat grabs my sleeve and pulls me around.

My father looks up, startled, glances at the sidewalk again, then stares at me, his eyes widening. "Bob?" he asks.

"Hello, Father."

"Bob, what the hell are you doing here?" There's the warm reception I was expecting.

"He…we…my friend here wanted to see where I lived." I turn toward Squat, who is smiling from ear to ear. "Squat, this is my father. Father, this is my friend, Squat."

The puzzlement on my father's face is understandable. We haven't talked since my mother died and here I stand in front of him with a man named Squat.

He's sixty-seven but seems fifteen years older. His hair was already gray when I left home, but little of it remains, and what is there has not been cut or combed in some time. He shuffles more than he walks, and one leg is reluctant to move. His eyes have a rheumy appearance, and one lid droops almost shut. There is a hearing aid in one ear and the fingers gripping the broom are twisted in a way I don't remember.

Removing his right hand from the broom, he slowly

extends it to me, but there is doubt in his gaze as if he's not sure he can trust me with his arthritic limb.

Taking it in mine, I am surprised at how soft it is. It was always hard when it smacked the side of my head, setting my ears to ringing. Just one solid squeeze and he'll understand the pain I used to feel.

I gently release it.

"Gracious," he says. "It's been so long." Is that sadness I hear?

I feel out of place and in the wrong time; I don't have a reply.

Squat saves me the trouble. "I mechanic, just like Bob," he shouts.

Father's head swivels, looking at Squat, then back at me. "A mechanic, huh?"

His eyes shift back to Squat and he says, "Well, you don't have to be too smart to be a mechanic."

"Hey," I snarl, "Squat wanted to see where I grew up, but if you can't talk without insultin' him, we'll leave right now."

My father eyes me for a moment then reaches out. I flinch as he brushes my left shoulder and says, "Get the chip off, will ya?"

"Let go inside," says Squat.

"Why do you want to go inside?" my father asks.

"See Bob room."

"Nothing there. Just a bed and a desk. No need," he replies.

"I see it," says Squat, the same determination in his voice that he shows when he's sweeping at Jacob's.

Father glances at me and asks, "You want to see your old room?"

"No, but I don't think we're gonna convince Squat."

"Then, let's go," my father says, heading toward the house.

"Oh, boy!" says Squat, following him.

It feels as if I'm entering a shrine; nothing has changed since the day of my mother's funeral. I'm not even sure the throws on the furniture have been washed, although the dishes piled in the sink are different. The only staple I don't see are the whiskey bottles.

We go up the stairs to my room, Father hanging on to the rail and pulling himself slowly along, and I remember how I used to live in fear of hearing his feet dropping heavily on those stairs as he came home from a bender.

When we get to the room, we can't move around much. He's using it for storage, and there are boxes all over the floor, on the bed, and the desk. Dust clings to everything, but Squat is happy. I notice the posters from the various rock concerts I used to love attending are gone from the walls.

"Let's go back downstairs," Father suggests.

Returning to the living room, he and I stand in the middle, watching Squat as he walks around examining everything.

Father nods at Squat and asks me, "Something wrong with him, isn't there?"

"His mind's a little weak, but there's absolutely nothin' *wrong* with him."

"I heard you moved out of town. You back?"

"Just for a visit. Squat wanted to see Chicago."

As if on cue, Squat says, "I go Chaago."

"Squat?" Father asks, glancing at me. "What the hell kind of name is that?"

"It *my* name," Squat says, flashing a smile at us.

"And a good name it is, too," says my father loudly.

I stare at him, eyes wide, and Squat laughs.

"Come on," he says. "Let's sit down and catch up." He gestures toward the sofa.

I sit with my hands folded awkwardly in my lap, the same

way I would sit as a child, waiting to be punished when my father was drunk.

He puts his hands on the arms of his chair and lowers himself into it.

I remember sitting in it once when I was five, and the spanking I got for that outrageous act.

We both watch Squat for a minute as he wanders around, gazing at pictures, asking who the people are, and quietly exploring this new world.

When he steps into the dining room, my father looks at me and asks, "Who is he?"

I tell my father about Steve and Lou and why Squat is with me. The only response I get is a grunt.

"These people are my fam—" I stop and look away, realizing what I was about to say to him.

"Well," he says after an awkward pause, "If I learned one thing about you it's that you're going to do what you're going to do. In fact," he lets out with a smile, "it's probably the only thing I know about you."

Holy shit. My father just made a joke.

"How *could* we know each other?" I ask. "We seldom talked."

"Your mother, God rest her soul, always said we did too much talking and not enough listening."

I realize this is probably as close to an apology as I will ever get from my father. Before I can respond, he asks, "Have you been out to see your mother, yet?" as if she was living in the 'burbs.

Shaking my head, I say, "We had a list of things to do."

"I'm gonna go tomorrow. You wanna go with?"

Just then, Squat walks back into the room. "Go where?" he asks.

"Cemetery to visit Bob's mother's grave."

"No cemetery. Spooky." Squat makes a face.

"Well, if yous guys change your mind, you can go with." The upper Midwest accent jars me every time I hear my father use an expression that at one time sounded so normal.

"I hungry," Squat says.

"Me, too," my father agrees. "Except I don't have a thing in the house. Let's go up to the corner for a sandwich."

"The old Spadie's place?" I ask. "Is it still there?"

"Yep." He groans as he pushes himself out of the chair. "Except it's not Spadie's anymore. It's Gilmore's. Food's not as good but it's just as expensive," he grouses. "Other than that, I can't think of a reason to go there."

When Squat laughs, I focus on the humor, where once I would have seen only sarcasm.

"I'm gettin' married," I tell him as he puts a jacket on.

"No shit," he exclaims. "I thought maybe you played for the other team, if you know what I mean."

"What other team?" asks Squat. Then, he says to me, "You Papa funny."

I decide to follow Squat's lead and treat his comments as humorous, so I just mutter, "Well, I guess I gave you cause to wonder."

"Nah, nah, you didn't. Guess I was just a distrustful old cuss. Who's the woman?" he asks, as we walk out the door.

I talk about Nellie and Jenny as we head to Gilmore's. He wobbles a couple of times, and Squat reaches out to gently take his arm. There were times when he would have swung at me if I'd done that, but his only response is "Thanks, Squat. Not as steady as I used to be."

Squat pats him on the back and says, "Welcome."

———

When we get to Gilmore's, Father is greeted warmly by several people who are vaguely familiar but way too old to be who I think they are. He asks them if they remember his son, Bob, and neighbors I haven't seen in years are everywhere, shaking my hand and slapping my back.

I turn around and see Squat retreating, a look of distress on his face. I wave for him to join me. "I want you to meet one of my mechanic friends from Waynedale," I say. "Everybody, this is Squat."

As they begin to push forward, I warn them, "Squat's a little uncomfortable in crowds."

Squat, however, says, "It okay." Then, as each one greets him, he tells them, "I mechanic, just like Bob."

After we sit down, Father asks, "So this woman you're marrying, she has a daughter?"

"That's right."

"Son," he declares as he takes a sip of a pop the waitress set in front of him without his asking, "It's a lazy man that marries a woman with children."

The phrase sounds familiar, and then it hits me. That's what Steve told me the first night I went out with Nellie.

Squat repeats, "You Papa funny," and for the first time, I smile.

———

We eat and spend several hours talking with Father and old acquaintances, none of whom seem to know, or at least don't care, about his drinking. It is only when I notice how late it has gotten that I realize he hasn't had anything to drink except pop. I want to ask him why, but we're getting along and it might spoil the mood if I do.

"How long are yous guys going to be in town?" he asks, when I tell Squat it's time to go.

"This is our last night here."

"Too bad. It would be nice to spend a little more time with."

"I have to be back at work day after tomorrow."

With him not drinking, I'm almost enjoying our time together, but I remember that some of my worst beatings came when I least expected it, so I don't let my guard down.

———

During the stroll back, no one talks much, but when we get there, we stop and talk in front of his house. Squat is reluctant to leave; Father seems reluctant to go inside.

"When's the wedding?" he asks.

When I tell him December, Squat blurts out, "You come. You come."

He mulls that suggestion for a moment then asks me, "Would I be welcome?"

I rub the back of my neck and shake my head. "It's been a long time."

"I know that. What are you, stupid?"

There's the temper I used to fear, but he doesn't realize how it sounds until Squat reacts.

"Bob not stupid. Bob mechanic. He fix. You wrong." Squat shakes a finger at my father so hard I'm afraid he'll hurt it.

Father is surprised by the ferocity of the words coming from this man who, until now, has been so amiable. I wait for him to attack with words or blows; there was a time when he would have. I step forward, ready to protect Squat, but my father says, "I'm sorry, Squat. Where are my manners? I guess the answer's no, I won't be invited."

He sounds so sad, I weaken. "I'll see you get an invitation. I'd like you to meet the people I live with," I lie.

"Bob not stupid," Squat repeats, shaking his head.

"I know, that Squat." He rubs his chin. "You be safe on the ride back to Kentucky."

Father turns and shuffles toward the house. He has to use the rail to pull himself up the steps. I wonder if he's going to start drinking when he gets inside.

Chapter Twenty-Two

Upon our return to Waynedale, Squat and I are treated as conquering heroes. Lou invites everyone to supper. Nellie, Jenny, Sally, and the Mafia are all there, and Squat regales them with his exploits. He is the center of attention, and no one is more pleased than Steve.

After telling everyone about our meal with my work friends, Squat announces, "I meet Bob Papa."

Just when I think no one is going to comment, Nellie asks, "*You did what?*"

Sally smiles at me, raises her eyebrows, and tilts her head to the side questioningly.

"Yeah," says Squat, focusing on Nellie. "He be sweepin'. We go supper, but he call it dinner. He come see Bob get married." Squat turns back to his plate and sends a big bite of Clare's apple pie to his mouth as everyone gawks at him with looks of disbelief.

Finally, Lou asks, "Saints in Heaven, what brought all this about?"

"It's no big deal," I declare, "we just drove by the house

and he happened to be out, so we stopped to talk. I doubt he'll come to the wedding. He's not in good health."

"Was he as mean as you remembered?" Jenny inquires.

"He's mellowed," I reply, holding my hand out and shaking it slightly, to imply it's hard to tell.

"I'm not gonna say I told you so," Nellie says, slapping her hand on the table, "but didn't I tell you? Didn't I?"

"Yep," Sally agrees.

"Yes, to every woman at the table who has ever told me anything, I was wrong, you were right. There, how's that?"

"You wanna be more specific?" Clare asks. "I think you should go around the table and tell each of us what we were right about and what you were wrong about. What say, ladies?" She swoops her arms wide to encompass all the women at the table, who quickly agree.

"Settle down, ladies," I admonish, as they all cackle. "You fill in the blanks. If you think I was wrong about something, I was."

"I'll drink to that," says Steve.

"Oh, Steve," says Clare, "you'll drink to anything."

When everyone except Jenny and Squat has a beer in their hands, Steve declares, "A toast."

"Watch what you say, Steve," Lou warns. "There's a minor here."

"You know I'm not gonna say anythin' crude in front of Little Bit," Steve drawls, draping his arm around Jenny's shoulders.

"I know nothin' of the sort," Lou replies, shaking her head.

"Anyway," says Steve, hoisting his beer in Clare's direction, "I've drunk your health in company, I've drunk your health alone." Clare rolls her eyes, and Steve sweeps the beer through the air in front of the other members of the Mafia, as he continues, "I've drunk your health so many times, I've damned near ruined my own."

Everyone laughs but Lou, who frowns at Steve and fusses, "I told you not to curse in front of the child."

"She just graduated high school," Steve says. He glances under his arm at Jenny. "Are you traumatized, Little Bit?"

She grins wickedly and blurts, "Hell, no."

Nellie shakes her head, but the rest of us laugh as Steve leans over and kisses Jenny on top of her head.

Later, after everyone has left, I join Steve, who is sitting on the porch by himself.

"So did you find out?" he asks me.

"What?"

"What you did to piss off your old man?"

I smile at this big bear of a man who manages to be friendly to everyone while still appearing grouchy. "It was nice," I tell him. "We didn't rehash anything. We just let it all go."

Steve smiles at me. "Squat have anything to do with that?"

"Yeah," I acknowledge. "He insisted we drive by; we stop; we talk. He's persistent, that's for sure."

Steve's smile gets wider.

I gaze at a car passing on the street and wave when an arm comes out of the window to greet us, then continue, "I couldn't believe how gentle my father was with him." I look back at Steve. "He treated him real good, just like you would have wanted him to. Still…" I shake my head.

"What?"

Frowning, I mumble, "I spent the whole time thinking that at any minute…never mind." I'm still not able to talk about his temper.

Steve's smile disappears. "Whatever you got stuck in your craw, boy, until you spit it out, it's just gonna keep chokin' you." His mouth pinches at the corners and his eyes narrow as he stares at me.

I nod but don't reply.

A minute later Steve speaks again. "I'm glad he's comin' for your weddin'. I wanna meet him."

"Don't get your hopes up. He *may* come."

Steve sighs and remarks, "Well, son, I'm wore out. Goin' to bed." As he walks by, he pats me on the shoulder and mutters something I don't quite catch. It may have been, "Things are gonna work out just fine."

———

Halfway through the summer, I find out that while Nellie and I have been making plans for Jenny's move to the University of Louisville, Steve has been making plans of his own. I hear them one evening when the women are in Louisville shopping for clothes for Jenny.

Steve, Squat, and I are on the porch enjoying the evening air. As I read, Steve and Squat are talking about the people they ran into during the day. I have tuned out Steve's low growl of a voice, until he clears his throat in a way he uses to announce he has something important on his mind.

I glance up.

Squat is staring at Steve expectantly, but Steve suggests, "Squat, why don't you go watch television?"

Without a word, Squat walks inside and we hear him mount the stairs. He'll be waiting for me in my room when I come in.

When Squat is out of earshot, Steve begins. "Bob, I'm worried about Sally and Squat."

I mark my page and close the book. "Why are you

worried? Sally's happy, and Squat may be the most contented person I've met."

"Yeah, and a lot of that is thanks to the attention you show him. But he needs stability. Change gets him agitated. He was a mess when Mama and Daddy died."

"When was that?" I set the book on the swing next to me.

"'Bout twenty-five years ago. They was older when we were born. Mama was near on forty when I came along, forty-four when she had Squat."

"You think her age caused Squat's problems? I hear women over forty have more babies with Down's syndrome."

"Nah, he ain't got Down's."

"I didn't think so. What is it, then? Do you know?"

"Not 'zactly. Doc said he may have not gotten enough oxygen when he was born. Somethin' 'bout the umbilical cord wrapped around him in a bad way. Whatever it is, he's always been slow. Can't read, can't write. Never went to school. In a small town, there just ain't any facilities, so Mama and Daddy just said, 'We'll take care of him here,' and Daddy retired. Squat was real close to Daddy and took it hard when he died. Then, Mama just gave up. She was dead in six months."

"Do you resent that Squat's care fell to you?"

Steve has been gazing toward the street but turns toward me so quickly his beard shakes. "What're you talkin' 'bout? He didn't just *fall to'* me. I *told* Mama and Daddy I'd take care of him. Told them, 'Don't worry 'bout a thing. He'll live with me when you're gone.' No way I was gonna let the state put him in one of them institutions where he wouldn't know nobody."

"Steve, I'm sorry. I didn't mean to offend you. Or Squat. I just thought you might have more time for other things if you and Lou didn't have to take care of him."

Steve snorts and waves at a car passing by. "What other things? You ever see me do anything? Mama and Daddy had money. They left it to me, knew I'd take care of my brother. I don't even work." He pauses then answers my unasked question. "Sally wouldn't have to either, but she wants to."

"I guess havin' money makes it easier."

"Yeah, it does. I don't have to worry 'bout Squat not havin' what he needs, 'cept stability. Understand?" He glances quickly at me.

I shake my head. "I'm sorry, I don't."

"Well, what if somethin' happens to Lou and me. I gotta face facts. Squat could outlive us both. Then, what happens to him? And there's Sally. She'll miss us. She'll be okay, but it'd be nice if someone was lookin' out for her. We all need someone to check on us ever' now and then."

I hold my hands out, palms up, and ask, "Steve, what are you gettin' at?"

He studies me for a moment, then says, "Squat's takin' a shine to you, an' you already live here. If Lou and I die, what if we left the house to you and Nellie? Would y'all watch out for Squat?"

"What?" I ask, shaking my head. "That's not fair to Sally. She should inherit your house."

"She's got her own place, and besides, she'll be taken care of. She knows Squat prefers the company of men. That's why he works at Jacob's 'stead of her café. She'll help with him, but we need a man to be there for Squat, talk with him, do things for him that he don't want Sally doin'. There's a trust fund. Money won't be an issue."

"Money's not an issue now, Steve, but I wonder if I'm the right person." I rub my forehead, a headache beginning right in the front, above my eyes.

"I don't need an answer right now, but I don't want it draggin' out, either. My doctor thinks I might not live as long as I want to iffn I don't lose weight. Course, as ole Willie Nelson,

says, 'There's more old drunks than there are old doctors.'"
Steve chuckles and rubs his ample sides, then smiles. His lips
move as he sings to himself a little bit of "ole Willie's" song.

He moves over to Squat's spot, next to me in our swing.
Putting his hand on my shoulder, he drawls, "So you talk it
over with Nellie, okay?"

"I'll talk to her about it, but I have to tell you, right now
I'm inclined to say no. It's a helluva sacrifice."

Steve stares at me dead on, his expression as intense as if
he's watching a fire consuming his house. He points his finger
at me and scolds, "You only *think* it's a sacrifice. Squat gives
more than he takes. Always has. It'll be the best job you ever
had."

"When do you need to know?"

"I've talked to my lawyer. We can change the papers
anytime."

"What are the arrangements right now?"

"Sally's gonna do it, but that ain't the best arrangement.
Squat needs *you*. Nice thing is, you can keep an eye on Sally,
too." He pokes me in the ribs.

I shake my head and frown, but Steve says, "Yeah, you
can. You can watch her without makin' your wife mad; they're
friends. Hell, you can tell Nellie I asked you to have her over
for supper like we do now. You don't think she's comin' over
'cause she *needs* to be fed, do ya? Hell, she's got a café. She
comes over 'cause she knows we worry 'bout her. She's so used
to bein' worried about, she'll worry if there ain't no one
worryin' 'bout her." Steve's lips move slowly, repeating his last
sentence to himself. Satisfied that he said what he meant, he
nods, silently.

"I understand. I think."

"So you'll consider it?"

"Yeah, I'll consider it."

"Good," says Steve, exhaling loudly.

———

Nellie is as reluctant as me at first. "It's not that I don't like Squat," she says, "But we don't know anythin' about what's wrong with him. We don't know what his health issues are, his financial situation. And we sure don't wanna take money away from Sally."

"Steve says there's a trust fund. Says his parents had money and everybody would be taken care of. He claims Sally's on board with it."

Nellie's eyes widen. "Wait a minute, Steve's last name is Matson, isn't it?"

"Yeah, why?"

"You ever heard of Matson Bourbon?"

"Sure, Steve drinks it all the time. I thought it was a coincidence."

Nellie shakes her head. "Maybe not. Matson Bourbon is one of the oldest in the state. It was family-owned, a husband and wife. When I was a kid, they sold it for about twenty-million dollars. Let's go to the library and do some research."

A quick inquiry at the library confirms Nellie's statement and fills in a few more blanks. Steve's great-grandfather had started Matson Distilleries in 1870. Connoisseurs from around the world prized the select bourbon but the company only made a limited amount, to keep demand high. Steve's grandfather and father ran it successively until the early 1960s, when his father learned that he was sick. To provide a trust fund for his disabled son, he and his wife sold the business to an international distiller for twenty-one million five hundred thousand dollars.

When his mother and father died, Steve and Lou, who had

been farming in downstate Kentucky, sold the farm and moved home to take care of his brother.

Nellie and I stare at each other, mouths agape, until she says, "I'll be dipped in shit. Steve and Lou are multi-millionaires."

I shake my head in amazement. "One thing's for sure. Steve's right when he says money won't be an issue, but is it right for us? The last thing I want is for Jenny to think we're pushin' her aside to take care of Squat, especially if she thinks it's because of the money."

"You're assumin' something's gonna happen and we're gonna have to take care of him right away. Wish Steve had told you what the doctor's worried about if he don't lose weight."

"How about heart attack, diabetes, stroke, bad circulation—"

"Okay, Doctor Bob. I'm just wonderin' if his overall health is good."

"I can tell Steve we have to ask him some questions before we agree. That's reasonable."

"Yes, it is. But Jenny's not the only one we gotta consider. What about Sally? And Squat? We need to know more about *his* health, too. Let Steve know we wanna talk to Squat's doctor."

Nellie and I start writing down our questions, and before we're finished, we've filled two pages.

As we walk home, I say, "I wonder why Steve never mentioned his money."

"Maybe he was afraid you'd be swayed by it. People can be. He might wanna make sure you're not bein' nice to Squat just to get ahold of his money."

"If he doesn't trust me, he should just let Sally do it."

"He told you why that wouldn't work. Quit thinkin' it's

about you. This says more about him, Lou, and Sally. They wanna be accepted for who they are, not 'cause they got money. They're just ordinary country folk. I like that."

"True, but…" I shake my head.

Nellie takes my hand in hers, and we walk home holding hands.

Chapter Twenty-Three

A few days later, Steve, Nellie, and I meet with Doctor Talbott, Squat's doctor. He's short, thin, and balding, appears to be about forty, and laughs a lot. A sign on the receptionist's desk declares, *Dr. Talbott. Doctor of medicine, reader of the stars, and part-time vampire.* After referring to Squat's chart, he tells us Squat's horoscope then settles down to business.

"I've only treated Squat for about ten years," he reminds us. "The records indicate Squat suffered from perinatal asphyxia, a lack of oxygen at birth. This would cause him to be developmentally challenged."

"That's right," Steve agrees. "He was always behind the other kids. Didn't walk 'til he was almost four. Didn't talk 'til he was about six. Clare Jackson used to come over and work with him when she was home from college. She tried to teach him to read when he was a kid, but he just couldn't learn."

I glance at Steve, and he nods. No wonder Squat is so fond of Clare.

"Doctor Talbott, would you classify Squat's condition as severe?" I ask.

He shakes his head. "Moderate. After all, he dresses himself and works outside the home, doesn't he?"

"Yeah, but his job don't require him to do much," says Steve.

"Be that as it may, he can communicate basic needs and perform simple tasks, although I suspect autism, also. He's never been tested for it and at this point it would serve no purpose." Doctor Talbott closes the file and smiles. "Of course, he can't live on his own. Any other questions I can answer?"

"No," I reply, "I think you've laid it out for us."

Steve groans as he stands. When we leave the doctor's office, Nellie says, "That sounds like havin' a kid that never grows up."

I wonder if I'm ready to be a father to a perpetual child. Steve sees my frown.

"A kid that's never gonna wreck your car, or knock up the neighbor girl, or burn your house down," he argues.

———

The next day, I ask Lou to invite Nellie over for supper. Nellie insists we include Jenny, as well.

"We're bein' asked to be Squat's family," Nellie explains. "That's gonna include Jenny somewhere, sometime."

After supper, we all sit in the living room, Steve in his favorite chair with the cushion flattened from supporting his mammoth weight all these years. He immediately plows ahead, the proverbial bull in a china shop. His head swivels back and forth from me to Nellie as he asks, "Have you thought about what I asked you?"

Nellie peeks at Squat, gazing quietly around the room, then nods at me.

"First," I say, "I think we should explain to Squat what we're talkin' about. He probably has no idea."

Squat stares dully at me, but smiles when he hears his name, and asks, "Whaaat?"

"Okay," suggests Steve. "I'll explain it to him. Squat, you remember when Mama and Daddy died, don't you?"

Squat's smile disappears. He covers his face and squeaks, "I not here."

"Come on, Squat," murmurs Steve. "We have to talk about this."

Squat uncovers his face then covers it, again, and demurs. "I don't wanna hear it."

"We know you don't, Honey," Lou croons, "but it's somethin' we need to talk 'bout, and we think you oughta be involved. After all, it's about you. Do you wanna hear it *now*?"

"Alriiiight." He puts his hands in his lap but frowns.

Steve plunges ahead. "Well, Squat, when Mama and Daddy died, Lou and I came to live here with you. We've done okay, haven't we?"

"Alriiiight," says Squat, still frowning.

Lou says, "Squat, I am so thankful you accepted us into your home. I love bein' here with you."

"Alriiiight."

Steve nods toward her and says, "Lou, you word it better than me. Will you explain what we wanna do?"

I've never seen Steve defer to Lou before, and I notice that his eyes are wet. Neither Lou nor Sally act surprised, and I wonder if the brash fellow I normally see is an act.

"Honey," Lou murmurs to Squat, "there might be a time when Steve and I can't live here no more, and we've asked Bob and Nellie if they'll come here and live with you if that ever happens. Would that be okay?"

"Noooo," he moans, putting his hands over his ears then quickly removing them.

"Well, then, who would you want?" asks Lou. I can barely hear her.

"You and Steve."

"But if we couldn't, who would you want?"

"Why can't you?"

"We can now, but we're talkin' about if something… happened, like…with your mama and daddy," says Lou. I have to lean toward Lou to hear her. "Do you understand, Honey?"

"I don't wanna hear it."

"A lot of things can happen. Maybe nothin'. Maybe we live here with you forever. But in case we don't, we think it would be good for Bob and Nellie to live with you. What do you think?"

"I want alllll of you to live with me."

Lou pauses for a minute, thinking out her response, but it is Nellie who speaks next.

"Squat, I'd like that, too. Y'all are our family now. Could Bob and me maybe live here if you need us?"

"I don't wanna hear it." His hands are over his ears, again.

"We don't want to talk 'bout it, either, but it's important that we do," says Lou, calmly. "We wanna make sure you've always got a happy home. You'd like that, wouldn't you?"

"Yessss." Squat lowers his hands and rubs them together. His eyes dart around the room, stopping to look at first one then another of us.

"If you could live with any two of us, who would it be?" asks Lou.

"You and Steve," says Squat in a tone that declares the answer obvious.

"And who would be your second choice?"

Squat covers his ears again and then lowers his hands and says, "Bob and Nellie."

"Well, then, Honey, that's all we're talkin' about, what your choices are."

"I go now?"

Lou smiles. "Of course."

Squat stands, pulls the back of his shirt up over his head, and walks out of the room, peering out of the funnel he has made of his shirt.

When he's totally out of the room, I suggest, "Sally, how about you, Nellie and I take a little walk uptown. Jenny, would you mind stayin' here with Steve and Lou?"

"Nah," Jenny says. "Big Daddy and Lou wanna talk to me about somethin', anyway."

Steve lights up when she calls him Big Daddy. I suspect that moniker was his idea.

I look at Lou.

She waves toward the door and says, "Y'all go on along and work out your business. Steve and I have an arrangement to discuss with Jenny."

"What?" asks Mama Bear, ever protective of her cub. She shoots a worried glance toward me, but I shrug and shake my head.

"Just never you mind," Lou responds, walking behind us toward the door, thereby blocking Nellie's path back to the living room.

As we start down the steps, Steve comes out on the porch and repeats, "Remember, he's a child that will never wreck your car, or knock up the next-door neighbor's girl, or burn your house down."

"We'll keep that in mind," I say, heading down the steps.

There's still about an hour of daylight left in the muggy evening. We walk slowly because of the heat.

Sally is the first to speak. "What's on your mind?"

"Nellie and I would like to know you're okay with this and that you understand if we do this, it's not for the money."

"You were asked before you knew about the money, and Papa's been talkin' to me 'bout you since Pam came down here to take you back to Chicago but you chose to stay in Waynedale."

"I didn't choose Waynedale over Chicago, I chose Nellie over Pam." I feel a gentle squeeze on my arm from Nellie.

"Okay," says Sally. "But Papa told me he really admired how you screwed up then took your lickin' like a stand-up guy and managed to convince Nellie to take you back."

"That was a feat," agrees Nellie, smiling.

"What clinched it, though, was when you came back from your trip with Squat and you were talkin' to your papa, again. He didn't approve of you not gettin' along with your papa. When you made up, he said that showed the kind of man you are."

I smile as I remember Steve's comment the night we returned and I told him Squat had gotten me talking to my father. "Things are gonna work out just fine," he had said.

"Well, anyway," I say to Sally, "How do you feel about this? Nellie and I did some research. We had no idea there was so much money involved."

"It's a lot, but there's a lot of checks and balances, too. All the money's in a trust fund down at the bank. You'll have to file reports with the probate court once a year tellin' them what you spent it on, and the bank will have to approve it before that. I'll get enough upfront to keep me happy. You'll get enough annually, as long as Squat's alive, so you won't have to work if you don't wanna. When Uncle Squat passes, you get the house free and clear, and the rest of the trust comes to me, less a lump sum to you. I'm happy. My uncle is taken care of by people he loves who are young enough to see it through. Oh, and by the way, I intend to show up at the supper table, same as I do now."

"That'll be fun," Nellie chirps.

"I can't ask for a better arrangement," agrees Sally. "I'm not up to discussin' with my uncle why his pee's slowin' down or why the doctor has to stick his finger up his butt and stuff like that. You'll get to do that, Bob."

"Be still my heart."

"Well, face it. Havin' a older man around is similar to havin' a teenage daughter. There're certain things they need to hear from someone of the same sex."

"Amen to that," says Nellie.

"Back to the financials," I prompt, always happy to avoid a discussion regarding teenaged girls, old men, and anatomy. "A minute ago, you spelled out the arrangements pretty specifically. So your papa's discussed this with you in detail?"

"Yeah, we went over it about ten years ago, but even then, I encouraged him to find a man to do it. I think he started sizin' you up that first day in the diner. Then, when you and Squat came back from Chicago, he said he wanted to make some changes and laid out how he would set things up. He could have just done it without tellin' me, but he wanted me to be assured I'd be taken care of." She pokes me on the shoulder and suggests, "I bet he even told you he expects you to take care of me."

Sally and Nellie both look at me, and my smile is the only confirmation they need.

"Well, just so neither one of you get the wrong idea," Sally says, "I'm pretty much okay on my own, but I *am* an only child. It will be nice to have a brother and sister, even if they are married to each other." She smiles like a naughty child then continues. "But Squat's the main thing. You gotta take care of him. Papa will haunt you if you don't."

"We will," says Nellie. "I just hope we don't have to do it soon."

"Yeah, me, too," says Sally, frowning. "Papa's been goin' to the doctor a lot lately, and they're both a little overweight."

I love Sally's understatement. Steve probably weighs 350 pounds, and Lou's not far behind.

———

We gradually make our way to Main Street then return to Steve and Lou's. After going inside to say goodbye, Nellie and Jenny set out for Grove's Point and Sally heads home. I go upstairs to my room and find Squat sitting on my bed, watching television.

"I see you, I see you," he smiles as I walk in and sit in my chair next to him. We watch *St. Elsewhere*. It has an autistic character, and every time he appears on screen Squat cries, "Tommy!" the character's name. When the show's over, Squat goes to bed.

I sit there, staring at a blank television, wondering what to do.

———

The following Sunday, I have dinner with Nellie and Jenny. While we're eating, I tell them that if it is okay with them, I am going to agree to be Squat's guardian.

"It's about time," says Jenny. "What took so long?"

Nellie laughs and agrees, "Yeah, Bob, what took so long?"

"I wanted to make sure it's the right thing."

"Now that you've made up your mind, we can tell you

somethin' else," says Nellie, her eyes shining. She smiles at me, and urges, "Go ahead, Jenny."

I look from Nellie to Jenny. They both have the same excited, happy smile.

"I'm gettin' the rest of my college paid for," Jenny says, grinning from ear to ear.

Jenny is a good student and has received a partial scholarship to the University of Louisville. It will cover about half of her expenses. Nellie and I will pay the rest, but she is going to need a job to have any spending money. "What do you mean?" I ask.

Nellie says, "Remember the other night when Steve and Lou said they had some business to discuss with Jenny? Well, they told her as long as she maintains a B average they're gonna pick up her college tuition, room, and board. Whatever's not covered by her scholarship."

"Isn't that great, Bob?" asks Jenny.

I frown. "It sounds like a bribe to get me to agree to the deal with Squat."

"But it's not," argues Jenny. "That's why I couldn't say anything until you made up your mind. Big Daddy said he was gonna do it regardless of what you did, but I couldn't tell you until you decided so you wouldn't think you had to. Isn't this great, Bob? I won't have to work while I'm in school. I can use my money from you and Mom to visit Aunt Pam in Chicago. I'm sooo excited."

"I'm not sure I'm okay with this."

Now, it's Nellie's turn to frown. "Bob, if they were offerin' to buy her a car, or pay for a vacation, or just give her money, I wouldn't be okay with it, either. But it's her education, and she has to maintain her grades. Nobody's ever helped us before. Steve and Lou, why they're just so wonderful and, and..." Nellie starts crying, then Jenny.

I sit there like a dope.

———

The next evening, after Squat has gone upstairs, I tell Steve and Lou. Their reaction is more subdued.

"Mark my words," says Steve. "You'll never regret it."

"I just hope I'm up for it."

Lou walks over to where I'm sitting and puts her arm around my shoulder. Planting a kiss on my cheek, she says, "Honey, if you ain't up for this, ain't nobody up for this. Clare was right. You're a good man." She ruffles my hair and adds, "For a Yankee."

Steve says, "Time for bed. Oh, by the way, Sally's takin' me and Lou up to Louisville in a coupla weeks. Gotta see a doctor. You need us to bring you anything back?"

"Let me think about that. Everything okay with you?"

"Sure. Just routine," says Steve, rubbing his ample girth.

Chapter Twenty-Four

Three weeks later, on a Monday, as I'm finishing my lunch, I hear my name over the loudspeaker. When I pick up the phone, the receptionist tells me that I've got a call.

"She sounds upset," the receptionist says.

Upset doesn't begin to describe it. Her sobs are so hysterical that, at first, I don't recognize Sally's voice, let alone understand her.

"Slow down," I say. "What's the matter?"

There's a pause, during which I hear her sucking air in like a jet engine, then I hear, "Oh, Bob. You've got to get here quick! *Oh, Bob!*"

"Sally where are you?"

"The hos...hospital in E-town. You've got to come right now."

Her words tumble one on top of the other. I understand that something terrible has happened, but nothing beyond that. Shouting to my boss that I've got a family emergency, I run out the door and drive to the hospital, cursing the traffic that is always light, the signals that are always green, always, until today. I couldn't understand who is in trouble. I'm scared of finding out what's happening and scared of not knowing. Was this the day Steve and Lou were going to Louisville?

I burst into the ER waiting room and immediately see Sally sitting in a chair, leaning forward, a nurse's arm around her. "There's my brother," she says and runs to me.

"Oh, Bob, she sobs, "Mama's dead, and they think Papa's gonna die, too."

"*What? What happened?*"

"They were goin' to Louisville. I was supposed to take them but didn't have anyone to cover the café so Papa said he'd drive. He don't drive the expressway much. Someone in another car said there was a dog on the road. Papa tried to avoid it and lost control. He ran off the road. They rolled over, and neither one ever use a seat belt. Oh, Bob, *why didn't I take them?*"

The nurse stands next to us, her hands clasped in front of her. "We've been waitin' for you," she says. "I'm Alice. Let's move someplace private."

She steers us down the hallway to a small room with a heavy wood door and a sign announcing, *Chapel.*

As we enter, a man with a clerical collar hurries down the hallway toward us. Alice waits for him at the door. Holding Sally around the waist, I guide her to a couch and lower her onto it, then sit next to her. She continues to sob, "Why? Why?"

The minister speaks quietly to Alice, who comes over to us and says, "This is Reverend Peterson, the hospital chaplain. He'll stay with you. I have to go back to the emergency room, but I'll tell the doctor you're in here." She clasps our hands, again, then strides out the door, closing it behind her.

Reverend Peterson asks, "Do you have a minister you want me to contact?"

I sit next to Sally, her face pressed to my chest, my arms around her. She shakes her head. I try to position her face away from the grease stains on my shirt, but she is oblivious to them.

"Were your parents members of a church?"

"Yes," I tell him. "They attended fairly regularly, but I don't...it would be over in Waynedale. Sally, what church do they attend?"

Sally's crying slows and she steps back. "Waynedale First Church of Christ. The minister's name is Gomez. Thomas Gomez."

"I know him," says Reverend Peterson. "I'll fill him in. I understand you are their children. Do they have any other relatives we need to call?" Rev. Peterson's voice is calm.

Sally shakes her head.

"Just Steve's brother," I say. "He shouldn't come here; he's mentally challenged. I'm not their child, just a friend."

"Family is what we want it to be, especially at a time like this," says the reverend. He sits in a chair facing us and holds one hand from Sally and one hand from me, forming a circle.

The door opens, and a man in lime-green scrubs enters.

Releasing our hands, Reverend Peterson stands and moves behind the chair. He nods at the man, and says, "Dr. Sanders." Looking at us, he says, "This is Dr. Sanders. He'll talk to you about your parents."

The doctor smiles grimly at Reverend Peterson, then sits in the chair with the minister behind him. The look on Dr. Sanders' face tells us what we fear. Sally's back straightens as if she is about to be hit, and she grabs my hand.

Even so prepared, when Dr. Sanders says, "Your father passed away about ten minutes ago," she collapses against me and I have to keep her from falling to the floor. His words make no sense, and I struggle to understand.

Dr. Sanders gives us a moment then questions, "Is there anything you want to know?" He glances from Sally to me then back.

"Yes," says Sally. "Did he ever regain consciousness?"

The doctor bites his lower lip and shakes his head.

"There's at least that," says Sally. "He didn't know Mama was gone. Were you with him when he died?"

"Yes, I was. He just stopped breathin'. He had lost too much blood. Even if we had been able to stabilize that problem, he had serious head injuries; he wouldn't have survived."

We sit for a few moments, and I continue to hold Sally. I can hear the minister praying, but his words of supplication on behalf of Steve and Lou make no sense. We don't need to pray for them; he's at home working in the garden, and she's in the kitchen planning supper. That's what they do in the afternoon.

Dr. Sanders waits a moment then says, "If you have no more questions, I have to get back to the emergency room. Please, stay here with Reverend Peterson as long as you want." He stands and walks to the door. Hearing Sally's sobs, he stops and tells me, "I can prescribe a sedative for your sister if that would help. This is quite a shock."

"Thank you," I reply. "We would appreciate that."

"I'll have the nurse bring it to you in a few minutes." He walks out, closing the door behind him.

The next few hours are a blur. I call Nellie, and tell her we're going to Sally's so she meets us there. Sally opens a desk drawer and pulls out a folder.

"Papa gave me this some time ago and told me I wouldn't have to do a thing; he had everything planned. I told him that was morbid but he said, 'You'll be glad when you have to use it.'"

Steve's right. He's got everything lined out with phone numbers to call. Once we make the first calls to the funeral home and their church, we start calling friends. We're so busy calling people and letting them know what has happened that it's only when I hear the clock at a church chime four times that I realize Squat will be leaving Jacob's in thirty minutes. And we have to tell him.

Oh, my God! I'm responsible for him now.

It's only been two weeks since Lou, Steve, and I met with their attorney and signed the papers naming me as Squat's guardian if anything happened to them. Steve had repeated then what he had told me when he first asked me to be the guardian. "I've got some health problems, so I need to have everything in order, but it'll be fifteen years or more before you ever have to worry about this." It ended up being closer to fifteen days.

"We've got to get to the house," I tell Nellie and Sally. "Squat will be there soon."

"Oh, no," says Sally, "I forgot about Uncle Squat."

———

We hurry to Steve and Lou's. As soon as Squat spots us on the porch, he starts calling, "I see you," and a smile brightens his face. "Where Steve? Lou, where Lou?"

Sally tries not to cry but can no longer contain it.

Squat looks at her, sees her sobbing and puts his hands over his ears. "I don't wanna hear it," he says then removes his hands from his ears, but he won't look at us.

"Squat," I mumble, glancing at Sally, who nods for me to continue, "there's been a bad car wreck." He puts his hands over his ears then removes them. He stares at the floor.

"Steve and Lou aren't comin' home."

"When will they?" He looks up at me.

"Squat, they won't be comin' home…ever. They were both killed in the wreck."

Squat thrusts both hands over his ears and says, "I don't wanna hear it." He begins pacing to and fro, no more than four steps in any direction.

"And I don't wanna tell you, but I can't change it."

"I don't wanna hear it. I don't wanna hear it," he repeats, pushing his hands against his ears. Removing them, he runs into the house calling, "Lou, Lou, where you?"

Sally sits in a swing leaning forward, her face in her hands, so Nellie and I walk inside.

Squat comes up to us and demands, "Where Lou? Where Steve?"

"They won't be here anymore," I advise him, and he stares at me blankly.

"Who fix supper?"

"I will, Squat," Nellie tells him.

"I need Lou and Steve. I want them *here*."

"We'll do the best we can to make everything stay the same for you."

"I don't like this," he moans.

Nellie tells him, "Honey, neither do we, but Bob and I will be here with you."

Nellie holds her hand out to Squat, who takes it in his. "Will you let me live here with you?" she asks him.

"I want Lou and Steve."

"I do, too," agrees Nellie, "and so does Bob, but we can't have that. Would you let Bob and me live here with you?"

"Lou fix my lunch to take to work."

"Yes, Honey. I'll fix your lunch."

"No, *Lou*."

"I'll be your Lou," promises Nellie.

"I no like this," says Squat.

"Neither do we," says Nellie.

————

Sally tells everyone she should have driven them to Louisville and, of course, they all say it wasn't her fault. Squat withdraws to his room.

"What do you think about Squat goin' to the visitation?" I ask Nellie.

"The coffins will be closed, won't they?" she asks.

"Yes. The funeral director said their head injuries were so bad there was little they could do."

The images of Steve and Lou that flash through my head are unpleasant. If I don't want to think about their injuries, I certainly don't want to see them. "Squat doesn't need to be exposed to that, but since they're gonna be closed I wonder if it would be good for him to see all the people who come to pay their respects."

"Probably," agrees Nellie. "But he hates cemeteries. What did Sally say?"

I shake my head. "She's upset, plus, she took that sedative the doctor gave her at the hospital. It's got her in a fog."

"Well, I guess you've got your first tough decision ahead of you."

But it wasn't so tough, after all. When Squat learns that the service will be a tribute to Steve and Lou, and all their friends will be there, he says he wants to be there, too.

"Do you understand that Steve and Lou won't be there?" I

ask. "It will just be all their friends sayin' nice things about them."

"That good," he murmurs. "I wanna hear."

———

Steve and Lou were popular beyond Waynedale. Visitors come from all over the state. The funeral director said we need eight pallbearers for each coffin because of Steve and Lou's sizes. I thought it would be hard to get that many, but I have trouble narrowing it down to sixteen, and we end up with honorary pallbearers.

Jacob sits with Squat in the lounge to keep him company. "Should I sweep?" he wonders when they first sit down.

Jacob and I both smile at him. "That won't be necessary," Jacob assures him. "We're just gonna sit here and take the day off."

Sally doesn't recognize all the people. She and I are standing near the caskets discussing who some of them are, when she looks over my shoulder and her face goes pale. "Oh, my God," she gasps, "what is *he* doing here?"

I turn around but can't figure out who she means, so I ask, "Who?"

She pleads, "Don't let him see me, please don't let him see me," and begins to slide sideways toward the door, so again I question her.

"Who?"

"Ah, shit," She blurts under her breath. "He sees me."

I turn, again in the direction she's facing, and there he is. He is the most handsome man I have ever seen, and he comes inexorably through the crowd toward Sally, like a malevolent plague-carrying fog. Ignoring me, he hugs her. I see her draw her arms up against her chest to keep them from going around him, and her body stiffens. She turns her head when he tries to kiss her.

"Sally," he prattles, keeping his arms around her, "I'm so sorry. Is there anything I can do?"

She keeps her face to the side and refuses to return the hug. "No, there isn't," she says. "Why are you here?"

He steps back, puts his hand on his chest, and declares, "Honey, I wanna be here for you."

"I don't want you here."

Before he can answer, I say, "Excuse me, Charlie, could I have a word with you in private?"

He glares at me, and I swallow hard. He is about six inches taller than me. He stares down, and sneers, "Who are *you*?"

Sally says, "Bob, thi—"

"You don't need to introduce us. I'd know him anywhere."

"Bu—" Sally starts.

Charlie ignores her. "I don't know you," he says to me.

"No, you don't," I agree, "but I know you. Let's go out in the foyer for a minute. I have a message from a friend."

Charlie points at Sally, makes a clicking noise as he winks, and says, "Don't go away, babe." He walks toward the foyer, moving as if he created the ground under his feet.

When we get outside the visitation room, he demands, "All right, who are *you*, and who is the message from?"

"It's from Steve."

"Steve's dead."

"Yeah, I know. Spooky, isn't it?"

"What are you talkin' about?" Charlie leans in, crowding me.

I have to tilt my head back to look up at him. "Didn't Steve once tell you that if you ever showed up in Waynedale again, he'd hunt you down, cut off your head and shit down your throat?"

He blanches then swivels his head around as if searching for Steve.

"Look at me." I touch his arm, wondering what I'll do if he takes a punch at me.

He jerks his arm away but looks me in the eyes.

I see anger in his, but I continue. "The message still applies. Leave right now, and if I ever hear that you're in Waynedale again, *I'll* do it." It is all I can do to keep from shitting down both legs, and my knees are about to buckle. One hard swing from him and I'm dead.

He laughs. "You and who else?"

"Us," I hear from behind me.

I glance over my shoulder. Clare is there, the Mafia standing shoulder-to-shoulder with her. Each clutches a purse in her hands.

"You heard him," Clare snarls. "Git."

Charlie laughs. He's being threatened by some stranger about half his size, backed up by five seventy-year-old women. He shakes his head but quickly stops smiling. His face goes white and he swallows hard as he stares at Clare.

I follow his eyes and shout, "Clare, put that away!" as she pulls a snub-nosed revolver out of her purse.

She lets Charlie see it then returns it to her purse. "I don't wanna have to tell you again to *git,*" she orders, glaring at him.

I notice that all the Mafia have their hands in their purses.

Charlie notices, too. He holds his hands up and turns to go, but before he can, Pauline pokes his left pants pocket several times with the end of her cane. The last one is right about where Charlie's balls should be. The grimace on his face says her knowledge of the male anatomy is good.

"And get that ring you put in this pocket back on your finger," Pauline warns. "We saw you slip it off when you came in."

He scowls and pulls a ring from his pocket. He starts to put it on then glares defiantly at us and puts it back in his pocket.

As he pushes past Louise, she puts her hand out and holds it against his stomach.

When their eyes meet, she tells him, "Don't fuck with the Mafia." She stares straight at him until he turns away. When she removes her hand, he walks out the door, shaking his head.

After a moment of silence, Wanda drawls, "He's a turd that just won't flush."

My knees are jelly and I hear Clare exuberantly exclaim, "I think that went well."

The other four members of the Mafia murmur their agreement.

Clare takes hold of my arm, pats it and says, "Bob, you're doin' just fine." She waits a moment then adds, "For a Yankee."

"Clare, why do you have a gun in your purse?"

She shrugs. "I always pack heat when I go out."

"We all do," says Mabel. She looks at the others. Their heads are bobbing.

"I don't believe it," I say, rubbing the back of my neck with my hand.

"Oh, you can believe it," Louise says. "That's just a little ol' pea-shooter Clare carries. The rest of us have Glocks. Between the five of us, we can hit you with sixty-five rounds."

"Sixty-six," corrects Mabel. "I got one in the chamber."

Louise's eyebrows rise. "I forgot that," she says. "I do, too."

"The Glock's too heavy for me," says Clare, shaking her head. "I like my revolver."

"Yeah," says Wanda. "But you only got five rounds. We got fifteen, plus one in the chamber."

I can't believe I'm standing in a funeral home having a discussion with five female septuagenarians about the relative merits of their firearms. "What in the world are you afraid of?" I ask.

They all laugh as Mabel says, "Absolutely nothin'."

I start to add something else, but just then my father comes in the door. I had called him the day before to tell him about the accident. When he said he was coming, I tried to dissuade him, but he was adamant.

Clare sees me gazing at the door. She reaches into her purse and pulls out her revolver, again. "Do I need this?" she asks.

The rest of the Mafia's hands are diving back into their purses.

"*No*," I reply. "For God's sake, put those away. It's my father."

Their heads swivel as if they're at a tennis match. They put their guns back in their purses, and Clare starts rooting through hers, at the same time saying, "Oh, my, he's handsome. Where's my lipstick?"

"Indeed, he is," agrees Pauline.

I shake my head as they rate my father an eight, maybe nine.

His cane clicks on the floor, and he appears lost, so I glare at the Mafia, tell them to behave, and walk toward him.

Clare calls out, "Don't you dare take him anywhere. I'll be right back." She ducks into the restroom, the rest of the Mafia scrambling after her.

My father looks relieved when he spots me.

"Thanks for comin', Dad," I say.

"I know this is a hard loss for you."

I hug him, not sure what kind of response I'll get, but he hugs me back.

"Come on," I say. "I want you to meet my friends."

We start toward the visitation room, but the Mafia is back,

lipstick aglow. They stand in a semicircle and block our path, just as they did with Charlie, but this time with smiles on their glowing faces.

"Dad, I want you to meet the belles of Waynedale, commonly known as the Mafia." As I introduce him, each hugs him. Clare is the last, and she finishes off her hug with a kiss on the cheek.

"Any father of Bob's is a beau of mine," she announces with a twinkle in her eye and a smile on her face.

I warn him, "They usually get what they want."

"Well, as pretty as they are, I can see why," he says, smiling.

He is charming and thoughtful, and I want to figure out who this is masquerading as my father, but I have other things to do first. "Have any of you seen Nellie or Jenny?" I ask the Mafia.

"They were in the lounge about fifteen minutes ago," says Louise.

"Yeah, that was the last time I saw them, too," agrees Mabel.

"Let's see if they're still there." I take my father by the arm and head in the direction of the lounge, but we are stopped every five feet by someone wanting to meet him.

"You've got quite a support group here," he says, as we finally clear the crowd and start moving toward the lounge.

"It all started with Steve and Lou." As I say this, I am brought back to why we are here.

"Yeah, I wanted to meet them," he admits.

I realize then what might have been.

I find Nellie and Jenny in the lounge, talking to a few of her regulars from the beauty parlor. As we approach them, Nellie excuses herself and walks up to us.

Before I have a chance to introduce her she says, "Mr.

Tingle, I'd recognize you anywhere. Bob looks just like you."
She hugs him.

"Dad," I say, "this is my fiancée, Nellie."

"Well," coos dad, "Since we're going to be family, maybe
you should call me Sam."

"Sam it is," Nellie agrees and puts her arm around Jenny's
shoulder. "This is my daughter, Jenny. We sure appreciate you
comin'."

"Now, are you Steve and Lou's daughter?" Dad asks.

Nellie looks confused, so I tell him, "No, that's Sally." I
glance around but don't see her. "I'm not sure where she is."

"Goodness," says Dad, "I'm not used to Bob knowing so
many pretty women. I'm having trouble keeping them
straight."

"Okay," I say, "quick rundown. Nellie and I are gettin'
married. Jenny will be my stepdaughter."

Each smiles as I mention her name, as if to announce,
"That would be me."

"The Mafia are friends, and you haven't met Sally yet."

"Don't forget Pam," Nellie adds.

"Pam? Who's Pam?" Dad scratches his head.

"You don't know Pam?" asks Nellie. "She's a friend of
Bob's from Chicago. I thought you knew her."

"No, I haven't met too many of Bob's friends in Chicago,"
Dad says.

Nellie surveys the faces around us, then says "Maybe we
oughta go find Sally and see how she's doin'."

The visitation room is overflowing. "Your friends had lots
of friends," Dad observes.

"They were good people," Nellie says. "Took to Jenny an'
me just like we was kin." Regret rolls across her face as she
adds, "I can still hear Lou callin' Bob and me an item."

Sally's standing at the coffins, talking to some church

friends of her parents. When she can break away, she hugs me and kisses my cheek.

"My Prince Charmin'," she drawls, "but how did you know who he was?" Turning to Nellie she asks, "Did you hear about Bob runnin' off my no-good ex?"

"No," says Nellie, looking at me, surprised. "How did you know about him?"

"Tell you later," I say. Extending my arm toward my father, I tell Sally, "This is my father. Dad, Sally is the lady whose parents were killed."

Dad offers his hand and his condolences.

Sally, taking his hand and pulling him toward her, states, "I sure 'preciate you comin', Mr. Tingle, but a handshake won't do. I consider Bob to be my brother, so we're kinfolk, and kinfolk get a hug."

Dad is at a loss for words, but after Sally hugs him, he regains his composure. "In that case, young lady I'll tell you the same thing I told this one over here," he says, nodding toward Nellie. "I want you to call me Sam, and if your parents were half as charming as you, I can see why Bob was so fond of them."

"Sam, Sam!" I hear Squat's voice coming up from behind my father.

Dad turns, surprised, and Squat engulfs him in a hug that catches both of them off guard.

"What happened to 'no hugs?'" I wonder.

"But it Sam," Squat responds.

"I hope you realize you just got a hug from someone who won't let me put my hand on his shoulder," I declare.

"And a good hug it was," he says, beaming at Squat. "How's my man?"

Squat's smile disappears. "Steve and Lou in Heaven," he replies.

For a few moments, Steve and Lou hadn't been dead. Squat's simple statement brings everyone back to reality.

———

The next two days are a series of highs and lows as we help Squat understand the finality of death, deal with our own loss, and introduce my dad around town.

Finally, we arrive at the graves. I don't expect Squat to go, but he never hesitates.

After the service, people begin to walk away, but Squat lingers. I stay with him while Nellie helps my father. Eventually, Squat and I are the only ones at their grave. I gently turn him toward the car, and as we walk away Squat gives Steve and Lou a no-look wave.

Chapter Twenty-Five

Steve and Lou's deaths have immediate repercussions. Nellie and I were going to be married in December and Lou was planning the event.

Now, we decide to scale things back. We have a small service with a justice of the peace when Jenny is home for fall break. Squat is my best man, and Jenny stands up for Nellie. Jenny insists we invite Aunt Pam, but she's on the road and can't get there.

Sally, the Mafia, and my father are the only others in attendance, and the mood is subdued, everyone missing the two who would never be there again.

———

Initially, Nellie and I stay upstairs in my room but after a few weeks, we move into the first-floor bedroom which had been Steve and Lou's. Squat and I still meet in my old room to watch *St. Elsewhere*.

As I take over paying Squat's bills, I notice how organized

everything is. It reminds me of something Steve told me shortly after I arrived in Waynedale, when I asked what he did for a living.

He handed me a card that said, *Steve Matson*. In the lower right-hand corner was his phone number. Under his name, it said, *Planning and Evaluation*.

When I asked what it meant, Steve smiled. He always liked it when he got someone to bite.

"In the mornin', I plan," he told me, "and in the afternoon I evaluate all the plans I made in the mornin'. It helps me keep everything organized."

———

Steve has accounted for every penny, and it is very easy to pick up where he left off, so it takes me by surprise when Jacob calls. It's a cold December evening, about four months after the funeral.

"Hi, Bob," he says. "Can we talk 'bout somethin'?"

"Sure," I reply. "What's up?"

"Here's the thing. I let Squat work here, and he keeps the place clean. But I don't really *need* him."

"Jacob, please don't let him go. He is so proud of that job. With all he's lost lately, I'm not sure he could handle it."

"Nah, I ain't lettin' him go, but the deal was, Steve *paid* me to let him work here. He'd pay me $400.00 a month and I'd pay Squat $200.00 of it and keep the other two for taxes and my trouble. Squat's so proud of gettin' that paycheck."

"I know. I hadn't lived here more than a month when Squat showed me his paycheck and told me, 'See, I mechanic, too.' But I've been all through the trust checkbook and I haven't seen any $400.00 payments bein' made to you."

"You won't find it there. Steve didn't wanna tell the bank

about it. He was afraid they'd say he was wastin' money, payin' me to pay Squat when he could just give it to him straight. But he wanted Squat to have the fun of gettin' a check, so he'd send it to me direct out of his own account. That's where you'll find it."

Something Steve told me when we were going over finances now makes sense. Steve had wanted me to get enough money so I wouldn't have to work if I didn't want to.

"But I'll probably wanna work," I told him.

"That's fine, long as you take care of Squat. But in case you don't wanna, you should be able to stay at the house for him. Like I do."

So we agreed on an amount, and then Steve said, "And in addition, I'm gonna leave you $100,000.00 outright. You invest it conservatively and you'll get about $5,000.00 a year interest with no risk to the principle."

"Why would I need that, Steve?"

"You might wanna spend about $400.00 a month on somethin' for Squat."

"For what?" I asked him, but he wouldn't say any more.

Now I know.

Then Jacob adds, "Hey, listen, I don't wanna rip anybody off. I tried to tell Steve $300.00 a month would be enough, but he insisted on $400.00. Let's drop it to $300.00."

"No way, Jacob," I reply. "A deal is a deal. Steve made it; I'll honor it."

"Whatever you say. Steve would just mail the payment to me. You can do that, too. Oh, oh, here comes Squat. Can't let him hear me talkin' to you 'bout this. Remember, Steve don't *ever* want Squat to find out."

———

Over the next few months, we begin to adjust as much as anyone ever adjusts to the death of parents. Squat and I leave for work every morning the same time as always. Nellie heads to the beauty parlor about the same time. If Squat has a doctor's appointment, I take off work. Gradually, I stop expecting to hear Steve's booming voice when I get home.

But it's impossible to live in a house that others so abruptly left without finding reminders of those people. For me, two things in particular bring on the memories.

The first is the trim around the door to the porch. Steve and I put it up a few years earlier in preparation for a visit from the Mafia. It never matched, but Steve refused to take it down. He even painted it. Now, every time I walk past it, I am reminded of something Lou said about Steve.

We were in the kitchen, talking about his attempt to repair the refrigerator with a hammer, which resulted in the purchase of a new refrigerator.

"What was he thinkin'?" I wondered.

Lou had just gotten a roast out of the freezer, and she turned to me, put her hand on her hip and said, "I'll tell you what he was a-thinkin'. He's just like a dog lickin' hisself. They do it 'cause they can. That's Steve. He does these things 'cause he can." She shook her head, set the roast on the counter, and returned to preparing supper.

The second reminder of the ghosts inhabiting the house occurs every morning when Squat comes downstairs for breakfast. When Lou was alive, he would come into the kitchen in the morning, kiss her on the cheek, and say, "Mornin', Lou."

Now Nellie's there, but every morning he kisses her on the cheek and says, "Mornin', Lou." The rest of the time, he calls her Nellie.

"We have enough money," I say to Nellie one night in January when we're getting ready for bed. "We could hire a cook. "

"I know, but what would Squat think? Besides, that's not what Steve and Lou wanted. They never had any help."

We talk about it and decide we want to keep things as much the same as when Steve and Lou were here. This means Nellie quits her job at the beauty parlor. She sends both her mechanics off to work in the morning and is there to greet Squat when he gets home.

———

One of the Mafia comes by about once a month with a pie, except for Clare. She's there every week or two and soon takes to having supper with us.

"How's Sam doin' up there in Chicago?" she'll ask me over supper. "Bet he's lonely."

———

One evening in April, after the most recent reference to 'Sam's lonely existence,' I ask her, "Clare, why don't you just say what's on your mind?"

She arches her eyebrows. "Well, you've got two empty rooms upstairs," she reminds me, gesturing toward the stairway.

"One," I reply. "One is for Jenny when she visits."

"You've got one empty room upstairs," she says, never missing a beat. "You should invite him to live here with you. It's too cold up there in Chicago for an old man like him." She ignores the fact that Dad is a few years younger than she.

"Arthritis, you know," she says, looking at Nellie. "Arthritis and cold weather don't go together." She shakes her head, and a 'Tsk, tsk' escapes her lips.

"If I'm not mistaken, Clare, we had eight inches of snow on the ground twice this past winter," I reply.

"Yeah, but if you got someone to snuggle up against it's not so bad." Clare winks at Squat, who smiles and winks back at her.

"Yeah," Squat says. "Sam need a teddy bear to sleep with."

"Not *exactly* what I had in mind," Clare laughs.

"I think it's an excellent suggestion," I reply. "The teddy bear, that is."

Later, after Clare has left, Nellie, Sally, and I are sitting in the living room while Squat watches TV. "What Clare said about your father is not that far-fetched," says Sally. "If you think I would be offended that you brought your father here, you're wrong."

"You've been gettin' along with him," adds Nellie. She says to Sally, "They talk every week." Turning back to me she says, "Why don't you ask him?"

"What, so Clare can sit out on the front porch like a vulture?"

"What Clare does and doesn't do is irrelevant to the question of what your father needs. Besides, if they hit it off, what's the harm?" Nellie grins.

"He's got his friends in Chicago. His life's there."

"Less than a year ago, you didn't even know if he was alive, so how can you be so sure about that? At least have him down for a visit."

"Yeah," Sally agrees. "Who knows what might happen?"

"You might end up callin' Clare 'Mama,'" says Nellie, as she pokes me in the ribs.

"Wonderful," I mutter.

"Quit bein' such a grump," says Nellie. "He ain't gettin' any younger."

"Yeah," says Squat. His voice rises as he mimics Nellie. "Quit bein' such a grump." Then, he returns to his normal voice and demands, "Bring Sam to *our* house." His eyes never leave the television.

I've only been married about six months. Besides a new wife, I've got a daughter home from college about once a month, Sally and Clare eating supper with us about four times a week, and Squat wanting me to make everything right. To Squat, everything is right if Steve and Lou somehow reappear at the supper table.

"I think we've had enough upheaval in our lives," I say. "Let's let things settle down for a while."

"I disagree," replies Nellie. "We've got all this upheaval goin' on. What better time to add a little more?"

Sally and Squat both nod.

When I look at Nellie, she twirls her hair around one finger. This means it's time for me to cave, a silent homage to the way she wraps me around her finger.

———

I talk to dad a few days later and ask if he had ever considered leaving Chicago.

"Not lately," he said. "Your mother and I used to talk about moving to Florida someday, least she did. I've always been pretty happy here. Never lived more than about a mile from where I am right now."

"Nellie and Sally think you'd be better off here. Clare does, too."

"Clare does?" he asks. "It'd be nice to have her waiting at the end of a move."

"Next fall, when it starts gettin' cold, you could come for a visit. Stay a few weeks, see how things work."

"I'll think about it," is all I can get out of him.

———

A few days later as I'm leaving for work the phone rings.

"Bob," the voice says, "this is Mac Gilmore. You met me last year in Chicago. I run the restaurant where you, your dad, and that other fella, what's his name? Squat? had dinner."

"Sure, I remember. What's up?"

"I'm worried about your dad. He usually comes in three or four times a week, and I haven't heard from him since Friday of last week. This is Wednesday. Just thought you'd want to know."

"Really? I talked to him on Sunday and he sounded all right."

"You want I should go down and check on him? Which house is his? He's in the next block down, but I don't know which house."

"I'd appreciate it." I give him the address and ask him to call me as soon as he finds out what's going on. "I was gettin' ready to go to work, but I'm gonna wait until I hear back from you."

"Okay," he agrees. "It won't take but about fifteen minutes."

When I tell Nellie, she asks, "What do you think we should do?"

"Nothin' to do until Mr. Gilmore calls me back."

I call my boss to inform him I'll be a little late. "Something's up with my father, but I don't know what."

"You think you'll be in later?"

"I think so. I'll call as soon as I can."

"Do that. We've got 'em stacked up into the street today."
He's been really understanding through everything lately, but
his voice is clipped and I hear the stress.

No sooner do I hang up than the phone rings. It's Mac
Gilmore.

"I found your dad lying on the floor in the living room.
He's disoriented, not sure where he is or who I am. He'd wet
himself. Doesn't know what day it is. I called an ambulance;
where do you want me to have them take him?"

"Mount Sinai." The hospital where I was born and my
mother died. "Can you go with him?"

"Sorry, no. Got to get the restaurant open. Is there
anybody I can call for you?"

"No, but see if you can find his wallet. He probably has his
insurance there. Also, give them my phone number. I'm gonna
arrange to get someone there as soon as possible."

"I wish I could do more."

"No, Mr. Gilmore, you've been a big help. Thanks. Not
everyone would have taken the time that you have."

Nellie comes into the room while I am talking to Mac.
When I hang up, she says, "You gotta call Pam."

"I was gonna call Joe, my old boss."

"No, Pam knows the doctors. You call her. Tell her you're
comin'."

"That's premature."

"No, it's not. You need to go."

"No," I say, deliberately, "You don't know my father." I
hesitate; then, unable to control myself, I shout, "He's a drunk.
He beat my mother, he…" I drop onto the edge of the bed,
my heart racing. I shake my head from side to side.

Nellie stands in front of me, frowning. She crosses her
arms and snarls, "You've always said you don't wanna talk
about it, and you pick now to talk? That's just great."

I feel the tears coursing down my face. She looks at me and shakes her head. "You're a grown man. You survived. You've thrived. Put some long pants on, Sonny Boy. Get your ass up to Chicago and take care of your father while you still have the chance."

I put my face in my hands and continue to cry. "You don't know," I cry. "You don't know."

"No, I don't, but that's 'cause you wouldn't discuss it." She stands in front of me, arms still crossed and fire in her eyes. "Every time I asked about him, you said you didn't wanna talk about it. Well, right now, I don't, either. Go take care of your father. If you wanna rant about what a bastard he is when you get back, I'll listen. But right now, we don't have time, and if you're the man I think I married, you'll take care of your father, regardless of the past."

"Squat..."

Her demeanor softens. "I'll stay here with Squat. But *you're* goin', regardless," she says. Spinning around, she takes her redheaded, country temper out of the room.

I compose myself then call Pam's office. When I ask for her, I'm asked who is calling.

"Bob."

"Just Bob?"

I hesitate. Pam probably knows a lot of Bobs.

"Tell her, B-O-B Bob." Only one of him.

"I don't go out with married men," Pam says when she picks up the phone.

"That's a new policy," I mock. She laughs, but I don't have time for joking. "Pam, I've got a problem."

I give Pam as much information as I have, and ask if she can get to the hospital.

"They won't tell me anything."

"I understand, but you can let them know the old bastard's got family, and that I'm on the way."

"If I put it that way, they probably won't let you in when you get there."

"I can't help it. I thought when he came down here for the funerals that I was over it, but I'm still mad."

"Where are you staying?" There's no invitation in the question.

"At Dad's."

She tells me she'll get to the hospital as soon as possible and call me when she does. Next, I call Squat at Jacob's and inform him I have to go to Chicago.

"I go Chaago with you," he declares.

"I think you should stay here with Sally or Nellie. I'll let you know what's happenin' as soon as I know anything."

"I go *with* you. See Sam." Squat speaks each word individually in the clipped style of a newscaster.

"Okay, Squat, I don't have time to argue. Tell Jacob, then walk home. We'll leave when you get here."

When I hang up, Nellie is standing behind me. "We'll be drivin'; Squat's goin' too," I say.

Her eyebrows arch.

"He insisted."

"Won't he be in the way?"

"Yes, but we'll deal with it. Let's get packed."

———

Three hours later we're north of Louisville, Squat in the back seat, giving his no-look wave to passing cars.

Chapter Twenty-Six

We stop in Indianapolis so I can call Pam. She tells me they've taken x-rays, which confirm Dad broke his hip. He is scheduled to have replacement surgery the next day.

We drive straight to the hospital.

When we get to his room he is sleeping, and the doctor says it will be best not to wake him.

"Does he have someone he can stay with during his rehab?" the doctor asks.

"Does he need that?" I ask.

Nellie glares at me and purses her lips then says, "He can stay with us, right, Squat?"

"Right," confirms Squat, nodding.

"We'll work something out," I say, not nearly as eager as Squat to have my dad with us. "But he's lived in Chicago all his life; we live in Kentucky. I'm not sure he'll like the move."

"He may not have a choice," says the doctor, staring at his notes. "Your father's overall condition is poor. He has osteoarthritis and hardening of the arteries. Now this. It would be best if he were living with someone."

"How long will he be hospitalized?"

"Two or three days, if he responds well. Then, he'll need to be in rehab for three to four weeks. When he leaves rehab, he'll need somebody with him."

"We be here," announces Squat. I glance at him, and he fusses me. "He your Papa."

Nellie pats him on the back, more affection than he allows from me.

———

Dad's house looks as if Attila the Hun and his Vandal hordes have been living there. The bath is dirty and dishes are in the sink. Weeks old unopened mail is piled on a desk. Not only is the house filthy, but it also needs repairs. There is a cracked window and the faucet in the bathtub drips steadily.

"He can't keep livin' alone," Nellie declares then calls Sally to give her an update.

"Bring Sam back here with you," Sally tells her. "You got plenty of room at the house and the warmer weather will be good for him."

"We're goin' to, if he agrees," Nellie replies.

———

The next morning, Dad has surgery. Squat sits next to me in the waiting room, periodically saying, "He be all right."

I'm troubled by my thoughts because I'm not sure I care.

———

Every day I call my boss from Dad's room to give him an update. "Bob," he tells me on the third day, "I'm gettin' a logjam. I gotta admit, I had a good mechanic apply for a job today."

I don't want to lose my job. It's who I am.

"Boss," I reply, swallowing hard and not meaning it, "Do what you have to do."

"I will, I just wish I knew for sure when you were gonna be back."

"The doctor won't release Dad yet, and we haven't begun to talk to him about where he's gonna live. His doctor doesn't want him to be on his own."

"You take care of things with your dad, but understand I've gotta take care of things here."

I begin to think about life after losing a job. When I hang up, Dad has awakened from a nap and has been listening.

"So he fired you over the phone, eh?" he asks.

"Yeah," I say. "You cost me my job."

"I didn't ask you to come. You did it on your own."

"Yeah," I say, beginning to pace, "It's never your fault, is it?"

"Oh, so you want to blame me for losing your job, do you? What else do you blame me for? Think I was involved in Jimmy Hoffa's disappearance, too?"

I stop pacing and glare at him.

He licks his lips.

I continue to stare at him; there is nervousness on his face. When he turns away, I walk to the side of the bed, forcing him to look at me. Putting both hands on the edge of the bed and, leaning over him, I growl, "What about Mom?"

He flinches; I've found a vulnerable spot. *Good.*

He turns away again, and says, "I don't know what you're talking about."

Still leaning over him, I reply, "Yes, you do. I'm talkin' about the times she needed a night out, but you were at the bar. The times a kind word would have made a difference, but you were too drunk to talk. The times she needed a new dress, but you'd spent all the money on booze."

He flinches at each example. I go for the kill.

"All the times you got drunk and beat..." My voice starts loud but then, as I feel tears on my cheeks, my throat constricts.

He looks at me, confusion on his face. His eyes wander over my shoulder.

I glance back and find Nellie and Squat behind me.

"Is that true, Sam?" asks Nellie.

"I don't know," he says, shaking his head. "The drinking, yes, I...I drank too much. The rest, I don't remember. If it happened, I'm sorry."

"He say he sorry," Squat murmurs.

"Stay out of it, Squat," I growl.

"Why?" he asks. "You and me, we mech—" I glare at him, my cheeks still wet with angry tears, and he stops. Then, gazing at me, he adds, "Sam shouldn't hurt you."

"Will you two let Bob and me have a minute?" my father asks, waving his hand toward the door.

Nellie takes Squat by the hand and says, "Come on, Bud. Let's walk down the hall."

When they get to the door, Squat turns back, points at Dad with his free hand, and says, "You should be sorry," then disappears out the door.

I have no idea what to do or expect. I shove my hands in my pockets and start pacing again. Dad's eyes follow me.

"I *am*," Dad says, as I make my third pass across the room.

I stop and glare at him. "You're what?"

"I *am* sorry. I know you're telling the truth. I don't remember any of it, and I don't want to, but I need to. I was a bastard, and I'm truly sorry."

His admission and apology stun me. I continue to stare at him, sensing his vulnerability.

"How could you have done that? We would have done *anything* for you? We didn't deserve to be treated that way."

"I know." He pauses and looks out the window. I follow his line of sight. In the distance, I can see the highway. Cars speed by, each containing its own little drama. There is a plane approaching the airport. People will get off and pick up their lives where they left off, some for the good, some for the bad.

He turns back to me; my eyes drill into his. "I know it, *now,*" he says. I'm sorry. That's all I have. I guess you want me out of your life forever, huh? Can't say I blame you."

"Doesn't matter what I want." The words fly out of my mouth like bats coming out of a cave at dusk. "You win again. The doctor says you can't live alone."

"I've got friends; I won't beg you to help me."

"I don't want you to beg me. I want you to understand how much you hurt me." I turn my back to him.

"You think I *don't?*" he growls, an old, weak wolf cornered in his lair. His voice commands my attention, so I face him. "You think I haven't thought about it every day since your mother died? I stopped drinking that night." He raises his head from the pillows. "I went to Alcoholics Anonymous four times a week. I rode the bus for an hour and a half every day for two years, just to put flowers on her grave. Gave me plenty of time to think."

He stops as if he's not sure he should continue. When I don't say anything, he does.

"According to AA, I'm supposed to make amends with everyone I've hurt. I put you off, didn't know how it would go. Then, when I was ready, you had moved, and I couldn't find you. Should have done it when you and Squat came by the house that day, but I didn't think I could speak freely with him there."

He takes a deep breath then says, "Okay, here it is, the final entry for step nine. I was a drunk. I hit your mother; never should have. Probably hit you, too."

I start to tell him there's no "probably" in the equation, and how hard his actions have made it for me to trust people, but he holds up his hand and says, "Don't tell me, I know I did. And I'll pay for it every day until the day that I die. You think I enjoy living alone? Or the way you look…" His voice breaks. "…way you look at me? You think I want to hear you talk about how great Steve was? Knowing you're comparing him to me?"

The door flies open, and a nurse comes in, shaking her finger at Dad. "What did I tell you, Mr. Tingle? I can hear you two all the way out at the nurse's station. You shouldn't be getting yourself upset." She points at me and says, "And you should know better, getting him all agitated. What are *you* thinking?" She arranges the pillows under his head.

"He's thinking I'm an old bastard, and he's right," my father tells her.

She frowns. "Now, Mr. Tingle, we don't need that kind of language." She checks his blood pressure and says, "I don't understand how you can carry on like that and not have your blood pressure sky high."

"Truth is an elixir," he says, "and confession is good for the soul."

Her angry expression calms. "That may be so, but you should take it easy. A man your age ought to be finished doing things that need confessing." She glares at me and walks out of the room.

I hear the clock again and count eleven ticks before Dad

asks, "So where does all this leave us? Still think I'm the devil incarnate? Won't get any argument from me."

"Yes," I say, this time quietly. "I think you're the devil. And you're right; you're not half the man Steve was."

Dad looks as if I smacked him, and I'm shocked by my deliberate meanness. I immediately add, "But neither am I."

"What do you want from me?" Dad's eyes glisten. Try as I might, I can't remember ever seeing him cry. Then I remember. He cried when Mom died.

"I don't know what I want, but I don't want what I've known," I tell him. I walk to the window and look out at the street. Then, my back to him, I add, "I'm tired."

"Of what?" he asks.

"Of bein' angry."

"At me?"

"At you for what you did." I turn to face him. "At me for runnin' away."

As those words come out of my mouth, I have an epiphany.

"But, when I ran, I found Squat and Nellie, and all the others, so why should I be angry at myself for runnin' when it gave me what I have today?" I pause for a minute as Dad and I mull over that thought. Then I follow it to its logical conclusion.

"And why should I be angry at you for drivin' me off when it led me to my family?"

"That's charitable of you to say that, but it doesn't address the issue of your mother."

Dad's eyes have been glistening; now, there are tears on his cheeks and he frowns. As I study him, really look closely, the truth hits me. He would change things if he could. He would bring her back, but he can't. I can hate him or I can love him, but neither will change the past.

The door opens and Nellie returns, followed by Squat, who's gazing at the ceiling and shaking a fist at some imaginary foe. I tell Dad, "We happen to have a savant on relationships available for consultation."

Dad raises his eyebrows.

Turning to Squat, I say, "Squat, I wanna ask you something."

He stops shaking his fist and looks at me expectantly. "Okay."

"My father has apologized for bein' mean to me. What should I do?"

Squat smiles broadly. "Lou say 'it better to be happy than mad'."

"Nellie?"

Nellie shrugs and says, "We have the most confusin' family I've ever seen; our daughter calls your ex-girlfriend 'Aunt Pam,' my best friend is someone whose father wanted you to marry her, Squat's like my brother and he's not even related to me, the Mafia think they're our old-maid aunts when they're really just busybodies, but bless their hearts, they're *our* busybodies. My entire family, except for my daughter, is made up of people I didn't know a coupla years ago."

She pauses to let all that sink in then turns to my father. "If you've *truly* stopped drinkin', come live with us. But so help me, Sam, if you start drinkin' again, or lift a finger in anger against *any* of my family, includin' your son, I'll personally throw you out on your ass."

Squat giggles, and declares, "Nellie say 'ass.'"

Nellie's gaze never leaves Dad. "I'll say a lot more if I ever find out you've hurt anyone in my family." She purses her lips several times. "But the truth is, my daughter could use a grandfather, and I could use a father-in-law."

She walks over to me and puts her arm around my waist.

"And Bob could use a father. From what I've heard, you owe him that." She pulls me tight and glances up at me.

I kiss her forehead, and Squat pleads, "Come live in *our* house, Sam."

Dad swallows. "If I do, it's not permanent. I don't want to sell my house."

"Then, rent it out," Nellie says. "If you wanna move back, you can. If I throw your a…" She peeks at Squat, who listens expectantly. "If I throw you out, you'll have someplace to go."

"The doctor says I can't go up and down stairs."

Nellie glances at me then says, "We can enclose the back porch, make it a bedroom with a great view of the field behind us. The bathroom is right next door."

He looks at me, a pitiful stare with none of the fury I used to see in his eyes. "How do you feel about this?"

I shrug. "Everyone wants you to come. I guess you should."

Nellie's arm is still around my waist. She continues to look at Dad but pinches my side, making me jump.

"I *want* you to come," I add, and she pats the spot where she pinched me.

———

We get Dad back to Waynedale and settle him into our bedroom on the first floor. Until we can get the porch finished out, he will sleep there.

———

The next night, Sally joins us for supper. Afterward, she starts clearing the table, but Nellie tells her, "Go look at the porch with Bob, and have him tell you what we're plannin' to do."

We walk down the hall from the dining room and stand in

the doorway while I tell her of our plans for making it into a bedroom.

Sally says, "While you're at it, you can fix that godawful trim around the door."

"I don't think so."

"Why not?"

"It's one of the things that help me remember your father."

She shakes her head. "Geez, you are sentimental."

"Yeah, well, that's the way it is, so get used to it."

"I don't have to get used to it; Nellie does."

We both examine the trim, then she turns to look at me, and I see tears in her eyes. "You're right," she says. "That trim reminds me of Papa." She puts her arm around my waist and her head on my shoulder.

I lean over and kiss the top of her head, and we stand there, admiring the mismatched wood like it was the *Mona Lisa*.

———

Nellie and I move into my old room on the second floor, next to Squat's. He's not used to my door being closed, but after he walks in a few times without knocking, Nellie starts locking it.

"Why can't I come in?" he asks through the door one night when we were feeling romantic and went to bed early.

"Because Nellie is a woman, and you're a man, and she needs her privacy," I reply, not wanting to lose the moment.

"You not locked out and you a man."

Nellie snorts into the crook between my neck and shoulder and says, "Yeah, Bob, explain that."

Ignoring Nellie's comment, I call out, "We're married."

"I family."

He wiggles the doorknob again.

Nellie barely contains her laughter.

"Yes, you are, Squat. But even in families, there is privacy. You didn't walk into Steve and Lou's room when their door was closed did you?"

"We Bob and Squat. We mechanics."

"I promise you, I am not workin' on a car."

Nellie holds me tightly against her and starts making sounds like a motor turning over.

I reach down and swat her butt. The sound of a hand smacking flesh rings out, drawing a scowl from Nellie and a question from beyond the door.

"What that?"

"Nothin', Squat. I just had to swat a mosquito."

Nellie sticks her tongue out at me, and I wag my finger at her.

I *really* want to get back to what we were doing, so I say, "Let's make a deal, Squat. If the door's open, you can come in, but you have to agree to leave when Nellie or I ask, okay?"

"I watch TV with Sam. He a man and I a man." We hear him walk downstairs.

"I think you may have lost your fan club to Sam," Nellie says.

Before I can reply she asks, "And why'd you have to swat me so hard?" Twisting on the bed, she strains to see over her shoulder. "Did it leave a mark?" she asks.

"No," I tell her, "but this will." I lean forward with my mouth open, prepared to bite where I swatted, but she shrieks and jumps up. There's nothing like a good chase.

———

Thirty minutes later, I go downstairs to check on Dad and Squat. Dad sits up in bed, asleep, and Squat is in a chair, dozing. When I turn off the TV, Squat wakes up.

"Time for bed," I tell him.

"Nellie different, isn't she?" he asks as we start up the steps.

"What do you mean?"

"She look different than us."

"That's 'cause she's a woman."

"Yeah," agrees Squat. "She pretty."

"Yes, she is," I say as we climb the steps.

"I like her a lot," Squat adds as he goes into his room.

"I'm glad. Goodnight."

When I go into the room, I tell Nellie, "Sam didn't steal my fan club. You did."

But she's already asleep, a smile on her face. I shoo Lou's cats out of the room and listen to the quiet of the house.

Steve was right; things have worked out just fine.

Chapter Twenty-Seven

Summer is quickly becoming fall, and we're enjoying one of our last meals before Jenny heads back to Louisville for her sophomore year. As he passes me some vegetables, Dad asks, "I've got an AA meeting tomorrow evening. Can you take me?"

"Yes."

"It's in E-town."

I stop loading my plate with beans, spoon in mid-air. "Why do you need to go so often? And to E-town, no less. That's thirty minutes there; your meetin' lasts an hour, then thirty minutes back. No sense in me comin' home. I'll blow the whole evenin'." I look at Nellie, hoping for some support, but if she heard me, she ignores it.

Dad says, "I'm tired of going to Grove's Point. Same alcoholics, same stories. I'd like to hear from some different drunks."

"Yeah, but you told me once that you haven't had a drink since mom died. Why go so much?"

"If you drank, you'd understand. It's a struggle every day.

All it would take is one drink and I'd end up right back where I was."

"In more ways than one," Nellie tells him, handing the plate of her homemade bread to Squat. "You start drinkin' again, and I'm buyin' you a one-way bus ticket to Chicago."

"See there?" says Dad. "I need all the help I can get, or the boss sends me packing."

Nellie smiles and points at him, but I roll my eyes. If Dad's ever sent packing, it'll be me who does it. He and Nellie have become thick as thieves, always planning something that he and I should do together.

Nellie points at Jenny and says, "Goes for you, too. If you don't wanna live by our rules, you don't have to live here."

Jenny's head snaps up. "What'd I do?"

"That boy that's been sniffin' round you, Wayne. He doesn't work and he's not in school. Last time we met y'all for supper, he smelled like a brewery. What is it you see in him?"

"He's sooo handsome, and he's always in a good mood. He's a great singer, he's strong, and he—"

"Drinks like a fish," Nellie finishes.

I frown at her, and Nellie asks, "You gotta problem?"

"You're goin' after everyone tonight. Who put a burr under your saddle?"

Squat's head swivels from Nellie to me, like he's watching a tennis match.

"Jenny needs to see the problems she'll be facin' down the road," Nellie says.

Jenny says, "Well, maybe if you weren't so hard on him, he wouldn't have to mellow out when he's gonna be with you." We don't see Jenny the Rebel much anymore, but when we do, it's usually male-related.

"He can leave 'mellow' in Louisville," says Nellie. "He brings it here and he won't be stayin' long."

"Have Wayne talk to me," Dad urges. "I can let him know how bad it is to be an alcoholic."

"He isn't an alcoholic. Why are y'all gangin' up on him?" Jenny shoves her chair back and storms up the stairs.

————

Dad has always enjoyed fall colors, and this season is especially beautiful. The nearby hills are spectacular, so I've taken him for rides several times to see nature at its best. When we return, he always thanks me.

"I can't believe it," I tell Nellie one evening as we prepare for bed. "He's never thanked me for anything before."

The porch has been converted to a bedroom for Dad, and Nellie and I have moved back into ours. She is sitting at the mirror in her nightgown and pauses from brushing her hair to focus on my reflection in the mirror.

"People change," she says, resting the brush in her lap. "That's what Sally and I keep tellin' you."

"I didn't think Dad could." I walk over behind her and we stare at each other's reflection.

"Why? You don't think you change? Trust me, Honey, you're changin' too."

She raises the brush and returns her gaze to her reflection, but only gets two strokes through her hair before I ask, "How do you think I've changed?"

Again looking at my reflection, she asks, "Are you happy?"

"Sure. At least, you tell me I am."

She rolls her eyes.

"So I'm happy, right?"

She points her hairbrush at my reflection and purses her lips.

I nod vigorously and say, "Right. I'm happy."

"See there? And your father's livin' in the next room. Ever think that would happen when you moved here?"

"No." I smile.

"And you stay 'round here so you can help him and be here when Squat gets home. Ever thought you'd be happy not workin'?"

"I help out when Jacob gets backed up."

"Yeah, you work some, but you no longer think you're a failure if you don't work, do you?"

"No," I admit.

"Those are some pretty major life changes. That's growth."

I step behind her and put my arms around her shoulders, my hands on her breasts. "I'm growin' right now. You wanna do somethin' about it?"

Mischief paints her face, and she slaps the brush down. "Race you to the bed," she squeals, jumping up.

I love an enthusiastic woman.

———

Despite her mother's warning, Jenny takes up with Wayne as soon as she moves back to Louisville. He's similar to Snake, the boy from her high school days, except Jenny is more under Wayne's spell. All she sees are the muscles, the curly hair, and the band he says he's going to start.

She takes him to meet Aunt Pam, hoping Pam will see all the things she herself likes about Wayne. They're probably not even out of Chicago before Pam calls.

Nellie answers the phone in the living room then tells me to get on the extension in the kitchen.

"She's really serious about this boy, and he's no good," Pam says.

"I know," agrees Nellie, "but what should we do?"

"Kill him with kindness. If you do, he'll show his true colors."

"What do you mean?" Nellie asks.

"Welcome him into your house, but don't criticize him. Before you know it, she'll be comparing him to Bob. Wayne exudes danger, and he's good-looking. Have you heard him sing? Really good. That's all Jenny thinks about. You can't tell her he's not right for her; she has to see it on her own."

"I don't know," Nellie worries. "Bob, do you think this'll work?"

"I agree with Pam. Let's pull him close. Maybe Jenny spots his true colors; maybe he changes. Somebody really smart told me one time that people do change."

"Hmmm," Nellie ponders. She doesn't sound convinced, but after we hang up, she and I talk about Pam's suggestion. She finally agrees to try but insists that I do the legwork. The next day, I call Jenny and invite her to bring Wayne for a visit.

———

The following Friday, they arrive in Jenny's car, two hours late. Squat, Dad, and I are just about to abandon the porch for the warmth of the inside when they finally pull up, Wayne behind the wheel.

He's tall, tan, and has a mass of dark curly hair, with a three-day beard. A sleeveless T-shirt, despite the chill in the air, accentuates his muscular shoulders, and I know from their bulk that he lifts weights. His dirty knees show below filthy, cut-offs, and when he opens his mouth, I see a gold-cap displayed prominently on one of his front teeth. He stumbles getting out of the car, and walks behind some bushes, fumbling with his pants.

"Not there," Jenny tells him.

"But I gotta pee."

"There's a bathroom inside," Jenny tells him, grabbing his arm, and pulling him and the guitar he's carrying toward the house.

As they approach, I hear Wayne ask, "Who's the retard?"

Squat immediately goes into the house, muttering, "I no retard."

As the door closes behind him, I hear Dad say, "Squat's a good judge of character."

I take a deep breath and wonder if Nellie's instincts are better than Pam's, but then I hear Jenny say, "That's my Uncle Squat. Don't call him that."

I glare at Wayne then look at Jenny.

When our eyes connect, she shrugs. The muscles in her neck are twitching. I decide that since she's taking up for Squat, I will bite my tongue. For now.

"Sorry we're late," Jenny says with no explanation as they mount the steps.

"What's up, old man?" Wayne greets me. "How they hangin'?"

I turn my head slightly, pretending I didn't hear his slurred, crude attempt at humor. Jenny struggles with her suitcase, so I take it from her, offer it to Wayne, and say, "I'll show you where to put this."

"First I gotta pee," he says, stumbling a little and ignoring the suitcase. He laughs mirthlessly, as if the need to relieve himself is both funny and serious at the same time.

"This way," says Dad, taking Wayne by the arm.

"No," he argues, jerking his arm away from Dad. "I said I gotta pee."

"That's where I'm taking you," says Dad, with more

patience than he showed me my entire three years of high school.

After they go inside, I ask Jenny, "Have you had supper? We waited for you."

"You should've eaten. Wayne couldn't wait, so we ate in Louisville."

"I can't believe you let him drive in the condition he's in."

"What's wrong with him?" Jenny asks.

"What's *not* wrong with him? You don't notice that he's stoned, or drunk, or maybe both?"

Jenny clenches her teeth and puts her hand on my forearm. "Please, don't tell Mom," she pleads.

I snort. "I'm not gonna have to, she'll spot it as soon as she sees him."

Just then, Nellie comes out the door. She's pumping her arms as she walks toward us, and there's steam coming out of her ears. "I can't believe it," she fumes. "He walked into the kitchen, smacked me on the butt, picked up a bag of chips, said, 'I'm goin' to sleep,' and walked upstairs. He's drunker'n a popcorn fart."

Jenny rushes inside and I hear her call, "Wayne!" as she runs up the stairs.

"I swear," says Nellie, "You put a pair of odor eaters in that boy's shoes, an' in three days all you'd have left was a guitar and a gold-capped tooth."

I spend the next fifteen minutes convincing Nellie that we have to stick to the plan.

———

The next day, Wayne sleeps until one in the afternoon. It's a warm fall day, and Jenny and I are in the middle of changing the oil in her car when he walks out on the porch, and shouts, "Hey, Jenny, fix me something to eat."

"I can't right now," she calls back to him. "Wait until I'm finished."

"I'm hungry."

"Is it okay if I go fix him some lunch?" Jenny asks me.

"If that's what you wanna do. I can run by Jacob's. I've got some things I can do there. You and Wayne can finish changing your oil after he eats." I slide out from under the car on my creeper.

"You're kiddin', right? He doesn't have a clue 'bout changin' oil."

"Maybe he should learn." I start to walk away.

Wayne is leaning on the porch rail. He yells, "Let's go, Jenny. I'm hungry."

I stop and stare back at Jenny.

"He's pretty needy," she says then smiles. "But I enjoy bein' needed."

"Even for things he should be able to do for himself? Hell, Jenny, Squat can fix his own lunch."

She looks at me, blankly.

"I taught you to change the oil in your car when we first bought it. You don't need my help, but I enjoy workin' on it with you. If you're gonna fix him lunch, I'm gonna do some things I need to do, and you can finish up."

Wayne starts walking toward us. "*Come on*, Jenny, what's the hold-up?"

"Just a minute," she calls out.

"Do you enjoy bein' needed that much?" I ask.

When she starts to respond, I tell her, "That was a rhetorical question. I'll be back in two hours. If you wanna wait until I get back, we'll finish this together, or you can finish it yourself. Maybe you should teach Wayne to do it."

He walks up as I say this and snorts. "Why do I need to know how to change the oil? Jenny's got plenty of money to pay somebody."

"You can do that," I say, "but then you never get the satisfaction of a job well-done."

"I got better things to do."

"Like what, sleepin' all day?" I set out for Jacob's.

———

Upon my return, I'm about a half-block away from the house when I hear the sound of a guitar, and a voice as good as anything I've heard on the radio recently. I can't make out the song it is singing, but I'm drawn to it. It's a slow ballad, mournful and lovely.

Everyone is gathered on the porch, and Wayne is singing. Jenny said he had a good voice, but I had no idea it was this good.

He finishes the song as I come up the steps, and immediately launches into a rousing version of "Are You from Dixie?" which allows him to show off his guitar skills. I'm impressed.

Dad and Squat are in one swing, with Nellie and Jenny in the other. They both scoot toward the ends, leaving me a place between them. When Wayne finishes, everyone applauds.

He looks at me, and says, "Hey, old man. Did you get the car runnin'?"

"I did. Those are some fine licks you were doin'."

"Nothin' special," he replies. "That's the kind of stuff people 'round these parts wanna hear. I prefer Nirvana."

"Who're they?" Nellie asks.

Wayne shows her a toothy smile. "They're out of the Pacific Northwest. Part of the grunge movement. That's why I dress like I do; I wanna be part of it, too."

"You don't have far to go," Dad vents as he gets up and walks in the house.

Wayne scowls.

"Don't mind him," I say. "He still believes music starts and ends with Sinatra. Play something else."

"Nah," Wayne says, standing and stretching. He's still got on the same sleeveless T-shirt he was wearing when they arrived, and now that I don't smell the booze on him, I can pick up a very strong scent of body odor. "I need a nap before supper." He heads in the house and I hear him lumber up the stairs.

"I told you he had a great voice," Jenny says.

"He may have a great voice, but if he takes a nap without takin' a shower first, I'm gonna have to burn the sheets," Nellie complains.

Jenny frowns, waves a hand dismissively toward her mother, and heads inside.

———

The heat hangs around into the evening, so when we finish supper and Sally leaves, Squat and I sit in our swing on the porch, with Dad in the other one.

Wayne, a bored expression on his face, drops into a rocking chair opposite us and drapes a leg over the arm. The material on his shorts is very loose, allowing, no, demanding, that I notice that he's commando. We can hear the low murmur of Nellie and Jenny in the living room, talking about classes she needs to take to graduate.

"So," I ask, carefully avoiding the view up his pants leg, "Why aren't you studying music?"

"Nothin' they can teach me." He sticks a finger in his

mouth and appears to be digging at some food stuck between his teeth.

"I imagine not," Dad says. I laugh, but Wayne doesn't understand sarcasm.

"Are you lookin' for a job?" I ask.

"I'm gonna start a band," he mentions, vaguely.

"Okay," I say, hoping to sound supportive. "You've got the talent for it. What are your goals?"

"My goal is to have no goals." He smirks at what he perceives is a clever retort.

"You need job," says Squat. "I have job."

"What do you know? You're just a retard."

I jump up out of my swing.

When I do, Wayne pulls his leg off the arm of his chair and puts his foot on the floor.

Placing a hand on each arm of his rocker, I lean toward him. "Listen," I growl, "you are talkin' to my best friend. You are Jenny's guest, and I will cut you a lot of slack because of that, but I will not allow you to talk to him that way. Do you understand me?"

He glares back, so I repeat, "Do you understand me? If you don't, I want you out of this house."

He says, "Get out of my face." Putting his hands on my shoulders, he pushes me.

I stumble back.

He stands up, and I realize how much taller than me he is. I'm still off-balance when he shoves me, again. The last thing I see as I fall backward down the steps is Squat lunging toward Wayne.

Chapter Twenty-Eight

I hear someone say, "I think he's comin' around." It's Nellie's voice, but the three figures next to my bed are blurry.

"Where am I?" I ask.

Someone takes hold of my hand. I blink my eyes several times. It's Nellie. She squeezes it gently as she reaches to soothe my forehead. "In the hospital. You've been unconscious for two days."

I groan. As my eyes begin to focus, I recognize Jenny and Squat, each looking over one of Nellie's shoulders. Squat has a black eye and the whole side of his face is bruised.

"What happened?"

"You got your ass kicked." My father's voice comes from the other side of the room. When I glance in that direction, I see him sitting in a chair, Sally next to him.

"I'm so sorry, Bob," says Jenny, "I didn't realize what a punk he is."

"What happened to you, Squat?"

"Squat's the hero," Nellie says, turning to the side and pulling him forward. "Wayne knocked you off the porch, and

Squat took him on. We heard Squat yellin' at him and came out the door just in time to see Wayne punch him."

Squat shakes his fist at the ceiling and mutters something unintelligible.

"Where's he now?"

"He in jail with bad people," Squat growls.

"I'm so sorry, Bob," Jenny repeats.

"Is anyone else hurt?" I ask.

Assured that no one else is, I look at Jenny and say, "Your mother is a pretty good judge of character. And you're not."

"Next guy that asks me out, I'm gonna ask him if he can change the oil in his car. If he can't, I'm not goin' out with him," Jenny says.

"Man, I've got a headache," I mutter.

Nellie grimaces. "The doctor says you'll be all right but will have to take it easy for about two weeks. You're lucky. You could have easily broken your neck. What did you say to him, anyway?"

"I don't remember."

"Well, what did he say to you?"

"I don't remember that, either."

"I do," says Squat. "He call me retard, and Bob call me best friend."

"That's right," says Dad. "When he knocked you down the steps, Squat went after him like a yellow jacket protecting his nest."

Squat beams and says, "Bob my best friend, too," as he pats my arm.

"You're both fools takin' on a college-age man. If either of you does that again..." Nellie's voice trails off. She turns her back on us and appears to dab at her eyes. Sally rushes to her with a hug.

"Yes, ma'am," says Squat.

"Yes, ma'am," I add.

––––––

Three days later, I'm discharged from the hospital. For the next week, if Squat is not helping my father get around, he is hovering over me. About the time his face heals, Jacob calls to check on us.

"How's the tag team doin'?" he asks.

"I had a headache for a week. Hope to be back in soon, though."

"I figured it might be a while when Squat told me what happened. Says you fought Wayne when Wayne called him a retard."

"Wasn't much of a fight. Just me flyin' off the porch, although I'm told my face really gave his fist a workout."

"Squat came by here to tell me about it. Looks like he took a lickin', too."

"That son of a bitch hit him. Can you imagine anyone hittin' Squat?"

"Makes no sense. Tell Squat I called. I'll see you whenever you can come back."

"Thanks, Jacob."

I hang up the phone then walk into the living room, where Squat and Dad had been talking. They're both dozing now, so I tiptoe out and sit on the porch.

––––––

For the next few weeks, one or the other of the Mafia comes by every few days. We've been seeing a lot of Clare since Dad moved in. She comes by to visit twice a week, and they go up to Sally's café for lunch on Wednesdays. Clare calls it their "mid-week, mid-day, mid-life fling." I don't mention that they haven't been middle-aged for years. As for Dad, I've never seen him this happy, and I realize how miserable he must have been when he was drinking.

Clare tells the rest of the Mafia that she's their scout; she's going to find out where Sam keeps all his friends then bring them back for the others. I don't tell them that might take a while.

The first time Clare stops by after I get home, she chews me out royally, ending with, "You should know better than to put Squat in danger."

"I didn't intend for any of this to happen," I reply.

"Well, next time, think, Mr. Big City." She pauses for a moment then pushes a bony finger into my temple. "Think," she says.

I promise Clare that I won't put Squat in jeopardy again.

She thrusts her jaw toward me and fusses, "I would hope not," as if that settles all the world's problems.

Jenny wants to stay in Waynedale to help Nellie, since she's got me to look after, in addition to Dad and Squat, but Nellie won't hear of it.

"You can't be missin' that many classes, young lady," Nellie tells her the following Wednesday, which is the first day I join the rest for a meal in the dining room.

"Don't worry," Jenny says, as she sets the table. "I've talked to all my professors. They said they'd help me make up what I've missed."

"Your mother's right," I tell her. "I'm able to get around now, and you need to be in class."

All through supper, she lobbies to stay, so when we finish clearing the table, Nellie and I practically carry her and her suitcase to the car, where she breaks away to run back to Dad. As she hugs him, I hear her say, "Thanks for everything."

When she returns to where her mother and I wait, I want to ask what it is she thanked him for, but before I can, she starts apologizing again for bringing Wayne home.

"The only thing I ask is that you be more careful in pickin' your friends," I tell her. "Trust your mother's judgment a little more. I can't handle gettin' beat up."

Nellie pats me on the back then leans on the car door and stares in at Jenny. "Have you talked to Wayne?" she asks. She sounds like an onlooker asking the bomb squad if a nuclear device lying in the street has been defused.

"No, and I don't intend to," Jenny says. "He asked me to come bail him out when they were haulin' him off. I was gonna, but Sam…"

Nellie pats Jenny's arm and says, "I know."

My mouth opens to ask what they mean, but before I can, Jenny says, "Take care of ol' hard-headed Mr. Big City." She smiles at me as the car starts moving. Sticking her hand out the window, she waves at us until she's out of sight.

———

Even though she has refused counseling since she was abused, Jenny starts seeing a therapist in Louisville. It's almost six months before she brings a man around, but he is a definite improvement. Still, we don't often see anyone more than once. After a second visit from one I particularly like, Nellie tells me not to get excited.

"He's not the right one," she states.

"Is it possible," I ask at supper the night after Jenny and the young man leave, "that Jenny will never find a man good enough to get your approval?"

"What's that supposed to mean?" Nellie scrunches her eyes together.

"Nothin' bad, just that mothers tend not to think anyone stacks up favorably for their children."

"That's more for sons," she retorts.

"Yep," agrees Dad. "I remember the first time you brought a girl home. You must've been a junior in high school. Anyway, your mother was scared to death you would run off with 'that tramp.' Nice young lady, as I remember," Dad says, chuckling.

"I want Jenny to be happy," Nellie says, as we start clearing the table. "This fella yesterday, what's his name? Chuck? Sure, he was nice, but Jenny didn't have that glow she gets when she's really happy. I think she's just markin' time."

"I mark time on calendar," Squat says, alluding to the fact that every night, just before going to bed, he takes a marker to the calendar on the kitchen wall and puts a large X through the day just ended. It is something he was doing when I moved here and he hasn't missed a day, yet.

"And a fine job you do of it, too," Dad tells him.

Squat holds his arms up, palms skyward, and says, "Ta da!"

"I don't think Jen's gonna meet anyone at school," Nellie says. "I think her future's in Chicago."

"Chaaago," Squat blurts then smiles at me.

"Lots of good, young men from Chicago," Dad says. "Present company excluded of course," he adds, chucking me on the arm.

———

For the next year, Jenny is very selective in who she brings home, but Nellie is right. We never see Chuck again. Each time she has someone home, however, she calls Nellie and me sometime during the next few days to ask what we think. We are as positive as we can be and are helped along by her not choosing to bring home any more Waynes or Snakes.

———

When the following summer rolls around and Jenny graduates, she heads off to Chicago alone. Pam has promised to help her find a job. I hope Pam doesn't give Jenny any dating advice.

———

The summer of 1994 is hot, muggy, and long. Even with the air conditioning, Dad is always uncomfortable. In late August, exhausted from the heat, he asks me to take him to Chicago for a few days. Nellie and Squat decide it's time to see Jenny, so I take my car to Jacob's to check it over before we go.

Satisfied that everything is shipshape, I eat lunch with Squat then tell him I'll see him in a few hours.

"Tell Sam, I get home I beat him," Squat says, shaking a fist in mock anger. He and Dad play a game of checkers every afternoon, with much shouting and bragging, although in the end Dad always snatches defeat from the jaws of victory, and Squat struts around all evening proud as a peacock.

The house is quiet when I get there. Dad went back to bed after breakfast, something he doesn't normally do. I knock quietly then open the door just enough to see him still in bed. But as I turn to leave, I realize something's not right. I look back; his eyes are not totally closed, just drooping a little.

"Dad?" I say, walking toward him. When I touch his cold hand, I realize that he and Squat have played their last game of checkers.

I sit in a chair and look at him for a few minutes, trying to figure out why he couldn't stop drinking until my mother was gone. The last few years had been pleasant, but they'd lacked something. My mother.

I was on my own from age seventeen to thirty-five, then I met Steve and Lou. Just as I reconnected with Dad, I lost them. In the four and a half years he lived with us, he became a checkers buddy for Squat, a companion for Clare, a father-in-law to Nellie, and a proud grandfather to Jenny. Eventually, to my occasional chagrin and Nellie's constant delight, he was a father to me. Nevertheless, there is no great sense of loss.

But, as it so often turns out, there are things Nellie knows that I don't.

————

I've already called the funeral home when Nellie comes in from the grocery. Her immediate concern is Squat.

"He's gonna be devastated," she says. Then, putting her arms around me, she asks, "Are you all right?"

I nod.

I'm relieved that the men from the funeral home have left with Dad's body before Squat gets home. I don't want him to see Dad being carried out. I am sitting in the living room looking at the checkerboard table when I hear Squat coming up the steps. Dad would usually be waiting there for him, and they would start trash talking as Squat came in the door.

He waves his hand at me, then shouts, "Where Sam?" when he doesn't see Dad at the table.

I give him a minute to realize Sam doesn't seem to be home before I tell him.

The words, "Sam died" are barely out of my mouth when Squat drops into a chair. A moan starts way down inside of him, and as it gets louder, it becomes recognizable as "Nooooo!" He puts his face in his hands and rocks forward.

I kneel next to him and put my hand on the arm of the chair. "I'm so sorry, Squat."

He raises his face and says, "Steve don't need him in Heaven. I need him *here*." He puts his face back in his hands and cries, something I never saw him do when Steve and Lou were killed. His face, what I can see between his fingers, is anguished, as if his losses, his parents, Steve and Lou, and now my father, have all hit him at once.

In a moment, he rolls out of the chair and falls to his knees on the floor, leaning against me. I'm not sure what to do since he normally doesn't want anyone touching him. Nevertheless, I reach out and put my hand on his shoulder. Feeling him lean against me harder, I put my other arm around him, and hold him tight as he cries. I start crying, too, but I'm crying for Squat.

Chapter Twenty-Nine

Sally and Clare go with us to Chicago for the funeral, and for the first time, Clare seems hopelessly adrift. Mac Gilmore and people from the neighborhood are there, and I introduce her to everyone as Dad's girlfriend, which pleases her.

"And how are you related?" Mac asks Sally.

"She's my sister from another mother," I inform him, and as Nellie and Sally nod, he smiles.

Pam and Jenny arrive a short time later, Jenny with a young man whom we haven't met but have heard about.

"I promise he won't beat you up," Jenny had told me a few weeks earlier when we first talked about him.

"High praise, considering some of the guys you've brought home," I retort. "But I'm not worried. Squat's got my back."

Squat was passing through the kitchen and heard me say that. "Yeah, I got you back," he said, loud enough for Jenny to hear him over the phone.

"Tell Uncle Squat I said hi," Jenny said. "I want you to come to Chicago and meet him. He works in computers. There's this new thing startin' up called the Internet. Bill says it's gonna let people link up computers. I don't understand it, but he tells me the things we will be able to do will be amazin'. Can you believe it, Bob? I'm goin' out with a computer nerd."

"Good. Most computer nerds have lousy left hooks."

"I told you, he won't beat you up."

———

Now we are in Chicago, and although this is not how I wanted to meet Bill, he is as nice as Jenny made him out to be.

"It's very nice of you to come for the visitation, especially since you never met my father or me," I say when Jenny introduces us.

"I wanted to be here for Jenny," he replies.

Just as he says that, Jenny interrupts, saying, "There're some people from my work. Excuse me," and walks off to greet three women who are scrutinizing the crowd for someone they recognize. Their faces all show relief when they see her.

"Jenny's told me quite a bit about her family history," Bill continues. "She's extremely grateful that you and your father have been in her life for the last few years."

"I'm the one who should be grateful," I say, putting my arm around Nellie's shoulder. "Jenny, her mother, and Squat have put meanin' in my life."

"Before we all start cryin'," Nellie says, as she dabs at her eyes, "when do you think y'all will be comin' to Waynedale?"

"Right now, I've got an awful lot going on. It'll probably be Christmas before we get there."

Nellie asks Pam, "What about you? Can you come at Christmas, too?"

"Sure."

"Bring a friend," says Nellie, not just being polite. She and

Pam are now friends, but she still prefers to see Pam distracted by another man whenever we're together. I've learned to accept that Nellie has a jealous bone that runs from the heels of her feet to the top of her skull.

Squat is standing next to Nellie staring at the floor. Bill has been watching him, even as he talked to us. Now, however, he speaks to Squat.

"Squat, I understand you're quite a checkers player."

Squat looks up when he hears his name but shakes his head. "No checkers. Only with Sam." He turns and stares at Dad's casket, which we've kept closed to avoid upsetting him.

I smile at Bill and mouth, "Thank you," but nothing we say draws Squat into the conversation.

Clare is just as morose. Since we left Waynedale, she has communicated with us through a series of grunts and growls.

———

The day after the funeral, it turns cool, even by Chicago's standards. As we head back to Waynedale, I worry about how subdued Squat is, and Clare goes the whole trip without saying a word. She simply nods her head when we ask if she wants to stop.

———

No one dares touch the checkerboard in the living room, but one day a few weeks later, it is gone. When I ask Nellie about it, she shakes her head and shrugs. A few hours later, though, I hear noise from inside what used to be Dad's room.

We've turned it back into an informal gathering area, the way it was before Dad moved in. The door is slightly ajar and

I peer in through the crack. The checkers game is set up on a game table, and Squat is sitting on one side of it.

Suddenly, he says, "Stupid move, Sam. You know better." He picks up a red checker and jumps three black ones. Then, he moves around to the other side of the table and in a darn good imitation of my father, says, "Gee, Squat, you play good." He moves a black checker one square.

Moving back to the red side of the table, he says, in his own voice, "Yay, I gonna win again. Don't worry, Sam; you win someday."

The red checkers are spread out all over the board, and after he moves one of them, he returns to "Sam's" side. Using Dad's voice, complete with Chicago accent, he says, "Now you done it." Picking up a black checker, he starts moving it around the board. Every time he comes down there's another red checker to jump until he has swept the board clean of all red checkers.

"You win, Sam!" he yells. "Sam, you win!"

———

At Christmas, we have an almost full house. Pam doesn't bring anyone, but she, Jenny, and Bill drive down Thursday night for Christmas on the following Sunday.

As soon as we are alone, Pam reveals to Nellie and me, "I think this is the guy for Jenny. I think if this week goes well, she'll be getting a ring, maybe on Valentine's Day."

"What do you think of him?" Nellie asks, looking up from a casserole she's preparing for tomorrow's dinner while Pam and I keep her company.

"I think you're going to be very happy," Pam tells us, reaching out to rescue a carrot before Nellie drops it into the casserole.

"We're sorry you couldn't bring anyone," I tell Pam as I open a bottle of wine and pour three glasses.

She finishes chewing the carrot then says, "No need to feel sorry for me. I might be getting a ring next year, too."

"Ohhhhh," Nellie squeals. "This is so exciting! Who is he?"

"A doctor I met in Chicago. After one date, I quit seeing everybody else."

Not even glancing up from the dish she's preparing, Nellie points a finger toward me and says, "I'm warnin' you, Bob. Not one word."

"Ouch," I say, and they both look at me questioningly. "I bit my tongue."

"Cute," says Pam.

"When do we get to meet him?" Nellie asks, ignoring me and carrying the now-finished casserole to the refrigerator.

"I'm almost positive we'll be coming next summer."

"Why will you be comin' next summer?" I ask, opening the refrigerator for Nellie.

"Because, father of the bride, I think there will be a wedding here that I'll be attending."

When Nellie hears this, she sits down, a solemn expression on her face. "I wasn't sure I'd ever see her with somebody decent."

"Here's to Jenny and her future," says Pam, raising her glass in a toast.

"Oh, I've got to call Clare," says Nellie after drinking to Jenny. "She really hasn't been herself since your father died."

"She's definitely in mournin'," I agree.

"Well, it's a good thing someone is grievin' for him," Nellie scolds me. Turning to Pam, she adds, "I don't understand it, Pam. His own father and he hasn't cried hardly any. Just a little when we told Squat Sam was dead."

"I thought you and your dad made peace," Pam says.

"We did, but come on, we were apart for all those years. I came to respect him, even like him, but I can't say there's a huge sense of loss. I think I miss the years we didn't have more than I miss him."

"That doesn't make sense," Nellie argues.

"He's a man," says Pam, dismissing me with a wave of the hand. "Why do you expect it to make sense?"

I can hear the direction this conversation is taking, so I make a tactical retreat and set out to find Squat. He's in Bill's room with Jenny and Bill. The TV is on, but no one is watching. Jenny and Bill are sprawled on the bed. Bill has his arm around Jenny, who is flipping through the pages of a gardening magazine. Squat is reciting to Bill stories about his work at Jacob's and our trip to "Chaago," and Bill, bless his heart, is hanging on Squat's every word.

As I walk in, Jenny glances up and asks, "Where are Mother and Aunt Pam?"

"Down in the kitchen drinkin' wine and waitin' for your Aunt Sally to come over. They think there's an event comin' next summer that they need to plan."

Jenny's eyes dance as she chirps, "Great." She unwraps herself from Bill, flips the magazine aside, and heads downstairs. Bill, meanwhile, gives me a puzzled look.

"What event next summer are they planning?" he asks.

I smile at him. "Just as soon as you need to know, they'll tell you."

"Oh," he says. He scratches his head but seems satisfied with that answer. "Okay."

Chapter Thirty

Jenny is twirling her hair around her index finger as we sit across from each other in the living room. It's a nervous habit that she inherited from her mother.

It's just the two of us. Bill took Squat to a car show in Elizabethtown, and Nellie went to the grocery. We've been talking about all the changes our family has been through during the last ten years, and I've been marveling at how much Jenny looks like Nellie, and how beautiful they both are.

But then Jenny goes quiet. As she twirls her hair, she squints her eyes and frowns, a sure sign she's troubled by something.

"What's on your mind, Sweetheart?" I ask her. She should be happy. Valentine's Day was the previous Tuesday, and yesterday she and Bill drove down to tell us officially that they are engaged, and for Jenny to show Nellie her engagement ring.

"I have a favor to ask."

"Okay."

"You've been about the best father a girl could ask for," she professes.

I wait for the "but."

"You've talked to me about things I didn't think I'd ever open up about; but there's one thing I've never talked to you about, and it's so strange, 'cause it's the one thing that probably relates to you more than anything else."

Her finger must be losing circulation the way she is pulling the hair tight around it. I tell myself to quit focusing on her finger and listen to what she's saying.

"What's that, Sweetheart?" I ask.

"My father, and the man that raped me."

If she wants to surprise me, she's doing fine. I hesitate, then ask, "Do you *want* to talk about them?"

She looks away. "No, but I owe you that if I'm gonna ask this favor of you."

"Then, can I suggest a ground rule?"

Jenny turns back to me and pulls the strand of hair taut.

"I'm not sure how awkward it is for you to talk about them, but if your hair-pullin' is any indication…"

She smiles and untwines her hair, which remains in a tight curl on the side of her head. Folding her hands in her lap, she says, "Let's hear the rule."

"We've gotten to understand each other pretty well over the years, haven't we?"

She nods and appears relieved that, for the moment, I'm doing the talking.

"Okay, let's agree that neither of us will be shocked by anything that is said, neither of us will think less of the other one for sayin' it, and both of us will still respect the other person when we're finished, regardless of what is said."

When I finish, she sighs, audibly. It's only then that I realize she's been holding her breath.

"Can I add one thing?" she asks, latching onto the strand of hair, again.

"Of course."

"We will both still love each other as a father and daughter love each other, regardless of what is said."

"I think that's perfect. The floor is yours."

She scans the ceiling, then the walls, and finally the floor. I think back to the night her mother told me of her rape. Nellie didn't know how to start and didn't begin to talk until I turned away from her. I decide to try it, again, so I gaze out the window, the same as I did with her mother. Then, I wait.

Sure enough, in a moment Jenny says, "I loved my father, but he was a no-good drunken bastard."

"So I've heard."

"I thought all men were like that. I thought you were all bastards and women loved you, anyway, 'cause we had no choice. When my father died, he had no insurance, no money, nothin' to leave Mom and me, but I loved him; I didn't think I had a choice. Then, Mom started datin' Simon."

This is the first time I've heard his name, but I know exactly who "Simon" is. I feel as if I've been smacked, and I flinch, despite my promise not to be shocked.

Jenny turns away as if nothing happened, and I think, "Lord, thank You for giving me this young lady to love."

She stands up, inserts her fingers into the back pockets of her jeans, paces the length of the room, then turns around and retraces her steps.

When she stops and sits down, I wait, again. After all, I gave her the floor.

"At first, I was flattered by what he said. Then, what he said became what he did. I knew it wasn't right, but in a way, it felt good."

Despite all my efforts, I must be showing some of the

anger that is raging in me because she immediately leans forward and pleads, "Please don't judge me. I was confused by how I should react. And I didn't know any better. After all, I was only eleven when it started."

Calming myself, I hold my hand up, and say, "I'm not judgin' you. I'm not shocked; I don't think less of you; I still respect you." I remember her addition and add, "You are my daughter, and I love you."

She seems mollified, but says, "This is so hard for me, but it's important that I tell you."

"I know." I hope that I can live up to my promise to contain my emotions, but what I'm hearing is making me very angry at a man who died before I even met Jenny.

She leans forward and puts her face in her hands. She stays that way for about fifteen-seconds then sits up. Placing her hands on her knees, she looks at me, almost defiantly. It is the same way she stared at me when her mother and I talked to her about Snake. Then, she was angry at all men; now, I perceive that she blames only Simon. I hope I'm right.

"So as I said, I knew it was wrong, but at the same time it felt good. I told my friends about it, even though Simon said it should be our secret. I didn't care that it was wrong; I wanted to brag about it. I had a man, not a boy, a man. But they knew it was wrong, and they told me it was. They told me I had to tell my mother, but I wouldn't."

She pauses for a minute, and a tear runs down her cheek. Her voice catches in her throat as she asks, "But I lured him, didn't I?" She looks at me when she asks this, and I see the question in her eyes, along with the tears.

"Do you want me to respond to that?" I ask. "I think you know the answer, but you *must* understand what I think about what you just said." I smack my hand on the arm of the couch and add, "What every man with a *shred* of decency would think about it."

"Tell me," she responds with tears in her eyes. She grabs a tissue out of her pocket, then continues. "I've got to know if you think I did anything wrong."

"*Hell, no!*" I thunder.

She blinks and appears stunned at the ferocity of my response.

"You did *nothing* wrong! Only in the perverted imagination of some sick, twisted, control freak does an eleven-year-old lure an adult into a sexual relationship."

She exhales and closes her eyes. When she opens them, she puts a tissue to her face. "I needed to hear that from you," she mutters then blows her nose. "It wasn't until after I started goin' to a counselor that I finally accepted that it wasn't my fault, but I needed to know that you didn't blame me." She pauses. Then, even though there are still tears running down her cheeks, she smiles and advises, "You can shut up and listen, again."

I laugh, and Jenny stands up, staring out the window with her back to me and continues. "So for a long time, this was my new image of men. I no longer thought they were just bastards; I thought they were perverted predators, too."

She turns to face me and for the first time I get a look from her that I get occasionally from her mother; she is staring into my soul.

"That included you," she says.

Neither of us speaks for a moment, then I slowly dip my head and reply, "I know." Actually, I didn't until now, but I have always suspected it, and I don't blame her in the least.

She stands facing me and says, "There has always been one constant in my life, even before I knew you. That is my mother. I pushed her away, but she never left my side. She protected me, *loved* me, regardless of what I threw at her. When you came along, she allowed you in on one condition, that you help her with me. I hated you both for that, just as much as I love you both for that now."

She walks over and sits on the chair across from me, again. She pulls her legs tightly together, leans forward, and folds her hands on top of her knees. "Without you to show me what a man should be, without Mother understandin' that I needed to be shown, and without her knowin' you were the right person to do it, I would have always thought the sex I was havin' with Snake and Wayne and all those other boys was love. I would have never fallen in love." As we look at each other, she pauses, then smiles. "Bill is wonderful. He's so good to me. I've told him all about this, by the way."

She laughs suddenly, and rocks back in the easy chair, a twinkle in her eyes. "He felt so bad for you when I told him how Mom made you tell me you wouldn't have sex with me, and I was such a jerk to you." Then, she becomes serious, again, and says, "Don't think I ever told you, but I'm sorry I was so hard on you."

I shake my head, still embarrassed after all these years. When I look back at her, she smiles at me so sweetly that I know she is my daughter, and I am her father. I have a child; her name is Jenny.

"So," she adds, "There you have what Bill and all his computer geek friends would call 'Jenny 1.0.' I hope this will help you understand the favor that I'm gonna ask of you."

A few minutes ago, Jenny sat before me twirling her hair around her fingers, barely able to face me. She didn't appear to be sure what she was going to say, or how she would say it. Now, her gaze bores in on me. She sits there, proud of herself, not asking, but demanding, that I be proud of her, too. And I am.

"What is this favor?"

Leaning back, she blurts, "Would you be terribly hurt if I didn't have you walk me down the aisle?"

I frown. "I'll definitely be disappointed, but it's your weddin'. What do you have in mind?"

She is so sure of herself that her eyes are two shining beacons, flashing her confidence at me from across the room. "I've always felt that the person that walks you down the aisle should be someone very influential in your life. You agree with that, don't you?"

"Yes, I do."

"It breaks with tradition, but…"

When she hesitates, I start smiling, pride swelling in my heart. "Say it, girl," I encourage her. "I think I know, but I want to hear you say it."

Her voice cracks as she says, "I want my mother to walk me down the aisle. Is that all right?"

"All right? Sweetheart, it's perfect. Your mother will be thrilled. I'm thrilled."

Jenny jumps from her chair and sits next to me on the couch. She throws her arms around my neck, plants a kiss on my cheek, and announces, "You're the best father anybody could have."

"That was my goal," I reply, returning the kiss to her cheek. "When are you gonna ask your mother?"

"Ask me what?" Nellie wonders as she walks into the room and sets her purse on a table.

"Oh, we didn't realize you were home," I say, glancing in her direction.

"I came in the back door. Ask me what?" she repeats, concern on her face.

Jenny looks at me. I nod, so she says, "I want you to walk me down the aisle when Bill and I get married."

Nellie sits in the chair occupied by Jenny until moments ago and extends her arm toward me. "But I thought you would want Bob."

"We've talked," says Jenny, taking my hand in hers and smiling at me. "We decided I should have the person who has been most influential in my life." She turns back to her mother. "We both agree that's you."

Nellie gawks at me, her eyes wide. "But it's just not done."

"Maybe it should be," I reply. "You have until September to practice."

———

"I need help," Squat says. He is standing in the hallway with cufflinks and studs for his tuxedo in his hand. I step outside the bedroom and pull the door closed so Nellie can finish dressing.

"Let me see what I can do." I hold my hand out for him to drop the accessories into it. "I haven't worn one of these in a while, but I think I remember how they go."

Squat drops them into my hand and says, "I never wear tuck. This what birds at zoo wear."

I laugh at his joke then go to work pulling his shirt together with the studs. When I'm finished, I follow him into the bathroom so he can see the effect in the mirror. He smiles at his reflection, and I tell him he is handsome.

"Yeah," he agrees. "I look good."

When Nellie comes out of the bedroom she asks, "How do I look?" I'm dumb, but even I know there is only one correct answer to that question.

"Wow," I say.

"Yeah," says Squat. "Wow!"

"You say that, but I took Jenny to the shop this mornin' to

fix her hair, and when we were finished, oh, my goodness. That girl is drop-dead gorgeous."

I laugh, prompting Squat to laugh along. "And where do you think she gets her drop-dead gorgeous looks?" I ask.

She waves her hand at me dismissively, but I can tell she's pleased.

———

When we get to the church, I realize I haven't been inside since Steve and Lou's funeral.

Steve. Once again, that man lives up to his reputation as a planner. When we first met with the rector to work out details for the wedding, he said, "Don't worry about a thing. Steve paid for it."

"What're you talkin' about?" I asked.

The rector shrugged, smiled awkwardly then said, "About a month before he died, Steve came in and made a nice donation to the church. He told me I probably wouldn't be seein' you and Nellie too much. Said you weren't really church people."

He paused, then said, "Actually, his exact words were, 'When it comes to churches, Bob's a little less dependable than the prodigal son, but Nellie and Jenny are gonna want Jenny to have a church weddin', so I'm gonna give you a contribution, and when it comes time, I expect you to give them the best darned weddin' this town's ever seen.'" Shaking his head and laughing, he said, "Only, Steve didn't say 'darned.'"

I never heard, nor did I ask, how much Steve had given the church, but any time Jenny asked for anything, the rector said, "We can do that."

As soon as we're inside, Nellie disappears to be with Jenny, leaving me to my own devices, so I greet our friends as they arrive. Except they're not friends, anymore. Now they're my family.

Clare and the Mafia are there, along with Pam and Sally. They gather with Squat and me, and, of course, Clare has something to say.

"Well, father of the bride, are you ready to walk your daughter down the aisle?" she asks.

"I think Jenny's got a little surprise for everyone."

"What?" asks Pam.

"Yeah," says Sally, "what's goin' on?"

"All in good time, my pretties," I say, in a voice I hope sounds like the Wicked Witch of the West.

Squat and Bill's brother escort Sally and Pam to the bride's family pew, then Squat returns for Clare, Jenny's honorary grandmother. After Bill's mother is escorted in, I walk down the aisle and sit next to Clare, who is staring at me. I check Squat, afraid he might be uncomfortable because of all the strangers, but he beams at me from where he's standing on the other side of Bill then waves.

"Where's Nellie?" Clare asks in a not-so-discreet whisper. I smile, but before I can make a wisecrack, the organist transitions into that most recognizable of all processionals, and everyone stands and turns to the church vestibule.

I hear an audible gasp as they see Nellie with Jenny. Then, as the congregation realizes what is happening, they begin to applaud.

Clare lets out a whoop, and slaps me on the back, shouting, "You're the best damned Yankee I've ever met."

I shake my head. "This was Jenny's call."

"It may have been Jenny's call, but I bet you told her you were okay with it," she says then grabs me around the shoulders and aims a kiss at my cheek. It lands on my ear, though, since I've turned to see Sally and Pam's reaction.

Pam gives me a thumbs up, and Sally mouths the word, "Yes," makes a fist, and brings it down in front of her body.

As the congregation settles down, I see that Jenny, in addition to her bouquet of flowers, has a single red rose. Nellie does, too. They draw closer and are both staring at me.

Nellie comes to me and hands me her rose. Then, she kisses me, and I hear an audible "aww."

When she steps back, Jenny holds her rose out to me.

I take it and hug her.

She kisses me on the cheek and says, "I love you," then pulls back so that we are face to face, about six inches apart, and adds, "Daddy."

I immediately decide that someday, no matter what I have to do to arrange it, and no matter how withered and dry they are, those two roses will be buried with me.

Nellie escorts Jenny to Bill then joins me. That's when it hits home; my family is about to get a little bit bigger.

Bill is going to be a good addition.

Chapter Thirty-One

We're on our way to another wedding. This one is in Chicago, and Nellie is almost as excited as two years ago when she walked Jenny down the aisle. I can tell that she's looking forward to Pam being married. Nellie told me on several occasions that she appreciated the kindness Pam has shown to Jenny, and the advice Pam gave us in helping Jenny through some rough patches, but the gratitude came with a heavy dose of jealousy.

For a long time, she didn't approve of the two of us talking privately, but after Pam started dating only Todd, Pam and I have had several one-on-one conversations. After each, Nellie asked what we talked about, and simply nodded when I told her, "The usual; family, happiness, work." She grinned, however, when I always added, "And how I made the right choice by stayin' in Waynedale."

Before Todd came on the scene, Nellie would cling to my arm when Pam was around, as if she might have to pull us apart; she quit doing that with Pam's engagement, and I no longer worry that Nellie's got a bucket of cold water around to throw on us. It was then, also, that she stopped making comments to me about Pam's appearance, like when she used to ask me if I noticed the crow's feet around Pam's eyes.

Now she says things like, "I think Pam looks ten years younger, now that she's engaged." With coaching from Sally, I've learned not to credit Pam's makeup, but to observe, "I guess that shows what finally meetin' the right person has done for her."

Nellie enjoys hearing that.

———

As we travel to Chicago, Squat rides in the back seat with Clare, cranking out no-look waves to the passing cars as if he has an inexhaustible supply. Sally and the three remaining Mafia follow in a separate car. Pauline Wilson died right after Jenny's wedding.

Before we left Waynedale, I asked Clare, "Are you sure you're up to this trip? Pam would understand if you couldn't make it." The last time she went to Chicago was for my father's funeral.

"Of course, I'm up to it," she fumed. "I'm young enough to be your sister."

"Only if our mother had you at age fifteen and me at age forty-five," I tease.

"Just never you mind," she said. "I'm goin' to Chicago and I'm gonna have a good time."

We stop first at Jenny and Bill's. Bill, Jr., all of three months old, is just finishing a feeding, and we sit and visit until it's time to go.

At the wedding, all eyes, except mine, are on Pam. She is a picture of beauty, but for me, Nellie steals the show. She turns to me frequently and smiles each time she sees that I'm looking at her, a sleeping Bill, Jr. in my arms. Billy wakes up long enough to grin at Pam when she comes by on her walk down the aisle. She pauses to kiss him on the forehead, ignoring me, which earns her a hug from Nellie.

After the wedding and reception, Sally and the Mafia set out for some "clubbin'," as Clare calls it.

"Do you think you'll be able to keep up?" Clare asks Sally.

"Why wouldn't I be able to?" Sally asks, putting her hands on her hips.

"It's been a while since I've seen you strut your stuff. I hope you're still able to."

"Don't you worry 'bout me! You worry 'bout yourself." Sally waves her hand, dismissively.

"I will worry 'bout you when all the men are flockin' to me," says Clare. "I don't want you gettin' your feelings hurt."

Sally rolls her eyes.

While they go clubbing, Nellie, Squat, and I spend a quiet evening with Jenny, Bill, and young Bill. This is Squat's first time meeting our family's newest addition, and he is enthralled. I watch him gently hold Billy on his lap then lean over to kiss his head.

Billy laughs and waves his arms, catching Squat's nose.

"He grab my nose," Squat says, to no one in particular. Looking at me, he announces, "He be mechanic. I teach him."

My father would have loved hearing that.

———

The next day, Nellie and I swing by the cemetery to visit my parents' graves, while Squat stays at Jenny's to give Billy his first lesson in being a mechanic—sweeping.

When we get there, I'm pleased to see a cluster of roses next to their headstone and surprised that they're real.

"Who put them here?" I wonder. Nellie smiles, so I ask, "Do you know?"

She nods. "Jenny. She told me she comes here every other week."

"Why?" I ask. "He was impossible to get along with, and she didn't know my mother."

Nellie puts her hands on her hips. "You don't get it, do you?" she asks. "Just 'cause you could barely tolerate your father don't mean everyone felt that way. He was *good* to Jenny. He and you were the first men she trusted."

"She was that close to him?"

Nellie rolls her eyes. "Yes!"

I put both hands on top of my head. "How did I miss that?"

Nellie looks at the ground and shakes her head then stares at me. "Maybe you didn't wanna see it, 'cause it started right after he moved in. Whenever she came home from Louisville, she'd make a beeline to his room. Sometimes they'd talk until supper."

"About what?"

"Everything, but most often, about bein' kinder to the ones we love. It wasn't long before she'd do somethin' like thank me for fixin' spaghetti and meatballs for her 'cause she got good grades, or she'd see me cleanin' the kitchen, and she'd start puttin' dishes away. Little things, but she never did that before."

"She would've done that on her own eventually."

"Maybe, but she wouldn't have gone to counselin' on her own. I know that for a fact."

"He didn't have anything to do with that."

Nellie cocks her head to the side. "You think she decided to go on her own?"

"Yes."

"Well, she didn't. Your father convinced her to go. It was after Wayne beat up you and Squat. Sam was insistent, told her there are some things we just can't do by ourselves and talked about all the people that helped him get sober. You were out cold in the hospital, and they talked the whole afternoon. I heard the love in his voice, for her and for you. She wanted to bail Wayne out, but he told her that if she ever saw him again, it would be a slap in your face, after how good you'd been to her."

I shake my head. "No way he told her that."

Nellie wheels around so we're face-to face and, with hands on her hips and fire in her eyes, she glares at me until I look away. When I do, she pokes a finger into my chest, demanding that I face her, again, and says, "You *listen* to me, Mister. He told her that, and a lot more. I heard him say he was wrong 'bout you, that he couldn't be prouder when he saw how everybody," she raises her arms, then drops them, so that they smack on the sides of her thighs, "even *Pam*, looked up to you. Jenny told me he treated her like an adult and made her feel safe, just like you."

I clench my fists in front of me, and snarl, "He and I had *nothin'* in common." I glare at his name on the headstone, an all-too-familiar knot tightening in my stomach as I remember him hitting my mother. *Did I really miss this side of him, the one Nellie's describing?* Shoving my hands in my pockets, I blurt, "I take after my mother. I got *nothin'* from him, except beatings."

She waves her arm at me, dismissively, and walks to the other side of my parents' headstone. She glances down then seems to be working her toe against something. Reaching down, she pulls a few random weeds then stands and tosses them to the side.

After rubbing her hands together to wipe the dirt away, she places them on top of the stone and looks at me. "You and he were two peas in a pod. You talked alike and walked alike. Both of you widened your eyes and smiled when you were surprised by something. Sometimes when I was talkin' to him I had to remind myself it wasn't you." She frowns. "You really think it's a coincidence that everyone that loves you loved him?"

I pull my hands from my pockets and spread them wide. "If I treated you and Jenny the way he treated my mother and me, you wouldn't have anything to do with me."

"That's right, 'cause I'd have your ass thrown in jail. Your mother chose a different path, but that's beside the point; we're talkin' 'bout him, not you. Your daddy drank, and drinkin' made him mean as a snake. I get it." She shakes her head. "Jeez, Bob, we all get it. But you're the only one that ever saw that side."

"My mother did," I assert, sweeping my arm toward her grave.

"You were the only one *in Kentucky*." She tilts her head back, and says, "And another thing. You claim you left Chicago 'cause of Pam. Are you sure that's the only reason?"

I squint at her and turn my head slightly to the side. "What do you mean?"

"Pam may have contributed to your leavin', but I think you got tired of not havin' a family, so you went down to Kentucky and put one together. You started it with Steve, Lou, Sally, and Squat. Then, you added me and Jenny. At some point, the Mafia joined. I didn't want Pam to be part of it, but I accepted her 'cause y'all seem to need each other." She smiles, her voice softens, and she says, "Besides, Jenny calls her 'Aunt Pam.'"

Her voice is hard, again, and the smile disappears as she declares, "Then, even though you didn't like it your father joined our family. He got himself sober, and he was good to everybody he met, includin' you." Her eyebrows go up, and she extends a hand toward me. "For goodness' sake, he even tried to help Wayne."

I flinch in surprise, and she mocks, "Yeah, didn't know about that, did you? After tellin' Jenny to cut him loose, he went to see Wayne in jail. He saw the potential the boy had, even if he didn't want Wayne hangin' around Jenny, so he offered to sponsor him with AA."

"Well, he didn't," I smirk.

She shakes her head. "No, and I can't say I was sorry when Wayne refused to go. But it proves that once Sam moved to Kentucky all his meanness was gone."

Nellie's glare dissolves, and her voice softens as she pats the headstone and says, "They're at peace. When will you be? For my sake, for our family's sake, hell, for *your own* sake, it's time to let go of your anger."

She walks around their monument and comes over to me, putting her hand on my cheek. "Remember that night you told me your father thanked you for takin' him out to see the trees changin' color?"

"Vaguely. Why?"

"I said then that you both had changed, and you agreed with me."

"Maybe," I say, hesitantly.

"So what's different now?"

I clear my throat. "Why should I let him off the hook for seventeen years of beatings 'cause he managed to be nice for a few years? Maybe he was just an old man who saw the grim reaper sneakin' up on him, and he was tryin' to get into Heaven."

A look of exasperation crosses her face. "Let's go home," she says. She tugs at my hand, but I refuse to move, and her hand slips from mine. Halfway to the car she turns and yells back at me, "I hope you don't believe that."

I probably don't, but I don't want to forgive him, either, even though I know Nellie's right. I gaze again at his name on the monument. The dad I knew in Kentucky was not the drunken, abusive dad I knew growing up. Kentucky Dad loved the people I loved. He treated them with kindness, even humor. He was a friend to Squat and an advisor to the rest. If he didn't help me after he came south, it was only because I wouldn't let him.

I recall how he let Squat win their checkers games, and I feel the tears on my cheek. I remember him in the hospital when he apologized to me for his drinking and his abuse. I couldn't accept it, then; I realize his ineffable sincerity now.

I told him at that time, "I'm tired of bein' angry," but I realize now that I still hadn't let it go. If I was tired, then, I'm downright exhausted now. I cry harder as I picture him at the dinner table the last Christmas he was alive, joking with everyone as he carved the turkey, teasing Squat that he was going to give him the gizzard.

Oh, my God. Steve used to do that. How had I missed that?

I walk across their graves to the monument and drop to my knees. Leaning forward, I press my head against his name as sobs rack my body. Grabbing the flowers from the ground, I clutch them to my breast, oblivious to the thorns penetrating my hand.

Nellie touches my shoulder. I hadn't heard her come back. I stand and clutch at her so clumsily she almost falls. I cling to her as if trying to avoid falling off the face of the Earth.

I realize what Dad's apology meant five years ago. He wanted to tell me that he had loved Mom and me all those years. At the same time, he had hated himself for drinking, and he took out his hatred on those that he loved because he was a drunk and drunks won't blame themselves. When Mom died and he sobered up, I was too angry to accept his love, even as he showered it on all my friends.

What Nellie has been telling me makes sense. When he came to Kentucky, he was no longer the bastard I once knew. I can accept that, or I can become the bastard; I have to choose.

Nellie kisses my tear-stained cheeks, and I tighten my embrace around her. As I release my hold on the flowers, the thorns pull away from my hand, leaving blood on my palm. I feel a burden lifting from my soul.

I let it go.

Chapter Thirty-Two

Squat is in the front office where we have a television for the customers. He's yelling something. I hear the TV blaring and recognize fear in Squat's voice, but can't make out what he's saying. I'm working on a car in the repair bay but quit and walk toward the office.

Halfway there, he meets me, shouting, "Plane! Plane!"

"What about a plane?" I ask him. Jacob is standing in front of the TV and on the screen, I see smoke pouring out of a tall building.

"Plane fly into building," Squat tells me. As we watch in horror, we see a plane hit a second tower. "People die," Squat moans, visibly upset. "Nooo." He turns abruptly and goes into the garage area, where he walks around in a very agitated state until finally he picks up his broom and starts sweeping very fast.

Jacob and I watch the TV screen for about five minutes, until Jacob asks, "What has the world become?"

I shake my head. "It's crazy," I reply. "I think I better take Squat home and spend a little time with him. Okay with you?"

"Sure, sure, you go on ahead. I can handle what I got here today."

"I'm doin' a brake job on the car in the bay. The back two are finished. You just need to do the front two."

"Okay. I'll finish it."

Just then, Squat yells, a random noise expressing distress, and Jacob says, "Get him on home. He is really upset."

I walk into the shop area and say, "Come on Squat. Let's go home." Usually, if I want to pull him away from his job, he objects, but today he just leans the broom against the wall and walks out with me.

As we walk the three blocks home, Squat is silent but occasionally shakes his fist at the sky, muttering.

All I can do is say, "I know, Buddy."

Nellie is in the yard putting mulch around the bushes in anticipation of cooler weather and hasn't heard what's happening in far-away New York. Squat stands silently as Nellie and I talk, then he quietly drifts into the house.

"Is Squat all right?"

"No," I reply, shaking my head.

"Go to him." She puts her hand on my shoulder and steers me toward the steps. "I'm gonna turn on the television to see what's happenin'."

"Keep it low," I say, as we walk into the house. "Squat doesn't need to hear it."

As Nellie goes into the living room, I walk upstairs to Squat's room. He is sitting in his rocking chair, slowly rocking and patting his stuffed bear that Steve and Lou gave him the first Christmas I was in Waynedale. Squat is singing to it softly, and occasionally he kisses it on the nose, so I sit quietly on the bed for at least a half-hour, Squat comforting the bear and me wishing I could make it better for him.

When he stretches out and falls asleep, I go downstairs and watch the news reports with Nellie.

That evening, Sally comes to supper. Squat eats in silence as we talk about Jenny, Bill, and their children.

"Billy is in pre-school and Beth is finally potty trained," I tell her, avoiding the subject of the day.

After supper, the four of us go for a walk, and Squat surprises me when he announces he's going to work the next day.

"Really?" I ask. "I thought you might wanna stay home."

He shakes his head. "I sweep. I go in."

"Well, then, I guess I will, too. I imagine Jacob will need some help."

"Yeah," says Squat. "We mechanics. People need us."

"Indeed, they do," says Sally. "You go to work tomorrow, Uncle Squat." As she says that, she pats me on the back; I'm Squat's surrogate affection receiver.

"Yeah, I go work," he says.

I reach to put my arm on Squat's shoulder, but he twists away, saying, "No hugs! No hugs!"

———

For the next few months, we grieve with the rest of the country. While the country goes to war, Squat and I return to our schedule; Squat isn't happy if we get out of our regular rhythm.

———

I notice we're getting busier, and, during the spring of 2002, I realize that I've been at the garage nearly every day for the last month. It's early April, and warm for this time of year, or maybe I'm still expecting April in Chicago, cold and dreary. Squat is sitting outside, eating his lunch and watching the birds build nests.

As I finish an oil change, Jacob calls me into his office. He was late coming in this morning, so Squat and I opened up. We've hardly spoken this morning.

I drop onto the leather day bed he's got against the wall. "What's up?" I ask.

"I'm wore out," he says, rubbing his forehead.

"You look wore out." He's got bags under his eyes, and they're not twinkling, as they do when he's got a new joke or is having a good day, which is most of the time.

"Go home," I add. "Squat and I will take care of anything that comes in. We can close up."

"Not what I mean. I'm not just wore out today. I'm long-term wore out. Plus, I can't keep up with all the changes in these new cars. Hell, I'm sixty-nine now."

As I begin to wonder where this is leading, Jacob continues. "I've decided it's time for me to hang it up permanently." He wipes his brow with a handkerchief, then says, "End of June, I'm closin' the garage. This will upset Squat, so I thought I'd tell you first."

"Yeah, he's gonna be devastated. I don't think he's ready to quit."

"I know, but he just has to keep up with that broom and I've got to keep up with all these different cars. Someone brought one of those hybrids in here last week. First one I've seen. How've you kept up with them?"

"I got Bill. He keeps Nellie and me up with all the latest technology. If I can't find somethin' on the Internet, he finds it for me."

Jacob nods then says, "I got an idea I wanna run by you. Why don't you buy the business from me? I'm just gonna shut it down. You'd be able to let Squat work as long as he wants. My customers like you; they'd be happy to have you take over. Won't have to go over to Grove's Point to get their cars worked on. Best of all, I'd get a little money out of the deal."

I sit back and cross my legs. I hadn't seen that coming. "Hmmm. I'll have to talk to Nellie about that. I kinda enjoy havin' the time to do what I want. I'm no spring chicken, either."

"What are you talkin' about?" Jacob laughs. "What are you? Fifty?"

I smile. "Fifty-one."

Jacob points at me. "Nailed it."

I shrug. "Close." I pause then tell him, "Steve ruined me, fixin' it so I don't have to work. Now, I enjoy havin' my independence."

"You think about it," he says, standing up, "but I'm shuttin' down the end of the June. That's in eleven weeks. You want me to tell Squat?"

"Let me. If I was to buy the place, would you help me with any overload?"

"You mean, flip jobs with you? Hadn't thought of that." He stands behind his desk, rubbing the back of his neck. After a little bit of thinking, he says, "Sure, I could work ten or fifteen hours a week. But let me know if you're gonna buy me out by the end of May so's I can let my customers know."

That night, after supper, Sally has the solution.

"Let Squat buy the garage," she says. He's got gobs of money in his trust that's gonna come to me when he dies, and I don't need it. He'll be thrilled."

———

On July 1, 2002, we open for business under new management. Nellie takes a picture of Squat and me standing under a sign that reads, *Squat's Auto Repair. Squat, Proprietor.* Now, instead of telling people, "Bob and me mechanics," he tells them, "Me and Bob partners."

If it's possible, Squat is more enthusiastic about his sweeping now than he was before, and I tell him not to hurt himself by swinging the broom too hard.

"It my garage. I keep it clean. People comin'," he declares, and he's right. We are so busy that Jacob comes in a couple of hours a day.

Quickly, though, I realize that after working only part-time for so many years, it is hard for me to go back to full-time. With Jacob and Squat both in their late sixties, we need somebody younger to help us, so I contact the technical school in Elizabethtown and ask if they have an auto mechanic student who'd want to work part-time, then go full-time when he graduates.

"I'll get back to you," the instructor says. "I've got somebody in mind, but I want to talk to her first."

"Her?" I ask.

"Oh, yeah," the instructor says. "She's gonna have a hard time fittin' in a large shop. She's gonna need someplace that will take the time to get to know her. I've heard about you and Squat. This might be a good fit." His enthusiasm is scaring me.

"Wait a minute," I say. "It's just me, Squat, and another old-timer that helps us out a few hours a week. I don't wanna take on someone that needs raisin'."

"Oh, you won't have to raise her, just accept her for how she is. She's not, how shall I put this, not the most feminine young lady you will run across."

Margie blows into the garage a few weeks later like a hurricane crossing into land. She's a deputy sheriff's daughter, has a tattoo of barbed wire around her bicep, which is much larger than mine, and a piercing through her nostril. She's built like a refrigerator, but with a head.

Every morning when she walks in the door, she rolls her shoulders forward as if preparing to lift something heavy. She frequently runs a hand over her closely-cropped hair, and she's ornery as they come, but a hard worker and a dandy mechanic, with the best computer skills this side of my son-in-law, Bill. Most importantly, she takes to Squat immediately, and within days they are dueling trash-talkers.

She calls Squat "Old-Timer" and he calls her "Young-Timer." When things are slow, she turns up the radio and dances him around the repair bay, Squat laughing and singing and watching their feet. If he's too tired to dance, Margie asks him what it was like to repair stagecoaches.

Anytime she gets his goat, which is frequently, he yells at her, "You're fired," a grin creasing his wrinkled face and a hand randomly rubbing his now mostly-bald head.

"You can't fire me, I quit!" she yells back.

Then, they both point at each other and laugh.

Squat tells customers, "Me and Margie and Bob, we be mechanics." Then, he turns to Margie and hollers, "Ain't that right, Margie?"

Margie doesn't even pull her head out from under the hood. She just yells, "That's right, boss."

When Squat can remember who we are, it seems as if the good times will go on forever.

Chapter Thirty-Three

Arthritis ravages Squat's knees, but he never asks me to drive him to the shop. When I ask him if he wants to retire, and tell him he's certainly earned it, he screws up his face and says, "Now, Bob, we talk about this. I be mechanic. People need me."

So every morning, Nellie packs us lunch and off we walk, albeit more slowly. I notice that Squat doesn't give his no-look wave to people nearly as often anymore.

"Where my broom?" he begins to ask every day, even though it's leaning against the wall in the exact spot he has left it for all the years I've been working here. I also notice that he doesn't change his clothes unless Nellie or I remind him; he used to change them as often as three times a day.

I suggest he have a check-up with Dr. Talbott, and he says, "Oh, boy!" He always enjoys a visit to his doctor. I can understand why.

The sign declaring Dr. Talbott to be a *Doctor of medicine, reader of the stars, and part-time vampire* is still on the receptionist's desk. When we see the doctor, I tell him that Squat's acting a little peculiar.

"Peculiar, huh?" he replies, letting the word roll around on his tongue as if it has an unusual texture. He studies Squat's chart as he sits on a chair with wheels and no back. As he moves back and forth, six inches toward, then away from me, he mumbles, "Squat's birthday is September twelfth."

His head snaps up. He stops scooting the chair and, staring at me over the top of his reading glasses, asserts, "Of course he's havin' trouble. Do you realize how his stars are aligned right now? Why, I'd be surprised if he *wasn't* havin' problems. And you come to me, a mere mortal, and expect me to do something about it?" He shakes his head, and I hear an audible, "Tsk, tsk" directed my way.

Squat smiles, broadly; he's seen this routine before. It puts him at ease, and I find it a refreshing change from the manner of most doctors.

"All right," he says, rolling his chair toward Squat, "Let's take a look at things." He shines a light in Squat's ear, and asks, "What are you doin' with all these beans in here?"

"No beans in ear," Squat replies, laughing.

I've seen some pretty good magicians in my day, but I will never figure out where Dr. Talbott gets the bean he holds up and says, "Look what just came out."

Squat's eyes grow wide but he sticks to his guns. "That not come out my ear."

The doctor continues the exam, constantly befuddling Squat with more beans, a quarter out of his nose, and an observation that he can see fish swimming around when he looks in his eyes.

"Oh, brother," Squat replies. He seems puzzled, then growls, "Get out of here."

Dr. Talbott leans back. He raises his eyebrows and squints at Squat over his glasses. "But it's my office," he protests.

"I say get outta here," Squat yells, laughing and pointing at the door.

"It's a good thing I'm finished with the exam," the doctor says as he rolls his chair back and stands up. "Pull your shirt on and let's step into my office."

When we're seated in his office across from him, Dr. Talbott asks, "Squat, who am I?"

"You silly doctor," Squat answers.

Dr. Talbott smiles, then asks, "Yes I am; do you remember my name?"

"Dr. Friend."

This elicits a big smile from the doctor. "That's the nicest thing anybody's called me in a long time," he says. He folds his hands in his lap and turns to me. "It's possibly Alzheimer's," he says, and I flinch.

I feel tears welling up in my eyes and rather than wiping them away I let them run down my cheeks.

Dr. Talbott reaches into a drawer, puts out a box of tissues, and shoves them in my direction then continues. "His memory lapses may be due to something new or just a progression of the same mental challenges he's always had. We may never find out, but they've got more equipment in Louisville. I'd recommend goin' there for some additional testin'."

"Is there anything else we can do?" I ask, taking a tissue and blowing my nose.

"Absolutely," Dr. Talbott replies. Turning to Squat, who is glancing at the pictures of the doctor's family that decorate the wall, he says, "Squat, I have something I want you to do."

Squat looks back at the doctor, and says, "Go onnn."

Dr. Talbott says, "I'm gonna give you a Hindu mantra that I want you to recite twice a day." He bows his head, raises his hand as if taking an oath, and begins to chant something totally unintelligible.

As he goes on for ten-seconds, Squat begins to smile. When he reaches twenty-seconds, Squat laughs, and Dr. Talbott stops.

"Did you get that?" Dr. Talbott asks, "Because with the mess we've got with your stars and planets, regular medicine isn't gonna work."

Squat ducks his head, raises his hand, and makes noise for a few seconds.

"You got it," the doctor says, standing up. "Very few people get it on their first attempt, but you got it."

Squat grins, and he and I stand.

I hold my hand out to Dr. Talbott, and say, "Thank you for bein' silly with him."

"He's my favorite," the doctor replies, shaking my hand and smiling. "Good luck. This could be serious."

"I know," I reply, sighing.

Doctor Talbott nods then says, "Squat, you take care of Bob, ya hear?"

"Alll rrrright," Squat says, but sounds dubious about the assignment.

"I like him," Squat tells me as we walk to the car.

"You like everybody." I want to put my arm around his shoulder but refrain.

"Yeah, but I like him more."

———

Even Squat has to work at liking Dr. Cronen, the specialist we see in Louisville. There is no joking, and he's only able to confirm what we already knew; it might be Alzheimer's, and it might not. Squat enjoys the drive to

Louisville, though, so we go every few months for follow-up.

On our third visit, Cronen says, "Squat's a little heavier than he should be. It wouldn't hurt him to drop thirty pounds."

"Maybe so," I reply, "but why take away candy bars, when he has such few pleasures?"

"It can shorten his life," the doctor warns.

"He's already lived thirty years longer than the doctors told his parents he would live when he was born."

Cronen frowns and turns away, but I've made up my mind; if this is Squat's last illness, I'm not going to deprive him of pleasure on the outside chance he might live a few months longer.

So Squat eats his candy bars and sweeps the floor while Margie and I work on cars. Sometimes he turns a wrench for one of us or holds a part in place. At night, he watches TV with Nellie and me.

Eventually, I have to remind him to take a bath, something he used to do the minute he came home after work. When reminded, he bathes, and it's actually a relief that he doesn't change clothes so often.

But one night when I tell him to take a bath, he looks at Nellie and says, "No bath. Okay, Lou?" Then, he turns to me, and says, "Why you shave beard, Steve?"

When he goes upstairs, Nellie says, "What was that about?"

I shake my head and exhale as if that will expel from my mind the memories of my conversations with the doctors.

I wait about fifteen minutes, then go upstairs to say good-night. When I knock on his door, he says, "What?"

"It's Bob," I tell him.

"Bob who?"

At first, I think he's joking, but when I open the door, there's fear on his face, and he yells, "Go away! Who you?"

I say, "Excuse me," close the door, and go downstairs.

Nellie has turned off the TV and is in the bedroom. I start changing into my pajamas, but she picks up on my somber mood and asks, "What's wrong?"

I can't bring myself to tell her. Shaking my head, I sit on the edge of the bed.

She sits next to me and puts her arm around my shoulder. "He didn't recognize you, did he?"

I shake my head, and she says, "He hasn't called me 'Nellie' in some time. I didn't want to worry you, but I've been 'Lou' for at least two weeks. He's always called me that at breakfast, but now it's all day long."

"Do you think he should go to the doctor, again?"

Nellie shakes her head. "Not unless they have some new miracle drug. Nothin' they've done has helped. I think he's better off just bein' here with us."

———

The next morning, after breakfast, I'm putting on my work shoes when I hear Nellie calling me frantically. I run toward the sound, and when I meet her in the kitchen, she shouts, "Squat's gone."

I run for the door, shouting, "Call Sally. Tell her we need her to watch for him. Call the sheriff, too. You stay here, in case he comes home. I'm gonna see if he's on the way to the garage."

He's not at the garage, so I circle the town in ever-larger loops. It takes forty-five minutes, but finally, Nellie calls me on my cell phone.

"Sally called," she tells me. "He's at her house. She saw

him comin' down the street, totally befuddled. Didn't know who she was; thought she was me. He hasn't recognized me in weeks, then he thinks *she's* me."

I drive to Sally's, and as soon as I pull up, I see them sitting on the steps. "Bob! I see you!" he hollers, as if everything was normal.

———

Margie is hurt when he starts forgetting who she is. I tell her not to take it personally, he's been forgetting who Nellie and I are, too. A troubled look crosses her face.

"Is it Alzheimer's?" she asks.

I sigh and lower my head.

"Dammit!" she yells, smacking one of her big fists into the palm of her other hand. It makes a popping noise loud enough that I'm very glad she's not blaming me. "He don't need that, not on top of everythin' else."

———

Later that day, I find her out behind the garage, crying.

"It's not fair," she sputters when I ask her if she's all right.

"I know," I say, putting my hand on her shoulder.

"I want someone to explain how this is fair," she demands, between sobs. "He never had a chance from the start. It ain't right. It just ain't right."

I use my hand on her well-muscled shoulder to guide her to a bench against the back wall of the shop. She enjoys sitting here during her breaks, eyes closed, lips moving, lost in the music coming through her headphones. We both sit down, and I smile at her.

"You haven't been around him as long as I have," I tell her.

"Let me tell you about something that happened one time shortly after I became his guardian."

She tucks away her handkerchief and looks at me. If I didn't know how kind she is, her nose piercing, barb-wire tattoo, and muscular shoulders would intimidate me.

"We had gone to Louisville, and we were on our way back. We had to stop 'cause of a wreck. All the lanes were closed. We must've sat there for an hour, not movin'. I began to get mad. I had things to do; I had places to be."

"Been there."

"Squat listened to my complaints for a few minutes, then told me, 'Calm, Bob. Sometimes things just...' he thought for a minute, then said, 'happen. It good you not in wreck.'"

"That's our boy," says Margie, now smiling.

"Yes, it is. Squat doesn't expect anyone to feel sorry for him. He's always accepted the way things are. He is normal for Squat; you and I are normal for Margie and Bob; his philosophy is, 'Life is good; we could be in the wreck.'" I smile then ask, "Now, how can you feel bad for someone who thinks that way? To tell you the truth, I wish I was more like him."

"Really?" asks Margie, raising her eyebrows.

"Really," I reply, nodding. She holds her fist out to me, and we do a knuckle bump just the way she's taught me to do it.

———

About two weeks before the end, Squat asks Nellie and me to let him stay in Dad's old room.

"Honey, will you be happy in a different room?" Nellie asks him.

We're both flabbergasted when he replies, "Sam want me there. He say we be together soon. What he mean?"

Nellie and I exchange glances, then she asks, "Do you see Sam a lot?"

"Yeah. And Steve and Lou. Yesterday I saw Mama and Papa. They all say they ready for me."

We move Squat to Dad's old room. It was a porch, then it was Dad's room, then it was a porch, again. Now, it's Squat's room. Through it all, it's had the mismatched door trim that Steve and I put up a few months after I moved in. Squat touches it as he enters, and I realize he's always done that.

As soon as he's in the room, Squat gets in bed. He never leaves under his own power again.

———

Everyone has left but the two of us. I stare at the casket sitting over the grave. In my peripheral vision, I see the dirt vultures leaning on their shovels, anxious for us to leave so that they can finish and go home.

Steve and Lou's headstone is to the right of Squat's grave. On the left is Steve and Squat's parents' marker. Strangers to me, and yet I feel a kinship. Lying between the two couples, Squat will be protected by them in death, as he was in life.

My world is inside that casket. Everyone who has become my family, Squat either led me to or helped me stay. He was why Steve wanted me to board with them. He calmed me, and made me see the mistake I was flirting with if I broke up with Nellie over Pam. He stepped between Wayne and me and got beat up for it, but he was as proud of his shiners as he was anything he'd ever had. He held both of Jenny's children in his lap, kissed them gently on their heads, and showed them that a man can be different, and still be a man. He showed me the good in my father. For close to twenty years, my day started at breakfast with him on my right. It ended with us watching TV, me in a rocking chair, him stretched across my bed. In between, we worked on cars and he gave no-look waves to anyone who happened to come his way.

My parents are buried in Chicago; my family is here. Mom and Dad would understand. The stone just beyond Steve and Lou's reads, *Robert Tingle* and *Amanda (Nellie) Tingle*. Our birth dates are there, the end dates blank, and when they are engraved in the stone, I will lie here next to my one, true woman, surrounded by my family in this small town, my town, home at last and forever. Every road I've traveled has led me to this moment, and I appreciate every last bump in every rough mile.

I cry, but not for Squat. He didn't want tears any more than he wanted hugs. I cry for me because I want to hear him tell me one more time, "We mechanics, you and me."

Nellie has tears on her cheeks, but a smile on her face. She takes my hand in both of hers and says quietly, "We need to go. Everyone's comin' to the house."

I nod, and we turn to walk to the car. Halfway there, I reach into the air and wave. A no-looker.

About the Author

Erv is a lobbyist, continuing education instructor, and attorney. He is also on the adjunct faculty at Indiana University Southeast. He is a member of the board of Louisville Literary Arts as well as being in Second Draft Writers Group and Louisville Writers Meetup. Erv's first book, *Subterfuge*, an historical fiction mystery, was chosen Best Historical Fiction at the 2020 Imaginarium Author's Fair in Louisville. He is currently working on a novel about a man who is attempting to survive causing the accidental deaths of five people, including his immediate family. Erv lives in Louisville, Kentucky, with his wife Linda, their dog, and cat.